Perseid Press
P.O. Box 584
Centerville MA 02632

Hell Bound

Cover art and cover design by Roy Mauritsen.

Cover design © Perseid Press
A Perseid Press Original

First Perseid Press Kindle edition October 2015
First Perseid Press Trade edition October 2015
First Perseid Press Electronic Edition October 2015

Trade version, ISBN-13: 978-0-9964289-4-1, ISBN-10: 0996428941
Kindle version, ISBN-13: 978-0-9964289-5-9, ISBN-10: 099642895X
ePub version: ISBN-13: 978-0-9964289-6-5, ISBN-10: 0996428968

Published in the United States of America

10 9 8 7 6 5 4 3 2 1

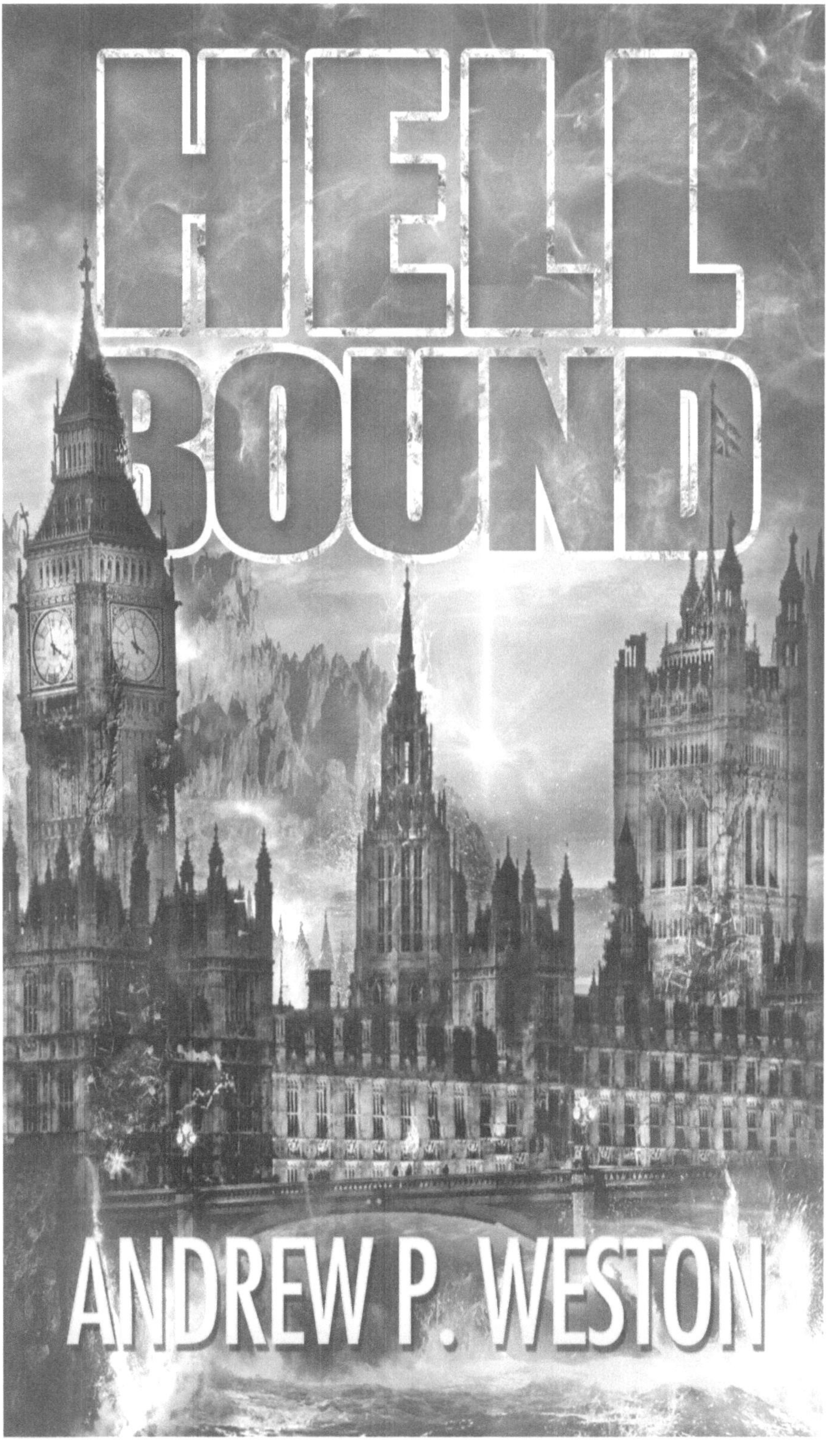
HELL
BOUND
ANDREW P. WESTON

Acknowledgement

To Janet, who graciously allowed me access to a dark and wondrous playground.

HELLBOUND

ANDREW P. WESTON

Dedication

"Hell is empty, and all the devils are here. . ."
— William Shakespeare

Dedicated to all those who know the truth isn't just out there . .
it's much closer to home than you think.

TABLE OF CONTENTS

HELL BOUND

Arising thunder from the vast Abyss

First roused me, not as he that rested wakes

From slumberous hours, but one rude fury shakes

Untimely, and around I gazed to know

The place of my confining

— *Dante Alighieri, The Divine Comedy*

Prologue

Lost in shadow, I surveyed my surroundings and took my time to ensure the area was deserted. The squall outside fell in stinging gusts, creating a tympanic frenzy of contending melodies. I paused for a moment to savor the erratic beat of rain against metal, glass, and corrugated roofing. Only with the greatest effort could I break free from its hypnotic discord to concentrate on the task at hand.

This didn't take long, for I'd chosen my location well. It was past midnight, and my position at the top of the stairwell afforded me a commanding view of the parking lot outside. Apart from a sole discarded coffee cup tumbling its way along a line of stationary vehicles like a demented gymnast, I was completely alone and invisible to the detritus of humanity sleeping fitfully beneath makeshift shelters throughout the different levels of the garage.

The scant security lighting that still worked did little to illuminate the area. If anything, each lamp created a swathe of gloom that I would use to my advantage, for my assignment here would end shortly: it was almost time to go home.

At last.

Just the thought of getting back sent a twinge of pleasure tingling along my spine. While my work afforded me a degree of freedom enjoyed by no one else, I always felt fatigued the longer I stayed away. And a week was simply too long.

Still, it's been a good harvest. Not only was I able to sort out a major problem for the Boss, but the latest candidates should go a long way toward calming his frustrations.

A faint echo portending ravenous hunger intruded at the edge of my astral perceptions. Adjusting my awareness, I sensed my quarry coming closer. Forewarned, I used the opportunity to mentally review his rap-sheet.

Jesus Toledo Perez. Born 1980, in New Mexico, to Alberto Toledo and Christina Perez. A fraternal twin introduced to his true vocation at the tender age of just five years, when he smothered his sibling, Alana, in her sleep following an infantile spat. Authorities weren't able to pin anything on him at the time, and how would they? An innocent child, rolling over in the night to cuddle his sister as they slept? Little did the Toledo family appreciate the monster born into their midst that day.

But *we* did, and that act had drawn him to our attention. For as little Jesus grew up, his crimes progressed from random acts of asphyxiation as a child to the more opportunistic, premeditated, hormone-driven angst of a teenager. By the time he graduated, Jesus had strangled, drowned, and pushed seven people to their deaths.

Hmm. Judging from what it says here, he always acted as if he was daring the authorities to catch him. Just what we want. A cold, calculating killer with a God complex.

I watched him from my place of concealment as he edged his way out onto the top tier from the opposite side of the level.

Hiding beneath an oversized golf umbrella, and dressed to the nines in an expensive suit and raincoat, he looked every bit the highflyer currently establishing himself as a philanthropist and charity worker among the city's homeless.

The perfect cover.

Or so he thinks.

I noticed he was carrying a plastic bag. Despite the wind, I could hear the contents clunking as he moved.

Aha! Going with the poisoned hooch option tonight, are we?

I suppressed a snort at the poignancy of the situation.

I've got a real-life Jesus of suburbia right in front of me, but the only salvation he'll be bringing one of the poor and lowly to-night is a release from the suffering of their miserable lives.

Time to intercede.

Like a wraith, I detached myself from the gloom and stepped out into the night. Within moments, the rain had soaked my hair and beaded my trench coat and sunglasses in a chainmail of trans-lucent pearls. Gliding silently between parked vehicles, the only sign of my advance came from the momentary dimming of the overhead lights as I passed.

I neared my target, and noticed Jesus had stooped low over a congregation of cardboard boxes between two large trucks. The soft *chink* of glass scraping on concrete signaled his preparations, and in moments several bottles stood on the floor before him.

"There you go," he crooned, "this'll help keep you warm on a night like this."

Several pairs of grubby hands snaked out from darkened al-coves. Grasping at the unexpected gifts they fought among them-selves, frantic for any solace that might ease the drudgery of their existence, if only for a little while.

A cap popped, and necks craned as bottles were lifted to-ward eager lips.

Oh no you don't!

I swept forward and slapped one of the bottles away from desperate fingers. Full of liquid, it bounced once before exploding in a shower of liquid-crystal splinters.

Jesus spun to face whoever had intervened in his machinations. His look of anger blanched into one of fear as his gaze met mine.

I couldn't blame him. Despite the glasses, I'd always had that effect on people.

Dressed from head to toe in black, and coming in at over six feet tall, I exuded an air of menace and barely suppressed aggression.

Without taking my eyes from him, I grabbed Jesus by the collar, lifted him off the floor, and addressed the bums now cowering inside their rain-sodden caves. "Ladies and gentlemen, if you value your existence I strongly suggest you stay where you are for the next few minutes. Enjoy your beverages, and the fact that each of you will now live to see the dawning of a brand new day."

As I concluded my sentence, I flexed, and sent Jesus sailing through the downpour behind me. Only then did I pause to regard the occupants within their shelters.

Nervous, owl-like expressions stared back.

Holding their attention, I nodded once to reinforce my point, then turned on my heels and stalked toward my mark.

Jesus hit the deck with a tooth-jarring *thud*, and the air whooshed from his lungs. He rolled onto his side, groaning and coughing up blood. Shaking the moisture from his rain-sodden brow, he attempted to push himself up on his hands and knees.

I slowed my advance and unfastened the buttons of my coat. With infinite care, I pulled my left-hand glove off by its fingertips.

A gust of wind brought the coffee cup careening our way.

Tap, tap! Splat! Tappiddy-splat, tap, tap!

Mesmerized, we both stopped to watch as it scudded past and commenced dancing around us in circles. Jesus used the interlude to stagger to his feet. Swaying, he forced down a ragged breath and threw me a dirty look.

Idiot! You're just making your last moments on Earth all the more unpleasant.

I surged forward, balled my right fist and punched him in the face. His nose shattered with a satisfying *crunch*. Spinning head over heels, Jesus spiraled away from me, smashed through the doorway, and landed in a heap at the top of the stairwell. I was on him in seconds, but allowed him the courtesy of regaining his wits before I continued.

Jesus struggled to regain his focus. Blinking furiously, he clutched his face and peered up through tear-laden eyes. Although unsteady, I hadn't quite knocked the stuffing out of him. "Who the fuck are you?" he hissed. "What do you want?"

Sweeping the vent of my coat to one side, I exposed my weapon for the briefest fraction of a second and removed an official-looking document sealed in blood-red wax from an inside pocket.

He caught sight of the hi-tech sickle and froze.

I cracked the seal, unfolded the scroll, and said, "Jesus Toledo Perez. Listen carefully. This is an official Hellegal Declaration. For your crimes against humanity, you have damned yourself, and your life is forfeit. I am authorized by His Satanic Majesty to reap your eternal soul. Sentence is to be carried out immediately. Are there any last words you'd like to say?"

"What?" he spluttered. "Are you kidding me? Are you seriously trying to make out you're some kind of Grim Reaper?"

Why do they always say that?

"No, this isn't a joke." I stepped forward and held out my exposed hand, as if offering to help him stand. "We've been watching you ever since you murdered little Alana, all those years ago. Mind you, I've got to be honest. Even then, you didn't stand condemned, childhood naivety and all that. However, because of your course of action since then—" I shrugged, my left hand still proffered. "Well, that's a whole new ball game."

I smiled like I was his new best friend.

That did the trick. Reaching out, Jesus accepted my offer.

As we made contact, the letters etched across the parchment glowed white hot. Jesus gasped and his eyes widened in shock. Then the writ itself burst into flames. At that exact moment, he stiffened, as if impaled on a spike of unimaginable agony. All tension drained from his body, and Jesus folded silently onto the floor.

"Another fool successfully bound for hell," I mumbled. "Speaking of which . . ."

I glanced back out across the parking lot, and checked to ensure my activities had remained unobserved.

Nothing.

Satisfied, I leaned over the internal rails and stared down into the darkness of the sub-basement.

Excellent. Nice and clean, just the way I like it.

The tempo of the rain drumming against the roof increased, as if bidding me a fond farewell.

Time to go.

I removed my other glove to ensure both hands were free, then slid my scythe from its sheath. Depressing the center gem adorning the handle, I listened as a faint whine confirmed a build-up of power. A tingling sensation crawled across my skin. Gripping the staff firmly, I channeled my energy along its length and slammed the butt into the ground.

"Dorash! Mi dreósgadh ânise!" I intoned in ancient Hellanese. (Portal! Open to me now.)

The floor sagged and fell away, as if a sinkhole had opened beneath it. Moments later, a swirling vortex created a void between dimensions. Tongues of lightning played along the edges of a boiling corona. Stabbing out, they probed the walls and railings in a sizzling discharge that sent sparks dancing along my clothes and across the surface of my skin. A stiff breeze erupted in response to the sudden vacuum. Redolent with sulfur and charred flesh, it put me immediately at ease.

With a final glance at the body of the late, not so great, Jesus Toledo Perez, I jumped into the jaws of doom. Engulfed within a maelstrom of kaleidoscopic contradictions, I felt as if I were floating on air before the heady rush of an insane descent swept me away.

Eternity became encapsulated within an instant, and before I knew it I'd slammed into an entirely different type of ground; I felt my spirit resonate to a familiar vibe.

I inhaled the sweet fragrance of home.

Tappiddy-tap, tap, plop!

Eh? I glanced down.

The coffee cup obviously liked my company; it had decided to string along on my descent into hell.

Well, look at that! It got sucked into the vortex along with me.

I determined that perhaps it would be nice to keep this little memento of my latest trip topside. I stooped toward it, but the polystyrene had already blackened, bubbled, and begun to melt.

Bugger! I sighed. *Ah well, this place isn't for everyone.*

Chapter 1: No Rest for the Wicked

A hollow, rhythmic reverberation imposed itself upon ancient solitude.

Ching! Ching! Ching! Ching!

Penetrating the rocks, each resonant chime grew in pitch and volume. Grit and shingle that had lined the roof of the vault for an age became dislodged, adding its substance to the layer of dust and grime already coating the floor.

The assault continued. Disturbed from their rest, heavier pebbles fell from once sturdy emplacements. Inevitably, the growing cascade attracted larger clods of mixed earth and stone. A hole appeared, illuminating the interior with filtered gray and yellow phosphorescence. Ruddy overtones and sporadic roaring from beyond the makeshift ocular indicated conditions outside the cavern were far from ideal.

The rim widened and a hand encroached into the sanctuary, armed with a long cylindrical object.

Click!

A bright concentrated ray of light stabbed down. After circling the chamber once, it withdrew, only to be replaced by the weighted end of a rope ladder. Knotted rungs squeaked under the weight of the new arrival, and their protests created a tremulous counterpoint against deeper grunts of physical exertion.

Nearing the bottom, the intruder interrupted his descent to survey his surroundings.

Like an ethereal searchlight, the beam from the torch washed across the interior of the room until it came to rest on the goal of this day's efforts.

"Well, well, well," an incredulous voice spluttered, "the dreams would appear to be accurate after all. And there's me thinking I'd finally gone and lost it."

Chuckling, the adventurer released his grip and dropped the final few feet to the floor. Slight of build and dressed as he was in nineteenth-century garb, his formal jacket and bowtie seemed oddly out of place with his environment.

With a reverential air, he walked toward the bizarre image before him. As he did so, he subconsciously flexed his fingers and massaged his hands, as if his exertions had cost him dear.

Arriving at his prize, he paused to contemplate the scene.

A huge effigy, over twelve feet in height, dominated the center of the cavity. Depicting two giant beings locked in mortal combat, it looked as if they had been impaled upon an incredibly long weapon of mystic origin.

Hmm. It appears to me that my friends were fused together at the moment of their deaths. Calcified bone to carbonized flesh, the perfect congruence of good and evil.

The explorer staggered as a shockwave from another eruption pulsated through the region. Once it had passed, he reached out to caress the device that had immortalized the pair forever. His gesture disturbed a skin of ash overlaying the metamorphosed relic. The crust crumbled at his touch, revealing the gleaming hilt of a huge sword. A jewel in its pommel flared in the dark, filling the cavern with a cold, electric-blue radiance.

Can it be true?

Closing his eyes, the overawed soul grasped the gem in both hands. In moments, the power contained within the artifact had imbued him with a hint of its potential.

He released it and backed away, grinning.

"Oh my," he hissed to himself, "with this, the success of my aspirations is virtually guaranteed. Not only will it mean I'll be able to stay one step ahead of His Infernal Asshole's bounty hunter, but it confirms that my intelligence about Grim himself is correct. I'll bait him and tempt him and dangle him on a string until he explodes with frustration. Then, once I've led him to me, I'll have the luxury of a choice . . ."

Elated, the mystery intruder fingered the unusual bracelet adorning his wrist.

"Then we'll be reunited at last."

A rare moment of lucidity heightened the reality of the situation he faced.

"Of course, the execution of my plan is fraught with peril and unseen hurdles. But now I know I can trust the visions, perhaps the other, more arduous route will also furnish me with the outcome I desire. After all, Cream *has* served his usefulness . . ."

His mind made up, the tomb raider removed a simple pocketknife from within the folds of an inside pocket, and advanced upon his prize once more.

*

For one of my regular nightmares, this particular dream was incredibly realistic. Both focused and lucid, it was so vivid that a full range of everyday sights, sounds and sensations washed over me.

Despite this, I knew it was only a fantasy. It had to be. For in it, I commanded legions of angels with a mighty hand. Flying above a battlefield of utter ruination, I led a charge that unleashed death and destruction upon God's foes. Thunderbolts raged through the heavens. Screams of outrage and terror pierced the clamor, and the distinctive aroma of ozone and incinerated quintessence filled the air.

Nothing *everyday* about it at all, really.

This nightmare was glorious. But it was anathema. Recoiling from my dilemma, I fought against the tide threatening to sweep me away. A tongue of vermillion flame blazed from the darkness, sundering my connection to the vision. Free at last, I fought my way back to consciousness.

Heart thudding, my eyes snapped open. The darkened but familiar surroundings of my bedroom met my eager gaze.

I've been away too long. Once I'm up and about, I'll check in with the guys and then arrange with the Boss for a dose of Bãlefire. There's bound to be a whole pile of new contracts waiting for me, so it'll be best to resume my duties with all guns blazing.

I was about to relax again when I noticed the drapes curling indolently in the breeze. Then a stronger cool draft of air intruded, and teased the hairs along the exposed flesh of my torso and legs.

I don't remember leaving the shutter open . . .

Intrigued, I slid quietly out of bed, padded buck-naked across to the window, and drew back the curtains. Sure enough, one of the stained glass vents had been unclasped and jammed open with what looked like a folded piece of card, allowing the soothing gloom of a brand new day in the underworld to filter, unhindered, into my room.

I wasn't too concerned. My suite took up the entire top floor of the southeastern corner of Black Tower, in what mortals would call the Tower of London. But that was a literal lifetime away. In the netherworld, we call this ancient fortress the Den of Iniquity—or the Den for short. Located at the center of the sprawling edifice that was Olde London Town, within the Juxtapose level of hell, it was a fitting tribute to one of the greatest symbols of oppression ever completed by William the Conqueror, for here my department and I wielded authority.

As Satan's bounty hunter, it was my job to run rebels down and reel them in. For those especially difficult assignments, I'd employ the services of my personal posse of trackers: Nimrod, Champ Ferguson, and Yamato Takeru. Known collectively as the Hell Hounds, the mere mention of their names struck fear into the festering hearts of Juxtapose's every denizen. And well it should, for my team was ruthlessly efficient and showed no mercy.

But as infamous as the Hell Hounds were, there was another section under my jurisdiction which the simpering masses feared more.

On those occasions when someone gained unauthorized access to sensitive information, or was stupid enough to really piss off His Infernal Majesty, their reassignment would most likely be deferred. Such instances were rare, true, but when they happened the Boss usually allowed the Inquisitors to come out to play.

And *play* they did.

The extraction of information—as well as teeth, blood, nails, and all manner of other bodily fluids and appendages—was their business. They were very good at it.

Sequestered in Blood Tower along the inner ramparts of the southern wall, the Inquisitors ensured only the darkest and most despicable standards of foul play were meted out. So enthusiastic were they in the application of their arts that very often there was hardly enough essence remaining in their victims' mutilated remains for the Undertaker to work his magic.

Yes, an ambiance of morbid dread saturated these environs, and the regular serenade provided by the ululating shrieks and screams of those being tortured only exacerbated the atmosphere.

No wonder the rank and file avoided this place like the plague.

Thus, as I looked across the smog-laden, filth-stained roof-tops toward the city itself, I wasn't too concerned that someone might have gone to the bother of breaching my inner and outer defenses, scaling the walls, and opening a window, just to scare me. I get death threats all the time. They come with the job.

"Death threats." I snorted in barely restrained contempt. "Bloody idiots! Most of them still think we're alive in some way, and cling vainly to what remains of their humanity. As if that will ever count in their favor in a place like this."

I leaned across the sill and inhaled the fetid stench of rot and decay. Up above, the dusky glow of Paradise fought to pierce the gloom but, as usual, its pathetic attempts only served to halo the clouds in a repulsive golden-yellow backdrop. Down below, a flock of ravens took flight as a plaintive howl issued from the dungeons.

Someone's started work early.

The cry rose into the air before being snatched away on the breeze.

Thank purgatory I'm back where I belong. I took another deep breath and smiled. *This is where I was meant to be.*

That same gust of wind knocked the window shutter against the ancient granite of the tower's buttress. The impact caused the wedge holding it in place to fall loose. Dropping to the floor, it bounced once with a crisp scrunching noise and came to rest against my feet.

I glanced at the offending article and noticed it wasn't card at all, but thick, expensive paper.

Are those letters?

Retrieving the parchment, I unfolded it, marveling at its texture.

Hey! This stuff is luxuriant and hard to come by. Most of those wanting to make a statement in New Hell go for vellum made of human skin. But this? This looks handmade. And the characters are exquisite.

Written in blood, the words of a poem called to me:

> *I will catch these stars of midnight black,*
> *Of foulest thoughts*
> *In mirrored halls of polished sheen,*
> *Where exquisite acts of murder sublime*
> *Foster rose-blood gardens,*
> *And foes*
> *Reaped upon a sea of bitter dread.*
>
> *I know what you are, chrysalis,*
> *And what you purport to be.*
> *For scarlet blooms and accusations*
> *Shadow your every step,*
> *And memory's ancient wrath*
> *Will seal the fate of your immortal coil.*

"Yup," I chuckled, "another death threat, and a prosaic one at that. Where do they get this drivel?"

I was about to toss this latest waste of time into the bin when I noticed something distinctive about it. Holding the passage up to the light, I confirmed my suspicions.

Look at that! The writing markedly deteriorates as the verse progresses. It's almost as if the author was in a rush to finish, or something marred his hand.

My deliberations were interrupted by a soft growl of frustration from the other side of the room. "Are you coming back to bed, or what?"

All thoughts of intrigue forgotten, I dropped the note and looked toward the source of the query: Strawberry Fields. She lay like a goddess, curled across my black satin sheets, where her venetian-blonde hair had fanned out to form a halo of fire about her. A heat matched only by the color of her lips and the first flush of arousal now gracing the surface of her radiant and incredibly curvy flesh.

Yum, yum.

Among the elite of Hellonian society, we were allowed the luxury of unrestrained sex. Just as well. Strawberry was one of my best Inquisitors, and one of the few people I could make physical contact with. Her appetites were as inventive as they were demanding.

Not that I minded. The Boss had imbued me with a whole arsenal of arcane and physical attributes; among them, increased reactions, stamina, and strength, as well as the ability to heal quickly. Such enhancements were necessary to allow me to fulfill my duties unhindered.

Of course, at times like this, I had a whole host of additional perks to enjoy.

Green eyes blinked open, and an insidious look crossed a set of impeccably formed features. Strawberry uncoiled herself from the covers, exposing flawless porcelain skin and perfectly formed breasts.

"Get your body over here," she purred. "My first interrogation isn't for an hour yet, so we've just got time to—"

Her most welcome invitation was drowned out by the shrill interruption of a phone ringing.

Hellfire! Whoever that is better have a damned good reason for calling.

Without shifting my gaze from the bittersweet promise of perversion and pain before me, I stomped across the room, fiddled for the deck, and then snatched it from its cradle.

"Yes?" I snapped. "Who is this?"

"Ah, Daemon Grim," announced an oily, nasally whine. "I thought I might find you still ensconced within the splendors of your most magnificent castle."

I recognized the smug, arrogant bastard on the other end of the line straight away. We hated each other with a passion, and his voice always reminded me of nails grating down a chalkboard. He realized that, and used his advantage as often as he could, for he knew I would never willingly communicate with him telepathically.

The Undertaker.

When I didn't reply immediately, he continued: "With a lady friend, are you? Do apologize to Strawberry on my behalf for interrupting her meal, but I'm afraid she'll have to satisfy her urges elsewhere, and at another time."

Is he daring to read my mind?

"What the fuck do you want?" I growled, slamming my mental barriers into place at the same time. "I'm busy."

"Busy?"

The disdain in his reply was evident. In fact, I could envisage a sneer stretching its way across his ugly mug right this second.

"You heard me. Think of it as recharging my batteries after a successful hunt. I'm back at work later today. If you've got a retrieval request, submit it through proper channels like everyone else."

"Ah yes, about that *successful* hunt. Would you be so kind as to drag your sorry ass over to my mortuary? On the double would be more than sufficient. We've things to discuss."

"What's the matter?" I retorted. "Aren't you happy with the latest batch of freshers from topside? Not good enough for you?"

"On the contrary, I've spent the last few days giving them a cursory examination, and they'll prove more than suitable. His Satanic Majesty seems enamored by one Josephine Abigail Reed in particular. How did he refer to her . . . ? Ah yes, 'a Black Widow among spiderlings, if ever there was one.' As much as it pains me to admit it, you did very well—"

"Good." I was becoming impatient with the obvious maneuvering by one of the biggest backstabbers in the underverse. "So what's your problem? And who do you think you are, imagining for one moment you can tell me to drop everything and come halfway around hell just to satisfy your overblown sense of self-importance?"

A moment's silence followed before the Undertaker finally revealed his hand:

"The list is—how can I say this—a little short?"

Eh? "Short? Look, I've only been back three days, and in the hectic carnival that always follows such a mission, I simply haven't had time to catch up on everything. Stop frigging about and get to the point."

"If you insist," he simpered. "While the latest recruits were indeed satisfactory, I'm afraid to say your list was missing the cream off the top."

Cream off. . . ? The penny dropped.

Even when alive, Dr. Thomas Neill Cream had possessed all the virtues we looked for in a potential Hellonian. Although a qualified doctor, he was nonetheless a narcissistic sociopath who'd used his skills as a backstreet abortionist to purge the dregs of nineteenth-century London with an élan both detached and merciless. His proclivity was best expressed by his habit of poisoning his victims and then staying to watch, so he could enjoy the prolonged misery of their slow and painful deaths.

Reviled as the Lambeth Poisoner, Cream had such a penchant for celebrity that he basked in the notoriety bestowed upon him by the mistaken belief he might be Jack the Ripper—a myth publicly dispelled shortly before his death by hanging in 1892.

Although we welcomed him with open arms, Cream was never one to accept the fact that, in a place like this, he'd never be top dog. So he did something monumentally stupid in an attempt to boost his standing.

Not only did Cream manage to drug Satan with one of his foulest concoctions, he also took something from His Diabolical Majesty. This item was extremely sensitive. Designed to serve as an inducement, and to lure rebellious hearts and test their loyalty, even the knowledge of the artifact's existence was a closely guarded secret, limited to a privileged few.

Cream simply wasn't important enough to be on that list.

That's where I came in. Dispatched with all haste to retrieve both Cream and the article he'd stolen, I managed to track him down and ensure that any evidence relating to the fiasco was brutally sanitized. No one else would ever discover how close the Boss had come to public embarrassment.

Of course, job done, I'd consigned Cream's sorry ass back to where it belonged.

At least, I thought I had.

Taken unawares, I gasped, "Are you saying Cream never arrived?"

"You are a sharp one, aren't you? At first, I thought your Inquisitors might still be toying with him. After all, I can only imagine how exasperated our infernal master was to discover one of his subjects had tried to run rings around him. And you know how much Satan hates to be vexed. So, I presumed they were enforcing those sentiments, and ensuring our dear doctor labored under no illusions as to the eternal consequences of his error. I must confess, I was rather disappointed to discover Cream never actually made it to your Den of Incompetence in the first place. Therefore, my next assumption was that *you* must be overseeing his reeducation, personally. In light of recent information, I see I was sorely mistaken."

"Recent information?"

"Oh yes, did I forget to say? I have something with me that you might like to cast your eye over."

I ran my gaze along Strawberry's exquisite form once more.

"I'm already 'casting my eye' over someone. And I doubt that what *you* have would beat what I'm looking at right now."

Damnation's biggest thorn in the flesh didn't accept my blatant invitation to expand on his statement.

"So?" I snapped. "Are you going to tell me what it is, or not?"

Once again, Mr. Obnoxious didn't even deign to reply.

Or not it is. One of these days, you annoying prick. One of these days . . .

I let images of my fondest wish come true soothe the cauldron of my rage for a moment before daring to speak. I didn't want the Undertaker to know how much he irritated me.

With a final glance at what could have been, I turned away from Strawberry and hissed, "I'm on my way, and Satan help you if you're messing me about."

The line went dead.

What a jerk!

Chapter 2: Slab A

Ever since His Satanic Majesty thought to separate the various circles of hell into different levels, long-distance journeys had become something of a nightmare, for each sphere could endure at times and in places that did not mesh with its neighbors.

In some cases, adjoining domains adhered to seasonal rhythms completely at odds with those around them. In others, like Juxtapose, pockets could manifest whereby a multitude of different dimensions co-existed within the same borders. The trouble was, this didn't prevent them from bleeding into each other on a random basis. In Olde London Town, for example, you might be walking along a street covered in asphalt and flagstones one moment, and find yourself stumbling across cobbles and jumping out of the way of horse-drawn carriages the next.

The variety and complexity of the situation was mind-boggling. No wonder, then, that when forced to travel, most citizens would try to use the Bridge, a multidimensionhell construct capable of transmuting itself into any number of forms to safely reach its objective. As it presented the easiest and most relaxing method of transportation, it was by far the most popular option.

If slumming with the vassals was beneath you, another alternative was afforded by a host of gateways, scattered here and there throughout each province. Most of these were officially sanctioned by the Department of Injustice, and used by those in positions of responsibility, such as Satan's intelligence agency, the Devil's Children, or his bureaucrats, the Blue Suits.

Some of these gateways looked like actual doors or archways and were incorporated into the structure of official buildings. Others were hidden in plain sight and disguised as brick walls, streetlamps, or telephone booths, and could only be used by those with the ability to distinguish occult energy.

No matter who you were, however, we all had to be careful of the rifts. Insidious tears in the Sheolspace continuum that warped the fringes of reality and turned everything on its head.

If you walked into a rift unawares, you might find yourself fractured into a million pieces, in two or more places at once, or forced into a situation where you overlapped the same moment in time. People had been driven insane by the experience of reliving their own everyday lives, again and again and again.

*Talk about d*éjà—*I'm well and truly fucked up*—*vu!*

Needless to say, the ever-present hazard of enforced lunacy didn't stop the plethora of revolutionaries infesting the underworld from exploiting these loopholes as often as they could. It was either that or pay Tesla a fortune for one of his multidimensionhell rift projectors.

And our dissidents hate to part with their hard-won campaign money.

Fortunately, I didn't have to stress myself too much in this regard. Due to the nature of my duties, I must be able to move about swiftly. To facilitate this, the Boss had given me an ethereal anchor to prevent any unforeseen mishaps: the Bālefire. An abstruse power source of untold potential, it ran through my veins like precious lifeblood, enhancing my abilities and negating obstacles at the drop of a hat.

Of course, the Undertaker's tantrum meant I hadn't had time to recharge my eternally damned soul since returning from the land of the living. Nonetheless, I'd still felt grounded enough to make the trip.

Having arrived, incident free, in New Hell via the Azazel gateway only seconds ago, I decided to use the short walk to the Mortuary to clear my head and remind myself why I disliked the Undertaker so much.

When a condemned soul first awakens here, they are tormented by a measured dose of Satan's Grace, an inscrutable concentrate of pure, unadulterated, diabolical tincture. This cryptic essence first discerns what an individual holds most dear, then warps it, so it becomes their greatest bane.

A poet, for example, might be unable to remember a single verse, or be forced to recite perfect prose in languages undecipherable to all who listen. An athlete could awaken with joints that shatter at the slightest exertion. A talented singer may find themselves mute, with no vocal cords whatsoever. Or, in a particularly inventive move, realize their voice has been enhanced to a superlative degree, but the actual words of their chosen songs burn like acid in their throats. Lovers would be cursed with detailed memories of their former devotion, only to realize they could no longer stand the sight of each other.

And fair enough in my book. It's what hell is about, after all. If they'd sinned enough in life, they'd pay for it here, eternally, and with no chance of reprieve.

Wiser hearts accepted this, and knuckled down to make the best of their situation. Others rebelled, fought tooth and nail to do whatever they could to deny the reality of their predicament.

They couldn't win, of course, but part of me admired their balls. Such souls faced un-life bravely, come what may.

The same went for those who died, again, after they had arrived. Termed "reassignment," reanimated existence was a very fragile thing, a minefield-riddled assault course, compounded by the stark fact that murder—both official and unofficial—was the most widely promoted hobby here. Practiced with zealous aplomb by most of the populace, it turned everyday life into a marathon filled with constant hazards and impending death.

An uphill treadmill leading nowhere.

But, to their credit, the majority of my fellow subjects adapted to this drastic change in circumstance and simply got on with it.

Take, for instance, my own situation. I had a job to do that brought me up-close and personal with the most offensive dregs of Hellistic society. Radicals, scumbags, traitors, despots. They were my daily fare. Week after week, year after year, day in, day out. I also must adapt to face the unending challenge and get the job done.

And then there was the Undertaker.

As you can imagine, a place like this has no shortage of candidates especially deserving of further torment. But the Undertaker wasn't satisfied to leave things to fate. Oh no. *He* preferred to hide away in his stinking laboratory like an obscene cockroach waiting to feed on the unwary, and his choicest tidbits were those who couldn't bite back. The weak. The needy. The maladjusted and confused.

Hell's biggest coward seemed to relish the fact he could do whatever he wanted, to virtually whomever he wanted, without fear or consequence. His unconscious victims would materialize on his slab, helpless and alone, and be subjected to a whole catalog of invasive alterations. And the intrusions this twisted, depraved little insect inflicted on others were as obscene as they were plentiful.

He made things much too personal in my opinion. So much so that I was increasingly suspicious he got some kind of sexual gratification from his egotistical little power trips.

Power trips? Bah! He's just a closet rapist, is all, hiding his own inadequacies behind the façade of his rank and privileges.

So lost was I in my personal stew of bitter resentment that I hadn't realized how far nor how quickly I'd traveled. Checking my step, I found myself staring across the street toward the imposing columns of the entrance portico to the Mortuary. Constructed of Black Widow marble, it created an ominous area of deep shadow that frowned upon passersby and leached into the fabric of the sidewalk.

The legend inscribed across the pediment, *Abandon Hope, All Ye Who Enter Here*, bade a chilling welcome to the throngs doing their best to give the steps as wide a berth as possible. Difficult to do, seeing as the edifice filled an entire city block.

Without waiting for a gap in the traffic, I made eye contact with the driver of an advancing taxi, flicked back the vent of my coat, and stepped out. It took a moment for the poor soul to register my presence and that I was now right in front of him. His bulldog features clouded in anger. That classic look was replaced by one of shock, a split second later, as he recognized the scythe, my clothes, and what it meant to cross me.

A squeal of brakes split the constant drone of engines and horns. He shuddered to a halt only inches from my legs and breathed a huge sigh of relief. Then his cab bounced as he was struck from behind by a truck. The continuous stream of vehicles in both directions paused to enjoy the entertainment, while I seized the opportunity to saunter casually across to the other side whilst tactfully ignoring the sudden torrent of obscenities unleashed behind me.

As I closed on the Mortuary, my heightened awareness tingled. The nearer I got, the more I recognized the muted presence of devilish power. Aroused, I opened my senses fully to capture the full flavor of its essence and began to salivate.

Dark and foreboding, ancient crystallized walls radiated an air of misery, an effect exacerbated by the red-veined exterior, which made it appear as if lifeblood ran through its very structure. Ascending the steps, I detected an unsavory exudation, as of meat left to rot and fester in the sun. Repelled, I wrinkled my nose. The odor increased as I pushed through the smoked-glass revolving doors.

Within, a maze of interconnected passages and walkways awaited me. Stretching off into the gloom, none of them gave any indication of the nature of the work taking place in the bowels below, for they gleamed with a pristine radiance that revealed someone here had developed a somewhat obsessive attitude toward cleanliness.

And since his run-in with Astarte, Queen of the Dead, I can guess who.

The place looked deserted. I was just about to call out when a sad-looking fellow with sorry eyes peeled himself away from the shadows. Skeletal beyond belief, his skin had a bleached, gray-white pallor to it that reminded me of molten wax.

"Follow me," he announced solemnly, "my master awaits you in the main studio."

Master? Studio? I sighed. *Only a total ass-wipe would have such illusions of grandeur, imagining the butchery he practices is an art form. Wait until I tell the guys.*

Without waiting for a reply, Mr. Happy spun on his heels and shuffled quietly off along the main arterial corridor. I followed at a discreet distance, only to be led past a series of vacant bench-seats and individual waiting rooms, mysterious, hushed offices, and empty elevators.

We eventually arrived at the end of the hallway and descended a ponderously wide, wrought-iron spiral staircase. As if it were determined to refute the standards displayed by the rest of the building, it creaked ominously under our weight. I could actually see the dust falling away from the wall as the restraining bolts groaned in protestation.

Round and round we went, descending gradually. With each passing level, the general hubbub increased. Thirteen floors later, we arrived at the bottom in what I could only describe as a hive of activity, and a jaw-dropping tribute to the immaculate conception of bacterial-free efficiency.

There were minions everywhere. Buzzing from one side of the subterranean corridor to the other, they pushed, pulled, carried and dragged all manner of orthopedic, vascular and pathological appendages from this lab to that.

I couldn't resist glancing into each of the cold rooms as we passed.

The Mortuary was renowned as a palace of death and resurrection. A hovel, where intestines should lie intertwined with sinews and arteries but often didn't. Skin and bone with eyeballs and teeth. The mere mention of this place conjured visions of filthy, blood- and feces-stained walls, where the liquefied remains of those incurring His Auspicious Majesty's displeasure dripped through grilles in the floor.

I didn't see any evidence of that. Instead, I witnessed endless racks of numbered boxes and musty sacks neatly filling shelves or hanging from meat-hooks like prize joints in a butcher's emporium. Floor to ceiling high, each refrigerator overflowed with the well-kept remains of those awaiting mutilation and reactivation.

In smaller storehouses, ranked tiers of sarcophagi and pallets lay open for inspection, their occupants afforded a degree of dignity sorely absent elsewhere.

Obviously Blue Suits or other privileged dignitaries of the Satanic Intelligence Agencies.

I couldn't believe what I was seeing. Even in those theatres where autopsies were currently underway, the substantial assortment of drills, cutters, handsaws and chisels adorning each of the pegs on the walls showed clear signs of lavish care and maintenance.

And this place is much larger than you'd ever imagine from the surface.

Lingering at the entrance to one of the side cells, I noted with interest how the technicians within the receiving area managed the ongoing situation.

Fluorescent lighting, harsh against the white-tiled backdrop, illuminated the sterility of their working environment. The smell of bleach and antiseptic spray stung my nostrils. Four orderlies held a limp, comatose female subject in position, whilst a further pair strapped her into restraints. After a final check of an accompanying chart, an assortment of scalpels and meat cleavers were laid out in order upon a starched, green surgical cloth. With a flourish, the assistants set to, and in no time every stainless steel bowl adorning the surrounding trolleys was overflowing with ruby-red entrails and bone-white appendages.

A further flurry of activity followed. I watched, enthralled, while a mishmash of body parts and organs was expertly sewn into a conflicting patchwork of utter mayhem.

In response to an unspoken signal, the close-knit team loosened the fetters holding their patient in place and jumped back. A sizzling discharge energized the air with abstruse potential. The corpse twitched, shuddered, then lay still once more.

Satisfied, the minions filed into an adjoining cubicle to start the procedure anew on a fresh victim, while waiting ghouls scurried in to devour the leftovers.

Having noticed my curiosity, the guide explained: "Although many of us assist with preparations, final inspections are always carried out by the Undertaker himself or his principal deputy, Gorgonous. Only then will they be fully reanimated."

I suppressed a shiver.

The mere thought of the control exercised by hell's slimiest turd made me realize how fortunate I was, for I had never graced the Undertaker's lair.

Who I was or what I did before I arrived here, I'd never known. I had a void in my mind that effectively swallowed all knowledge of my previous existence. My first ever recollections of the netherworld were of waking up in a comfy chair before a roaring fire, in the presence of the Dark Majesty himself. For reasons I still can't understand, he welcomed me into the fold like a prodigal son.

Empowered personally by Satan, I was infused with the diabolical puissance to carry out my special duties and ushered into a whole new, privileged way of life. I'd taken to my role like a duck to water and never looked back. As far as I was concerned, my previous existence didn't come into it. It wasn't important then, nor would it ever be.

I cast a final glance toward the body on the block.

There, but for the grace of Lucifer, go I. These poor bastards don't stand a chance . . .

The guide took my silence as an indication that I'd seen enough. Without a further word, he turned and we continued on our way.

We eventually arrived at the end of the corridor and paused before a set of double-swing gates. This chamber appeared larger and more ornate than those we'd passed so far. The threshold itself and decorative kick-strips along the bottom of each flap were of highly polished brass. Despite its spotless appearance, however, this room stank to high heaven.

Unholy shit! It smells as if the odor permeating this place emanates from in here. Is he distilling skunk-piss hooch on the side?

A sign above the lintel declared: Private—Slab #A1.

I had to smile.

Private? Who'd voluntarily want their nasal cavities and eyeballs melted?

We were expected. Before Mr. Happy could announce us, an ingratiating voice pronounced, "You may enter."

Biting back an instant retort, I pushed past my escort, kicked the gates wide and stepped in. I had to admit, what I saw astonished me. Whereas the other rooms were overflowing with equipment and all sorts of other ancillary paraphernalia, this one was surprisingly Spartan.

A massive chunk of gold and cream marble dominated the center of the workspace. Shaped exactly like an embalming table, its bulk dwarfed the solitary cabinet and double-wheeled trolley positioned to one side. A large butler's sink graced the opposite wall, and I noticed with interest that the entire floor was one huge grate.

The Undertaker himself languished on the far side of the slab. His slicked-back hair and So'vile Row suit looked oddly out of place with his surroundings, and he appeared totally at ease within the confines of his own little kingdom.

Time to rectify that!

"Well, here I am," I snapped. As I strode purposely forward, I cracked the knuckles of each hand. "Now, why don't you start explaining why you dragged me half way around the underworld before I start rearranging your face?"

He glided toward me like a stunt double of Bela Lugosi from the 1931 black and white classic, "*Dracula.*" As he drew near, the fetid stench saturating the air intensified.

Prince of Darkness! I'd forgotten just how bad his breath is.

"My dear boy," he tittered, "a picture paints a thousand words. Or in your case, a personal message does. While Cream himself appears to have eluded my abode, something else took his place." Gesturing toward the slab, he explained: "*This* is why I felt it prudent to demand your personal appearance."

I glanced toward the surface of the table, and for the first time noticed a piece of card positioned across the plug. A calcified lump of what looked like pumice had been placed on top of it, to hold it there. Pale red letters peeked out from under the stone. Snatching it up, I confirmed my suspicions.

Another note written in blood. And by the same hand, too.

The words inscribed upon it said:

> *Listening,*
> *You resolutely ignore the injustice of your actions.*
> *A mockery,*
> *You judge others by your master's opinion.*
> *Guilty,*
> *All stand condemned, and mock your integrity.*
> *Now freed by a trifling passion,*
> *I long to possess what you have.*
> *Please, accept this small token,*
> *For Arthur's folly leads the way,*
> *On blood-stained, piss-soaked sheets.*
> *An inferno of wasted passions*
> *Dedicated to your most lavish attentions, awaits.*

Sure enough, the text degraded the longer the passage went on, as if the author had once again rushed to complete his message before being discovered.

The Undertaker stepped closer. Nodding toward the note, he said, "Our mutual loathing aside, I think it may be in our best interests to investigate this matter together."

"Why do you say that?"

"To put the matter succinctly, I'd like to know *how* Cream managed to avoid my net. And all outward vocalizations aside, I have no doubt our master's confidence in you is well founded. Your loyalty to him is, after all, without question, and your competence, renown. Up until now, you have never failed him—"

"And I never will!" I waved the parchment in his face. "This is far from over. If you knew the specifics of Cream's misdeeds, you would realize he is far more resourceful than he appears. Why do you think I was dispatched topside to retrieve him in the first place?"

That got him. The Undertaker fell silent, and had the decency to look deeply troubled.

I added, "That's why I'm going to let him play this little game through. He's obviously got contacts: well connected contacts who, for whatever reason, were not only able to assist him in planning his crimes but also had the wherewithal to add a little insurance policy to cover his ass if things went wrong. It took me two days to catch up with him the first time, so I want to know who they are, too. And by the way, you should know, I didn't just consign his soul back to hell, I *bound* him here."

"You bound his essence?" The Undertaker looked shocked. "But that should have meant . . ."

"Yes, I know. No one should have been able to interfere with my machinations. No one! The fact that someone did has made this personal. Big mistake." I tapped the top of Slab A with my finger. "One way or another, I promise you now, Cream will wind up here. The Reaper guarantees it."

"So, what are you going to do?"

"Besides recommending you use a stronger breath freshener . . . ?"

I scanned the poem again. Although it conveyed a different tone to the one left at my apartment, both seemed imbued with a veiled challenge.

Cream obviously wants something from me to help achieve his goal. To discover what that is, exactly, it looks like I'll need to be patient.

Aloud I suggested, "He's taunting me, daring me to decipher the clues and follow him. Can't you see? These rhymes are nothing but the bait I need to catch him."

"Catch him?"

"Yes, look." I held out the note and read aloud, "'Now freed by a trifling passion, I long to possess what you have. Please, accept this small token, for Arthur's folly leads the way.'"

I came to a decision—one I thought I'd never entertain where the Undertaker was concerned. "I'll ask His Excellency to update you with what he deems you should know. It'll probably be necessary anyway, to ensure the appropriate mind-wipe takes place before his next reassignment."

In reply to the look of confusion that clouded the Undertaker's face, I explained: "Basically, Cream is doing what he's doing in a vain attempt to increase his notoriety. He doesn't simply want to stand condemned; he wants to revel in it. Don't let appearances fool you. He will do anything, risk everything—even a thousand years in Hades and Purgatory—to go down in history as . . ." I caught myself just in time. "Let's just say, he's having a dig at me, and hinting where I might find a further breadcrumb or two. Something about Arthur's folly? Evidently, it will lead the way to the next clue."

"So *that's* why he left this?" the Undertaker gasped, holding out the strange stone toward me. "I thought it an odd choice of paperweight."

Taking possession of the rock, I got an instant hit of residual, ancient power. Its texture was much smoother than I expected.

The Undertaker continued, "The token he's left you isn't what you think. I've examined it myself and was shocked to discover it's actually a piece of carbonized bone . . . of angelic origins."

"Angelic? How the blazes did it get here?"

"Such things are rumored to exist." He shrugged. "Remember, after the war that led to the ousting and the division of the brethren, both Yahweh and Satan lost many of their strongest advocates. Scores perished in deep darkness, thought to be lost forever."

"So you're suggesting this fragment is from one of the Heavenly Host, fallen in battle? But if that's true, where did Cream find it? *How* did he find it, come to that? And what does all this have to do with me?"

"Perhaps this 'Arthur's folly' will begin to lead the way?"

Something the Undertaker once said now gave me an idea. *It can't be that obvious . . .* can it? I suppressed a snigger, and turned to my new best friend. "You were involved in quite a public spectacle last year, weren't you? I remember reading about it in the Sinday Times. Couldn't miss it, really, seeing as they splashed your antics across the entire front cover. What was it again? Ah yes, the InfernoCon 666 Convention. When asked *why* you caused such carnage, you were quoted as saying, 'the folly of this debacle shouldn't be—'"

"'The folly of this *pretentious, poetic* debacle shouldn't be allowed to detract from the fact that there is no such thing as salvation, here in hell,'" the Undertaker interjected, quoting himself, "no hope of redemption. No chance of deliverance. No possibility of escape."

"Precisely. And that was just across the street from here, wasn't it?"

"Why, yes it was. Do you think . . . ?"

"I do. Not only was Cream here, but he had the nerve to remain close-by. Close enough to include a jibe that links your

antics to Arthurian legend and Excalibur. Or, as we refer to it here
. . ."

"The Hexcalibur Hotel!"

"Give the man a cigar. From what I've heard about the place, blood-soaked and piss-stained sheets are an everyday occurrence. Cream's leaving a trail for me to follow. So, while you determine exactly how the little fucker managed to avoid reassignment, I'm going to start pecking at breadcrumbs."

Chapter 3: The Game's Afoot

Arranged over sixty-six levels, the Hexcalibur Hotel was a dominant feature of the New Hell skyline. Ideally situated for Dr. Thomas Neill Cream's purposes, it not only attracted denizens from both ends of the social ladder, but also from far-ranging time periods and other realms.

Kings, queens, and despots graced the penthouse suites with their extravagant excesses; princes and princesses the staterooms; from where they would plan minion-hunting purges and engage in drunken revelry. Even the mundane, everyday riffraff were welcome since the establishment regularly hosted all manner of themed soirées popular among the masses. Many an illicit tryst and murderous plot had been fomented within the eight hundred and fifty-eight rooms that made up this shining beacon to depravity. So ready, in fact, were the staff to turn a blind eye to just about anything except sedition that the hotel regularly attracted the likes of fallen angels and demon lords, and agents of Satan's intelligence network who wished to remain anonymous.

Due to its proximity to the Mortuary and a nearby rift gate, the Hexcalibur had become a fashionable rendezvous for huge ranks of Blue Suits gathering in force to welcome back colleagues slain in the line of their ever unpopular duty. Indeed, at this very minute both the ground and first-floor foyers were packed with well-heeled clientele. As such, the distinguished-looking gentleman sitting on the tearoom balcony overlooking the busy street attracted no attention whatsoever. And although his top hat and tails, heavily waxed mustache, thick-rimmed glasses and ornate walking cane set him apart from the usual briefcase-wielding crowd, nothing about this soul appeared exceptional.

But that was exactly the effect that Cream hoped to achieve.

Come on, come on. Where are you, for goodness sake? I'd have thought your golden-balls would have cottoned on by now.

He replaced his bone-china cup on its saucer, fished about inside his jacket, and removed an antique pocket watch. Flipping the lid, he assessed the time.

Just after noon. He's been in there for nearly two hours. Surely . . . ?

The revolving door of the building opposite began to turn. Cream caught his breath and sat forward in his seat. Moments later, he whistled a sigh of relief as his target stepped out into the midday gloom.

"There you are, my boy," he muttered. "So, you've taken the bait, have you, Grim?"

He looked on as Satan's Reaper stopped for a moment, checked his watch, then appeared to evaluate the bulwark of the hotel's façade.

Cream tensed again, absentmindedly fiddling with an ornate bracelet about his wrist as if the action provided a degree of security. Hatred welled up from the depths of his dark and embittered soul.

"You thought to deny me my rightful place among the elite of the underworld. A foolish endeavor, for while I don't deny your power, you are nothing but a blunt instrument, a tool to be used and discarded at whim," Cream muttered aloud as Grim strode purposefully out into the traffic without looking left or right.

Brakes squealed. Horns blared. The sound of shattering glass and metal rending metal cut through the din. Curses rang back and forth until the creature below made eye contact with his hecklers. Then all protestations abruptly ceased as people scrambled to get out of the Reaper's way.

"I rest my case" Cream said softly.

The chaos below filled Cream with a surge of optimism. Grasping his walking stick, he caressed the neon-blue gem in its handle, allowing its radiance to infuse him with a calm that soothed his beating heart.

He glanced down at the street for a final time. "Oh yes. It would appear the game's afoot. Let's see how good you are, my boy, and if you can keep up after you've tasted my little distraction."

*

I stepped out of the Mortuary and into blissful fresh air, or at least, whatever it was that passed for fresh air here. To be honest, after a visit with the Undertaker I couldn't think of anywhere in the underverse that wouldn't smell like roses in comparison.

A quick check of the time revealed it was just after midday.

Is that all? I can't believe it was only this morning I was still in Juxtapose.

A fleeting image of what I'd left behind fluttered through my mind.

Strawberry.

I glanced at my watch again. A Rolhex Sky-Fall, it was brand new, and a gift from Strawberry herself. She'd bought it as a replacement for my previous timepiece, a Denizen 6000, smashed to pieces three months ago by Kroyel Ash Fangs, an overly ambitious demon lord who'd violently disagreed with Satan's ruling that he be relocated to the frigid depths of Niflheim. Part of me could understand his reticence at being banished to freeze his ass off for a thousand years.

But he didn't have to take it out on my Denizen 6000. Bastard! I'd had that for over two centuries. It never lost a second . . . until he put his fat cloven hoof through it.

For Strawberry to buy me a present like this meant something. Not that we could get engaged or anything. One of the quirks of unlife here—privileges or not—was that such relationships were simply not allowed. Exclusivity was frowned upon, unless it was directed in His Satanic Majesty's direction, of course.

Still, we have what we have . . .

Shaking my thoughts clear, I stared up at the imposing height of the Hexcalibur Hotel and studied the gargoyles adorning its weathered crown over eight hundred feet above me.

From what I remember, it covers sixty-six floors and has thirteen apartments on each level. Where would I stay if I was leaving a trail to follow?

A cacophony of horns and intermingled shouts of alarm intruded, and my attention abruptly snapped back to the here and now. I was greeted by a sea of angry faces and shaking fists. Without realizing it, I had started to cross the road , paying no heed to my surroundings.

My trademark death's-head stare silenced the dissenters almost immediately, and I breezed across the broad street unhindered.

The wash of malevolent energies that bathed my senses as I entered the hotel's main foyer was overpowering. Some patrons scrutinized my presence with disdain. Others tactfully ignored me, refusing to make eye contact. A few blatantly sized me up, as if eager to test their strength against the Reaper. But that was to be expected. This was hell, after all, and the halls of this establishment were as blighted by the ignorant and foolish as they were by the elite and proud.

So long as they don't try to interfere in my business, I'll let them walk away.

My romantically naïve sentiments were crushed almost immediately:

The moment he saw me, a hulking great brute with no discernible neck detached himself from the cocktail bar. Dragging his hairy knuckles along behind him, he approached with the swaggering confidence of one newly dead, someone who hadn't yet found his place in the greater scheme of things.

I was puzzled. *Does he normally look like that, or was the Undertaker tripping when he experimented on this one?*

A sense of imminent conflict radiated around the room, and between us grew an empty space. A hush descended. More worryingly, it actually went dark as the Neanderthal loomed over me.

"Hello, Chuckles, I don't believe we've met?" I began, hoping to diffuse the situation with humor. "My name's—shit a brick!"

Despite his size, the missing link was exceedingly swift.

A huge club of a fist appeared and buried itself up to the wrist in the lobby's highly polished granite floor. I stared in amazement at the cracks spiderwebbing outward from the exact spot where I'd been standing only a split second before.

If I hadn't been fast enough, my new watch would have been buggered! Or my head, come to that. Aloud, I advised, "Whoa, big boy. I suggest you rein in the aggression, or aim it at someone else . . ."

Chuckles wasn't paying attention. He seemed more content to work himself into a frothing frenzy as he struggled to retrieve his hand. With a mighty heave he wrenched it free amid a shower of stone chips and debris, and immediately took another swing.

"Look," I continued, ducking, "I appreciate you haven't been here long but if you don't listen, this will end badly. Now, *back off.*"

My words were like a red flag to a bull. No sooner had I spoken than he dropped his head, threw his arms wide, and charged. Once again I was shocked by his speed, for he managed to catch me around the waist and lift me off the floor. With a roar, he slammed us both into the nearest coffee table.

Wood and glass flew in every direction as furniture disintegrated under our weight. Several bystanders, too slow to get out of the way, were pulled into the fray. We tumbled over and over in a tangle of arms, legs, and briefcases. Fortunately, the confusion gave me the opportunity to kick out and roll sideways, away from danger. I regained my feet and circled my opponent.

My skin tingled as I automatically healed the multiple lacerations covering my face.

Something about this situation doesn't feel right.

I stared into his eyes, trying to get a clearer picture of where this guy was coming from. Nothing concrete came back, except that I was dealing with someone stir-fry crazy and wound to fever pitch.

But why? How does he know me?

He gathered himself to leap again.

In the name of all that's unholy! I don't have time for this. I was faced with a choice. If I manifested, this debacle would be over instantly. The trouble was I'd use up precious vitality; vitality I simply didn't have to spare as I hadn't yet recharged my essence within the Bālefire. I needed my remaining potency to close on Cream. With so many witnesses, however, I couldn't let this challenge against Satan's authority go unanswered.

Time to make a statement.

As the meathead launched himself toward me I jumped forward, putting all my strength into the Hail Mary of sucker punches. Our combined momentum did the trick. As my fist connected with his face, a tremendous shockwave ran the length of my arm and down through my boots. The sharp report of snapping teeth and crushed cartilage rang out, loud and clear. I went numb to the shoulder.

Stunned, I stepped back, doing my best to hide my discomfort.

Hellfire! What's this guy made of, steel?

Chuckles stood stock still, disbelief etching his features. Blood flowed freely from his shattered nose and pulped mouth. With infinite slowness, he raised one hand to his face to check the damage. When his fingers came away scarlet, he stared intently at them, as if fascinated by the fact he was injured. He turned to look at me, and his gaze managed to convey an unspoken question just before his eyes rolled into the back of his head. A brief pause followed; then his knees folded and he crashed to the floor like an avalanche run amok.

The entire room quaked from the impact.

A red and green gem rolled out from one of his pockets.

Is that a bloodstone? That's worth a hundred diablos. Where did he get money like that so quickly?

The penny dropped.

I spun in a tight circle and drew my telescopic scythe from its sheath. People screamed in alarm and drew back, fearful of being reaped. I scanned the foyer, searching for anyone else who might be involved in the distraction.

When I found no one, I positioned myself above the poor dupe who had been conned into delaying me, pictured the Undertaker's gut-churning face, and opened my mind. Despite our agreement, I still felt dirty.

Did you see that?

I did, the Undertaker replied, *it would appear you are on the right track and Doctor Cream is keen to ensure the trail doesn't go cold.*

That's what worries me. He knows how costly a trip topside can be, and seems intent on preventing my rejuvenation. I'm about to send you my mystery party-pooper. Before you go all Picasso on him, would you please ensure his memories are extracted and examined thoroughly?

Seriously? With the obvious forethought Cream has given this little venture, do you honestly think there'll be anything of evidential value in there?

It's doubtful. But aren't you supposed to be an expert? Of course, if you don't feel up to it . . .

I left my thought unfinished, and instead conveyed a vivid scene of my Inquisitors getting down and dirty with the Neanderthal's brain.

No! No! The Undertaker shrieked in panicked alarm. *The extraction of detailed recollections is a delicate procedure, best conducted on a freshly revived corpse. Do* not *let your butchers anywhere near his skull; otherwise I might never discover how my own security was breached.*

Very well, but don't forget. There are larger fish to fry here than your pathetic security measures. Anyone and everyone with knowledge of what Cream's up to must be caught and interrogated. Get what you can, then permanently zombify him. Understood?

The Undertaker failed to reply, but I knew he'd heard me. The astral finger he projected through the ether was a dead giveaway.

That settled, I cleaved my attacker in two.

He disappeared amid a sulfurous cloud of vapor, and as the last whiff dissipated, a momentary pulse of approval thrummed along my nerves from someplace else.

Hmm. It seems my Infernal Father is also keeping an eye on events.

It didn't surprise me. He was never far away.

I glanced around the lobby again, trying to assess how many in the crowd might be members of one of his many secret intelligence agencies. Even I couldn't keep tabs on all of them.

Then I had a spur of the moment idea.

Boss? You know how important it is I keep this situation sanitized. If you can think of a way of reenergizing my spirit without me having to lose a day in limbo, I'd be grateful.

A vision of another finger, this one even larger and with a bloody great talon on the end loomed toward me, accompanied by a throb of echoing laughter and a sound like boulders being crushed.

His parting thought was crystal clear. *Stick that where Paradise doesn't shine and pull your socks up . . . or else!*

He was more annoyed at Cream being on the loose than I had first appreciated; I sobered instantly.

Right, I'd better get down to business.

I approached the reception desk, where a diminutive woman with ridiculously large, beaverlike front teeth studied my every step through thick-rimmed spectacles. A duty manager, her whole soul smacked of fastidious attention to detail.

The name tag said it all: Nora Woods.

Another stunning example of the Undertaker's razor-sharp wit.

Flashing my ID, I graced her with what I hoped was my best smile. Nora glanced at the badge and frowned, remaining unimpressed.

"My apologies for the disturbance. I'm here on official business, sanctioned by His Infernal Majesty. May I see the register? I'm particularly interested in guests who have stayed here over the past few weeks."

She clicked her fingers twice and gestured impatiently toward the debris littering the main foyer. For a moment, I thought she was telling me to clean up the mess I'd just made. I was about to remonstrate when a bellboy standing behind the counter snapped to attention, grabbed a dustpan and brush from beneath a table, and rushed to comply. As I watched him go, Nora slammed the ledger down on the desktop in front of me. Startled, I jumped back, and only then did I see the faintest of smiles flicker across her rodentlike face.

Ignoring her challenge to engage in a pissing contest, I cleared my mind and scanned through the list.

It didn't surprise me when the name Thomas Neill Cream failed to appear. So I started again, this time looking for clues. I was glad I did. Ten minutes later, my gaze came to rest on an entry from the previous week, only a few days after I'd supposedly bound the infamous doctor back to hell. It read:

Mr. Jack Lambeth. Purveyor of TLC
(Tonics—Lotions—Concoctions)
Floor 13. Room 13.

"So, the Poisoner couldn't resist yet another passing reference to his idol, the Ripper," I mumbled, piquing Nora's interest at last.

"Are you saying we had a Very Important Denizen staying with us who had to make do with a substandard room?" she gasped. "Why in Purgatory didn't he ask for a suite?"

She looked genuinely distressed.

"He's no VID," I snapped, and projected an image of him in the ether between us. "Mister *Lambeth* is a fugitive from injustice. I need access to that room. Now."

"But Mister Lambeth checked out this morning. The room is currently occupied."

Only this morning? "And?"

For emphasis, I peeked over the top of my sunglasses.

She started, fumbled with the contents of a top drawer, and produced a master keycard. Anticipating the next hurdle, I said, "There's no need for security to come with me. I'll return this once I'm done."

Without giving her a chance to argue, I snatched the card and strode away.

I needed time to think, so I took the back stairs.

What the hell is Cream's game? It looks like he's definitely watching me, baiting me so I stay hot on the trail. But even without a boost I'm more than a match for him. I must be missing something. I know, I'll have my contacts at the Fiendish Bureau of Investigation check into Cream's background, aliases, and recent movements prior to the topside incident. Perhaps they'll have something that will give me an edge.

Taking out my Spirit Hextel Blacktooth I placed the call, and spent the next few minutes giving my associates, Bella and Donna Nightshade, a rundown of the things I needed. Identical twins, they were as thorough as they were deadly. What these girls didn't know, they or their extensive network of informants would find out.

Satisfied, I exited the stairwell on the thirteenth floor and scooted along to the desired room. The place appeared deserted, just the way I liked it. Putting my ear to the door, I extended my senses and was rewarded by the sounds of someone inside.

It would seem they're engaged in a spot of physical activity. I grinned. *This'll spoil their day.*

As quietly as I could, I swiped the keycard through the lock, turned the handle, and crept inside. I wish I hadn't.

An obese walrus of a man filled the only couch in the room. Naked from the waist down, he'd positioned himself on the edge of the seat and hitched his knees back toward his shoulders. Some kind of wire trailed out of his ass and along to a control unit by his side. A regular, muffled buzzing noise intruded above the sound of his grunting. Bathed in sweat, his hands clenched and relaxed in time to a rhythmic humming.

He caught sight of me and jumped up in surprise. Vainly trying to cover his modesty, he gasped, "Would you mind knocking before you enter my room?"

Too late! The image of a landed whale was now indelibly etched on my fragile mind.

"Disturb you at a crucial moment, did I?"

"What? Who . . . ?" His gaze skipped from me to the sofa and then back again. His eyes widened as he registered my identity for the first time. "The Reaper! No, no, no. I haven't done anything wrong. I'm just charging my mobile phone."

I strode farther into the room and peered down at the couch. What I'd assumed to be a control pad was in fact a Hate & T Mobility deck. Cheap and nasty, they were one of Satan's fun little ways of constantly reminding you the afterlife was out to fuck you, as they could only be charged by way of an obscenely large butt-plug. So large, in fact, that regular users talked with a limp.

Now disconnected, I noticed the battery indicator on his screen flashing.

"Aren't you going to reconnect to the charger?"

"Er, no . . . Not while you're here, if you don't mind," he stammered fretfully.

"Don't worry, I'm not here to collect from you," I reassured him. "I'm merely trying to discover more about the previous occupant."

"Previous occupant? I . . . I wouldn't know. The room had been tidied before I got it."

"I see. And did you notice anything unusual? Had anything been left here that appeared out of place?"

"Not that I know of."

I wracked my brains, drew out the note from the Mortuary, and read it once more. When I reached the end, my eyes lit up. I scrutinized those last few lines again:

> *For Arthur's folly leads the way,*
> *On blood-stained, piss-soaked sheets,*
> *An inferno of wasted passions*
> *Dedicated to your most lavish attentions.*

"An inferno of wasted passions . . ."

"I'm sorry?" my blubbery friend mumbled, obviously thinking I was talking to him.

"It's nothing. Where's this room's Dante?"

"I . . . I don't know. I never read them."

My attention fell upon the bedside cabinet. Scooting over to it, I edged the top drawer open and found what I was looking for. A copy of Dante's *Inferno*. Its gilt lettering and red-stained jacket were badly worn, but a fresh piece of paper protruded from beneath its back cover. Picking it out, I unfolded the parchment and discovered my hunch had been right.

The message said:

> *Words cast in acoustic streams*
> *Flow in darkest alternating currents,*
> *Chilling and fluidic.*
> *A night to remember,*
> *Where the ink-blood rivulets of humanity's pulse*
> *Sink beneath the waves in Olympian failure.*
> *A white star of fallen potential,*
> *Staining your record red*
> *Born amongst bitter accusations.*

I read the passage again and only then noticed the text was still wet. I'd smudged some of the final words where my thumb held the parchment.

It's still fresh? I must be closing the gap . . . or he wants me to think so. This clue is way too easy. Acoustic currents. A night to remember. An obvious reference to the Olympic class White Star liner that went down with massive loss of life. We gained a lot of souls from that tragedy; and here I am, just a short cab journey away from the very place it sinks every night. Very clever. Or very stupid.

I'd only ever been out to New Hell Harbor once, but I remembered a few bars down that way where I'd collected several juicy debts in the past.

I glanced at my watch and then at my fat, sweaty acquaintance.

Hmm. Not too early for a lunchtime tipple. And who knows? If I drink enough, it might help me forget.

*

Safe at last, Cream sat back, removed a silk handkerchief from his top pocket, and wiped the perspiration from his brow.

That was most . . . exhilarating, though somewhat perilous.

He hefted the walking stick in his other hand, and ran trembling fingers across the oval-cut gem crowning its hilt. Although it looked like an aquamarine, it was much, much more.

But at least I now have confidence in our latest acquisition.

Tightening his grip on the pommel, he pulled lightly, and the end of the cane came away with a gentle *click*, revealing the gleaming silver edge of a concealed blade within.

"So it worked then?" a voice behind him queried.

Cream turned to find his partner-in-crime had just entered the room.

"It most certainly did." Cream replaced the handle and continued, "This jewel fragment worked admirably. As you surmised, the cutting contains sufficient dominion to accelerate just one person. But at what speed! It was a remarkable experience, one quite breathtaking."

"Does this mean you're now confident enough for the next stage of our little caper?"*Am I . . . ?*

Cream gazed from the upper-story window of their shared apartment. In the distance, the silhouette of the Awful Tower dominated the melodramatic backdrop of the ancient city brooding beneath it.

Am I really prepared to take this venture to a whole new level?

He took a deep breath, and imagined the glory he would bask in if it actually worked.

"Yes," he replied, "I do believe I am. Let's go and see if we can improve our chances by tracking down our man. And while we're about it, why don't we procure ourselves some real killers?"

Chapter 4: Breadcrumbs

Despite my reputation, it proved impossible to find a taxi driver willing to take me all the way to New Hell Harbor. Because I hadn't been that way in a long time, I'd forgotten how renowned it was as a hub for mercenary activity; activity which invariably attracted the more disgruntled and confrontational stereotype. Needless to say, a large concentration of "shoot first and shoot you again when you're down" mentalities had turned a hornets' nest into a boiling cauldron of ever-fomenting trouble.

Most sensible people avoided the place like the plague. But I wasn't most people.

Delayed considerably, I'd been forced to walk until I happened across a convoy of Armored Combat Earthmovers heading in the right direction. The rear ACE commander took pity on the lone hitchhiker strolling headlong toward danger and pulled over to give me a lift. When they found out who I was, I got VID treatment all the way: I was invited to sit beside the commander on the bare frame of what had once been the main gunner's seat. I felt like royalty.

Thus, by the time the outskirts of the harbor district loomed large, I'd not only recovered some of the time I'd lost, but the frayed edges of my temper as well.

Clouds as thick as forever blotted out the repulsive glow of Paradise along the far horizon as rain moved in from the west. Fortunately, I didn't need the flickering light of salvation to know I was in the right place.

A staggered series of heavily defended switchback checkpoints dotted the main roadway leading down to the bay itself. The farther we progressed, the more evidence of fighting I saw. Streets were lined with the ruined shells of commercial properties. Burnt out, bullet-riddled vehicles lay abandoned everywhere, forming impromptu barricades. And at every turn, a patchwork of dark stains marred pockmarked sidewalks, as if each blemish were desperate to tell its own story.

And then, after we passed the most heavily-defended fortification, signs of conflict simply faded away.

Places of work looked to be open and trading once more. Delivery trucks, bristling with armed escorts, trundled to and fro between warehouses and docks. Those streetlights still standing actually worked.

Seeing my look of surprise, the ACE commander explained: "We had a spot of bother here a week or two back. A surprise attack by the Communist Coalition and their new allies. It caused a lot of damage but, as you can see, it's all sorted now . . . this area is back under our protection."

"Really?" I mumbled. Unconvinced, I scanned the rooftops for hidden snipers and ninja assassins. "We can't have a little rebellion ruining business now, can we?"

"Actually, it was great for business," he chortled. "We've never had so many new recruits clamoring for a bit of action. My unit alone, the Flying Fifth, has grown by over thirty bods. And very welcome they are too . . . Aha, here we are. Hang on a tic."

We veered away from the main convoy and into the entrance of a large parking lot. While most of the spots were filled by an assortment of military vehicles, spaces here and there contained evidence of everyday abnormality. A beat-up Chevy looked strangely at home wedged between two APC carriers. Across the way, a red Corvette gleamed brightly under a flashing neon sign, right next to the camouflaged outline of a hulking tank. And right in front of me, a VW camper van—abandoned diagonally across two slots—dared to interrupt a precision line-up of over a dozen neatly parked jeeps.

Home sweet home . . . to someone.

The commander tapped me on the shoulder and pointed to a squat slab of a building near the water's edge. "Sam's Oasis Bar. You might want to wait out the coming storm in there."

No sooner had I jumped down onto the tarmac than the ACE pulled away. "Good luck, Reaper," the commander yelled above the roar of the engines. "Any time you want to turn apocalyptic, just give us a call."

I grinned. Then fat globules of rain started to spit from the sky.

Out in the mouth of the harbor, I noted the HSMS (His Satanic Majesty's Ship) *Titanic* had refused to let the worsening weather dampen its party atmosphere. That would come later, when she underwent her nightly dunking. For now, revelers had illuminated the balustrades and walkways in an assortment of gaily-colored lights, and despite the wind I could hear the sound of clinking glasses and lively music wafting across the open water.

The spitting got heavier, sizzling as it turned more acidic.

I think I'll take the commander's advice. I've got a little time to kill, so I might as well ask a few questions and stay dry until the main event. You never know.

The building before me was a tribute to stark efficiency and lack of imagination. Sprawled across half a block from the harbor's edge and out toward North Road, it was a featureless chunk of concrete, three stories high. The only windows I could see appeared to be horizontal firing loops on the seaward side. Apart from that, the exterior was featureless except for an encircling halo of razor wire three-quarters of the way up the wall and a series of machine gun nests on each corner of the roof. Movement around the parapet betrayed the presence of ever-vigilant sentries.

Next moment, the clouds burst, and the acidic shower turned into a downpour.

A heaving, mixed throng of mercenaries and civilians crowded around the entrance. They'd obviously had the same idea as I and were falling over themselves in an attempt to get in out of the torrent. Although the large oak doors had been thrown open, so many people were trying to get inside at the same time that it had become a logjam.

Time to live up to my name.

I took off my gloves and drew my sickle. Now heavy, rainfall masked my approach. That didn't last long. Activating my weapon alerted those closest to me of imminent danger. People turned, gasped, and struggled to get out of my way. Most of the soldiers were quicker. Diving for cover, they parted like the Red Sea and left a wedge of unfortunates in front of me, too slow to avoid the touch of death.

Damned souls dropped like flies. In moments I'd swept in through the entrance, leaving a line of freshly mown corpses in my wake.

A door manager stalked toward me. Cursed with a body the size of a gorilla and the teeth of a rabid chipmunk, he caused me to experience a momentary déjà vu.

Is New Hell hosting a missing link convention I don't know about?

The hatcheck girl minding the weapons cage called out, "Hey, mister. We don't want any of . . . Oh, Mister Grim . . . ? I'm sorry; we weren't expecting you."

King Kong raised two huge fists.

I raised my exposed index finger in warning.

"Shanidar, stop!" the woman screamed.

The brute paused and turned toward the woman, looking for last-minute direction.

Amazed, I watched as she communicated with him using sign language.

He's deaf? Then how . . . ? That was fortunate.

"Shanidar," she repeated, speaking aloud as she signed, "back down. That's the Reaper, His Majesty's bounty hunter. We must extend him every courtesy."

Behind me, a murmur of discontent broke out among those who had never seen me before. A few idiots even cocked their weapons. Planting my staff firmly on the floor, I stared at the fools until they fell silent, noting with satisfaction the fear now spreading like an infection through the growing press. When I turned back, however, I discovered Shanidar had maneuvered even closer, and interposed himself between me and the girl at the counter. By the look on his face, he was trying to intimidate me and make a point.

Okay, so will I.

In view of the fact he was obviously being protective, I decided on a lenient course of action. First, I collapsed my scythe and put it away, demonstrating clearly that I didn't feel a need for it. Next, slowly replacing my gloves, I resolutely ignored Shanidar. Finally, I extended one hand toward him and in ancient Hellanese intoned, "*Air bhurg dì-meas, abaid thu deônaich falaing.* (For your disrespect, you will suffer confusion.)"

"Watch out, a curse!" someone hissed.

The sound of shuffling feet became louder as people backed away.

To ensure Shanidar would receive the full effect of my hex, I delivered it both verbally and mentally. In only a few moments the big guy succumbed to its influence. He blinked, staggered, and with an air of bemusement clouding his features, turned to the cashier for support.

He signed toward her. Apparently baffled by what he had just said, she shrugged her shoulders. He tried again and then gawped at his fingers with a mystified expression.

"What's happening?" the cashier complained. "What have you done to him? I can't understand him anymore."

I strolled closer to the cage. The name badge balanced precariously on her well-formed chest identified her as Eileen.

"Don't be too upset, Eileen," I said. "The jinx will only last a day or two. Think of it as an attack of digital dyslexia. Until then, Shanidar will have time to reflect on his attitude toward His Infernal Majesty's officers. Speaking of whom . . ."

Spinning to face the rest of the dripping throng now packed into the entrance hall, I projected an image of my target into the ether.

"In my official capacity as the Reaper, I'd like to know if any of you have seen this man. He is an absconder who, despite his looks, presents a very real danger to public insecurity."

Thomas Cream's profile rotated a slow three-sixty in the air before them. As I waited for a response, I seized the opportunity to scan the crowd's emotions. While I wasn't mind reading, the scan nonetheless afforded me an opportunity to zero-in on someone who might have useful information.

Not a damned thing! What a waste of—

"Would you like to speak to Sam, the owner?" Eileen asked, suddenly eager to please. "He's downstairs and has a good working relationship with a number of His Majesty's officials, including the Ombudsman. I'm sure he'd be keen to offer his assistance."

He knows Job? I glanced at my watch. *About five minutes to go.*

"That would be most helpful. Thank you."

Eileen nodded toward Shanidar and picked up a phone. Now contrite, the big man beckoned me toward a set of stairs to one side of the weapons cage, and lifted a frayed burgundy rope from an adjoining brass hook.

As I passed, I glanced at a couple of signs affixed to the grille and couldn't help but laugh. In bold letters, the first proclaimed: One Weapon, One Magazine, No Shit.

A bit late for that. I've already caused quite a stir.

The second was smaller, but no less important in a place like this: Rooms to Rent. By the Minute, Hour, Day, Week, and Month.

An entrepreneur too. No wonder the parking lot is full.

I descended into the gloom and emerged into a perfect haunt for wannabe death-dealers. The room looked much like the inside of an open warehouse, all brickwork and metal walkways above, unadorned concrete below. Machine gun nests filled each of the four corner gantry junctions; on the main floor its booths and tables were packed with an assortment of marines, soldiers and sailors from assorted eras of history.

The air was saturated with the vile stench of stale beer, vomit, Camel Dung cigarettes and, from what I could discern, other substances too. The only ventilation I could see, apart from the firing ports, was high on the roof, where a single skylight failed miserably to vent the voluminous clouds chuffing from it like a runaway steam train.

A group of braver souls, oblivious to the choking brume, gyrated wildly to the racket scratching and screeching from a 1950s jukebox over in the far corner. By the way they moved, the dancers were either attempting to demonstrate techno-style hip-hop or being electrocuted. I couldn't quite fathom which.

A sensible-looking guy behind the bar, wearing a beige suit and pencil tie, replaced an old-style telephone in its cradle and made his way around the counter. "I'm Sam," he shouted above the din.

He paused at the last moment and looked at my hands.

Nice one!

I smiled and waggled my gloved fingers at him. "It's completely safe," I yelled back, "especially as I understand you have a good working relationship with our Dark Father's servants."

"I try my best," he replied. "We get a lot of people passing through, and the Hall of Injustice likes us to keep tabs on certain individuals for them."

"In that case, I'd like to ask a favor . . ."

I concentrated and displayed a front, side, and full profile representation of Cream into the air. A burning sensation emanated from inside my breast pocket. I focused more intently, directing my will, and superimposed those images upon a physical manifestation of my choosing. The smell of singed fabric became apparent, Finished, I removed a completed wanted poster from within the folds of my coat.

"Would you be so kind as to display this in a prominent position? Anyone providing information that directly leads to Cream's apprehension will be amply rewarded . . . and earn the Reaper's gratitude."

Sam took possession of the notice and gave it the once over. He seemed surprised.

"This guy doesn't look up to much," he mused aloud. "Still, if Satan wants him, it'll give this lot something useful to do." He glanced toward his clientele, and his eyes popped wide: "And if I turn the whole thing into a contest between factions, this poor shmuck won't stand a chance. I take it you won't mind if they use him as a punch bag before you take him into custody?"

"Not at all. The more suffering he endures, the better. The only stipulation I've ensured to add, as you can see in bold letters along the bottom of the notice, is that Cream is *not* to be interrogated under any circumstances. To do so would be *unfortunate* for those involved. And any friends or extended family they might have."

"I understand. I'll make sure that's passed o–"

The deafening sound of a siren brought our first meeting to an abrupt end.

All necks craned toward the skylight, and quite a few people headed for the exit.

"Is that . . . ?"

"The *Titanic*." Sam nodded. "She'll be going down, *again*, in about a minute's time."

"I'll be leaving you, then. Duty calls." Nodding to the poster, I emphasized, "Just make sure you pin *that* in a prominent position."

"Will do. Ping Pao to go, on the house?"

"Thank you, but no. My usual tipple's Diabhalvulin 18. I like the way it burns on the way down."

Sam laughed. "It figures." As an afterthought, he added, "Hey, if you're meeting someone off the boat, try the south side of the parking lot. Look for a trailer with a motorboat on it. The stairs there lead down to a tiny cove. It's away from the harbor, but it's where most of the revelers like to come ashore. And watch your boots. You're not wearing waders and the term "in the shit" doesn't even begin to describe what the tide brings in."

Forewarned, I bade Sam a hasty farewell, joined the growing surge toward the door, and made my way back outside.

Thank Beelzebub, the main body of the squall had passed by, and now only a light drizzle remained to coat the streets in a slick film of sweat. Most of the patrons were heading toward the docks, so I hung back. As the crowd thinned, I spotted the speedboat Sam had told me about and phased toward it. Sure enough, a weathered set of steps sat beside it, leading down onto a tiny reinforced breakwater. Behind it lay a small beach, swamped with the flotsam and jetsam of one of the most volatile districts of New Hell.

The stench was appalling.

I see what he means about protecting your footwear.

The rotting detritus of hellkind had congealed into a definitive mass that puckered and pulsated with a life of its own. I peered closer and realized the entire shoreline was seething with crabs and giant centipedes.

Pick the bones out of that! I think I'll stick to dry land.

After climbing down, I strode to the end of the jetty and looked back out to sea.

Just in time.

Another long blast from the *Titanic* announced the moment of truth had arrived. As the final warning groaned across the harbor, a seething mass of bubbles erupted near the bow. The ship began to dip, and a loud cheer rang out from the revelers on board. In response, the party music screeched to a halt, and the musicians struck up a slower melody. A rousing toast introduced the sonorous notes of our national anthem, *Nearer To Satan Than Thee*.

With infinite grace, the stern lifted higher into the air, creating a glittering waterfall that caught the waning glow of Paradise and refracted it into a million prismatic needles. The myriad fairy lights adorning the railings winked out, only to be replaced by a kaleidoscopic fireworks display. Chrysanthemum bursts in a plethora of bright, scintillating colors threw back the gloom. Silhouetted against the night sky, the imposing bulk of the *Titanic* hung suspended in midair for a second. Then the effervescent froth at the bow increased, and she knifed into the icy depths.

As she did so, the orchestra fell silent, all sounds of gaiety cut off. Moments later, the HSMS *Titanic* disappeared beneath the waves amid hissing clouds of steam.

Awesome! No wonder everyone wants to watch.

Now it was simply a question of waiting for the stragglers to come ashore. To pass the time, I retrieved my most recent clue, and read it again:

> *Words cast in acoustic streams*
> *Flow in darkest alternating currents,*
> *Chilling and fluidic.*
> *A night to remember,*
> *Where the ink-blood rivulets of humanity's pulse*
> *Sink beneath the waves in Olympian failure.*
> *A white star of fallen potential,*
> *Staining your record red*
> *Born amongst bitter accusations.*

"So, I've been waiting for the damned thing to sink, but who the hell am I supposed to look out for? There's nothing concrete to tell me anything, except for the last stanza, which doesn't really seem to fit."

Born amongst bitter accusations?

"Is that a literal hint of some sort? Someone born again in hell? Newborn perhaps, who feels they shouldn't be here . . . ? *Like most of the other complainers.* "Born free. Born to be wild?"

A disturbance out at sea caught my eye.

One moment the black, glasslike surface of the water was calm, the next it rippled. Bubbles fizzed and popped. A wave of poodle-perm wigs appeared, strung out across the bay like luminescent jellyfish. Strontium silver and yellow, pink, violet, plasma-purple and neon-blue. The gaudier, the better. Heavily powdered profiles were everywhere, adorning bearded faces decorated by running mascara and smudged lipstick. The entire host sported unsavory physiques, and every one of them was squeezed into ill-fitting Victorian bustles. There must have been close to a thousand drag-artists leading the charge.

Ever the dutiful chaperons, each of the men escorted a lady on his arm. Pencil thin, the women seemed to have gone with a black-tie approach. Stenciled mustaches, greased back hair and monocles made it look as if they had taken a chance, and lost badly at a Monopoly Guy lookalike convention.

The sea was awash with floating false eyelashes, fans, and cocktail sticks.

Then a second wave appeared, closing rapidly on the first.

More debauched than their fellows, this crowd was naked, and had obviously said "to hell with the risk," and submitted to their lusts.

A morbid assembly of erections and bouncing curves bobbed and waddled toward me, their owners doing their level best to avoid the swarm of scorpions and spiders now in hot pursuit. While some were successful, none could avoid those arachnids spawned within them.

You live by the rules, you die by the rules. No sex for vermin . . . or else!

To say the experience was surreal was an understatement. Some of the biggest pollutants in hell were inappropriately dressed, fat, sweaty bastards. And here I was, forced to watch hundreds of them waggling and flopping ashore.

They were sickening. Some specimens were so overweight I could have slapped their flab and ridden the undulations on a surfboard. My hand twitched toward my scythe, and it was only with the greatest restraint that I was able to resist the urge to cleanse my beloved environment.

And I'm supposed to get my next lead from one of these fuckers?

The two groups met and went down in a tangle of blubbery flesh, coifs, cuffs, and evening wear. Presented with a possible new food source, the crabs and centipedes scouring the shoreline made haste to leap for dangling morsels of flesh and shiny tiaras. Fresh screams and curses punctuated the night, a welcome accompaniment to the catcalls emanating from the bar crowd, now watching from the docks.

This is a complete waste of time.

Just as I was about to give up and vent my fury, I saw him. Or should I say, I saw *part* of him.

A single head appeared above the waterline. Held aloft by its blue-black hair, it calmly sipped on a cocktail through a brightly-colored straw. As his lips drained the contents, all manner of unsavory aquatic *things* began squeaking and leaping from the tumbler to the safety of open water.

His torso emerged, and he handed off his drink to one of his attending retinue. With infinite care, he slowly maneuvered the two body parts back together . . . almost, for a gaping wound still separated one from the other. Careful hands smoothed every hair back into place, and then he tied a scarlet silk cravat around his neck to hide the deformity.

Recognition hit me like a thunderbolt.

That's Bertran de Born, the guy accused of sedition by Henry II! Bloody hell. He's portrayed by Dante as a sower of schism.

I glanced at the last line of my clue again and laughed out loud.

"Born amongst bitter accusations."

Literally? But how . . . ?

Bertran heard my outburst and altered course toward me. As he waded into the shallows, I realized he had dressed for the occasion as a modern-day version of Dracula. Very fitting, for his widow's peak, goatee beard, and piercing eyes fitted the mood perfectly.

"Reaper?" he said, by way of greeting.

"Bertran de Born," I responded, "I wouldn't have thought this was really your scene."

He turned to look about him as the ensuing debacle unfolded. The crabs, centipedes and voracious other insects appeared to be finishing off the stragglers in double-quick time.

Unconcerned, he held out his hand for a boost onto the quayside. "Just Bertran, please." Cocking a thumb toward the dead and the dying, he explained: "I do like people who have broken out of their shells, even if they tend to squander their time in folly. Call it a fault of mine. I thought to liven up their pointless carousing before it's too late, for surely our Dark Lord must chafe at such wasted exuberance. After all, what's the point of endless suffering and resurrections if you don't capitalize on it? There's nothing like a rousing bit of campaigning to get the juices flowing. Along with all the blood and gore, of course."

"Wouldn't your message have been better received in there?" I countered, pointing back at Sam's Bar.

Bertran snorted. "Bah! I wouldn't be seen undead in that hovel."

In a quieter tone, he admitted, "And in all truth, the mercenaries frequenting my competitor's establishment fight the fine fight and keep the Undertaker's minions busy enough." Bertran cast a critical eye over me. "But I doubt you've come all this way just to exchange pleasantries. Are you are you here to help me with something?"

I showed him the note. "To be honest, I think it's *you* who're going to help *me*. But I'm damned if I can really make head or tail of the conundrum."

I had trouble staying quiet as Bertran read the passage through, but somehow I managed to give him the solitude he needed to work things out.

At first, he appeared puzzled. His gaze flickered from side to side, and he whispered a few undecipherable phrases under his breath. As he scanned the contents again, one finely formed brow arched upward. Then his face brightened with a look of comprehension.

He chuckled. "How fortuitous."

"What? What's fortuitous?"

"That phrase about alternating currents."

In reply to my look of utter confusion, he explained: "I had someone stop by my bar asking about Tesla only last week."

"Tesla?" I echoed, appallingly slow off the mark.

"Yes, Nikola Tesla. The genius responsible for the discovery of many scientific inventions"—he shoved the note in my face and pointed to the second stanza—"including the *alternating current* electricity supply system."

Of course!

"Is *this* the guy who asked the questions?" I showed him a photograph of Cream in all his slimy glory.

"No, I'm afraid not . . . Er . . ."

For some reason, Bertran had suddenly become coy.

"What's the matter?"

"Reaper . . . you must understand. Because of the nature of our friend's enquiry, I didn't even ask his name. I'm sure you're aware the subject of Tesla's work attracts an unsavory element that our Satanic Father would rather have . . . um, obliterated. I . . . Let's just say I'm . . ."

I understood completely.

"On my authority as Reaper, I can offer you full immunity if you cooperate with my enquiry. Believe me. His Infernal Majesty is very keen for me to take the man I'm after into custody. In fact, I'm prepared to overlook certain illegal practices, if it ensures I capture him promptly."

Bertran cogitated for a moment, then stepped closer. "Very well. The individual in that picture bears little resemblance to the one I saw only six days ago."

"Wait a minute! Six days?"

"Yes, that's right. The person I spoke with was a rather sour-faced chap; to be honest with you, he looked a bit nuts. He spoke with a French accent, was obviously well educated, but kept mumbling on about this and that, and about someone called George."

I did the math in my head.

It took me forty-eight hours to track down Cream. Then I spent the rest of the week collecting contracts before returning to the Den. Three days later, I got the call.

I reverted to fingers. *For this other guy to be here, so shortly after I'd dealt with Cream, suggests a possible connection . . . and an urgent need for sanitization.*

Aloud, I said, "I see. And what was he after?"

"There's been quite a lot of chatter on the white market recently, regarding one or two of Tesla's latest products. You'll probably be aware of the rift generators he manufactures? You know, the ones that can create a short range, short-term portal? They're all the rage with mercenaries at the moment, as it helps them get one over on their opponents."

Bertran glanced around to ensure we weren't being watched, dropped his voice even lower, and continued: "Well, rumor has it that Tesla's made a breakthrough which will revolutionize the way warfare is conducted. From what I heard, it relates to a new form of acoustic cipher, which will generate huge doorways. Anyway, the chap who dropped by last week had an obscenely large budget, and a very specific shopping list. One that not only included the new phonic generator, but details about a number of other . . . er . . . mythical and therefore banned items."

"Such as?"

He paused again, took a deep breath, and murmured, "Dare I say, relics of a bygone age? Perhaps even, from the Time of Sundering?"

A shock coursed down my spine; for a moment my legs felt hollow.

Knowledge of such history and the artifacts it referred to was proscribed by law, for it related to the fall of Satan, and angelic weapons of untold mastery and purpose. Not only had all record of them been destroyed—at least, that's what *should* have happened—but public archives since then had been altered to completely avoid any reference to those times. Few were privy to such matters, for even talking about it would render a transgressor top of my list, and consigned from there to a thousand years roasting in Hades.

I understood now why Bertran was so reluctant to speak.

And yet, it seems Cream and his friend display a blasé attitude about incurring my Awful Father's wrath.

"So, how did you help him, Bertran?"

"I directed him to my cousin, François, in Perish. He traffics mercenaries and Foreign Legionnaires for several of the causes over there. Obviously, because of his contacts, he has exclusive ties to the white market as well."

"How far developed are Tesla's latest models?"

"At the moment he's only got short distance prototypes of his latest model working. Thanks to the idiosyncrasies of the Undertaker, Tesla keeps making mistakes in his calculations, so his toys keep fritzing out. But he's removing those obstacles one by one."

"And this new device can go anywhere?"

"From what I'm told, yes."

"Thank you, I won't forget this. Is there anything else you'd like to add? Remember, no detail is too small."

Bertran thought for a moment. "Now you come to mention it, I think our mysterious friend might be suffering from a form of OCD. Although our conversation was brief, he couldn't stop massaging his hands. I thought he might have cramps or something similar, but there was a desperation to his actions that bordered on the schizophrenic."

"Good, people will remember him then, and that makes it easier for me to track him down." I glanced at my watch. "Look, I'd better get going. I've lost enough time as it is."

I turned and jumped back onto the lip of the parking lot.

"You're sprightlier than you look," Bertran shouted in surprise.

"It goes with the job," I replied. As an afterthought, I called, "You say your cousin is in Perish?"

"That's right. Just ask for François de UnBorn. He lives in the fourth district, or as they say over there, the Hotel-de-E'ville Horrondissement. But be sure to mention his name. Despite your standing, Perish is a dangerous place. Even by hell's devious standards. If they realize you're there to see François, you'll be able to avoid a lot of deliberate hassle."

"Thanks, I'll bear that in mind."

Now all I have to do is think of a way of getting back to Juxtapose without expending too much energy.

As I began walking toward the docks, my Despicable Father demonstrated, once again, he had been keeping a close eye on events. Before I'd even had the opportunity to think of anything myself, a congealing miasma descended over the entire bay.

All traces of the surrounding jeering and heckling fell away. The insects on the shoreline paused in their carnivorous rampage. Everything seemed to hold its breath.

Then from out of the mists came a metallic, baying resonance. A rhythmic reverberation made its presence known, becoming more pronounced as the groaning sound got nearer. A voluminous wash of water came cascading out of the gloom, followed moments later by the cause of the commotion. The Bridge itself.

Thank Purgatory for that! It looks like I'll be riding back to Juxtapose in style.

Chapter 5: Perish the Thought

My journey was somewhat bizarre.

Having climbed aboard the Bridge in New Hell, I found it promptly morphed into a vaulted gondola, ascended into the heavens, and spun a wormhole between realities. The view from inside appeared much like a fluidic kaleidoscope, and as I punted my way along the wormhole's length I had the opportunity to peek into myriad other fragments of helltime.

Here, souls roasted alive in the fiery pits of Hades. There, denizens fought for their lives against a leviathan from the depths of Purgatory. Before me, demons and shape shifters fought over the bloody remains of adventurers that had strayed where they shouldn't. And behind, insurgents, intent on wiping out their antagonists, had detonated an *ADAM* (Advanced Demolition Atomic Munition), a tactical nuclear device. The maneuver not only vaporized their enemies but most of the northeast sector of Hellview Estates as well.

What was even more disconcerting was the fact that although my journey seemed to stretch on into eternity, it was over almost as soon as it began.

Before I knew what was happening, the roiling mass of cloud encompassing me parted, and I looked down from a vast height upon my destination: Perish, or as the world above knew it, Gay Paree. But nothing was gleeful or merry about the sprawling conurbation stretching off into the distance below me.

It was sinister. It was brutal. Earthy and crass. Souls here were as cruel as they were merciless. Embittered and hardhearted, their Gallic charm was reflected in their view of existence where *joie de vivre* had definitely been replaced by *joie de la souffrance*.

Me? I loved Perish. It was so gothic I never had to worry about what to wear. Black went with absolutely everything, and I was looking forward to immersing myself among the uncultured once more.

A chime sounded, notifying me of my imminent disembarkation.

So, how will the Bridge put me down?

I was about to find out:

First the starboard arch of the gate glimmered with a spectral radiance that beckoned me forward.

Next the tone sounded again, and the plane of the portico flared.

I stepped through, my stomach leaping into my mouth as I experienced an unexpected drop. Disoriented, I found myself plummeting, then tumbling forward onto a raised platform. Thankfully, my heightened senses allowed me to arrest my fall and use the momentum to gambol to a safe landing.

The inference was clear: My Despicable Father was demonstrating he was still pissed, and expecting me to stay on my toes.

Nice one, Sire! Thank Beelzebub I didn't make a complete tit of myself.

I took stock of my surroundings.

Behind me, two inverted metallic horns marked the threshold of a displacement vortex. The event horizon still glowed like the surface of a pond illuminated by moonbeams. As I watched, a static display shimmered between the spines, and the field collapsed in on itself and died.

An unsanctioned gateway? And one that Satan knows about? Interesting . . .

My acrobatic display took me halfway along a metallic gantry that sloped down into a small, circular reception foyer. From what I could see, that area was protected from the portal run-off by a number of security guards, and a transparent screen running from floor to ceiling.

Tiered shelves lined either side of the aisle, upon which sat hundreds of glass vessels. Arrayed in all sorts of outlandish shapes and sizes, each contained what looked like severed body parts in some sort of fluid.

Comprehension struck me like a thunderbolt.

Satan's really thrown me into the lion's den.

Although I'd initially been confused by the temporal doorway—which was a brand-new feature—I now recognized where I was, for I'd been here once before, many years ago.

Perish was governed by a number of crime lords, who ran the city with a ruthless efficiency matched only by Satan and his fallen angels themselves. One of the most notorious of these gangsters was a soul named Don Pérignone, a cutthroat bootlegger of impressive stripe. Together with Al Catraz, his gunrunning deputy, he controlled most of the districts south of the River Inseine with an 'iron fist in titanium glove' approach. A policy reflected by the Don's habit of keeping souvenirs of those who had displeased him in kill jars.

I cast my gaze along the racks of prize specimens about me and instantly felt envious of such a fine collection.

Damn, but I want one for a paperweight! Rumor has it that those who really annoy Pérignone are kept alive at the edge of dissolution, just so he can serve them their severed limbs, fried, with garlic and onions. He's been known to extend their suffering for months that way, before allowing them to fade for reassignment. Very clever.

Both hoods conducted their affairs from a number of different venues, but their main base of operations sat below the place where I now found myself. Called *Infernos*, the nightclub was a heavily fortified hive of iniquity atop the Awful Tower, from where they spread fear and extortion in equal measure. They'd obviously added the portal to help move their merchandise about. And really, where better for them to display such a fine reminder to the consequences of disobedience?

I looked back toward the reception area and noticed that the grunts making up my little welcoming committee were undecided as to how to respond.

The one behind the desk picked up a phone and babbled incoherently into the receiver. His buddy next to him lowered some kind of visor over his eyes, cocked a mean-looking Hellishnikov 7.62, and leveled it right at me. The final goon also pointed a gun my way, but appeared distracted by whoever was speaking to him on the other end of a walkie-talkie currently pressed to one ear. They reminded me of hell's version of the three wise monkeys, or in their case: 'Speak only evil, see all evil, and hear nothing but evil'.

Radio Guy nodded and said something I couldn't hear to his buddies, whereupon they all began backing away toward a set of sliding doors.

"Before you all go scurrying off to whatever rocks you like to fornicate under," I shouted, "or start overtaxing the drainage system with a strenuous bout of panic flushing, you can relax. I'm not here for you, or any illegal contraband that might be deposited around this establishment . . . without your knowledge, of course. I just need to see your boss. It's urgent."

They all froze. No one replied.

"J'ai besoin de voir votre patron," I repeated mentally and verbally in my best French, a completely unnecessary exercise for I knew they understood Standard English perfectly well. Everyone in hell did.

Each one of them sneered at my effort to communicate. Mr. Machine Gun even had the audacity to hawk up half his lungs and spit on the floor.

In response, I removed my scythe, extended the shaft, and held it out in plain sight.

Their gazes flicked repeatedly between me and the blade. The muzzles of their guns inched upward.

"Gentlemen," I warned, "I'm trying to be polite. Don't make me regret it."

Neither their eyes nor their weapons stopped moving.

Your choice.

"Very well . . ." Depressing the bottom of five studs, I slammed the heel of the sickle into the ground and unleashed a shockwave that rocked the entire edifice to its foundations. As the monkeys were thrown to the ground, a wide crack split the fabric of the metal at my feet. Splintering outward, it zigzagged along the floor and radiated toward the walls on all sides. Jars danced on shelves; dust motes, dislodged, fell from the ceiling. One of the fissures wormed its way down to the security screen, hit the glass, and fractured the entire barrier from top to bottom. Miraculously, the barricade held.

In the ensuing silence, a trio of stunned faces looked my way.

"Do I have your attention now? Good. That was a little taste of the power at my disposal. Think of it as a demonstration. I haven't bothered to manifest the full might of the Phage, *yet*, so on a scale of one to ten, that was a *one* . . . bordering on a two. Would you like to see what happens if I up the stakes?"

Radio Guy shook his head vigorously. His buddies continued to stare.

"Excellent. I've already asked to see your boss twice"—I raised my staff and wiggled my thumb over the button again—"there won't be a third time."

As one, they rolled onto their hands and knees and scrabbled for the doors. Before they'd covered half the distance it swished open, and a heavyset individual looking like a cross between Marlon Brando and a bulldog chewing a wasp stalked inside. Al Catraz. *Not* the person I'd asked for.

We made eye contact. I could see he was far from happy.

Then his scrutiny flicked past me and on to the display cases. A near disaster had been narrowly avoided, for at least a dozen containers had been shunted to the edge of their shelves where they now teetered precariously, only a hairsbreadth from oblivion.

Al's anger fell upon his flunkies.

"Well, don't just lie there groveling, you dopey morons!" Waving his arms furiously, he shepherded them toward the racks. "Put the blasted things back in their places before they fall."

Now he was grumpy. At this rate, we'd be through the rest of the seven dwarves in less than a minute.

Mind you, I appreciated the slick distraction his ruse had furnished.

So smoothly I hadn't realized what he was doing, Al used the cover of his wildly gesticulating outburst to disguise the fact that he had removed a Hell-Brass 6.66 Magnum from a concealed holster beneath his jacket. Its barrel was now pointed directly at me: not a welcoming sight.

"If you know me, Reaper," he snarled, "then you know I don't really care for authority. What's to prevent me from testing how resistant to injury you really are? Perhaps you'd make a fine addition to my collection."

To your *collection? So that would mean . . . ?*

"Where's Don Pérignone?" I demanded. "I'll only speak with the man in charge."

"You are speaking to him." In response to my look of surprise, Al explained: "I retired the Don a few years back. Let's just say I didn't like the direction he was taking us, so I arranged for a very generous pension plan. One weighted with all sorts of fringe benefits."

"Concrete benefits of the lead-lined variety?"

"Most definitely. You could say he's immersed in a whole new way of life now."

The neutral veneer of his emotions revealed he was telling the truth.

So there has *been a change in leadership . . .*

"Very well." I paused to replace the scythe within my coat and stepped slowly toward him. "As I was trying to emphasize to your lobotomized flunkies, I'm not here to cramp your style. I *am*, however, on a time-constricted mission. Bertran de Born suggested I might be helped in my endeavor if I enlisted the help of his cousin, François."

"François? François de UnBorn?" A huge grin split his gnarled face.

"Yes, why?"

"He's my partner in, er, no criminal activity whatsoever."

This time, Al's aura blushed scarlet, with strontium-red whorls. And it wasn't the fact that he'd just lied that was firing him up. Oh no. He was one of those who had obviously heard the tales about my regenerative powers, and he was itching to put them to the test.

Our little exchange had given me time to close the gap between us. Walking up to him, I pressed myself against the Magnum's muzzle. "By all means, test your little theory. But if you waste my time by forcing me to heal myself, there won't be enough jars in this place to hold the pieces I'll cut away from you."

The barrel was now positioned above my heart.

As if I ever had one to begin with.

An urgent buzzing disturbed his deliberations. Using his free hand, Al reached inside his jacket and removed a Denizen Guileless mobile phone. As he held it a few inches from his head, his eyes glazed over.

I was intrigued. Not so much by the fact that he was using telepathy, for such decks incorporated an enhancement function to allow users to convey accurate thoughts and impressions across all the levels of hell. No, I was disturbed because those particular models were premium, and supposedly only available to Satan and his fallen angels.

So, that's either a white market imitation, or we've got a few leaks that need plugging in the higher echelons of power. I think I'll give the Hounds a call once my enquiries here are finished. It'll be nice to give them something to chew on for a while.

The pressure against my chest eased as Al's eyes came back into focus. Moments later, both gun and phone were things of the past, tucked away in dark, deep pockets.

"You're not going to believe this," he mumbled, "but that was François. Not two minutes ago, he received a call all the way from New Hell. Veeery expensive. Evidently, his cousin Bertran was keen to stress the urgency of assisting you. Having been apprised of a few details, François is inclined to agree." His face deformed into a smile, and he beckoned toward the double doors. "Please follow me, and I'll show you to your carriage."

"Carriage?"

"Yes. The sixth metro ley line runs directly below this tower, so we've turned it into our own personal chauffeur service. It grants us freedom of movement throughout the whole of our territory, as well as access to the twelfth and sixteenth horrondissements. You'll still have to travel north, of course, but at least you'll get most of the way in safety."

"I see . . ."

"My apologies." Al was quick to make amends. "I thought you were sent here to snoop. We're a stubborn lot and don't take kindly to authority, nor do we trust anyone sent by His Satanic Majesty."

I stopped and turned to face him.

You've just earned yourself a future visit.

"Mr. Catraz. There's one thing you need to understand about me. I'm a very different kettle of fish to the small fry you've no doubt come across. Nor am I like any Blue Suit or Infernal Agent you will ever meet. I never lie to achieve my objectives. I don't need to. My record speaks for itself. The worst thing you can ever do is try to impede my enquiries or engage in unnecessary pissing contests. They don't impress me and will only ever work against you. I hope you take the hint, because I'll never extend the benefit of another one."

"Are you threatening me?" His hands twitched toward his pocket.

Snorting, I resumed my march across to the exit. Over my shoulder I emphasized, "And I *never* issue idle threats."

The doors opened, and I was treated to the stunning view of Chomp-de-Marsh. As one of the most prestigious cultural centers Perish had to offer, the swamplands had been specially manicured to attract tourists from across the many-layered circles of the underworld. From my vantage point atop the tower, I could see its crazy-paving network of walkways and footbridges stretching off to the southeast. What's more, even from this height, the gentle drone of the park's mutant, flesh-eating insects provided a relaxing counterpoint to the urgent thrum emanating from the city itself.

Al managed to restrain his ire—just—and directed me toward an old style elevator at the very center of the upper deck. The place was crawling with thugs armed to the teeth with Hellishnikovs and M666s. At first, I thought my trigger-happy friend was still overreacting to my presence, but then I realized I was walking across the transparent polycarbonate roof of the nightclub itself. The muscle was obviously here to dissuade any antisocial behavior. No easy task, for Infernos attracted only the vilest and most affluent of patrons.

Talk about a volatile mix of perversion and privilege.

I tapped the resin with the toe of my boot.

But how thick is this stuff? I'm right on top of the DJ's position, and can't hear or feel a thing. Impressive. I'll have to see about getting some for one or two of the special interrogation rooms back at the Den.

I never had a chance to ask, for moments later I was ushered into the cage. The doors clanged shut and my host depressed a red button at the bottom of the control panel. Al must have been eager for me to leave, for he kept hitting the thing so hard and so often it sounded as if he was tapping out an emergency SOS signal.

At last, the lift began to descend, albeit at a snail's pace.

With a look of relief, he said, "Stay on the shuttle until you reach Gyre-Monpar le-Massacre. It's a main station. You'll know you're getting close when you've passed Sèvered Limbe. Once at the Massacre, cross over the thirteenth track and head for the Pitched-Fork line. It runs north until Châttered Let, on the far bank of the Inseine."

"Change at Gyre-Monpar le-Massacre. North to Châttered Let," I repeated, "got it." Then I remembered something important. "Hey, hang on . . . where does François actually live? All I know is that it's somewhere in the Hotel-de-E'ville Horrondisse-ment."

"That's where you'll be getting off," Al shouted back. "When you emerge at street level, just walk east onto Rue de l'Hôtel de E'ville. François' place, Bistro Noir, is on the third street corner you'll come to."

Bistro Noir? I had to smile. *Do they choose these names to deliberately reflect the nature of their undertakings?*

As the car departed the top tier, its momentum picked up considerably. Its pace continued to increase, accelerating until its rate of descent bordered on terminal velocity.

Sneaky bastard! Is he trying to get one over on me again, like he did with the gun? Once this is all over and I've replenished myself in the Bâlefire, I'm definitely going to serve him up a huge helping of attitude adjustment.

Overhead cables screamed through the pulley system. Taking a deep breath, I summoned the power to phase, and held it at the threshold until I judged the time was right. The black and gray jigsaw of the surrounding city was looming larger at alarming speed. My gaze remained fixed on one focal point in particular; as it drew ever closer, I flexed my knees in anticipation.

Sparks flew as the hydraulic brake bit into the line. A tooth-jarring squeal split the air. The carriage abruptly decelerated so that I was catapulted to the floor. Regardless, the ground still rushed up to embrace me.

Too little, too late.

In an instant, my molecules were streaming through the ether toward my goal. I coalesced opposite a groundside ticket booth, just in time to see the cart flash through the safety lattice and disappear below ground.

A muffled boom and accompanying vibration signaled the moment my carriage smashed into the floor of the tunnel below. Armed goons sprinted from an adjoining building and down the stairs, only to run into a billowing cloud of choking dust and acrid fumes. Coughing, cursing and sneezing rang out amid the ensuing hullabaloo.

"Oh yes, very clever," I mumbled aloud, "I can imagine his reaction if I were to confront him about this unfortunate *accident.* 'Oh, sorry, Reaper. The brakes, line, emergency stop—whatever—must have failed'. As if."

Denizens tend to forget I am a lot older than I look, and have been around the block a few thousand times. And yeah, I do talk to myself at times—an occupational hazard for those who can trust no one. But I also understood the rudiments of this style elevator enough to know that the disaster I had just witnessed was nigh on impossible. Even if the cable had snapped completely, special ratchetlike devices on either side of the car should have clamped the carriage in place.

Should have.

"Oh, I'll be back for you, little king. I'll be back."

A quick assessment of the situation revealed that my would-be assassin had, in fact, done me a huge favor. The central control column was housed in a building adjacent to the main metro entrance. Because of his botched attempt to kill me, all of Al's monkeys were now tied up, swinging from debris-coated tires in the basement. Judging from the hoots and hollers currently echoing up from below, they'd be there for a good few minutes yet, as it would take quite a while to dig through the rubble to confirm the presence of my poor shattered body.

In the meantime . . .

A group of bewildered sightseers stumbled past. Adjusting my hood, I blended in amongst them, and together we made our unhurried way into the station foyer. Once there, I joined the queue at the ticket gate, paid my due, and descended onto the waiting area.

The platform environment was a tribute to photonegative chic. Sterile white bricks and a brightly paved platform conflicted sharply with the coal-black gravel that had somehow leached into the iron-workings. Everything on the track—rods, rails, cross-ties—had been stained a brittle cobalt color.

CCTV cameras sprouted from all the walls and every overhead joist, so I employed the extra precaution of a glamour to alter my appearance. Thus protected, I settled back to await the next train. I didn't have to wait long. Less than a minute later I stepped aboard a pristine shuttle, and sped on my way to my next rendezvous.

The journey in itself offered a surprise; understandable really, as I was used to the Olde London Underground, where travel was a dismal affair. There, soot-lined passageways ran along endless tunnels that resembled yawning black holes. On many occasions, they literally swallowed passengers whole. Where such travelers went, nobody knew, but those denizens were never seen again, not even on the Undertaker's slab.

Here, however, the route was a monument to disparity.

One moment we'd be clattering through echoing stations, their cathedrallike environs creating a backdrop of mystery and shadow. The next we'd emerge into the baleful glory of the Perishian cityscape, resplendent with baroque architecture and rickety but quaint iron bridges that appeared far too flimsy to support our weight.

The sight was mesmerizing.

My change at Gyre-Monpar le-Massacre made me realize how well Al Catraz governed his territory. He obviously liked things clean and efficient. Sanitized. Bespeaking his clinical approach to leadership. Elsewhere, standards were obviously different.

The subway car serving the Pitched-Fork line was a mortuary on wheels. Headless corpses and disembodied entrails lolled and sloshed indolently within the carriage as it negotiated its sniper's-alley gauntlet along the line. Those seats still upholstered were stained a morbid claret and brown, testimony to the skill of gunmen lining the roofs. Wire-mesh windows—mostly smashed, or decorated by bullet holes—gave little cover from ubiquitous cross-hairs and telescopic laser sights.

Conditions weren't any better outside.

Burnt-out vehicles and sizzling body parts lined the track. The closer we got to Notre Damned, the worse it got. Street gangs engaged in running battles, using the carriages themselves for cover or escape routes. Every so often the shuttle would rock from an explosion too close for comfort.

Now this *is what hell is all about. Beelzebub, but I love it here!*

My growing delight was tempered by a familiar ringtone: "You're just like poison—"

So my friends at the Fiendish Bureau of Investigation had something for me. Ducking down, I tucked myself between two seats, removed my phone, and confirmed a call from either Bella or Donna Nightshade. Although they were way over on the other side of hell, I opened my mind to their astral signatures. Hopefully, I'd be strong enough to receive some cogent mental impression behind their words.

I wish I had a Denizen Guileless like that bastard upstart. It'd make this so much easier. Perhaps I'll just take his when I'm finished with him.

"Hi girls, find anything useful regarding Cream?"

"It's what we *didn't* find that's more interesting," Bella replied.

"In what way?"

"Our initial enquiries showed the usual flitting about that all normal denizens engage in. Especially those hoping to ingratiate themselves among the highflyers and other notables in the employ of our Despicable Master. You know the type: Shakespeare, Marlow, Sulla, Attila, Frankenstein, and so forth."

"Yes, he likes to suck up in an effort to glorify his own position. I know this already. So what's new?"

"What's *new* is the fact that three months ago his usual pattern of activity stopped, almost as if he dropped off the face of the netherworld. Now, we know he didn't, because of the monumental fuck-up involving Victor's vaccine."

"You know about that?" A cold chill thrilled along my spine.

"Only what we need to know. Compartmentalization is our middle name. After all, we've been doing this long enough to prove that too much digging in the wrong area can induce a severe case of mind-wiped early retirement. Something we are keen to avoid."

I breathed a huge sigh of relief.

"So, what *do* you know?"

"Either that Cream developed a sudden desire to stay in one place—highly unlikely—or, he reverted to *other means* of travel."

I was momentarily confused. Then I recalled the information Bertran de Born had provided regarding the mysterious buyer, and that party's interest in Tesla's latest discovery.

"Go on . . ."

Donna took over the conversation: "Well . . . *my* investigation has revealed the *other means* we discussed remain fraught with danger. I'm still gathering all the details and will update you when I have specifics, but I'm starting to think that Cream may not only have illegal access to His Infernal Majesty's bureaucratic network, but also to alternate channels which are strictly prohibited."

"Are you referring to Tesla's new acoustic work?"

A pregnant pause followed before Donna replied, "Yes, I am. How the bloody hell did you find out?"

"Hey, I'm Satan's bounty hunter. I wouldn't be much use if I didn't have ways of uncovering secrets. And before you ask, yes, my source is reliable. For the time being, he or she will remain anonymous."

Another silence ensued before Donna stressed, "I take it we can trust in your discretion? Such information cannot be bandied about willy-nilly."

"Girls, please! Me, blab? Perish the thought. No, part of my assignment actually involves hunting down and silencing those who may have access to such knowledge; and since I've arrived here, the list is growing by the second."

That thought reminded me of another important facet provided by de Born. "Actually, I may have something for you . . . Can you hang on a tic?"

Without waiting for a reply, I rolled out from my position and scoured the interior of the long carriage. Only two other passengers were traveling within this particular car. One looked like some kind of spiv in a zoot suit, while the other was a stinking lawyer, tail and all.

Wrong place, wrong time, guys.

In the blink of an eye, my sickle was in my hand and pointed straight at them. The shock of what was happening barely had time to register on their faces before I depressed the second gem down from the top. Two bright bolts of blue energy flashed from the tip. An anathema to their damned condition, the dual blast of God's Grace caught them full in their chests. Writhing in agony within a sapphire nimbus for just a second, their desperate cries abruptly cut off as their forms disintegrated.

I spun back into position and resumed my conversation. "Sorry about that, ladies. I was just removing a few unwanted distractions."

"Obviously, what you have to say is for our ears only?" Donna breathed huskily.

"You could say that. Although so many people seem to know about it, I'm beginning to think we have a leak."

"A leak?" Bella snapped, strident and direct.

"Yes. From what I understand, Tesla's latest innovation is still in the experimental phase, correct?"

"That's right, go on."

"And yet it's already common knowledge among many within the criminal underworld. They could only have found out about it so quickly from one of the Devil's Children."

"That's a bit of a sweeping statement, Daemon," Bella argued. "You know how resourceful some of the condemned can be. This is hell, after all, filled to the brim with psychopathic geniuses and narcissistic overachievers. They have their own means of gaining and exchanging information. It's a form of currency down here."

"Point noted. And I would be inclined to agree were this confined to just this one aspect, but it's not. I find it highly suspicious that I am involved in the pursuit of a subject—or subjects, I'm still working that bit out—who not only want access to instantaneous travel throughout our entire multiverse, but who also seem intent on gaining possession of ancient relics proscribed by law."

Such as? the twins thought simultaneously, adopting the security of mindspeech.

Artifacts from the Time of Sundering.

I sensed their alarm, even at this distance.

Daemon, Donna sent, *All knowledge of those times is banned.*

As is any reference to the articles involved, or their history, added Bella.

"You needn't tell me that," I replied, reverting to open verbalization once more. "Few are privy to such sensitive matters, and on the short list of those who are, even we are near the bottom."

"So there are bigger fish to fry." Donna stated. "Or in this case, roast in Hades for millennia after being mind-wiped."

"You can see the urgency of my dilemma."

"Actually, we may be able to help you there," Donna offered and Bella concurred.

"Really? How?"

"Well," Donna continued, "before we got sidetracked, I was explaining how Cream may have illegal access to the Blue Suit portal network. Now, because of the security features incorporated within the Sheolspace continuum, he'd need to employ various glamours, pseudonyms, and disguises to get away with it. Even then, continued travel would be fraught with danger."

"I'm already aware of that, Donna. How does it help me?"

"Well . . . what you don't know is that everyone using the grid gets chipped."

"Chipped?"

"Yes. Our Awful Father likes to keep tabs on all his subjects' movements, no matter who they are. So he's added an additional secret firewall to the matrix. Anyone passing through hydraspace gets DNHA-tagged."

DeoxyriboNewHellcleic Acid? But . . . The penny dropped.

"Because no matter what kind of portal you use, legal, illegal, or one of Tesla's dimensional rents, you must pass through hydraspace to get from one point in the continuum to another." *Brilliant!* "And it won't matter what disguise you're wearing: you can't change your DNHA."

"I thought you might like it. We've got tapeworms interrogating the system as we speak. It'll take the rest of the week, but we'll have Cream soon, one way or another."

"I like your—" The train entered a tunnel and everything outside went dark. Inside, things looked little better, since only one of the bulbs was working. Fortunately, I didn't need any illumination to see clearly. We began to decelerate, and a faded sign affixed to a sidewall indicated we were arriving at my destination, Châttered Let.

I'm almost there. "Look girls, I gotta dash. I'm meeting someone who can clarify some of the points we've been discussing." I was struck by a sudden brainwave. "Before I go, I've got a quick question."

"Shoot!" they replied in unison.

"If you *do* get a result, can you run a separate diagnostic to identify anyone who has recently made a journey similar to Cream's? I was thinking, if we get two or more corresponding patterns, those might give me a big clue as who his accomplices are."

"No problem at all," Bella replied. "We've got our own Hell Data Net servers, so I'll begin a separate cross-tandem search along the parameters you suggested. Doing so might take a few days longer, but will save time in the long run."

"Great news. I'll catch up with you both soon."

The shuttle pulled to a stop and the doors swished open. I received an instant hit of ammonia, feces, and rotten vegetables. The warbling tones of a busker strangling an out of tune accordion somewhere along the platform didn't do much to ease the welcoming ambience.

Excellent. That reminds me to give the café bars and restaurants a miss while I'm here.

Chapter 6: A Step in the Right Direction

All this unexpected running hither and yon had proved more fatiguing than I cared to admit. But that was to be expected. The last time I'd managed to refresh myself within the roaring heart of the Bãlefire was a few days before my topside assignment began. Such undertakings were always draining, both on my mystic and physical libido. And my previous mission was no different, especially as circumstances had contrived to keep me away from home much longer than usual. My energy reserves were second to none, but they weren't inexhaustible. I could feel myself growing weaker with every passing hour.

If not for Cream and his blasted schemes, I would have revitalized my essence by now. I don't know how much longer I can carry on before waning potency starts to affect my performance, especially with scumbags like Catraz getting in the way at every turn.

I pondered how things had turned out so far:

I'm obviously on my own for the foreseeable future, and it's clear that's the way it'll be until my Diabolical Father decides I'm producing tangible results. So I'd better change tactics. No more blasting my way through obstacles with brute strength and bad attitude. Perhaps it would be better to save energy and start cultivating allies. After all, recent events have proven the criminal element is a goldmine of information and resources.

This snippet helped make up my mind, especially in relation to the de Born family. I could exercise a great deal of leeway in achieving results, and if I played things right today, I'd have the vast resources of the white market's intelligence network at my beck and call.

Of course, by helping me they'll unwittingly be turning themselves into Lucifer's pawns. But I shan't emphasize that fact.

Emerging onto the sidewalk, I determined to foster new ties as quickly as I could.

I was stunned to discover Al Catraz had been true to his word, probably because he thought I'd be dead by now. Bistro Noir was a literal five-minute stroll from the metro. Situated on the corner of Rue de l'Hôtel de E'ville and Rue Geoffroy l'Asinîne, its elegant presence dominated the block, making an instant impression.

Wolfsbane, devil's claw, and rattlesnake blooms hung from a score of first floor window boxes. Arranged into a Hanging Gardens of Babylon feature, they festooned the stark bare stone in various shades of lilac, red, and green. Highly polished brass fittings accentuated wide double doors and floor-to-ceiling, glossy black surrounds. Quaint little wine tables and Louis XVI gondola-backed bureau chairs lined the pavement, while stenciled glass windows allowed passersby a glimpse of the privileged elite inside. A plain cream Perishian awning with the café's name emblazoned in gold along its length added that final touch of class.

Here, if anywhere, was a place fit for a crime boss to preen like a peacock whilst entertaining his flock.

Obviously, I was expected.

A maître d' waited for me at the door. Dressed in a black waistcoat and bowtie, a crisp white apron tied around his waist, he was 'welcome to our establishment' personified. Or he would have been, but for the starched towel hanging from his left forearm possessed a telltale lump.

For me, or difficult customers perhaps?

I glanced at the other attendants, busily scurrying to and fro. They also displayed telltale bulges that had nothing whatsoever to do with taking orders for drinks.

Are they a simple front line of defense for a cautious gangster, or is de UnBorn privy to the attempt on my life? I guess I'm about to find out.

Making eye contact, I showed the waiting escort my hands were gloved and casually peeled back one side of my coat to reveal my scythe, safely within its pouch. I held the flap open as I walked up to him.

"My name is André, Mister Grim," he said by way of greeting. "Mister François is waiting for you on the exterior VID balcony. He thought you might like to speak in private, well away from prying eyes."

"Thank you. That would be nice." I paused in the doorway. "As a gesture of respect and good faith, would you like to take possession of my weapon?"

His gaze flicked to the jewel adorning the shaft, and lingered for a moment. Nonetheless, his reply was swift: "That won't be necessary, Mister Grim. Your name precedes you." Pointing to a younger waiter standing at the bottom of a set of ornate winding steps, he added, "If you follow Pascal, he will guide you to Mister François. In the meantime, may I get you a drink? Cognac, coffee, premium paint stripper?"

"Diabhalvulin 18, if you have it?"

André nodded and stepped aside.

I quickly wove through the pressing throng, and was ushered upstairs. The VID area was a wide open patio to the rear of the premises. Decorated in a similar style to the exterior of the café, the terrace had the added protection of a trellis-style gazebo, over which decorative flowers had been encouraged to grow. From my position I had an unobstructed view of the Parc d' Injustice, containing one of the most renowned monuments in all of hell: the Mèmorial de la Sheol.

I always thought of that place as a shrine to my work. After all, I'd lost count of the millions of souls I had committed to an eternity of suffering.

François de UnBorn sat waiting in one of two loose-cushioned Chippendale recliners, flanking a wrought iron table. With his widow's peak, slick blue-black hair, and goatee beard, he looked very similar to Bertran, albeit François, more muscular, and had his head firmly attached.

Like his cousin, François also sported a fine silk cravat. In his case, this sprouted proudly from the chest pocket of his quilted smoking jacket like a fleur-de-lis on steroids. I grinned at the sight of it, and François took my smile as a sign of warmth.

He gestured to the seat next to him. "Welcome to my home, Reaper. I've had a long discussion with Bertran, so I know why you're here. He's gone to great lengths to assure me I can trust you. I hope that's true."

"As I've recently had to emphasize to your partner in . . . er, business, although I represent the very highest echelons of Satanic Injustice, I am allowed to operate within a very flexible remit. I don't need to lie to achieve my objectives. So long as I realize my goals, Satan is happy. Very happy, for they are an expression of his will. And those who help me—even in an unofficial and off the books capacity—well, I can only imagine the favor that might curry."

François looked at me long and hard. I could almost see the cogs clicking over in his mind as he weighed the pros and cons of dealing with someone like me.

"Very well," he replied, "excuse me for one moment while I take certain precautions."

He reached below the table and retrieved a small ornate box covered by a number of glowing, arcane symbols. With rapt deliberation, he closed his eyes, mumbled a brief phrase, and then pressed his palm against a spike sprouting from the lid.

Scarlet flowed, and I felt power coalesce about us.

François opened the cover and removed a miniature dryad, wings batting, from within. Extending his hand he allowed the creature to lick his wound, then said, "Protect."

Bound by the blood-tie, the sprite took to the air and began orbiting the terrace. As she circled above us, her female form glowed green and a shower of tiny sparks fell from her hair. Whatever she was doing set my teeth on edge and made my eyes water.

"Now we can talk without fear of telepathic eavesdropping," François explained, "which I fear may be necessary, given our agenda."

He took a deep breath. "As you know, while Al's forte lies in gunrunning, mine relates to those who use them. I traffic a wide range of mercenaries and Foreign Legionnaires for several of the parties currently engaged in conflicts throughout the various realms of hell. Obviously, this entails the unofficial transport of produce between venues. That brings us into frequent contact with the underground facilitators of the white market, people peddling all sorts of services and equipment. Sometimes that might relate to the people themselves, or the stuff they have to offer. But more often than not, one of our most precious commodities is information.

"After speaking with Bertran, you'll be aware there's been a great deal of chatter lately regarding the single-plane rift generators which Tesla keeps churning out. I can confirm such rumor as truth. Tesla has not only constructed a stockpile of new, short-range, short-term models, but he's also made a breakthrough on his long-range sonic prototype that will transform the way future campaigns are organized and conducted. Because of *my* particular area of expertise, ours was one of the first organizations Tesla approached. He was keen for us to test his device's effectiveness in the mass relocation of troops between all the realms simultaneously—"

"Wait a minute," I cut in, "a multi-phasic amplifier that can access *every* level of the underverse at the same time?"

"That's right."

"And did the bloody thing work?"

"I must say, despite the fact it kept overheating, I found it to be very promising. We lost fifty percent of our troops to the quantum flux, but half is better than nothing. Tesla said he's confident he can remove the glitch in a relatively short time, and from what I've heard, is close to realizing that goal."

"When was this?"

"He originally approached us several months ago. The trial run took place two weeks later. News has gradually leaked out since then."

"So how does all this help me?"

"Indirectly. Let me explain." François shuffled forward in his seat. "As gossip about Tesla's breakthrough started to circulate, it understandably led to a number of tentative enquiries from the more notorious militia groups currently on the market. The portals are obscenely expensive, you see, and they're the only ones who could readily access the funds to buy one."

"How much?"

"The going rate is ten million diablos."

I whistled.

"Precisely. Then we started getting offers from the more reputable brigades, those who obviously restructured their finances enough to willingly put a huge dent in their bank balance. Do you see the point I'm making? Because of the cost involved, they're the only interested parties we've had. Imagine my surprise, then, when about a month or so ago a strange little chap walked in here, bold as brass, and demanded to buy one of the new models."

"Cream?"

"No, not at that time. This gentleman was dressed like a native Perishian, but acted in a very odd manner. Almost as if he was having a conversation with someone who wasn't actually there. Oh, and he kept wringing his hands all the time."

A surge of pleasure warmed my heart.

"And I take it this gentleman wished to remain anonymous?"

"Of course. He stated he was a well-funded archeologist who wished to obtain a transportation device that would allow him to pursue his dream of . . . to . . ." François became reticent and his aura darkened.

He's afraid. "Please continue," I said in as gentle a tone as I could muster. "I'm sure Bertran will have told you I offered him amnesty. I extend that same courtesy to you. You have the word of Satan's Reaper."

He didn't look convinced. "It's just that . . . this person possessed a great deal of knowledge about things that shouldn't be spoken of. Things from the Time of Sundering."

Above us, the dryad gasped and faltered in her flight. A sharp glance from her master quickly focused her concentration where it belonged.

"What *things*, specifically?" I couldn't prevent my tone from becoming harder.

François swallowed, hard. "Initially, I found that difficult to make out. He twittered on about all manner of subjects. But amongst his ramblings he made specific reference to Vidium Swords, the Scroll of Divergent Union, some cup or other, and possibly—and I'm not quite sure about this—Goliath's Skull?

Reaper, he was not only aware of their existence but willing to part with a vast fortune to gain information as to the possible whereabouts of one or all of those artifacts."

Very few people would have ever heard of the Time of Sundering. Even fewer about Vidium Swords, the heavenly weapons wielded by God's angels during the final battle.

This goes much deeper than I thought. "And did you help him?"

"I wasn't sure I had, at first. Now I can say for certain that I did."

"Explain."

"Think about my position for a moment, Mister Grim. I'm a crime boss in one of the most notorious cities in one of the most despicable levels of hell. Here, I have wealth and influence. The power of life and death over others. And I'm cannier than most you'll meet. I value intelligence above brute strength, information over possessions. I use my head where others would act without thinking. But even *I* don't know about such things. Whispers, yes. Rumors, most certainly . . ."

"So how did you *unwittingly* help our mysterious buyer?"

"I sold him one of the acoustic prototypes Tesla had given me . . . and . . ."

"And?"

"And I told him what I knew. Just a snippet I'd heard from some half-crazed idiot many moons ago, regarding the likely site of a fallen . . . you know what."

"Where?"

"Hades. A place that still suffers greatly from tectonic instability. I suggested that perhaps the fragile crustal areas were the result of a great external upheaval and thus might indicate the resting place of those who can't be named."

"That sounds a little farfetched to me. How much did our nutty citizen pay for this unsubstantiated information?"

"Two million diablos."

"Two million!" My jaw dropped.

François noted my reaction but waved for silence. He hadn't quite finished:

"Imagine my shock then, when only this past week Cream entered my establishment looking for a specialist gem cutter. He claimed that he had a further million to spend if we could find someone willing to do the job quickly, without fuss or too many questions."

"*Further* million?"

"That's what I thought. I'd heard of him, of course, but it was the first time I'd ever met the Poisoner in the flesh. I took his inference to mean he was working with the other guy, the crazy one with all the money, although he never directly confirmed that fact."

"Tell me, did you find a suitable craftsman?" As I asked the question, I scanned François' emotions.

"It took some doing, but we found the perfect stooge. Henry Cheval, a shady double dealer from the Twelfth Horrondissement. We had him here within the hour. He ended up working on what I can only describe as a huge blue stone. I've been in this business for nearly nine hundred years, and I've never seen a jewel like it. But I've heard the legends, and really, where else could it have come from? It looked like a cross between an aquamarine and a topaz, and was bigger than my fist."

A cold tingle wormed its way down my spine. Something in François' words and the feelings behind them was invoking a powerful reaction within me. I was lost to the echoes of distant battles, where flaming swords shattered worlds and enemies alike.

Only with the greatest difficulty did I break the spell.

"How soon can you locate this Henry Cheval again and get him here?"

"Mister Grim, I'm afraid that won't be possible. Part of the agreed fee imposed by Cream was the requirement that the gem cutter submit himself to a ripcord. As soon as he'd completed his task, Henry was mind-wiped and sent for reassignment."

Crap! Go figure. Cream and his OCD little friend are starting to get on my tits.

François was quick to appease my rising temper: He reached beneath the table again, removed a gray baseball-sized object from within a bag, and tossed it to me.

I caught it in one hand and found it warm to the touch. Several studs in its surface made a triangle formation around its crown. The device emitted a high-pitched whine whenever my fingers strayed too close to one of the buttons.

Just like some women I know.

"What's this?"

"That is a working prototype of the new multi-phasic portal generator. Cream made a point of emphasizing that it is glitch-free but has been manufactured to function only twice before self-destructing. He said to think of it as a gift . . . and a sign of things to come. Evidently it incorporates tech that removes any trace elements added to the traveling medium . . . whatever that means."

Does he mean the tags? If so, anyone using it would be invisible to surveillance!

"How did Cream get one of these?"

"I think it's obvious when you connect the dots, don't you? Especially as he went on to stress that should I be interested in putting the word out on their behalf, there'd be a twenty percent cut from future purchases."

"Generous."

"No, just good business. They know they'll need my extensive white market acumen."

"Tell me, what does your partner think about these latest developments?"

"He doesn't know. After what happened to Don Pérignone, I'm choosy about what becomes a mutually shared concern."

Really?

My eyebrows twitched upward. Subconsciously, I hefted the orb up and down. François waited, calmly returning my stare, allowing me time to process his startling revelation.

Time to make an offer.

"How does this generator work?" I asked, intrigued by the apparent simplicity of its design.

"The three buttons operate like a dead man's switch. You press down with your palm and they pierce the outer layers of your skin to mesh with your spirit. Then all you do is envisage where you'd like to go, release the pressure, and *shazam*!"

"So you need to keep a clear image in your head?"

"Most certainly, otherwise you'll spread your atoms across hydraspace."

"And this new model literally can go anywhere?"

"From what I'm told, yes."

As casually as possible, I asked, "I don't suppose you know where I might find any of the other articles on this fruit-loop's shopping list?"

François went quiet again. As he stared into my eyes, his aura flickered through every color in the rainbow.

He's still weighing me up.

A knock at the door disturbed his process.

"Come!" he called.

André entered with two crystal tumblers on a silver tray. Each contained a rich amber liquid that swirled lazily around the inside of the glass. Without a word, the maître d' strode confidently across the terrace, deposited the drinks at our table, and left.

"Efficient ship you run," I murmured. "I like that."

Picking up my glass, I paused to inhale the heady fragrance of Diabhalvulin before downing half its contents. It burned like a welcoming fire in my throat.

"So, can you help me or not?"

François followed suit. After sampling his drink, he said, "This is mere speculation of course, but I hear the underworld's most obscure reference archive has a special section where restricted materials might be researched. Access is denied to all except the highest tier of Satan's Blue Suits and intelligence network."

"The Hellexandria Library?"

"No, no, no. That's what everyone's supposed to think. I'm referring to the vaults below the Sphincter, in S16, ancient Egypt."

There are catacombs below the Sphincter?

The surprise obviously showed on my face.

"You didn't know?" François spluttered. He looked worried. "Hey, I told you the nature of my work means I get to hear things. I just keep my ear to the ground and listen. It's not my fault if people find out the wrong things and blab about them."

I hunched forward.

He glanced toward my hands and I sensed his rising fear. "You're not going to . . . ?"

It's not you I'm pissed at. "Relax, François, I've bigger fish than you to fry. It's quite refreshing to meet a denizen of hell who values information so highly and keeps his head in a crisis. No offence intended to your family . . ."

"None taken."

"In fact, how would you like an expanded circle of contacts? Or enjoy the luxury of knowing you could dig into any affair under Paradise without the Department of Injustice ever knocking on your door?"

His eyes bulged as he caught my inference. "At what price?"

"Think of it as an interest-laden investment where I'll be a silent partner. A necessary evil, I'm afraid, as most souls balk at the idea of working with the Reaper. Now, while this means you'll have to do all the work, I'll nevertheless be busy in the background, keeping away any unnecessary heat. This puts a few noses out of joint initially, but when your opposition or any dissenters wind up banished to Hades, or reassigned without memory, word will soon get round that you're untouchable. Of course, it might also entail your elevation amongst the criminal elite."

"What about Al?"

"Oh, don't you worry about him. I have a feeling he won't be in a position to cramp your style for much longer."

I raised my tumbler. "Do we have a deal?"

A broad grin split his face, and our glasses chinked together.

"I believe we do."

Chapter 7: Beginning of the End

Sonorous tones of utmost complexity swelled into the air. Enfolded in majesty, Frédéric Chopin clung to every note, allowing the cadence to soothe the agitation crowding in on him. Soon the harmonies began to weave their magic. Compelling and sublime, the tempo lifted Frédéric's heart and transported him to another time and place, a world of utter tranquility, a world the likes of which could never be found elsewhere in the multi-layered misery that was hell.

His fingers flowed like liquid silk across the keys as he reminisced about the golden years before his illness, when triumphs and accolades were still parts of his life.

As was my beloved George.

No sooner had the comfort of a rare smile touched his face, however, than a shadow fell across the rose-tinted landscape of his memories.

Ah, I was wondering when the Undertaker's little "gift" would interrupt my reverie.

A spasm seized his hands. Rippling up his arms and into his shoulders, the pain intensified before slamming into the vault of his skull. His sight expanded, and images of places he had neither seen nor visited cascaded through his mind. Despite the pain, Frédéric chuckled.

If only the fool mortician would acknowledge that unexpected side effect of his malevolence can occur, he wouldn't be so smug. The visions almost make the discomfort worthwhile.

This vision took hold. Magnified beyond comprehension, it filled the vast horizon of his consciousness with memories and emotions he could never have imagined or experienced otherwise. Reaching the limit of his endurance, myriad possibilities hung, suspended in time for just a moment before rebounding back toward him at alarming speed.

Frédéric braced himself. The incoming wave was all-consuming and, sure enough, no sooner had it struck than his perspective twisted. The ground opened up beneath his feet. He fell through the reticulation of time itself, and the anguish of his decline cascaded anew through his mind:

Again came the shock he had felt at the diagnosis of his temporal lobe epilepsy and the neurological imbalance this created, which plagued him with hallucinations and unprovoked seizures. The gradual ossification of his intellect, along with the helpless sense of impotency he was forced to endure, became an emancipation that gnawed away at his soul as it robbed him of the competence to retain his popularity and prestige. The bitterness of separation from the one he adored. The inevitable embrace of death. The horror of awakening in the underverse, where his suffering was recognized and gleefully compounded—For how better to torment a virtuoso than deny him the ability to express his creativity?

Frédéric gripped the lover's knot adorning his wrist. Made from links of agate-of-hell and another unknown stone, both intertwined with locks of thick, luxuriant hair. Its luster anchored his soul against the tide of indomitable resentment that threatened to sweep him away. Thus armored against the rush, he forced himself to relax and struggled back to the here and now.

My, my, how the Undertaker must enjoy the fruits of his efforts.

In defiance, he caressed the tresses securing the bracelet in place.

I love you, George, my Amantine. This is all for you.

The air sizzled behind him, and the smell of ozone filled the room. A muted thud reverberated through the floor. He jumped in his seat, and a fresh surge of arthritic agony coursed along his fingers. Frédéric cursed, massaging the back of his knuckles to ease the pain.

Without turning from the piano, he asked, "Is it done?"

"Of course," Thomas Cream replied indignantly. "Do you think me entirely incompetent?"

No, just expendable. "Tell me."

"As you predicted, de UnBorn spilled his guts and gave Grim everything we hoped he would."

"Everything?"

"Absolutely. The dryad witnessed it all, not ten minutes ago."

"And what is our illustrious Reaper doing now?"

"As we speak, he's making his way to Sulfurous Sands with all haste, gloating over the presumption that he's closing the gap."

Frédéric pondered with satisfaction on the success of his plan. Doing so caused reality to dissolve about him until he was graced by a fleeting vision of a beautiful woman with a long dark mane. She was dressed in black, her hair adorned with flowers that added a femininity few had ever been privileged to witness.

"Out of the frying pan," he mumbled under his breath.

"What did you say?" Cream asked, confused by the reference.

Realizing he had been daydreaming again, Frédéric shook his head. "I said . . . did you stick to the plan?"

"Yes, it was nice to walk the streets of Olde London Town so freely again. I'd forgotten what a riot Unholy Covenant Gardens can be. Do you know, they attract all manner of vendors from—"

"I'm not interested in semantics. Did you secure the bloody contracts or have our efforts been in vain?"

"I acquired the first, but once I'd stated our proposals to the second, they were keen to remind me their skills are not for sale. However, they were so intrigued by the prospect of testing their mettle against a worthy adversary that they offered to face him anyway."

"Face him anyway?" Frédéric was shocked. He turned to regard his partner in rebellion. "Are you sure there are no hidden agendas that might come back to haunt us?"

"On the contrary, they were delighted by the audacity of our undertaking. Evidently, they feel it complements their very reason for existence here."

A surge of overwhelming satisfaction eased the relentless ache in Frédéric's hands.

And into the fire.

Then he noticed a travel chest on the floor. Curiosity roused, he walked toward it and discerned a faint hum emanating from within. A gentle prickling sensation crawled across his skin the closer he got.

"It would seem you've been successful."

Cream squatted down by the case and opened the lid. The room filled with a warm, golden glow. "Come and see," he breathed, "and savor the fruits of our labor."

Frédéric made his way around to the other side.

A huge amber scroll lay across the top of the chest's interior. At over four feet in length, it might have been penned by giants. The case was tied tight by a jet-black ribbon. A gilded radiance infused the parchment, appearing to originate from a swathe of arcane letters transcribed thereon.

Beneath it, strapped securely to the base, was a pearlescent gray goblet. Frédéric noted with interest how the otherworldly resonance permeated from the bottomless well of its depths.

"And what damage did you leave in your wake to secure these?"

"None, for it was far easier than I thought. Because of the proscription, hardly anyone is aware of their existence, and those privy parties have been relying on obscurity and ignorance to shield them from discovery. Using both orb and gem, it was a simple matter for me to breach the temporal barrier and drug the librarian. Once under my influence, she helped me take what we wanted." He grinned. "Such laxity marks the beginning of the end."

Frédéric was struck by a sudden notion.

"Talking of endings, have you taken care of the dryad?"

"Already done. Remotely, of course."

"And de UnBorn?"

Cream laughed aloud. "He was so enamored by the Stone of Seraphim Swiftness that I was able to spike his drink with consummate ease. My little concoction included blue mist, firethorn, and devil's trumpet. All memory of my suggestive impulse will fade within a day or two, so we're in the clear."

"Then it would appear *we* are in need of a toast?" As an afterthought, Frédéric suggested, "I'm sure you'll understand when I say I'll fix the drinks myself?"

*

Events were proceeding well. Not only had I managed to cultivate a major new informant, but it appeared I'd confirmed that Cream was indeed in league with the mysterious hand-wringer: a person who was not only well funded and uncannily knowledgeable, but someone, it seemed, who had friends in the highest of places.

That fact gave me something to chew on.

The thing about hell is there's always a catch. Things might seem to be going well, but something will always sneak up on you and bite you in the ass. The Devil's Children are puppets. Outwardly privileged, their lives are controlled to such an extent that there's no real semblance of free will. Here in Perish— and everywhere else, for that matter— the crime bosses can never relax. There's always a wannabe ready to stab them in the back and take their place. Every day denizens contend with whatever personal foibles they brought with them, ingeniously compounded a thousand times over by the Undertaker on assignment. Nobody does anything for free. So, whoever's financing Cream has an agenda. If I can discover what it is, I'll be well on the way to smashing a major conspiracy that seems to run throughout every level of society . . . And perhaps my Awful Father's mood will improve.

As droll as that thought was, it reminded me that even I was not immune to the idiosyncrasies of the netherworlds. I was one of its most feared and hated denizens, and yet I was forced to replenish my essence in the Bālefire on a regular basis—at His Satanic Majesty's pleasure, of course— otherwise my enhancements would quickly wane and I'd become as weak as a kitten.

I watched the vermin in front of me as I stalked along the sidewalk toward the Palais de L'Injustice, the closest official site of a major inter-dimensionhell gate. They scattered like rats, fear and loathing etched across their faces, an evident reminder of my standing.

If only they knew how drained I am right now, most would probably try their luck.

I hated it when this happened. It made me feel somehow corrupted. Incomplete, as if there was something crucial missing from the core of my being. A huge distraction when so many questions demanded answers.

Who's the leak among the Blue Suits? Where's the money coming from? What's Tesla's actual involvement? How did they ever unearth the details about prohibited knowledge? Have they been successful in discovering such artifacts? If so, why did Satan allow it? I thought he was omniscient and omnipresent here? How could he have let things slide so far? Is he losing his grip, as some have dared to suggest?

Blasphemous thoughts. Soft thoughts. Punishable thoughts.

The sooner I get to S16, the better. If de UnBorn is telling the truth and I uncover further clues, I'll get the Hounds involved. Prioritize my objectives with a targeted response and put the rebels under pressure. No mercy.

However, the orb in my pocket proved that things weren't quite right.

And what exactly was that gem they had cut? From what de UnBorn described, it sounds as if they actually have possession of a Vidium Sword. But how? Sweet Azazel! Even I *thought they were the stuff of myth and legend.*

Just thinking about the jewel and what its discovery meant set my pulse racing. Abruptly, my vision blurred, and I was transported to a time when the universe was much, much younger.

The firmament writhed within a crimson storm of chaotic energies. Around me, seraphim and cherubim rallied as the battle entered its final phase. Above, the indescribable might of the heavens massed. Below, a vast maelstrom opened its jaws. The sudden gravity well created by its presence generated a vacuum that sucked a third of the spirits into a downward spiral.

Angels fell, wings burning, and were consumed by darkness. Bright Lucifer fought back. Beautiful, shining, transcendent and evil, he challenged someone by name.

I raised a sword of living lightning in my hand. We clashed and . . .

Heart pounding, I cleared my head and realized I had stopped walking. For some reason, vapors had gathered about my feet and now clung to my boots and legs like melted tarmac. Ethereal voices whispered to me. Then I recognized where I was.

I've walked this far already?

To my left, the murky waters of the Inseine were broken by a series of low arches that faded into the gloom. The roadway itself was lined on either side by ranks of miniature battlements, as if an attack were expected at any moment. Moans exuded from somewhere far off within the brume, calling for aid that would never come.

Pont Snuff, the oldest bridge in Perish. A place synonymous with eternal suffering, for those who fell into its inky-black depths were drained of essence until they became shadows of their former selves. Wraiths without substance, who could never be reassigned.

Perishians avoided this area like the plague, and I could understand why. Even here, the siren call of the shades inhabiting the river's depths was hard to resist. Both alluring and heart-rending, they pleaded for mercy in an attempt to lure me closer. But I knew that if I was unwise enough to reach beneath the surface to offer my assistance, they might take advantage of my weakened state and condemn me in their place.

Thousands had gone missing over the years, for only the strongest wills stood a chance of crossing intact.

I stepped warily onto the span and made my way forward. Within seconds, my sanity was assaulted from all sides by a fresh deluge of appeals and empty promises.

"Help me, please, I beg you . . ."

"I have information. Priceless information. Surely it must be worth something?"

"Over here. I'm near the edge. That's not too much trouble, is it?"

"I can help. Get you across safely if you'll just—"

"Don't listen to her! I'm the one you want. You only have to dip your hand in . . ."

I resolutely ignored them all. To help me focus, I opened my senses to the full range of emotions behind the barrage. A necessary, yet risky gamble.

Insipid darkness leached into my mind, confirming my suspicions. While a few of the lost souls were indeed genuine, most were motivated by desires as black as pitch.

Then I heard someone call a name.

"Goliath!"

"Who said that?" I shouted.

A chorus of voices yelped all at once: "Me."

"Don't be stupid. It wasn't them, it was me—"

"Liar! I'm the one who called. Here I am . . ."

"No, he didn't, I did. Look this way . . ."

The resultant clamor was deafening, and threatened to ruin my concentration. Straining hard, I cut through the chaff and scanned what remained of the phantom auras below me. A feeble star sparkled patiently amid a veil of obscurity.

Who?

"Golgotha!" the same voice called out.

Place of the skull! Recognition flared, and my astral sight zeroed in on the entity.

"Don Pérignone? Is that you?"

"What remains of him," he admitted wryly. An overwhelming wave of bitterness cascaded toward me, along with scarlet thoughts of revenge.

"I'd ask you what you're doing here, but I think that's obvious. I see what your former subordinate meant when he said you were 'immersed in a new way of life.'"

The Don didn't bother responding. Instead, he thrust a catalog of spectral images toward me. I reeled under their weight but was drawn to one in particular, for its theme depicted the same event across differing periods of history.

An open plain, lined on both sides by opposing armies. Two contenders faced off. One towered toward the sky, his spear and shield dwarfing the insects about him. The other looked much less imposing: a mere shepherd, armed with a sling. An unavoidable climax occurred, and the ground reverberated as the titan crashed to the floor. A sense of falling through the ground followed, leading to an awakening beneath leaden skies, dark with ash. Rebellious thoughts resulted in an intervention by a higher power and, soon after, the true death followed. An age passed by. Sealed and silent, a crypt filled with dust. Within, an ornate sarcophagus of impressive proportions faded into antiquity. Upon it, in pride of place, an armored helmet sat forgotten. The scene receded until all that remained was an impression of a grinning skull. Its eyes gleamed like hot coals as it sank into murky depths . . .

As I regained my balance, Don Pérignone immediately got down to business.

"Right, let's dispense with the crap and get straight to it. You might prefer it if we converse mentally. Some of the things I have to say shouldn't really be bandied about."

This should be interesting. "Go on."

My erstwhile partner thought he was so clever dumping me here, just so he could avoid any chance that I'd die and regenerate. Well, tough shit for him. We hear things in this river, things that shouldn't be spoken of. Although I've no way out—unless some poor shmuck takes my place, of course— I still possess knowledge. And knowledge is power. A baleful reminder throbbed from lidless orbs. *I can help you, Reaper, if you're willing to trade. Possession of Goliath's Skull protects the free will of its wearer. They cannot be influenced. From what I've gathered, entirely the wrong group of zealots seeks to claim it, for if they succeed, that heralds the beginning of the end. No one will be able to manipulate them, not even his Satanic Butt Plug.*

So what have you got to offer, exactly?

Of all the denizens in this godforsaken place, you're known as someone who never lies. Someone who values truth. Well, actions speak louder than words . . .

Before I could ask what he meant, the streamers coiling around the embankments wrapped themselves around my entire body. They thickened, gleaming with an eerie phosphorescence that clung to my form like wraiths. Sparks capered through my hair, and a static charge danced across my skin. Everything went gray, all sensation ceased. *Something* changed. No sooner had I registered that fact than the miasma simply melted into the floor and clarity returned. Stunned, I found myself standing outside a huge building amid a crowd of startled passersby.

"What the fu–?"

A voice echoed from out of the receding haze.

I can help you, Reaper. Remember what I've done, and act as you see fit.

A reflection of burning eye sockets appeared again.

It took me a moment to recognize where I was.

Hey! This is the Assemblée Diabolique et Niveaux, the new Inter-Circles of Hell travel junction. I spun on the spot. *I've completely skipped the Palais de L'Injustice. But why? The Palais is an official—*

A sudden thought occurred to me.

Did Don Pérignone just help me avoid someone? Is that where the one of the moles works? Well, bugger me!

I thought about the implications of what had just occurred, and grinned. Just like that, the perfect solution came to me:

Oh, I'll "act accordingly" all right. If this pans out, I have the perfect candidate to swap places with the Don.

Chapter 8: The Sphincter

Like Perish, known throughout the many circles of hell for uncultured brutality, District S16 was renowned for chaos and riotous disorder.

Not that the District's denizens had much choice in the matter, for the Spouting Pyramids of Geyser dominated life, keeping everyone on their toes. Erupting with monotonous frequency each day, the monuments flooded the crowded streets and souks of Dark Cairo with a cascade of fire and brimstone so overwhelming it made Pompeii in nearby New Hell look like a day at the park by comparison. Here homes and businesses had been reduced to molten slag so often that locals nicknamed their city Sulfurous Sands. The ultimate holiday destination so long as you remembered your Paradise-factor million.

The only place in the entire district to escape wanton destruction was the Sphincter, an edifice I now found myself regarding in close detail.

And now I know the reason it's left alone.

Facing east toward a nonexistent sun, the slimestone rock that comprised the man's head and lion's body of this great monument was stained deep brown from the acidic air of its environs. I noted with interest how the rear end of our Hellistic version had been altered, raised high into the air like a cat in heat.

Typical!

The roiling clouds shrouding Paradise moved away to the south. In dwindling light, I quickly made my way around the entire structure. So far as I could see, the monument had no discernible entrance of any kind.

Then I remembered. *Of course! The bloody thing is supposed to be inconspicuous. If I want to get inside, I'll have to use my head.*

Sitting back on my heels, I took a moment to consider my options:

Brute strength is a no-no. I can usually pick up on the presence of enchantments, but this thing isn't emitting a bean. That means it'll be shielded all the way to Old Nickmas and back. So trying to hammer my way in will be a complete waste of time. And knowing my luck, if I try to force the wards with dark magic, the hex would likely rebound and fry me where I stand.

Next, I tried to think laterally.

Of course, I could try the travel orb. But do I want to expend one of my options? Or what about calling His Infernal Majesty? No! That's no good either, especially while he's still pissed at me. He'd probably tell me to go stick my head in a meat grinder.

Then it hit me.

Why don't I try a simple blessing? I'm one of the few souls empowered to use that filthy language . . . and its repulsive nuance just might work.

Encouraged by that thought, I moved back a dozen or so feet, spread my arms wide, and in the divine tongue, said, "*A-mad ha-pâ-tah.* (Stand revealed.)"

Power radiated outward from my location. As it rippled across the surface of the Sphincter, a glittering network of fireflies burst to life, highlighting a skein of concealment. Somehow, the bubble recognized my presence and expanded to encompass me. My vision warped, as if I were now looking at things through a slightly viscid medium. Then I felt a shift in the substance of Gehenna Mean Time (GMT): The entrance stood revealed.

And it was one hell of an entrance. Situated at the rear end—where else?—I found myself gazing at a large multi-leaved iris positioned exactly where the Sphincter's butt-hole should be. Stairs leading to it had been cut into the monument's hind legs. Climbing them, I made my way to a small platform positioned immediately in front of the annulus.

No sooner had I placed my foot on the top step than a metallic scraping sound set my teeth on edge. Fascinated, I watched as the blades in the doorway dilated to form an opening. A strange moaning sound issued from the now wide-open orifice, accompanied by the reek of ammonia, methane, and rotting eggs.

I reeled backward, gagging. "Jesus!" I blasphemed. *Where did they find that combination of stenches? It makes the Mortuary smell like a summer meadow by comparison.*

A squad of reavers skittered out onto the ledge. One of the Undertaker's finest achievements, they were an unholy bastardization of humanity, arachnid, and scorpion: the perfect guard dogs. Steel talons clicked on stone as the pack's alpha edged forward. His tail reared up, its wicked-looking stinger hanging poised, dripping with venom and ready to strike. He bared his fangs, and his yellow eyes glared with barely suppressed rage.

"You are exxxxpecteeed," he sibilated. "Follooow meee."

Expected? Unbe-fucking-lievable! Is nothing censored in this place?

Through gritted teeth, I snarled, "Lead on, please."

The pack parted, making an avenue for me to proceed. As I stomped forward, they tightened up to form a living halo of hair, teeth and claws around me. Only then did they usher me inside. The iris screeched shut behind us and the roof and walls closed in. I suddenly felt like a stubborn turd that didn't want to leave the comfort of a warm and cozy colon. A fitting analogy, as the constant lapses in security were now grating on my nerves and making me feel constipated.

My discomfort didn't ease once we were within the Sphincter itself. Although the hallway furcated in a number of different directions, the heat was oppressive, and exacerbated the stench a thousandfold.

I was led downward, along a series of switchbacks that took us deep into the not-so-secret workings of the monument. In the confined space, the reverberating resonance produced by my escort made it sound as if I was in the company of a tap-dancing troupe. The longer we walked, the more I had to resist the urge to show them my Elvis shuffle.

Eventually we turned a corner and arrived at a dead end.

"Remaaaaain heeeeere," the alpha hissed.

Without a further word, he turned and led his squad of mutants, clicking and clacking, off into the darkness.

Talkative bunch. I wonder if they do weddings.

I waited, but nothing happened. Just as I was about to call out, a bright thread of light appeared on the wall in front of me. Intensifying, it appeared to sink into the rock itself. It grew until the outline of a double set of ornately carved doors appeared. Once clarified, the unknown illumination cut off, and the entrance silently swung open to reveal a sumptuous office lined with bookshelves and overstuffed leather chairs. A familiar odor assailed my nostrils.

That smells like...?

"Please come in," a sultry voice called.

I stepped inside and sure enough, my suspicions were confirmed.

Inside, a pair of Blue Suits stood close together behind a cluttered desk on one side of the room. The first was one of the most outstanding librarians I have ever seen: close to my height, she had curves in all the right places and legs that reached all the way up to her armpits. Her crisp white blouse and navy-blue skirt accentuated her form perfectly. A pair of horn-rimmed spectacles hung from a chain around her neck, drawing my eyes toward the gleaming name badge pinned between her ample breasts: *Joy.*

I can only imagine.

Joy wore her wavy dark hair scrunched up in a bun. For some reason, I liked that a lot. Sadly, I didn't like it enough to prevent a sneer from souring my countenance. But Joy wasn't the cause of my displeasure. It was her companion, and the source of the stench—a literally reptilian, stinking lawyer.

At nearly seven feet in height, his emaciated form reeked of cheesy feet, stale sweat and cabbage. Like his companion, he wore a neatly-tailored dark blue suit, and a high quality collar and tie. Weeping sores and popping pustules covering his exposed hide spoiled the effect of his attire. He wore glasses, attached to the side of his head by two oversized bolts. The name emblazoned in smoldering letters across his breast pocket identified him as *Vernon.*

Vernon had taken a cunning position so that the bulk of the desk hid his tail and the pool of slime where he stood. Almost.

I couldn't help myself. I hated his kind with a passion.

"What the fuck is a lawyer doing here?"

"I'm here on behalf of the Attorney General, Mister Grim," Vernon replied. He removed a white parchment from his briefcase and held it up. "Here's our confidentiality agreement. Anything you see or hear within this establishment may not be discussed without the express permission of His Infernal Majesty or his appointed spokesperson."

"It's a bit late for that!" I retorted. "Do you realize how many denizens are blabbing about this place and its contents as we speak? I'm Satan's bounty hunter, for Azazel's sake, and even *I* wasn't aware of its existence until I encountered a few loose-tongued criminals during the pursuit of a fugitive. If not for them, I wouldn't be here now, following up a lead. So quit stalling and—"

"Hang on," Joy cut in. She appeared puzzled. "You mean you're not here about the break-in?"

"Break-in?" *Oh, this gets better and better.*

"Yes. We thought you were the specialist dispatched by the Fiendish Bureau of Investigation."

My head dropped. I clenched my fists at my side and made a conscious effort to maintain a hold on my temper.

I've wasted enough time. "*Do mo géill, cumhach'd.* (Submit to my authority.)"

Both Blue Suits staggered as the compulsive power of the hex took hold. Then they relaxed to await my instructions.

"Right," I said, "when did this burglary occur?"

"I'm not exactly sure," Joy replied, "but sometime within the last week."

"Why do you say that?"

"Because I have to complete an inventory every Sinday evening, and that was what? six days ago?"

"Isn't that a long time to wait between checks?"

"Not necessarily, especially considering the protocols we have in place."

In response to my look of confusion, she continued: "As you're no doubt aware, almost all of the items stockpiled here are prohibited; so we keep them in what we call 'cold storage.' Deep underground. Out of sight and out of mind. Outwardly, we don't have an overly elaborate security system like you'd find at the Hexagon, or Bunker of England, as our Dark Lord doesn't want to draw attention to this facility. So he relies on distraction instead.

The location of this particular archive was chosen because of its proximity to the Geyser pyramids. They cause widespread pandemonium that's effectively masked its existence for centuries. In turn, this gives us the luxury of being able to dispose of unwanted artifacts in a fully automated dump. We can literally forget about them . . . Unless there's an alarm activation, of course, or it's time for the weekly audit."

"I see. So how many vaults like this are there?"

Joy looked to Vernon for verification. "I believe there are thirteen, but I'm not quite sure. Part of my contract stipulates the compartmentalization of information. I only have access to the stuff I need to know. And once I've served my term . . ."

She removed a ripcord tag from between her breasts. Only then did I notice the fine chain dangling down from around her neck. That I'd failed to spot it earlier made me better appreciate the principle of distraction.

"You'll be reassigned?"

"After I've been mind-wiped, yes. I can't wait."

"Why's that?"

"I'm five years into a six-year solo tour, with no one except reavers and imps for company—" Joy glanced to her side "—and the occasional visitor from the department . . ."

Then she made eye contact with me. "But *he* doesn't count. That's why it's so nice to get a real visitor for a change." Joy's eyes smoldered longingly. She made her way around to the front of the desk, whereupon she arranged herself in such a way as to flaunt the shape of her figure to stunning effect. I felt as if I were witnessing the results of pouring liquid ivory into high heels and stockings.

Five years? I think someone's hungry.

In another part of hell, I could imagine Strawberry sharpening her claws.

I was forced to cough and clear my throat before I could speak. "I noticed that the chameleon sheath around this structure has a temporal aspect to it. While I appreciate that's a powerful deterrent in itself, surely it can't be the only defensive precaution. What else do you have, apart from your reavers, in the way of security?"

"Oh, there's infernal-red detectors and so forth, like everywhere else. But for the heavy-duty stuff, you have to go farther below ground." She sauntered casually toward me and linked her arm through mine. "It would be better if I just showed you."

As she led me toward a raised platform in the corner of the room, Joy explained: "The artifacts that have been stolen are imbued with great potency. Even the mention of their names causes a well of esoteric energy to coalesce in the ether which is something we don't want in such close proximity to a defense matrix. So, if you don't mind, I'd rather deactivate certain aspects of the grid before we speak further."

"Ahh, I see." I cocked a thumb over my shoulder. "Won't Vernon be coming with us?"

"I have to stay here, I'm afraid," Vernon replied. He waved the parchment confidentiality agreement. "Remember, we're waiting for an investigator to arrive, and I've got to get him or her to sign this before they can go anywhere."

"So it's just you and me then?" I murmured to Joy, who by now had decided to rest her head on my shoulder.

"It would seem so." She gave my arm a brief squeeze and managed to snuggle even closer. A heady bouquet teased my senses.

"What perfume is that?"

"Ah, thank you for noticing. I hardly get a chance to wear any since I've been here. It's a brand new fragrance by Jean-Paul Guillotine, called Plagus, eau de toilet." She flushed with pleasure. "Why, do you like it?"

Shit!

"Er, yes. It's very nice." To keep my mind on business, I asked, "You mentioned artifacts have been taken? So that obviously means more than one treasure has been removed?"

"I'm afraid so, yes."

Has she been slacking . . . or is she on the take?

We stepped onto the pad and stopped before a small control panel. An amber radiance lanced down, bathing us in a glimmering cone of light. Joy managed to detach herself from my arm long enough to submit to a retinal scan. Once it was over, she spoke into a microphone attached to a control panel.

"Joy Winters. Infernal serial number: Nineteen, eighty-eight, delta, epsilon. Thirty, eighty-one, thirteen."

She stepped aside and invited me to follow her lead. I did, concluding, "Daemon Grim. Infernal serial number: Six, six, six, alpha. Zero, zero, thirteen."

No sooner had I submitted myself to the process than the nimbus surrounding us changed to green. A prickling sensation crawled across my skin, and immediately we were someplace else.

I found myself on a floating platform, very similar in design to the dais in Joy's office, only this one was situated within a huge central bore nearly twenty yards wide. The shaft stretched off into the gloom above and below us, and its outer wall was lined by hundreds upon hundreds of tiny blue winking LEDs.

I adjusted focus to compensate for the reduced ambiance, and discovered each of the displays signaled the presence of an elongated metallic hatchway. The overall impression was similar to that found within a bank vault's strong-room, but on a much larger scale.

"How many are here?" I asked.

"Two thousand three hundred and forty-five," Joy answered proudly, "and this is the largest of all the chambers."

Our voices echoed off into the abyss, to be answered by the whine of a hydraulic system kicking into gear. Two concentrated beams of light stabbed out of the darkness, illuminating our chests in the red-wash of dual laser sights. Then I saw the source of them: a pair of double-barreled .50 Brimstone-Gehenna cannons with auto-track feature.

Nodding toward the guns, I said, "I take it those are part of the internal security measures you mentioned?"

"Yes. Sound and motion activated, and enhanced by an AI seek-and-destroy recognition system. We also have nerve-agent backups that can flood the entire shaft in seconds."

"So how in Satan's name did your intruder get past?" *Apart from you fucking up, that is.* "From what I see, it's state of the art."

"That's what's so disturbing," Joy responded. "Even if someone *did* overcome the lethal deterrents intact, they'd still need to defeat the DNHA lockout protocol, and *that* has an explosive response. Let me demonstrate how elaborate it is."

Joy moved toward the control panel and pressed her hand against a flat indented surface. *Phhut!* When she stepped back, I saw small beads of blood welling from her fingertips.

"DNHA sample analyzed," a metallic voice intoned. "Agent Winters, J., recognized. Please enter passkey."

Joy leaned over the microphone and in a deliberate voice, stated, "*Cuídhhtích dòigh uile se cò inntrig a-bos.*" She then repeated the same phrase in Standard English. "Abandon hope all ye who enter here."

I was impressed. "You speak ancient Hellanese?"

"Of course. It's required for all those with level six clearance. And it's the only way to prep the actual boxes." She signaled for me to wait. "Just give me a moment . . ."

"Please enter the required code," the same automated voice directed.

"Recognize item one. The Scroll of Divergent Union. Reference: *neoni, neoni, neoni, aon, còigh.* (Zero, zero, zero, one, five.)"

"Scroll of Divergent Union, neoni, neoni, neoni, aon, còigh, recognized," came the reply. "Transferring now."

Power bloomed. In moments, the deck commenced a dizzying ascent. As it did so, it scrolled around to the opposite side of the borehole and stopped in front of an access cover. I noted with interest how the .50s shadowed our every move.

A blue-white light sprang out from the LED unit. Once both of us had been scanned, I heard the faint hiss of a vacuum breach. Then the hatch slid open, revealing a compartment empty inside, save for a note written in blood:

> *There's nothing better*
> *Than a bright-eyed, soft skinned,*
> *Little doll.*
> *The perfect guinea pig*
> *For the strychnine candy cane*
> *That cures all ills.*
> *You will die this night,*
> *An exceptional death of pent-up frustration,*
> *Bottled for so long, and released at last,*
> *Like a volcano, against those who sin against God.*

The inscription was different from the notes I'd seen before. It was bolder, less graceful, and didn't degrade as the verse progressed.

Did Cream write this himself?

"Do you know what it means?" Joy asked, using the situation as an excuse to drape herself across me again.

"I'm afraid I do. Tell me, what exactly *is* the Scroll of Divergent Union?"

Still submissive to my will, she was helpless to resist.

"It's an acoustic seraphim incantation that causes the veil to drop between realms."

"Which realms? Heavenly or hell?"

"All of them."

Oh crap! "And how often can it be used?"

"From what I understand, the manifest indicated that due to the extraordinary power incorporated within the fabric of the invocation, it may only be uttered once."

"That's once too many in the wrong hands." Then I remembered an important facet of our earlier conversation. "You mentioned there were other boxes that had been broken into?"

"Yes, hang on a second."

Turning away from me, Joy dipped her head to the mike. "Recognize item two. The Cup of Tartarus. Reference: *neoni, neoni, neoni, dà, naoidh.* (Zero, zero, zero, two, nine.)"

"Cup of Tartarus, *neoni, neoni, neoni, dà, naoidh,* recognized," came the impassive reply once more. "Transferring now."

Immediately we plummeted in a virtual freefall for over a thousand yards. When the stomach-turning descent came to a stop, we found ourselves level with a similar but smaller cover. Joy opened it. As before, the drawer was bereft of its true contents, and another bloody message had been left in its place.

I picked it up, and inspected the passage:

> *Do I remind you of someone who should be dead?*
> *I've killed the sky,*
> *And its curdling reflection greets me anew each day*
> *With the burning flesh of a sadistic conflagration.*
> *Soon, you will be mine to command,*
> *A puppet, whose strings I'll dangle*
> *Above the abyss, on the edge of tomorrow.*

My hand-wringing tormentor was back, but on this occasion the last few lines of an otherwise elegant script were barely legible.

So, were they here together? Or did one person leave both notes?

I felt I was on the verge of making an important connection.

Absentmindedly, I asked, "And what does this Cup of Tartarus do?"

"This cup grants the Power of Command to anyone who drinks from it. As with the scroll, the sheer dominion of the spell involved means the user may only wield it once, otherwise they'll be consumed. However, the sovereignty of this particular icon remains active until the diktat has been fulfilled, or redirected."

My blood ran cold.

I read the contents of both poems again, looking for clues.

Well, it's clear they're aiming their rhetoric at me, and . . .

> *An exceptional death of pent-up frustration,*
> *Bottled for so long, and released at last,*
> *Like a volcano, against those who sin against heaven . . .*

I glanced at the second elegy:

> *I've killed the sky,*
> *And its curdling reflection greets me anew each day*
> *With the burning flesh of a sadistic conflagration.*

. . . they're making it obvious where I need to go.

"Joy, is there anything I need to know about the Geyser pyramids? Any other details that aren't common knowledge, even to the likes of me?"

"Other than the fact they erupt so often, at all times of the day and night? No. But we can talk about that later . . ." The look of ravenous hunger had returned to her eyes. "We're alone, we can't be disturbed, and . . . ?"

She let the inference hang in the air between us and chewed her bottom lip provocatively. As I watched, she then began to tease the ripcord chain from between her breasts with her fingers in a slow, lazy, circular motion.

I must admit, I was tempted.

"C'mon," she purred, "we all need some form of release. Who will know?"

That helped me make my mind up.

I held out my arms and smiled. Joy glided forward, her gaze fixed on mine, the first flush of arousal tinting her cheeks in a rosy blush. She molded to my body perfectly, and despite my centuries of discipline, I felt myself respond.

Joy sensed it too and raised her chin for our first kiss.

An all too brief taste of mint, and then it was over.

Joy caught her breath and stiffened. All the tension drained from her body, and her legs gave way. I caught her weight as she fell, maintaining eye contact until her pupils had fully dilated.

I inhaled the scent of her one last time.

"Only a fortunate few can touch my flesh and avoid the consequences," I whispered.

Very gently, I laid her out on the platform floor.

"And you're not one of them."

Visions of Strawberry's alabaster skin floated through the outer vestiges of my mind.

"Your incompetence cannot go unpunished."

Grasping the ripcord tightly, I interfaced mentally with its subprocessor and included the details I had only recently uncovered.

Pick the bones out of that!

Whoever her handler was, they could argue it out with the Attorney General and the Undertaker as to how things needed to proceed.

Me? I had other fish to fry, evidently, at the Spouting Pyramids of Geyser.

Chapter 9: Fish to Fry

Vernon took the news of Joy's demise and reassignment surprisingly well. But then, as a lawyer, and they were experts at toeing the line and looking after their own asses. After placing a few calls to FBI headquarters and the Attorney General's office, all agreed he would be left in charge of the depository until the appointment of a replacement librarian and the arrival of the special investigator, sometime in the morning.

He seemed quite happy, and from what I read in his emotions, considered this as a step toward promotion. Except that in his case that would only mean he would stink even worse than he already did: his tail would grow longer, and he'd make much more of a mess on the carpet.

Still, whatever rocks your boat, I suppose.

I paused to take stock of my situation.

I'd been inside the Sphincter for well over four hours. In that time, Paradise had departed and true night had fallen. The dusky glow of Dark Cairo did little to stave off the all-pervading gloom that infused the twilight hours here with an inevitable sense of menace. What's more, my waning strength meant I was losing the advantage of my enhancements; and the ability to see clearly in the dark was one of them. Thankfully, fire pits situated at the base of each pyramid blazed high, and by their light I could distinguish the silhouettes of all the major structures. The flaming beacons aided me to keep on the right track, for I was currently making my way toward the cemeteries positioned on either side of Kung-Fu's pyramid.

I mean, with all the threats regarding my imminent death, where else would I start?

The breeze picked up, and lightning branched across the sky in the distance.

That's rather sudden. I didn't get any warning of a storm moving in.

I started counting.

One thousand, two thousand, three thous–

A reverberating boom made the ground shudder.

And close too. Weird weather systems they have here.

The tympanic process repeated itself, only quicker this time; and before I knew it the sky was ablaze with a superfluity of anvil-to-ground and cloud-to-cloud discharges. A telltale pitter-patter on flagstones signaled the arrival of the first heavy drops of rain.

My internal alarm bells started ringing. I turned on the spot and extended my flagging senses out into the growing tempest. As a precaution, I also removed my scythe from within my coat and fastened my buttons tight.

It looks like Cream and company might have the balls to increase their attempts at intimidation. This should be interesting.

An ululating cry warbled out of the darkness.

"Reaper—Reaper—Reaper—Reaper . . ."

Who's that?

"Over here—Over here—Over here . . ."

Despite my best attempts, I couldn't zero in on the voice, which skipped from location to location around me.

"Cream?" I bellowed against the wind. "Show yourself, dammit! You've brought me here, so don't be shy about facing me now."

With a flick of my wrist, I extended my weapon to its full length.

As if responding to my challenge, the rain dramatically increased into a torrent, drenching me. I completed another slow circle, straining to get a clear line of sight on anything that might present a threat. Mocking laughter wove its way toward me through the downpour, taunting me from a dozen directions at once.

"I said show yourself. Let's get this fiasco over with."

Another blast of lightning followed. Right overhead, it drove me to my knees. The deluge erupted into a frenzied dissonance of light and sound. Thunder raged and hailstones as big as golf balls danced hypnotically about my feet.

Midnight congealed around me. I dropped into a fighting crouch. My alarm was working overtime now, and I decided it might be best to remove my gloves while I had time.

Before I had a chance to do so, a shadow rose up not twenty yards in front of me. It boiled and churned about itself, growing until it transformed into an eight-foot tall mass of flailing black rags topped by an impenetrable cowl.

Whatever it was, it didn't appear to have legs. Immune to the effects of the weather, it glided toward me. Armored gauntlets slid down from the end of tattered sleeves, like cobras hunting for prey. Two pinpoints of light appeared, impossibly far back within the deepest folds of the hood.

At last, the penny dropped. That's not Cream, unless he's been abusing steroids. And I doubt it's his hand-wringing buddy either.

"You wish to test yourself against us?" The tone of the question was laced with hostility. "That is well, for we have waited for a worthy opponent."

Oh fuck! It's a Sibitti enforc–"

The wraith morphed into a vortex of surging water and came at me with surprising speed. The surge hit. I was snatched into the air amid a bubbling, cascading frenzy.

Round and round I went, locked within an irresistible current that spun me head over heels and out of control. Had I been one of those denizens who needed to breathe, I would have quickly succumbed.

I found the experience both frightening and exhausting. I was weakened. I needed the Bãlefire to restore my full potential. And I had no way of calling for help.

Focus, idiot!

I lashed out, but it was like trying to swim in rapids. I tried to grab hold of the Sibitti's essence in some way, but his substance flowed through my outstretched fingers like spray drenching the rocks on a shoreline.

How the hell do you fight water? In a moment of inspiration I unleashed a powerful blast of arcane might through my scythe. You boil it.

I needn't have bothered. My effort had no discernible effect other than a resultant pressure wave that boxed my ears.

The Sibitti, however, didn't like what I'd done: The waterspout began to spin much faster than before; so fast, in fact, that the blood rushed to my head. In seconds, my vision tunneled and started to dim.

Slammed into the ground, I hit the deck so hard; the air was knocked from my lungs. I saw stars. Overwhelming distress consumed me, surfing along my synapses in an unending wave that my healing ability struggled to cope with. I coughed, gagged, spat out blood—along with a chunk of my tongue—and struggled to push myself into a kneeling position.

"I find you wanting," my opponent mocked. "How disappointing."

"What can I say?" I retorted through clenched teeth. "You've caught me on a bad day."

That thought struck home.

Or have they? I was led here, to this place, at a time when I cannot manifest.

I looked around, carefully. The storm had dissipated, no longer needed as a means to approach and then ambush me.

Oh, very clever.

Derisive snickering reverberated through the night.

It was a bloody set up! Just how many people has Cream included in his little rebellion?

"Perhaps my brothers may find continuing amusement in your pathetic attempts to stay alive," the enforcer chided, "but I've grown bored with you."

Brothers?

Sure enough, two more phantoms detached themselves from the gloom and manifested as identical corporeal forms.

Now I was worried. The Sibitti enforcers were personified weapons under the mandate of Erra, the Babylonian god of pestilence and mayhem. They possessed the might of an angel, and were true forces to be reckoned with. Assigned to hell to mock Satan and expose his weaknesses, they had caused widespread devastation in one realm after another. Had I been at full strength and able to Phage, I'd have fancied my chances, one on one.

But against three of them?

For the first time in my long and endless existence, I felt a twinge of doubt.

Despite my dilemma, however, I realized I had to suck it up. So I grinned.

There's more than one way to fry a fish. Looks like it's all or nothing.

"Do you find your predicament amusing, Reaper?" a different voice hissed. "Or is that pain I see etched across your bloodied face?"

Instead of replying, I called upon my remaining reserves and attempted to manifest. A slow crawl of energy answered my summons. I showed no reaction, hoping to catch them off guard. What little lethal force remained was pooled in the pit of my stomach, awaiting the trigger. I sent the command.

My essence fluttered like a fragile heartbeat . . . and then frittered impotently away.

As I suspected, I'd become far too weak to even call on the arcane majesty that was my right. A tingling sensation coursing through my veins was a sure sign that nearly all my remaining vitality was devoted to healing my injuries. So I went with option two:

My thumb edged toward the second button from the top of my sickle. Finding it, I fixed my target in sight and relaxed a little, for what I was about to do would even the score.

Addressing my intended victim, I teased, "Three of you? Three against one? I never realized the mighty Sibitti were such cowards. Just wait until the damned hordes of the underworld discover you were too scared to face the Reaper alone."

"Your reputation preceded you, little puppet," it crooned in reply, "albeit undeservedly."

Faster than any of them could react, I dropped my center of gravity and jabbed my weapon forward. A coherent burst of God's Grace lanced out, catching the creature full in the face.

Gotcha, fucker!

The blob of midnight exploded into a tornado of screeching fury and bloomed like the petals of a giant unfolding rose. But instead of dissipating it flared and looped back in on itself. So concentrated was its rage that the churning maelstrom it generated gouged a trench through the earth as it passed.

Torn from their foundations, chunks of granite and slimestone were whipped into a lethal barrage of brutal hammers and razor sharp edges. Projectiles rained down, scourging my face and rending my clothes. In moments I was battered into a half-witted gory mess.

Somehow, I'd retained a grip on my staff. Rolling onto my front, I pulled my hood forward in an attempt to protect my head and reduce the effects of the blinding fusillade of grit and dust billowing about me.

How in the blazes is that thing still alive? All I've done is irritate it.

My thoughts were prophetic. As before, I was plucked from the ground and hurled, gamboling over and over, high into the air. Banshee howls of glee accompanied me on my rollercoaster ride, and soon I was rising and tumbling through a series of vortexes that flayed, slashed, and impaled my body at every turn.

Thankfully, the enforcer soon tired of his sport.

One moment I was whirling along at a sickening rate, and the next I felt as if I'd become momentarily weightless. Peeking out through bruised and swollen eyelids, I saw clouds above, and the city lights of Dark Cairo far below.

Oh, for the love of Satan!

Gravity claimed me once more, and my gut-wrenching descent began.

Unable to warp, glide or phase, the plunge now dominated my world. But I didn't bother to scream. I felt remote from it, as if this nightmare were happening to somebody else. Instead, I closed my eyes and fought to control the rising panic within me.

Any moment now. Any moment now. Any mo–

The terrible collision blasted the insides of my skull like a lightning bolt. Strangely enough, my sense of detachment continued. As if a mere spectator to the events unfolding around me, I looked down on my body and witnessed a glowing blue thread linking my shattered remains to the disembodied consciousness now floating above it.

From my vantage point, I could see I'd been fortunate. I'd landed in the cinder pits next to the eastern cemetery. The ground had given way beneath me on impact, producing a crater over three feet deep. Nonetheless, my injuries were appalling.

Then the line holding my immortal soul in place snapped back toward my inert form, and a sensation beyond agony ripped through me. As my senses reasserted themselves, I cast my sight inward to assess the damage. It was bad. Very bad because all my organs had been ruptured and virtually every bone in my body shattered.

My self-healing faculty kicked into gear, and a gurgling scream split the night. It took me a moment to realize that scream had come from me. Because of my wounds, the usual ripples I felt during the regeneration process had been replaced with crushing breakers of misery coursing through my system. I vomited blood, teeth, stomach lining, and other things that should never see the light of day. My vision refused to clear. Eventually, the brutal waves receded, and I regained an awareness of my surroundings.

Something was in my hand. With the greatest difficulty I started to rise, and realized I'd still managed to retain a hold on my scythe. In fact, I'd clutched the damned thing so hard my fingers had actually sunk into the medusanite alloy of the handle.

A sickening sound of popping and grinding signaled my sinews and joints realigning. I pushed myself up from the ground, climbed out of the hole, and staggered to my feet.

"Is that it?" I taunted. "You catch me with my pants down, and that's all you've got?"

"Now is not the time for bravado, Reaper," another disembodied voice warned. "It won't make your passing any easier."

I still couldn't see properly. It took me a moment to spot them, huddled together in a group against the inky backdrop of the desert plain.

"What? You think you can actually destroy me? Here? In hell?"

To tell the truth, after the beating I'd just endured I wasn't so sure of the answer myself. In any event, they totally ignored my jibe.

"Look at you. The mighty Daemon Grim, feared throughout the multiverse, reduced to a mere victim."

A whooping cackle echoed from all three. Thankfully, they seemed content to wait and see what I would do next. Fine by me, because I'd had enough of their bullshit.

Time to find out once and for all.

I glanced at the crystal atop my scythe. It indicated I had sufficient energy for one, maybe two, full powered blasts.

They didn't seem to like the essence of God's Grace. I still can't understand why it didn't just kill them on the spot. If I survive this, I'm going to have a long chat with the Boss. There are things that have been hidden from me, and—

"Afraid to face us?" the same Sibitti called. "Perhaps you're thinking of running? Pleading for your life?"

I stared at my trio of antagonists, and selected the moron who appeared to be speaking. A sneaky strategy came to the fore.

Maybe this will work?

I summoned the full force of my will and discharged my weapon. However, instead of simply zapping him in the face, I warped the flow of energy so that it manifested within his tangible threshold.

The specter was illuminated from within by a flash of scintillating blue-white light. From where I was standing, it looked as if a nuclear blast had taken place within a giant colander, for multiple shafts of brilliance lanced out from the myriad holes littering his rags.

As the radiance intensified, I took their advice and started to run. Before I'd gotten three paces the ground heaved, and a paroxysm of volcanic rage erupted about me. I thought the pyramids had chosen this moment to join in the fun—as if my afterlife wasn't difficult enough—but I was wrong. It was the final enforcer. And he was pissed.

I dropped to one knee and brandished my staff. Almost instantly, I was engulfed in an incandescent halo of flames. My hair shriveled and disappeared, my clothes smoked and crisped, and the skin along my raised arm began to bubble and crack.

Unfathomable power poured into his summoning. Rock liquefied at my feet and metamorphosed into glass. My jacket and trousers flared along one side. Then the blistering cocoon imploded, and I was smashed through the air like a greasy streak of soot.

I hit the side of Kung-Fu's pyramid so hard that a huge block cracked on impact. Blood smeared across the stone as I slid toward the base. Flesh rendered, exposed bones blackened, I collapsed in a rattling heap at the bottom of the slope. My ears were ringing. It felt as if my eyes had been fused shut; and when I tried to move, I discovered the right side of my body wouldn't respond. The smell of roasted meat was overpowering. Using my opposite arm, I tried to drag myself away.

Something grasped me by the throat and yanked me into the air. The pain was excruciating, as I couldn't let go of my scythe.

My hand must have melted to the handle.

Lifted higher, I dangled like a fish on a hook. A muffled, garbled drone intruded on the edge of my hearing, but as everything was still humming, I couldn't understand what was being said.

As luck would have it, my left side still retained a degree of function. I kicked out, feebly, and tried to reach up to gain purchase on whatever was shaking me. I felt cold sharp metal.

A Sibitti gauntlet?

Useless. I was too weak to do anything.

My arm flopped back down, and something banged against my hip. Something hard. Something I'd forgotten about, in my coat.

Hope dawned.

As casually as I could, I pretended to wriggle against my captor and edged my hand inside my pocket. My fingers closed around a circular object.

The orb!

I reacted instinctively. Slamming my palm against the studs, I thought of the one thing I craved above anything else.

Instantly, I was someplace else.

*

A Wyrd tree basked in sublime tranquility at the center of a snow-dusted ornamental garden. Its ruby leaves shone like lanterns, blushing the surrounding bushes and shrubs with a gentle infusion of rose-gold warmth.

The full moon shimmered in a cloudless, midnight-blue sky. Resonant with purpose, its argent purity focused the night like a lens, filling the square with an expectant hush.

Around the edge of the oasis, silent witnesses maintained a lonely vigil. Ancient sentinels, their obsidian wings were folded against the chill; their stony hands rested upon the pommels of inhumanly long swords, each crowned by an impossibly large jewel of a different color.

The soft crunch of feet upon icy flakes intruded as a lone female figure walked the pristine parchment of the path. Hooded in scarlet, her footfalls were light and left an indented score along its length.

Without a word, she approached one of the guardian statues and stood before it. Pale fingers drew back her cowl. Burnished honey-blonde hair blazing like fire in the moonlight cascaded down to her shoulders. She was beautiful, glowing with an ethereal radiance that signified her oneness with her environment.

The unknown woman climbed the pedestal on which the champion had been positioned. She studied it for a moment. Whatever she sought could remain a mystery forever, for she deemed it an appropriate time to act.

"Yes, you've slept long enough . . ."

A look of determination crossed her face. She stretched up toward the titan's ear, cupped her hand, and whispered, "Daemon? It's time to wake up, can you hear me?"

Chapter 10: A Hard Lesson

The mists clouding my senses turned opaque and bloomed white. As they thickened, a sparkling effervescence manifested, as confounding as it was mesmerizing. Something at the edge of my perception imposed itself.

"Daemon?"

I tried to ignore the sound, remain safe within my cocoon of obscurity, but it wouldn't leave me alone.

"Daemon, are you with us?"

Muted sounds reflected like ripples and tugged the surface of my consciousness. Although distant, they were nevertheless insistent and conveyed a sense of urgency.

"Daemon? It's time to wake up, can you hear me?"

With grudging reluctance, I blinked my eyes open. The scene swam for a moment before clarifying into the familiar surrounds of my bedroom. A concerned face loomed above me, and long silken tresses fell forward to tickle my nose.

Inquisitor Strawberry Fields, aka Red Riding Hood? What's she doing here?

I raised my head, and memories came crashing back.

But I . . . ?

Other people milled about behind her. I heard an argument under way on the far side of the room. From what I could discern, my Hounds were not only present, they were making their feelings clear.

A low, deep grumble dominated the disagreement. Although I couldn't quite hear the specifics of what was being said, that voice suddenly rose in volume, and issued a command:

". . . long enough! Put aside your personal issues and obey me in this matter."

Everybody fell silent, and I heard Nimrod reply, "Yes, my Lord, we bow to your will; it shall be done."

"And *you* in particular, Nimrod," that same person insisted, "make sure you carry out my instructions to the letter. Understood?"

"As you wish."

I struggled to sit up. "How the . . . ?"

"Here, let me help you," Strawberry offered.

A pillow was pressed into position behind me, and people crowded in. The Hounds were indeed present, as were my Inquisitors. They all came forward, one by one, to welcome me back to the land of the eternally damned.

Nimrod, King of Shinar, and my lead Hound: A mighty hunter in opposition to God, Nimrod never said much and lived up to that now. Striding confidently toward me, he shook my hand, nodded once, and stepped back into the press. His gaze said it all. *Revenge.*

Yamato Takeru came next. Originally known as Prince Ōsu, Yamato was a legendary ninja killer from first-century Japan who had brutally murdered everyone who ever stood in his way.

Wielding his fabled weapon, the *Sword of the Gathering Clouds of Heaven*, he was undefeated in battle, and an elementary titan.

"Sensei," he murmured, "I look forward to fighting by your side."

Champ Ferguson was close behind him. A notorious Confederate guerilla fighter during the American Civil War, Champ was as loud as he was insulting. He had a cruel and sadistic streak bettered only by his skills as a tracker. Nobody I set him on had ever escaped. In fact, he was almost as good as I was.

When he chucked me on the chin, I said, "Speak with me when this circus parade is over. I have a little job for both you and Yamato."

His eyes flared in comprehension, and one corner of his mouth lifted in an evil sneer.

Then came the rest of my Inquisitors.

Leonard Skeffington, a previous Lieutenant of the Tower of London, led the way. We affectionately referred to Leonard by the pseudonym Crusher, as he had invented several remarkable torture devices that were still in use today, especially within our little cadre of specialists. Deceptively quiet and gentle, his almost apologetic nature hid an intensely vindictive character that loved to watch people suffer.

"Glad to see you're up and about, old chap," he whispered. "Why don't you do us all a favor and disembowel the swine who did this to you as soon as you can?"

"Oh, I intend to, don't worry."

Baron Ferenc Nádasdy, a sixteenth century Hungarian nobleman, and his wife, Elizabeth Báthory, stood next in line. While relationships were usually frowned on in the underworld, His Satanic Majesty had made an exception for these two.

Ferenc went by the codename Red Baron, a tongue-in-cheek reference to the foes he had gleefully slain in battle. For a denizen of hell, he was an honorable man who preferred to give prisoners a chance to spill the beans before he spilled their guts.

His other half, however, was an entirely different kettle of fish.

History referred to her as the Blood Countess. We knew her as Nutcracker Sweet. Elizabeth was the most prolific of history's female serial killers. Her endless quest for eternal youth in life had burgeoned into a distinctive, if gory, fetish for which hundreds of young girls had suffered and died whilst being drained of their lifeblood.

This couple was one of my best teams, for they employed a "good cop, bad cop" scenario to great effect. The only problems we ever experienced involved Elizabeth's mental instability and lack of inhibitions. Given the opportunity, she would happily castrate every male prisoner who fell into her clutches, even those who had given up their secrets willingly. And for some strange reason I'd never been able to fathom, she always insisted on working in the nude.

I was glad to see she'd made an effort to dress today.

"Just give the ones responsible to us," Ferenc announced loudly, "and I'll make sure my Lizzie is stir-fried and bat-shit hyper before I let her loose on them."

Elizabeth squealed at the suggestion, and turned to gaze at her husband with a deep-seated lust in her eyes.

Someone's going to get some tonight, I mused.

Finally came Black Velvet, Myra Belle Star. An infamous outlaw from the end of the nineteenth century, Myra was a crack shot who had adapted to the position of Inquisitor rather well. She loved the theater of her role, and would amuse the rest of us by staking her victims out on the ground before blasting away at them with her favorite rifle whilst mounted on horseback. The mere fact that she usually blindfolded herself ahead of time made the spectacle all the more entertaining. Thousands had lost fingers, toes, and other dangly appendages to her most inventive and productive form of interrogation before they were consigned to the relief of reassignment.

"Just let me *be* there when you start slicin' em up," was all she said.

"You'll be top of the list, Myra," I grinned. "In fact, if I get my way, you'll all be there to enjoy . . . to . . ."

I choked up.

Fuck it! I can't let them see me like this.

Keen to hide my moment of weakness, I snapped, "Anyway. Who the hell is taking care of business while you're all skiving off and emptying the contents of my drinks cabinet?"

"Oh, we're not skiving," Elizabeth countered with a giggle, "we've a few exsanguinations under way, and I have a pretty young thing in my office at this moment, roasting slowly over an open fire. I believe you know her? Joy Winters? A shocking case of negligence that we're keen to get to the bottom of. By the time I've finished with her, the Undertaker may have his work cut out to reassign what's left."

"Miss Winters is here?" I gasped, completely taken by surprise. "How long have I been out?"

"Two days," Strawberry whispered. "It took two whole days to regenerate your injuries." She glanced behind her, along with everyone else, and not until they edged away from each other did I realize someone remained standing by the fireplace.

Boss?

His Satanic Majesty stared into my soul as he waited with his back to the fire. On this occasion, I could see he'd adopted his "CEO's business" guise. Clean-shaven, his slicked back hair was adorned by the slightest dusting of gray at the temples. It added a touch of sophistication to his So'vile Row navy pinstripe suit, and Pradator necktie and shirt. The gold chain hanging from his waistcoat pocket complemented the dark red rose in his buttonhole perfectly, adding to the overall effect.

He looked every inch the embodiment of pure evil.

"Give us a moment, would you?" he requested in a deep resonant voice. "I'd like a word with my Reaper alone."

As everyone filed from the room, I jumped out from under the covers. Thankfully, Strawberry had seen fit to ensure I was wearing a fresh pair of Killvin Kleins.

Good girl.

I hurried to my nightstand to retrieve a dressing gown.

My lord and master flexed lightly backward and forward on his toes as he waited. I wasn't surprised to note he'd helped himself to one of my finest malts.

"Yes, you two *are* rather attached, aren't you?" he said.

"I'm sorry?"

The intensity of his gaze abruptly vanished, and he appeared to change tack. "Fancy a little tipple?" He waved his own empty glass at me.

"Thank you, make mine a double."

Satan made his way across to the decanter at my bureau.

"The usual?"

I nodded.

Outwardly, he appeared calm and relaxed. But I knew appearances could be deceiving: This was when he was at his most lethal.

What's going on?

The chink of crystal and satisfying glug of viscid spirits being poured broke the growing silence.

"So, how are you, Daemon?" he asked over his shoulder.

It wasn't until that moment that I realized I felt . . . good. Hell, I felt better than good. When I flexed my palms, a plasmic discharge leaped from my fingertips and rippled its way along my epidermis.

"If you'd asked me that a few days ago, I'd have said the experience was what you'd expect from someone who'd been buggered inside out by an angry rhinoceros suffering from PMT. But now . . . ?" He handed me my beverage, and I balled my opposite fist. A globe of lightning sprang into existence and hovered in the air above my hand, spitting and sizzling. "I'm fully charged and raring to go."

The regent of all that was unholy studied me closely with dark, unblinking, hooded eyes. This time, I saw tongues of fire dancing like mirrors in their depths. He motioned me to sit and said, "With what's been happening to you, it's understandable the dream of revenge is to the fore of your priorities. Retribution is good. Healthy, even. But, if I may offer some advice?"

"If you're going to play dad, please do?"

He raised an eyebrow in warning at my jibe. "You need to stop trying to juggle so many things at once. I know you have a fiercely independent streak that tends to make you try to do everything on your own, but you need to rein that in a bit. Concentrate on your true objective. If you do, your chances of success—and your ability to get a grip on your own shit—will increase dramatically."

I knew where he was going with this.

"Sire, I've never let you down, and I don't intend to start now. This thing goes much deeper than you rea–"

"Daemon," Satan raised his hand, "you don't have to explain yourself to me. When you appeared so unexpectedly—and without permission, I might add—two days ago within the heart of the Bālefire, I realized something must be truly amiss. Wicked, vindictive, and unforgiving I most certainly am. Stupid, I'm not. So I took the liberty of interrogating your recent memories, to see for myself what events had contributed to your sudden and shocking arrival. I must confess, in my eagerness to punish your perceived gaffe in losing Cream after you bound him back to my realm, I overlooked the possibility that others might have had a role to play.

"Sibitti enforcers. Tesla. Cream, and goodness knows how many other sycophants, hiding away like cockroaches, all eager to uncover details that have been justly prohibited and excluded from public knowledge. This cancer is more widespread than I imagined. A blight that appears to be eating its way through the heart of my own Blue Suits and intelligence organization. I suspect Erra is to blame, of course, for only he would dare plague me on such a scale."

"Erra? Would he consort to fraternizing with those he was sent to torment?"

"To get at me? Most certainly, although he'd more likely resort to the use of his personified weapons." Satan ran long manicured nails through his immaculate hair. "I tell you, Daemon. What happened to you was a hard and painful lesson, but also a timely reminder that we all need to keep on our toes. Had I not been so consumed by the need to make an example of you in front of the scheming masses, I might have seen the larger picture all the sooner."

"Is that an apology?"

His countenance hardened and the flames within his eyes flared white-hot until he realized I was joking.

"Hey, hey," I quickly added, raising my hands in defense, "you never have to justify your methods to me. Your castigation will have served a useful purpose. When my fellow denizens witness that no one is exempt from punishment, it'll sober quite a few of the die-hards and make my job a whole lot easier in the long run."

"That's my man!" Satan chortled. "Loyal till the end."

"So, do you really think Erra's behind all this?"

"That's what I'd like you to find out." Satan placed his drink on the table and leaned forward. "You have been immersed within the Bālefire for two full days . . ."

I cringed at the reminder of the time I'd lost.

"I left you there for so long because I don't want you subjected to the indignity of public humiliation again. You will find I have increased your capacity to manifest. That will come in useful should you find yourself sequestered from your source of diabolical nourishment in future."

I knew I felt different! "Thank you. I must confess, I'm itching to get going again."

"As am I. But there's one condition. I want you to involve the Hounds."

"Agreed, and already done," I countered.

In reply to Satan's look of puzzlement, I added, "With your permission, I intend to pursue Cream and his cronies with all haste. Nimrod will accompany me in that endeavor, while Champ and Yamato track down the Sibitti. Don't worry. I'm not going to ask them to engage in battle. I just want to build up a pattern of their movements and known haunts for when all this is over and we decide to take a more direct course of action. Champ is second only to me when it comes to tracking, and Yamato has an uncanny knack for manipulating the elements. As I've come to appreciate, *that* will come in handy if they run into trouble."

"It sounds as if you have a plan. Just remember to exercise caution. Strong as you are, those mayhem-spreading bastards need to be kept at arm's length. Don't get cocky."

That reminded me of something.

"I appreciate what you're saying, Sire, but even in my weakened state I was able to sting them and piss them off, twice. With a refinement in strategy, I should be able to do more. However, one thing did surprise me. Why didn't God's Grace kill them?"

Thunder rolled. The overlord of all that was unholy stared into my eyes without answering. I waited patiently for him to respond. As a courtesy, I generated a modesty shield, and strengthened it until it was impervious to eavesdroppers.

After what seemed like an age, he said, "I'm going to let you in on a little secret, Daemon. Something that shouldn't be bandied about. Not even with your team."

"I understand."

"I've suspected for some time now that Erra and his merry band may have a rather influential silent partner backing them down here. Now, I know you understand the way things are supposed to be. There are, after all, only two sides of the line, and we should each stay where we belong. But sometimes I get the distinct feeling my thorns in the flesh get a little leg-up now and again, from someone who should remain . . . neutral?"

"Seriously?"

"Deadly. How else do you think they manage to resist what is, let's face it, anathema to anyone who is damned?"

While that was food for thought, I still needed to make a point.

"Boss. I know I'm not part of your inner circle, like Samael and the other fallen angels, but I am your Reaper. My name and reputation reflect directly on you. I need to know stuff like this, for Azazel's sake. So far as everyone is aware, I'm supposed to be indestructible. I thought I was! And yet, look what nearly happened because I simply didn't know what I was walking into."

Satan finished his drink, pursed his lips, and nodded.

"Point taken. You've always supported me, Daemon. Even when some of my angels questioned my modus, *you* always stood by me, so the least I can do is show my gratitude more openly in future."

I was surprised. Satan never usually revealed his thoughts like this. Before either of us could get embarrassed, he reached inside his jacket and handed me a blood-and-something-disgusting-stained envelope, and said, "When I first examined you and cut away what remained of your clothing, this was pinned to your chest. Take a look. It's obviously for you, and makes interesting reading."

I opened it, to find the latest message from my elusive antagonists.

It read:

> *Petals of blood,*
> *Like tears, hang from shattered ribs.*
> *A fractured cage,*
> *From which memory's eye*
> *Blurs in swollen, yet refracted splendor.*
> *Enforced,*
> *I create you anew,*
> *And thus rearranged,*
> *Your grumbling condition*
> *Presents a juxtapose of New possibilities,*
> *Pathways,*
> *Where the weight of truth is painful to behold.*

How kind. It's a double entendre reference to my recent ass-kicking. But how did they know I'd survive such an encounter? Unless I was meant to? But then . . . ?

I fought down the endless domino-effect that such questions created in my mind and studied its contents again, to verify the clue leading to my next destination.

It wasn't taxing at all.

> *I create you anew,*
> *And thus rearranged,*
> *Your grumbling condition*
> *Presents a juxtapose of New possibilities,*
> *Pathways,*
> *Where the weight of truth is painful to behold.*

"Do you understand what it means?" Satan asked.

"Put it this way: I know where to start. If you don't mind, I'd like to crack straight on? Those idiots have a two-day lead on me now, and I've got a statement to make."

Chapter 11: Discoveries

As the fleshy bag of skin and bone below him prattled on, Erra banished its whining monotone to the farthest reaches of his mind and daydreamed—recalling former glories, times when both he and his champions wrought death and destruction upon just and unjust alike.

Babylon, wonder of the ancient world, brought to nothing by the unleashing of my wrath through the Seven.

Such recollections brought a rare smile to his beatific face, for few and far between were the opportunities to bring greatness to its knees. Erra had slumbered long and peacefully after that task, thinking his work done. But fate had played its hand to intervene, and in the unlikeliest of places: for here, as nowhere else, was he free to exercise the legitimate ire upon a contemptible foe.

Foe! Pah, Lucifer is so afflicted by hubris that he is blinded to the consequences of his actions. As if this many-layered fabrication of his delusional conceit has the dominion to stave off my judgment. He cannot. He became the artificer of his own downfall the moment he rebelled.

The supplicant below him adopted a more earnest appeal. Erra decided that, for once, perhaps he'd better listen; this human had proven surprisingly resourceful:

". . . so, as I'm sure you can appreciate," Frédéric Chopin stressed, "I'm voicing my concerns because I want to keep our options open. Victory cannot be achieved by brute force alone. We need to be astute; we must diversify. I know you think me laborious, Erra, but I'm right in this matter. Yes, my precautions add extra time into the equation, making it likely we'll never reach our objective, but they will also give us something to fall back on should the worst happen."

He has a point . . . I'll grant him that. "Explain?"

"Remember, just because our primary target lies festering in solitude and chains doesn't guarantee he will be easily vanquished. The wards about him mute power. Yours included. Once they're removed, I fear your advocates may discover they are overmatched."

"And yet you feel he offers the best hope of resolution?"

"I do, for he will provide the most direct means of achieving our goals. We now wait upon the Infernal Equinox. When it arrives a full assault can be made, so we need to be prepared. The artifacts will assist in this regard, as well as provide us with an option B should everything go tits-up at the last minute."

Erra snorted as he read the meaning of the colloquialism within the mortal's mind.

An inventive term. I think I'll remember that one. "And what about Grim?"

"He's a safety net." Chopin shrugged. "A last resort we can employ if everything else fails. Do you see now why I was so keen to secure assurances that your enforcers exercised sufficient restraint that they didn't damage Grim's heart?"

"Heart?" Erra spluttered, fully attentive once more. "Are you insane, mortal? Despite the pretense he projects to those about him, that creature possesses no heart. My champions recognized that truth the moment they encountered him. Weakened as he was, he begged no favor. Asked for no quarter. He's a cold-blooded killer, willing to die by the tenets he follows."

"While I appreciate your view," Chopin retorted, "I beg to differ. He does indeed possess . . . possess a . . . oh my!"

The insignificant little man droned to a stop and stared vacantly off into space. He wrung his hands, wincing at the obvious discomfort such habits caused him. Then his jaw dropped open, and he kinked his head to one side as if witnessing a scene of soul-rending grandeur.

He's having one of those accursed visions. How a mortal was graced by such an enigma, I'll never truly understand. Regardless, each of them has been unnervingly accurate, so I'm forced to heed them.

A few moments later, Chopin shook his head and staggered forward.

"Another revelation?" Erra asked disdainfully.

Chopin could only nod. Erra watched as the weakling's eyes danced from side to side. He appeared to be struggling to absorb what he had just witnessed.

"Tell me," the god breathed.

"There is little doubt that Lucifer will imbue his puppet with further power," the composer began, "for he seeks to forestall a backlash that could undermine his authority. While this unnatural power may prove difficult to overcome, it could also work in our favor. We've been graced with a two-day buffer, during which my associate and I have contrived to leave a number of booby-traps in our wake. Each will test Grim's resolve to the limit, highlighting any weaknesses in the compulsion that drives him. Rest assured, the hurdles we have placed in the Reaper's path will expose Satan for the charlatan he really is . . . and ultimately bring about both their downfalls."

"That is gratifying to hear, human. Please accept my thanks and my blessing. In response to your earlier query, be aware: my champions never had the opportunity to inflict the abuses they originally intended, for Grim escaped their clutches before full expression had been achieved. In short, it is doubtful he was mortally wounded." *Much to my annoyance.*

The diminutive figure bowed gracefully. "Thank you. Thus assured, I shall take my leave and prepare the final stages of our scheme."

Moments later, Chopin had disappeared from sight.

It is unnerving to think how mere mortals may mimic the superiority of the gods by employing . . . how do they term it . . . technological advancement? Still, his aspirations have counterpointed my own goals significantly. Who would have thought such an alliance was possible?

Then another worrisome thought plagued the god's mind:

I wonder what on earth possessed Chopin to approach me and ask for my help in the first place?

*

Because of the blatant clue I'd so recently received, I found myself back within the stinking confines of the Mortuary.

As before, a sad-faced underling intercepted me in the main foyer and offered to escort Nimrod and myself down to see the most hygienically-challenged individual—orally speaking—in the history of the underworld. As we followed the flunky, I reflected more deeply on the ease with which I'd been able to work things out of late. An ease, I was beginning to suspect, that was not only deliberate, but hid a menacing, ulterior motive.

My beating was an obvious trap. But they must know I wouldn't make the same mistake again. So why are they continuing to make it so simple to follow them?

That point was really bothering me.

What could they possibly hope to achieve by having the Reaper and his Hounds on their tail? Is it a distraction? A ruse? Part of a bigger scheme I'm failing to appreciate?

One way or another, I knew I'd find out, because whatever it was, it kept setting off my inner alarms.

As we neared the bottom of the main staircase, the noise from below increased dramatically, far beyond the levels I had experienced on my previous visit. In fact, it sounded as if something of a commotion was taking place. I was about to ask what the problem might be when we cleared the final spiral and were presented with a sight of utter pandemonium.

Gone was the ant's nest of clinical efficiency. Instead, I saw what the Undertaker's lackeys got up to when they took a break.

Outside the nearest office, two gore-soaked bandages hung from light fixtures. These had been positioned in such a way as to create a goalmouth. Sure enough, a glance along the corridor confirmed the presence of an identical arrangement about one hundred yards away.

From what I could see, the technicians, having divided themselves into rival teams, were attempting to play a sadistic mix of football and polo. As I watched, one minion sitting comically atop a surgical trolley being pushed hell-for-leather by two of his teammates, wove expertly in and out among his opponents. As he passed, defenders tried to knock him unconscious with walking sticks. Fortunately, the brave little chap was wearing an inverted kidney bowl upon his head, which acted as a helmet. Clearing the final obstacle, he turned to look back over his shoulder. Something large and round came sailing through the air. Like an expert wide-receiver, he changed course at the last second to scoop it into his arms. A muffled cry rang out. Amid much panting and grunting, the attacker then aimed himself directly at the hanging bandages and slam-dunked the object onto the floor.

A squeal of protest rang forth, only to be drowned out by a loud chorus of cheering. The ball left a bloody trail as it came to rest between Nimrod's feet.

We looked down into a bruised and battered face. Through broken teeth the "ball" complained, "I broody well habe it when thesh little bashtards have a break. Thish ish the third chukka in a row they'fve 'ushed my shkull."

Although stoically silent, I knew Nimrod was perturbed, for one of his eyebrows arched upward.

As an unholy whistle-blast deafened us, the sounds of jubilation cut off. All heads turned toward the source, which was none other than the Undertaker himself.

"Coffee break is over," he boomed. "Now get back to work."

The corridor erupted into a focused frenzy. As I waded through scurrying underlings I was rewarded with a clearer view of our host. I noted with amusement he had gone for a much more casual look than usual. A blue cashmere turtle-neck peeked out from under a brown-plaid woolen blazer. The jacket itself was outdone by an outrageously yellow pocket square that literally vomited its way from his top pocket. Tuscan calfskin trousers and brown leather brogue boots completed the outfit.

That looks . . . absurd.

I could tell Nimrod found the outfit hilarious as well, for both of his brows curved upward now, and his mouth formed a perfect O as in *'fuck off! Seriously'*?

I didn't know if the Undertaker was dolled up on a bet, or if his attire had anything to do with the continuing influence of Astarte, but I'd bet on the latter.

As we closed on him, I discovered that not everything had changed. My eyes started to water and my nostrils closed up. I knew there'd be no use holding my breath: the stench would only permeate the pores of my skin to get at me.

"Why are you back so quickly?" the Undertaker protested. "I told you the extraction of altered memories is a delicate process, and that I'd update you about your Neanderthal from the Hexcalibur Hotel when I had something useful."

"And do you?" I shot back. "Or have I disturbed you at a busy time?"

To piss him off, I cast a critical eye about me as the corridor slowly transformed back into the sterile working environment for which this place was renowned.

"Ha ha, very funny. The pressures on my staff are as relentless as they are demanding. I allow my underlings the luxury of an exercise break to ensure they work off those stresses sufficiently. I don't want our standards suffering." He squared his shoulders. "Anyway, did you come here to criticize or to exchange information?"

"So you *do* have something for me?"

"I do, although you won't think it much. The candidate you sent me has been mind-wiped. The procedure was akin to what you'd expect from a ripcord, only this was done surgically and with great skill. What's more, his prefrontal cortex and temporal lobe have been permanently damaged. How, I do not know; reassignment should regenerate all injuries suffered while in hell. In view of this discovery, I took it upon myself to examine every part of his limbic system so as to determine who might be responsible. I have extensive files, and there are only a handful of surgeons I know who are capable of such finesse."

"Fair enough," I conceded, "it sounds as if you're being more than thorough. But let me know everything you find. And I mean *everything*. As I'm starting to discover, even the slightest detail might have bearing."

We stared at each other. Then the Undertaker recognized the presence of one of the Hell Hounds for the first time.

"Nimrod," he spluttered, "why are . . . ?" Then he made the connection. "You're not just here to catch up, are you?"

"No. I took you at your word, last time, that you run a tight ship. I realize now that's not the case. How long have you had a secret portal?"

To his credit, the Undertaker didn't betray himself.

"Secret portal? I don't know what you're talking about. If you're trying to . . . ." He caught himself mid sentence. "You don't mean the officially sanctioned gateway I use to summon the Grumbles, do you?"

Grumbles! Of course! That's it.

I laughed.

"What is it, Grim? Tell me. If someone's been sloppy, I need to know."

"I think I've just worked out how Cream might have eluded us." Removing the latest clue from my pocket, I held it out for the Undertaker's scrutiny.

After he had scanned it, I tapped the last half of the verse. "Did you see this particular reference? Please read it aloud."

"'I create you anew /And thus rearranged /Your grumbling condition /Presents a juxtapose of New possibilities /Pathways /Where the weight of truth is painful to behold.' The truth be damned. It is painful to behold. I can't believe they'd contrive to use such means." Crestfallen, he stared directly at me. "You do realize where the Grumbles postern leads?"

"I don't care where that portal leads. I'm more concerned as to how he's doing this, as it'll help me get one step closer to bringing this farce to an end."

The Undertaker looked thoughtful. "You remember the bother we had during that awful Damned Poets Society Slam last year?"

"The one where you went ape-shit at the Hexcalibur Hotel? Don't remind me. That was suicidal lunacy at its apocalyptic best. I've never been so busy. Why?"

"Well, the mayhem went deeper than you think. We had so many rapture-seeking loons swamping us here at the Mortuary that I remember thinking their ardor must be part of a larger conspiracy. I knew something wasn't right. There I was, working my darkest arts, only to have the victims thank me for my time. No matter what I did, every single one of them remained sickeningly happy. In the end, I was forced to take a break. That's why I popped across the road to the InfernoCon Six Six Six convention. But things were even worse in there: so sickeningly pleasant, in fact, that I lost all patience and took a hand setting the Grumbles on the revelers. Anyway, with what's been happening, I'm beginning to—"

"What if all that was arranged?" Nimrod asked.

His proposal caught me off guard.

"Arranged?"

"What if this 'problem' was arranged, and goes back further than you realize?" Nimrod turned to the Undertaker: "And someone made sure you got so wound up, so incensed, that they knew you'd eventually lose your temper and dispatch the Grumbles."

Ding-fucking-dong!

"Bastards!" cursed the Undertaker. "That's exactly what I was about to suggest."

"So you think that whoever's behind all this might have been planning this dust-up for years?" I gasped. "And they got someone to put themselves deliberately in harm's way, just so they could get reassigned and slip into the Mortuary's basement should the opportunity present itself? But why? What do they want to mess about with down there?"

"There's only one way to find out," the Undertaker snapped, "follow me."

In moments, he was leading us along the main corridor, toward Slab A. Before we had gone halfway, however, the Undertaker veered right and ushered us through a highly-polished door. The sign on the wall read *Collections.*

Inside, we found a handful of minions busy monitoring the readouts from dozens of computer terminals. I lingered to look at a few screens as I walked past, but all I could see was an endless list of names and symbols scrolling down each page. The Undertaker ignored them all, stalked toward an open staircase at the back of the office, and began to descend.

Like obedient chicks we tumbled along in his wake, only to arrive, after a number of switchbacks, at a set of barricaded doors. Bold red letters stenciled across the pitted metal read: *Hub.*

I'd never been here before but whatever was behind the armor plating set my sinuses ringing. *There's something immensely powerful in there. How did I not sense it the last time I was here?*

Then I felt the tingle of a dauntingly potent force field.

Aha! I glanced at Nimrod to see if he'd noticed, but he'd withdrawn into his shell and appeared as disinterested as ever.

The Undertaker caught the exchange. "Welcome to the heart of my considerable empire."

The prickling sensation cut off and the gates opened, revealing a yawning chasm. Measuring some two hundred yards across, this fissure was filled by a huge miasma of balled, ionized gas. The cloud roiled and sparked under the influence of a myriad miniature novas welling up from its core, and each bright report flared across its surface in streamers of scintillating color.

A metal walkway haloed the anomaly. Service stations positioned at various points around its circumference catered to the multitude of conduits, tubes and wires that disappeared into or sprang from the brume in apparently haphazard fashion. Some of the cables stopped abruptly in midair, as if swallowed by invisible jaws. Others linked into already existing circuit breakers and junction boxes that lined the inner wall of the cavern.

"This represents the totality of those newly dead, as well as those awaiting reanimation," the Undertaker announced. With a sweep of his arms and a wash of body odor, he continued: "Even if consigned to the Inquisitors, their essences are drawn together here first, where they are stored prior to allocation. Basically, what you are looking at is a diabolical conjuration that contains the unadulterated tincture of who they were and what they did, including a full sensory evocation of a lifetime's worth of memories."

Once again, I found myself impressed by the unknown and surprising depths of one of hell's most hated institutes.

Who knew?

The scene before me was utterly captivating and, although energetic, instilled a feeling of euphoric serenity.

As I studied its various features, I noticed the composition of the plasma field was disturbed every so often by certain blemishes. Darker than their sparkling cousins, these burst from the depths to swallow brighter colors whole. Having fed, they commenced a rampage across the surface, spreading havoc and generating violent storms. Then, satiated, they'd dissipate, allowing peace to return once more.

I couldn't help but ask, "What is that . . . incongruity?"

"That, my dear Reaper, is sin," the Undertaker replied. "Despicable deeds and foul secrets, peeled open and revealed for the master's scrutiny, then presented to me on a smorgasbord of hate. These are the nuances I examine when determining the fate of all who pass through my domain."

"So, you think Cream got someone to tamper with this?"

"No, that would be impossible. However, there is a back door. A very dangerous back door . . ." He beckoned us forward again. "This way."

Guiding us out onto the catwalk, the Undertaker added: "As you can imagine, the concentration of so much eldritch vitality in one place creates ripples in the very fabric of Helltime." He pointed to an area of nothingness, below him and to his left. "Here, for example, is a void that leads . . . well, to be honest, we still haven't fathomed where it leads. No test subject sent through has ever returned. Not even by way of Reassignments. Here"—the Undertaker gestured to his right—"is a realm so inverted to the natural course of life that it is impossible for anything to exist inside for long. Even by Purgatory's standards, it's a place of horrendous apparitions and twisted insanity. His Satanic Majesty saves that reality for some very *special* customers."

He stopped adjacent to a metal ladder and then began climbing down. We followed, emerging onto a sub-walkway that led straight back the way we'd just come.

Why are we retracing our steps? There's nothing there except solid rock.

The Undertaker didn't bother to explain. Without slowing, he marched directly toward the cliff face . . . and disappeared.

It's a glamour!

Moments later, both Nimrod and myself also passed the barrier.

I felt as if I'd stepped through a curtain of ice. The temperature dropped abruptly, my breath fogged the air with a fine mist, and my senses immediately registered a nearby concentration of magical energy.

Now we found ourselves in another cave, similar to but much smaller than the one above. Over on the far side, wide stairs were cut into a naturally occurring alcove. Leading upward, the flagstones looked worn and scarred, as if a multitude of clawed feet had passed that way over a protracted period of time.

An area had been set apart in the dirt before us, marked by a circle of white stones. The Undertaker walked up to the nearest one. "This is what I meant when I referred to a back door. The void here remains ajar, so I can summon the Grumbles to do my bidding in an instant." He shrugged. "I find it necessary to use them occasionally to eliminate the unwanted and unworthy. And as you're about to see, Grumbles are quite voracious, leaving little behind."

"Voracious?" I echoed.

"Yes. Gorgonous has just informed me, telepathically, that they were fed not two minutes ago with the results of one of your latest purges. You might remember some of them from out at Sam's Bar, only last week? You're in for quite a treat."

That mixed bunch of mercs and everyday Joes? But there were over thirty of them.

Our host didn't pause. Dropping his voice, he mumbled something that sounded like a rhyme. I heard the words "authority," "Grumbles," and "mirror."

Power flared. The floor between the marker stones rippled as if someone had drawn a finger across the surface of a pond. Then a moan filtered into the room, sounding uncannily like the death-rattle of a doomed soul, and followed by a fetid outpouring of wind and heat which dried my throat.

"Behold," the Undertaker crooned, "my private escape route into oblivion."

No sooner had he uttered those words than a caterwauling of terrified wails and agonized howls screeched up out of the darkness. I adjusted my vision to compensate for the variance between realms, and peered within.

The Grumbles were still feasting. I was stunned to realize they comprised both tangible and spectral aspects. Nonetheless, I was only able to catch fleeting glimpses of whirring fangs and slashing talons as they stomped, tore, rent, and ripped their way through a growing jumble of torsos, detached limbs, and spilt intestines.

Blood squirted, gore splattered, and feces sprayed. Everything and anything was on the menu: scalps, brains, genitalia and fat; organs, sinews, noses and toes. The whole lot was consumed amid a frenzied maelstrom of gnashing and snarling and gobbling that quickly silenced any and all desperate pleas for mercy.

Mercy? Not on this side of eternity, my friends.

The Grumbles were thorough. In less than sixty seconds all that remained of more than three dozen victims were splintered shards of skeletons, the odd bit of mangled flesh, several belt buckles, a few tattered strips of bloodstained cloth, and one eyeball.

Their meal over, the crowd of mutated savages wandered off into the endless desert of their dusty domain, to do what Grumbles do. I watched as the last of them shuffled away, picking its fangs with what looked like the sharp end of a finger-bone. The beast paused, farted, solidified into a more tangible form, and took an unexpected dump before fading away into the distance.

When a final belch echoed out of the darkness, Nimrod snorted.

The Undertaker closed the gate. "So, you think Cream would willingly divert his essence into a place like that?"

"From what I know of him? Not a chance." I expanded my senses to savor the unique flavor of the partially open event-horizon. "But what I can say is that, he—or the people he works with—would definitely make use of a semi-active geodesic archway like this. The threshold emits a very distinctive energy signature. I'm betting Cream or someone in league with him knew about this, and used its substance as a lodestone to draw his soul here, or somewhere close by."

We began scouring the chamber walls and floor in a hunt for clues.

My attention was drawn to an impressive-looking condenser by the stairway. A number of major relays led into it from several different directions. Something about the spherical shape of one of the devices attached to the top of the junction box made me look twice.

"What's that over there?" I pointed to the object of my concern.

As we closed on it, a thrill of recognition coursed through my body. "Unholy shit! That's a translocation device."

"Translocation device?" The Undertaker looked puzzled.

"You must know Tesla's been working on these for some time now. He's reached the stage where he can flood the white market with near perfect models." I tapped the globe. "This is very basic. And old. Must be an early prototype. If it does what I think it can, it's capable of teleporting one or two people anywhere within the underworld."

"Anywhere?"

"I'm afraid so. And any when, too. I was recently gifted a newer version. From what I understand, the later models have a temporal element added into their matrix. I bet this was placed here months ago in preparation for . . ."

I caught myself just in time. Very few denizens were aware that Cream had actually managed to get his worthless ass topside. It was my job to ensure things stayed that way.

". . . er, one of the secret phases of his master plan, whatever that is. These later orbs can be set to operate for a limited amount of times before they self-destruct."

"Well, this one hasn't blown up yet," the Undertaker countered. "Do you think it might still be active?"

Bam!

I jumped in surprise as the glowing, razor sharp edge of a four-foot long cronimium blade cut the ball in half.

"Not anymore."

Nimrod sheathed his sword and stepped back.

I managed to swallow a curse attempting to force its way between my lips, and picked up both segments. Inside I discovered a small metallic wafer. Like its casing, the wafer had been cut neatly in two. After removing the pieces, I placed the halves together and saw a prepared message stenciled into the alloy. Written in freehand, it displayed the same inconsistency of clarity as its predecessors.

How in buggering Hades do they keep doing this?
It read:

A Nightingale glides among gilded cages,
Her veined candle of melted wax
Fails to illuminate those wards
Where life's blood now lies congealing.
A stuttering flame,
And a puff of old smoke,
Marks the moment another lamp is quenched,
A poignant reminder of life's only certainty.
Tuscany,
Ah, it's beautiful at this time of year,
But fear not,
That's not the Florence you're after.

"Oh, you infuriating fuckard!"

"What's the matter, boss?" Nimrod was clearly amused by the ire in my voice.

"You're not going to like this, but I'm afraid we're going all the way back to Juxtapose."

"Juxtapose? But we just came from there."

I waved the two pieces of metal in his face. "Don't blame me. Blame the irritating little shit who's giving us the runaround. Look at this."

Both Nimrod and the Undertaker read our latest breadcrumb.

"Do you see?"

"Well, he's obviously referring to Florence Nightingale," the Undertaker bemoaned. "Any idiot can see that. But what makes you so sure you have to go back to Olde London Town?"

"Because of the double innuendo the text contains. Nightingale was infamous for her work with wounded soldiers in the Crimean War. Following that conflict, she established the very first secular nursing school in the world at St Thomas' Hospital, London."

"Riiight . . . but how does that relate to Cream?"

"In life, Doctor Thomas Neill Cream was a bona fide, fully-trained physician before he turned to murder. Guess where he studied?"

"I haven't a clue," the Undertaker admitted. "English history isn't really my strong point."

"Then I'll help you. None other than the aptly named St Thomas' Hospital, the very place graced by Miss Nightingale. Guess where in London that is?"

"You'll have to tell me."

"It was in Lambeth, or, as we call it here, Lambsdeath. The sneaky swine is taking us back to where he snuffed out his victims' lives, because as you are well aware, Cream eventually became known as the 'Lambeth Poisoner.' And, if you needed any more proof, the final clue comes from the phrase 'old smoke,' within the text. That's the Victorian nickname for the capital, and relevant to the time he was active. Do you see now?"

"Bloody hell! Talk about spot the connection. What do you think you'll find there?"

"Damned if I know. But I'm itching to find out."

Chapter 12: Just What the
Doctor Ordered

St Thomas' Hospital was a sprawling great structure that fronted on the River Tombs, opposite the Palace of Westmonster. Despite the fact I'd lived in Juxtapose all of my afterlife, and the grounds were only a couple of miles from my home, I did what most people do when such things are right on their doorstep: I totally ignored it. Yes, I'd seen it at a distance, but even then it had never attracted my attention, for it was nothing like the topside version. Ours was old, decrepit, and festering: a stark reminder of the futility of sacrifice and good deeds. Why?

Satan had seen fit to order the entire edifice and its estate abandoned. And so, year after year, century after century, no one had dared do otherwise. The mortar had crumbled, and the dark red bricks and fluted towers had gradually stained gray. Windows cracked and shattered, heavy doors tore free from rusted hinges. Open to the elements, it was now home to all manner of wild birds, rodents, and down-and-outs seeking refuge from the harshness of an eternity of suffering.

Parts of the roof had fallen in decades ago, giving acid rain and the cloying mists of the River Tombs unlimited access to the multitude of halls, wards, and corridors that crisscrossed the hospital's interior like a latticework of veins and arteries clogged by the detritus of accumulated grime and neglect.

Nimrod and I had been here just over an hour. Because the place was so huge, we decided to reconnoiter the grounds and exterior structures first. A fruitless experience, as anything of value had been removed by scavengers long ago.

Waiting by the main entrance for Nimrod to complete his final sweep, I peered inside. The interior seemed to swallow light and sound whole. Yet from what my enhanced senses could ascertain, it looked deserted.

Yeah, right!

As I'd so painfully learned, appearances could be deceiving, all the more so where Cream was concerned.

A flapping of wings overhead told me we definitely weren't alone. My presence, although elusive, had already panicked a nesting pair of hell-pigeons. They had been so cautious, I'd completely missed them.

And if they can be that silent, so can any other unexpected visitors who've decided to wait for us.

Nimrod's arrival disturbed my concentration. As he splashed around the corner of the building, I asked, "Anything?"

"No," he mouthed, adding a slight shake of his head.

"Right. Let's do this."

Alert for danger, we slipped inside and quickly made our way to the reception desk. Once there, we stood still and listened. As a precaution, I also projected my astral sight as far as it would go, hunting for stray emotions that might give away the presence of hidden lurkers.

Nothing! Not a damned thing. And it looks like a maze in there . . .

"Any ideas?" Nimrod whispered.

"With the cryptic reference to 'stuttering flames' and 'puffs of smoke,' I'm betting the obvious place to start will be the hospital's furnace. Hang on a moment." I sidled across to a *You Are Here* notice-board.

As if by providence, a single shaft of Paradiselight dared to pierce the veil outside. Stabbing down through a gaping hole in the roof, it illuminated the entrance foyer sufficiently for me to scan the listed departments. Where the paint had blackened and peeled away, I was able to trace with my finger the slightly indented outline of each letter.

"Mortuary and Funeral Services. Pathology labs. Ah, here it is . . . Cremation and Incinerator. Basement level, north wing." *The basement, where else?*

I stepped back to get my bearings. Old signs hung by rusting chains from hooks in the ceiling. "North wing is this way. You cover the left side of the corridor, I'll go right. We'll take our time so as not to disturb whatever makes its home here. And link to me mentally so we can share what we see and hear."

Nimrod nodded and moved to obey. Once in position we stalked slowly forward, making sure to soak up the ambiance as we went.

By the time we'd gone a few hundred yards I understood why vagrants were absent, and the myriad critters left behind so keen to remain anonymous. Something wasn't right. It was eerily silent. Too silent. Nothing moved. Nothing breathed or squeaked. Apart from the wind working its way in through broken panes and missing roof tiles, not a damned thing made a sound.

A glance toward Nimrod confirmed he'd picked up on the atmosphere too.

Telepathy only. Stay sharp.

We gravitated toward each other and, to the accompaniment of the ceaselessly moaning breeze, disappeared into the muggy gloom.

The sheer magnitude of isolation here was both strange and disquieting. Such quiet made me jittery. Whenever my awareness would latch onto something at the edge of perception, it faded away before I could identify its nature. I tried not to let on that I'd detected anything. Nonetheless, each episode only served to confirm my suspicion that we were expected.

We finally arrived at the central shaft to the northern wing. Steps as pale as bleached tusks vanished into the depths. In this setting, the well looked as wide as the jaws of a leviathan and equally as black. Direction arrows indicated we needed to descend. So we spent the next ten minutes gradually spiraling down into the bowels of the earth.

Each floor was comprised of hundreds of tiny offices and store cupboards. Their doors filed off into the distance like blank dominos stacked before opposing mirrors. Curiosity roused, we checked out a few rooms on the way, to discover that most had been ransacked, although a few were still chock-full of outdated surgical supplies. The farther we went, however, the more the evidence of decay, and the less the wind intruded.

Eventually we arrived at the bottom. If the surface had appeared surreal, the basement presented another world entirely.

Despite the humidity, a definite chill pervaded the air. Many of the fixtures and fittings that once lined the subterranean passages had been torn down and positioned at the exact center of the junction of four long corridors. Piled high and crowned by a torn leather chair, they had been arranged as if we were looking at a monument to an unknown deity.

Apart from our breathing, the only sound to punctuate the silence was a constant *drip, drip, drip,* from a broken pipe or missing skylight high above. Whatever had found its way into the pit now coated the walls and floor in an oily substance that made it difficult to move quickly.

The hairs on the back of my neck prickled.

We must be getting closer, I broadcast to Nimrod.

Yes, I agree. But which way now?

Well. The direction board told us the crematorium and furnace were in the northern wing. Now we're here, I'd say we have to—

"He's here—he's here—he's here . . ." intruded a declaration out of the darkness.

Suddenly, we were surrounded by overlapping voices:

"Yes, the Reaper has arrived."

"Quickly, brothers and sisters, call the others—others—others . . ."

"At last—last—last . . ."

Unwelcome recollections of a recent, similar surprise crowded in on me, but only served to strengthen my resolve. As any pretence at stealth was now unnecessary, I called out loudly, "Ah, company. Just what the doctor ordered."

"Reaper—Reaper—Reaper . . ."

"This way—way—way . . ."

"Make ready. He's here—here—here . . ."

The echoing warnings drew ever closer.

"I don't suppose you'd care to show yourselves?" I said. "After all, if you know who I am, you'll understand there's nothing to fear if you don't stand in my way."

Up ahead, a pile of leaves and other accumulated detritus swirled to life under the influence of unseen eddies.

A soft hiss alerted me to the fact that Nimrod had just drawn sword from scabbard. Sure enough, the familiar gleam of burning ice filled the bottom of the stairwell in midnight-blue radiance. I emulated him, a gentle click announcing the moment I extended my scythe into combat configuration. Back to back, we held our weapons at the ready and started to make our way along the hall, revolving slowly about each other as we did so. Our maneuver appeared to do the trick, for despite repeated catcalls our unseen hosts seemed content to merely lead us deeper into the guts of the hospital.

Progress continued in this manner for more than five minutes, until we reached an old-fashioned combined ablutions area and changing room.

To our left, a congregation of rickety metallic lockers had been pushed together into an untidy knot. Draped with cobwebs and covered in dust, they appeared hooded in sackcloth and reverent, as if deep in prayer. Beady eyes gleamed out from the spaces in between and underneath, a sign that a food source was nearby.

On the other side, the remains of a shower block stood out in glaring contrast to the shrouded lockers. The once white tiles adorning these walls had stained yellow long, long ago. Many were missing; most were cracked. The floor itself was littered with shards of glass, broken faucets, bits of pipe, and copious amounts of mold. More worryingly, I also noticed a fresh trail of blood leading from an adjacent doorway down to the main grille, positioned precisely in the middle of the chamber.

Old light fixtures sporting shattered bulbs hung limply from frayed brown cords. Despite the fact it should have been impossible for them to work, each lamp flickered on and off, betraying the presence of some form of deviltry.

With so many demons, mutants and monsters inhabiting the many layers of the underworld, it is sometimes difficult to work out exactly what you are dealing with. Some are a minor nuisance, while others are much more puissant, and therefore deserving of respect.

I decided to make my offer again, more formally this time.

"If you are aware I'm the Reaper, then you'll know I'm here on His Satanic Majesty's business. So long as you don't try to obstruct me in the course of my duty, you have absolutely no reason to fear me. I give you my word. Look, I don't really care what little enterprise you've got going down here. This building is abandoned. Nobody wants it. Bad luck to you. But show yourselves now, and state your intentions. Do you understand?"

"Oh, we understand, Reaper," a voice intoned, "but it's too late for us—us—us . . ."

"Like you, we are bound by our word—word—word," a second one said.

"Locked by our oath—our oath—our oath," rasped another.

The orbiting chorus faded as the lights flared; a squadron of glittering, dark vortices manifested around us. An overwhelming impression of fear cascaded down, as if a million instants of terror had been frozen at the point of realization, only to be encapsulated within living, diamond-encrusted storms of hatred.

"Dread-Locks!" I shouted.

I knew it important to stay calm around these beasts, for they killed to order and would grow stronger by feeding on the panic generated by their victims. Once set on you, they were bonded—or locked—into fulfilling their contract. Or they'd die trying.

Such ghouls are difficult to see clearly, for their spiraling substance expands and contracts in an alarming manner. From my perspective, it looked as if their very nature was in contention with itself.

If only!

"They're here to oppose us," I called to Nimrod. "Take them out, no mercy."

With no more time to prepare, our struggle commenced.

The atmosphere sang to a thrumming resonance as Nimrod's sword became a dazzling streak of blue-white plasma. I'd have loved to watch, for his grace and precision in battle was legend. Instead, I found myself busy contending with my own demons as a fusillade of deathly blows rained down on me from all sides at once.

I had a point to prove, both to myself and my team member, so I refused the urge to manifest the Phage and relied instead on my own killer instinct and considerable skill.

With a dexterity few could match, I whirled my weapon in blinding arcs and met their attack head on. High mêlée, low advance, left, right, and center. I reveled in combat and quickly found my rhythm. Needle-tipped claws skidded along my blade. It mattered not a bit: whatever action they employed I countered, and my staff grated in protest under the blurred assault of razor edged talons. The chamber flashed and sparks flew, providing a dazzling backdrop to the ringing cacophony of adrenaline-fueled engagement.

The Dread-Locks were giving their all. When they were unable to breach our defenses swiftly enough they began to howl, and their attack grew increasingly undisciplined. Some commenced darting runs in an effort to distract us, while others tried to phase up through the floor. When that failed, bolder wraiths attempted simply to storm us and take us down by sheer weight of numbers.

Their skirmish continued like this for some time. Overhead smash—block. Underhand lunge—parry. Sweep, slash, gouge, and thrust. Catch, counter, jab, retreat and stop-cut. Over and over. Again and again. Nonetheless, as minutes ticked by without either side giving quarter, it became evident that their attempt to wear us down by attrition had backfired. Not only was the timing of their forays disjointed, but it was clear the frantic pace of our exchange was taking its toll on them.

From what I could discern, neither Nimrod nor I had given way to fear. The Dread-Locks had nothing to feed on. The glittering scales encasing their semi-corporeal forms lost their luster. As they dimmed, scores of plates fell to the floor and shattered.

Keep it up, I sent to Nimrod, *they're shrinking. Now it's our turn to use brute force.*

I discerned a summoning of potential as my partner readied himself.

Now!

As one, we leaped forward.

Shrieks of anguish knifed into the night as a rapid swarm of blows found their mark. Our unexpected attack gained fluidity, and then we were among them, dealing death and destruction at will. Their panic increased. Cries of alarm added a potent mix to their growing desperation.

"Flee—flee—flee . . ."

The tinkling cascade of their ruptured essences was accompanied by more yowls of pain, each followed by a succession of pops as air rushed to fill sudden vacuums.

"Don't let any escape," I roared, "not a single one. We need to send a message . . ."

The scene before me receded, overlapped by another reality entirely. In this place, I was both spectator and participant in yet another battle, as seen from someone else's perspective.

Two juggernauts came together, their blazing swords colliding with the power to sunder worlds. A shockwave ran the length of my weapon and up through my arms. I thrilled at the challenge and reached out to grasp my adversary by the throat.

Celestial energies clashed, and my eyes shone like stars as I called on the sum of my potential. I exhaled, and the vault of the heavens disappeared amid a blinding flash of brilliant white light. Heat washed across me, and my opponent screamed before erupting in flames. Inhaling, I thrilled to the surge of fresh essence. With so much potential coursing through my veins, I couldn't contain it. My head fell back and I began laughing. Mortals cowered, for the sound was both exhilarating and terrifying . . .

... and somehow, its timbre continued to peal along the halls of the hospital as I came to my senses.

What the ... ?

I blinked, and realized our surroundings were wreathed in darkness once again. What's more, the withered husk of a sole Dread-Lock was hanging from my fist.

Are they all gone? Well, screw me blind, I must have been fighting on autopilot or something.

Unfathomable as ever, Nimrod stood off to one side. His hands rested lightly on the pommel of his sword, his head kinked to one side. He stared at me, a strange distant look in his eyes.

"That was ... interesting," was all he cared to say.

Before I had a chance to ask him what he had witnessed, a faint resonance caught my attention. I held my breath and cupped my ear.

"Is that singing?"

Nimrod listened. "It would seem so." He glanced through the same exit from which the blood trail emerged. "I think we're supposed to go that way."

"By all means, let's go and see what else our hosts have in store for us."

That doorway opened onto a long dark passage. In the distance, a strident, flickering glow illuminated our destination and made it appear we had entered a tunnel leading to a literal Dante's Inferno. With weapons yet drawn, we made our way toward the apex of our journey.

The corridor itself was lined with an assortment of abandoned trolleys and wheelchairs. That made the going slow, as we needed to push them out of our way to avoid the bloody mess smeared down its center.

The gore smelt fresh, so I stooped to examine it. I was surprised to discover chunks of sticky flesh, bits of bone, and quite a lot of hair attached to portions of scalp. Broken nails near several of the doorframes revealed that whoever had been dragged this way had been conscious and put up a valiant fight.

And I'll bet those parasites let them, just so they could feed on the misery of it all.

Here and there, rooms stood open to inspection. We were obviously heading in the right direction, for they were sparsely furnished with examination tables upon which moth-eaten sheets now moldered to gray. A few of them even contained body bags that had seen better days. Regardless of their condition I could see they were in use, for mutilated limbs protruded like porcupine quills from holes where canvas had perished.

How long have these cockroaches been in residence? Perhaps it's time to fumigate the establishment.

In due course we emerged into a long, low compartment, at the end of which squatted the source of the ruddy light I'd seen earlier. A giant metal incinerator. The hatch of the furnace was thrown open, and hungry flames crackled and snapped with an eagerness that was a delight to behold.

Silhouetted against the blaze, the female torso of the Dread-Locks' latest meal sat tied to a chair. Her head flopped limply onto her breast, and what remained of her long tresses hung down over her face. The woman's hair was matted with dried blood and what looked like strips of fat. But that was the least of her worries, for her severed arms and legs lay in the middle of a pool of urine on the floor where her feet should have been.

Two massive shadowy helices swirled about their prey, softly singing unintelligible words that somehow conveyed a sense of inevitable menace.

Dread-Masters.

One appeared larger than the other. From what I remembered of these beasts, that would indicate it to be the more dominant individual, and the one I needed to address.

The tones of the song faded, and the flock leader glided down to a position immediately behind the bound victim. Blackness condensed about it, whereupon it solidified into a more tangible form. It started humming, and its two great hands fussed the female's head as if the creature was suddenly mindful of the distress it had caused. Then it grabbed her by the hair and yanked harshly backward.

A sharp gasp indicated she was fully conscious, and a tear of pain stole from the corner of one eye. The drop froze in place on her cheek. Somehow, it then peeled away from her face and gravitated toward the shimmering outline of her tormentor. The crystallized expression of grief blended with the monster's substance, and another glittering scale appeared on the surface of its skin.

They're keeping her alive so they can feast off her.

"Why are you here, Reaper?" a taunting, masculine voice called out. "Have you come to offer yourself in order to spare this unfortunate wretch?"

To enforce his meaning, the Master reached around and traced the edge of a gleaming talon along the woman's chin and down her throat. He prolonged the torture by leaning down to place a tender fluttering kiss on each of her eyelids.

Her emotion-laden sob echoed around the chamber.

"What?" I countered. "Do you think that is going to intimidate or move me? Look around you. This is hell. You're just enforcing what this place is all about. All you're doing is pissing me off. As your little buddies just found out, that's not a wise thing to do."

"They were lesser drones, insignificant battle fodder. We, on the other hand, are far more potent and not so easily vanquished."

"Is that why you thought it would be safe to accept a contract to take me out? Did you imagine chaff like that would be able to distract me, or soften me up before *you* stepped in?"

The flock leader didn't reply. He didn't need to. His emotions did that for him. I watched as the very edge of his dark aura burned vermillion.

Gotcha!

The subordinate Master floated down to take a stand by its companion. It hovered in the background, and by the way it acted I suspected a closer, more intimate connection than was immediately apparent. Sudden intuition provided the answer.

They're mated.

I wasn't fooled by the difference in size, as the females of most species are much deadlier than the males.

For some reason I thought of Strawberry and smiled.

The Dread-Master took my grin as a challenge. Barbed claws raked across fragile skin and fresh blood welled to the surface. The woman bit her lip in an effort to contain her anguish, but that didn't prevent another diamond from appearing within the crux of her tormentor.

I'm getting sick and tired of this posturing.

Stepping forward, I planted the heel of my scythe firmly on the ground. "Who offered you the contract?"

Neither creature replied.

I moved closer and added a compulsive element to my voice.

"Who offered you the contract? And perhaps more importantly, why?"

The extremities of both ghouls flared in response, but they remained silent.

Okay, time to make a point.

"Very well. By the authority vested in me, prepare to be judged—"

"You cannot do anything, Reaper," the flock leader interrupted, cold humor radiating from him in waves, "for we are not of this realm, and you have no jurisdiction over us."

I lifted my weapon and slammed it into the floor.

"Oh, really . . . ?"

For the first time in more than a century, I manifested the Phage, the full Satanic might of my station. Power bloomed, and I stood encompassed within a midnight nimbus of stunning magnitude. Purple streamers burned along the tips of my corona, and a coronet of scarlet flames danced about my head. The concrete bubbled at my feet as the indescribable potency of Hellfire rushed to obey my summons. I felt myself swell as my aspect darkened.

"I beg to differ."

A name appeared in burning letters in the ether before me. *Gru'al*.

"Gru'al! *Troh a'* lùthse ain mi sealbġh (Gru'al! By the power invested in me), *do a'* fàs dorcha, se thu deòraich (I banish you to the black void). *Ansîn, toil thu bàsath ís críen* (There, you will wither and fade). *Faod uíl méoem bi lârmud am thu, gu-bràithe* (May all memory of you be forgotten, forever)."

"You cannot!" he screamed. "You have no—"

The weight of obliteration fell upon the Dread-Master like a singularity. One moment he was hovering in the air before us, and the next he was crushed out of existence as the hex swallowed him whole.

An abrupt silence filled the room.

I turned my attention to the final ghoul, and another name manifested: *Desh*.

"Desh of the S'gãth," I began, using their ancient name, "I will offer you one last chance. Comply and you may avoid the fate of your companion. Tell me, *who* bought your services?"

"I . . . I cannot . . ."

"You have seen what I did to your mate. Do you wish to join him in oblivion?"

"We are bound by our oath to fulfill—"

"Tell me!"

"I cannot say," Desh replied in haste, "I don't . . . I don't remember. Gru'al committed us by sealing the agreement in unholy concordat, although I know not why."

Alarm bells rang in the back of my mind. I could tell by her aura that Desh was speaking the simple truth. As a Master, she should have been consulted about the details of the agreement, but her flock leader had forged ahead and concluded the pact alone. Once signed, the rest of the squadron was locked into fulfilling its terms.

I tried a different line of approach.

"How recently were you obligated to this contract, and where were the details actually sealed?"

"Although we have resided in secret within this great structure for more than a year, an accord was reached only this past week, where all such covenants are made."

As I thought.

I had a sudden notion.

"What brought you to this realm in the first place?"

"An offer of unlimited access to all the levels of this netherworld. The grandeur of such suffering proved hard to resist, for we would be able to feed and grow as never before."

"And do you recall who made that offer?"

"It was . . . I can't . . ." Once again, her aura became agitated as she struggled to remember specific details.

As if I needed any further verification.

I'd heard enough.

I raised my staff and stabbed forward. A concentrated beam of God's Grace lanced out, enveloping the Dread-Lock within a skein of purifying power. Her threshold expanded alarmingly, and then she exploded in a shower of darkest distillate and tinkling scales.

"I thought you promised her she would avoid the fate of her companion?" Nimrod said.

"I did, and I kept my word. Although reduced to next to nothing, her essence will eventually filter back to the S'gãth home world, where she'll start all over again. Gru'al, on the other hand, won't exist for much longer."

"Fair enough." He cocked a thumb toward the woman still tied to the chair. "What about their victim?"

I studied her long and hard. Although her eyes were wild and staring, the light of hope now burned in their depths.

Silly girl.

The Reaper in me won out.

"Leave her to the rats and other vermin."

In reply to the stoic eyebrow raised in my direction, I said, "She'll suffer. She'll endure a prolonged death, and then she'll be reassigned. As I said to Gru'al, that's what hell's all about."

With a flick of my wrist I collapsed my weapon, spun on my heels and stalked from the room. Nimrod brought up the rear. Wails of protest followed us as we strode back along the main corridor. I blanked them from my mind, and soon the woman's pleas faded into the distance. I didn't give her entreaties a second thought, not even when the rats began to congregate for their unexpected banquet.

As we climbed the stairs back toward ground level, Nimrod asked, "Where to now, Covenant Gardens? I take it that's what the Dread-Master was referring to?"

"Right first time. It's the only place I know of where such binding contracts are commonly made. But we won't go by the direct route. I've no doubt someone will be watching, so we'll loop around and go by Hearse Guards Parade. And we'll go in disguise. I want to get the lay of the land before we go charging in and start taking heads."

"What about the truce governing the market?"

I paused to look into his face.

"It doesn't cover those who foment treason."

"I like the sound of that." He graced me with a rare smile.

We resumed our journey, and I began chewing something over in my mind.

The thing that gets me about this is the depth of planning involved. It goes back years, and seems to involve all sorts of realms which I'd never have dreamed would take an interest in Satan's affairs. And the S'gãth! Although they're scum, they are creatures bound by oath. So what in Azazel's name could force them to forget . . . ?

A chill ran down my spine

The Cup of Tartarus imbues its wielder with the power of command but once, and I can't see Cream wasting it on a mundane step in his strategy. Nor can I envisage him trusting its influence to anyone else. So that means he must have access to something else that can compel obedience in others . . .

. . . but what?

Chapter 13: Covenant Gardens

I looked about me as I waited in line. For denizens of hell, all were behaving themselves remarkably well, probably due to the truce that governed entry into one of the most infamous locations in the entire multiverse: Covenant Gardens.

Of all the many layers in the underworlds, this was the only place where you were guaranteed to find the truth—or one aspect of it, since agreements made here, within the Sinotaph, bound each participant to an unbreakable pact.

Breaking such pacts had been tried, of course. Over the centuries, there were always those who wanted to push the boundaries and test the waters, if only to see what happened. All of them wished they hadn't, for doing so invariably consigned their souls to an eternity of brutal, agonizing torture without hope of reprieve.

From what I'd seen, the fate of those transgressors made Hades and Purgatory look like a walk in the park on a rainy day. Even the Undertaker had special instructions regarding those who broke these rules, for our Infernal Highness didn't want them to miss a single second of the anguish they'd earned. In that special hell within hell, they were kept whole, sane, and fully conscious, so their unending screams could soothe our Father's dark moods.

This venue served its purpose well, since in recent years the world of the condemned was getting a bit overcrowded. The activities sanctioned here kept HSM's minions on their toes and cleared the dross from our ranks.

Except that I'm not dross!

As we neared the west gate, I checked myself over for the umpteenth time. I was a distinctive guy, hated by millions, so I didn't want to attract attention . . . until I was ready.

Attract attention, for fuck's sake! I look like a Camp Nazi torturer.

Pickings within St Thomas' had been few and far between; most things of value had been pilfered years ago. Nonetheless, I'd managed to grab several items from a mortician's locker, to find only a predominance of bloodstained rubber. When I tried them on, Nimrod reacted as would any warrior from around the world: He pissed himself silly.

I seriously fought the urge to plant one on his chin until he reminded me the latex hat, mask, and gown would help hide my identity. What's more, it was large enough to fit over my existing gear.

Okay, so I look like a fat *Camp Nazi torturer.*

What was most annoying was the fact that Nimrod could afford to laugh. The dusty gabardine overcoat he'd snaffled made into the perfect image of an iconic mercenary. I peeked at him as we shuffled along in the queue. He appeared relaxed and confident, scanning the crowd as if completely at ease. Despite his stature, head and shoulders above everybody else—or because of it—nobody paid him the slightest heed.

The same couldn't be said for me. Although I kept my head down, I seemed to be attracting glances from men and women alike. I didn't know whether it was the blood smeared across my disguise that appealed to them, or the ingrained smell of formaldehyde. Whichever, I didn't like it, especially when one of the burly bearded guards on the gate leaned in as I passed and pressed something into my grasp.

I opened my hand and found a crumpled bit of paper. Smoothing it open, I saw a phone number on it, hastily scribbled. I turned back to stare at him, and the cheeky bastard actually winked and blew me a kiss.

You—

A heavy arm round my shoulder steered me away from trouble.

"How come you get all the luck?" Nimrod teased. "Although I don't think he'll do justice to one of Strawberry's satin negligees. He looks a bit too hairy."

"Shut the fuck up," I snapped, "and keep going."

"He'd probably tickle and ruin the moment as well."

"Wanker! If I wanted to hear you spout utter shit, I'd shove my fist up your ass and work you like a glove puppet."

Nimrod was unimpressed. "I *knew* you'd attended the advanced-level rimming course. We invented that, you know, back in the day, when Shinar had only just become a dominant city. The first . . ."

Too late: Nimrod had launched into one of his rare discourses. He'd run dry of words in a few minutes and revert back to his strong and silent stereotype. Until that moment, I knew I'd just have to suck it up, zone out, and submit myself to the experience that was the market.

This was easier than you might imagine.

When Covenant Gardens was first established, it comprised only two main features: the Sinotaph—a miniature acropolis-style structure, the interior of which was based on the Forum of the Roman senate—and a small waiting area outside.

As its fame grew and citizens began flocking here by the hundreds and then thousands, the site and its infrastructure expanded. Now, a bazaar one mile square catered to the myriad opportunists and ancillary trades that serviced those wishing to buy and sell contracts. The variety of what was on offer was as mind-numbing as it was overwhelming.

Ramshackle pavilions and lean-tos lined the inner walls. Constructed from tapestries, tarpaulin, plastic sheeting and fabrics, they displayed a grandeur lacking among the smaller tents and open-air stalls filling the central aisles.

All stank to high heaven, and many had kindling fires or burning braziers adorning their entranceways where cauldrons and pots hubbled and bubbled, each containing mysteries best left unsolved.

Here everyday inhabitants mingled freely with ghosts and ghouls, monsters and demons. Even Blue Suits were represented, looking completely at home among mutant shoppers and minion hawkers.

Recruitment posters flapped and billboards towered everywhere, advertising the latest campaigns (where the bored and disillusioned could make their undead lives that little bit more eventful) or whatever trend was currently popular, as "sanctioned" by His Satanic Majesty. I noted with interest that Marlowe and Shakespeare had been commissioned to take another dig at the Boss's thorn in the flesh, as the Dreary Lane Theatre was featuring *A Comedy of Erra's, Part II.*

Of course, it'd be a huge hit . . . or else!

Some bright spark had set up a *bureau de change* just inside the gates. Paper money wasn't much use here, as it tended to spontaneously combust in the wrong hands. But from what I could see, most of the major currencies were represented; with blood bags, gems, coins, and slaves being the most popular forms of tender.

And the noise!

Music predominated, filtering from the background to assail our senses with a brash, contradictory mishmash from a whole plethora of natural and improvised instruments. And if the myriad tunes weren't distracting enough, we also were serenaded by the strident voices of the merchants, each of whom had something urgent to say.

I listened to a few as we waded through the press, anything to help me ignore my companion, still prattling on about the benefits of anal interrogation techniques.

"Empty promises for sale," shouted a particularly rotund, elderly gentleman with a carbuncle on his nose. "Political guarantees and hot air. Impress your friends with the depth of your deceit."

"Garbage," yelled another. "All the cast-offs and junk you can imagine. I guarantee you won't find better quality shite anywhere else."

"Skiddies!" whooped a wizened old woman, boldly waving an atrociously stained pair of underpants in the air. "Flatulently fragrant and full of goodness. And for tonight only, you get a used handkerchief free with every purchase. Only the very best encrusted residues."

"Dreams, nightmares, and amnesia," warbled an ethereal wraith hovering above a gleaming orb of alien origin. "Incriminating memories removed for only a smidgen of life force."

The choices ranged from confusing to mesmerizing, and the general hubbub generated by thousands of vendors all shrieking at once blended into a crescendo of ear-ringing white noise.

Then there were the smells.

With the number of blacksmiths, armories and tanning stalls in evidence, anyone would be forgiven for thinking the stench of horse shit, cordite, oils, and bleached hides could burn your nostrils. But the pungent aroma of curry tinged everything else with a soft, fragrant overtone.

A quick check of the menu boards revealed that the particular favorite of the masses appeared to be rat, with human limbs also high on the list. A surprising revelation until I remembered how appalling food could be in hell, and how almost anything tasted better when curried.

Amid an overload of sensory contradictions, we gradually waded through the milling multitude, working our way toward the heart of the market.

Then the mood changed. In some strange way, the frivolity and carnival atmosphere transmuted into a deeper, more focused vibe that told us we were nearing our goal.

Nimrod ceased his diatribe and became more alert. I noted with interest how the marquees in this part of the Gardens had guards stationed outside. Banners and standards hung from entrance posts, together with honors and posters advertizing each unit's campaigns and availability for hire.

The tribal men and women looked particularly menacing, as if attempting to convey the superiority of their unit or faction through their posture or by a simple glance.

Nor did your average mercenary type make up the balance of the damned crowd. Anyone looking to make a name for themselves or escape the drudgery of life in hell was free to mix here with hardened veterans and guerilla fighters present from all historical eras.

We lingered by a makeshift set of arenas to watch Roman Legionnaires vie with gladiators, Spartans against Thebans, tribalistic warriors against British colonial troops, in round after round of nonlethal competition. In one particularly large pit, a medieval knight squared off against a dragon. A billboard proudly announced that someone called Jin Two-Fists had managed to capture the storied reptile on an expedition to the northern continent of Crematoria, in Gehenna.

Somehow I doubted that the pails of water they had collected and stacked around the edge of the ring would suffice in an emergency.

My misgivings were confirmed only a few minutes later, when Sir No-Brains decided to stick his lance where Paradise never glows, in an effort to spur the beast to greater efforts. His ruse worked like a charm, for the enraged leviathan promptly snapped free of its restraints, flattened the unfortunate fellow with one mighty sweep of its tail, and then roasted him alive in his cuirass.

Condolences—along with a tactless amount of whooping—showered down as the knight was stomped into a sticky purée.

"Oh, hard luck," someone drawled.

"Shame!" cried another.

"Bad form, Sir George. Bad form," mourned the marshal.

Nimrod leaned in. "They obviously forgot to explain the rules to the dragon."

"And then some . . ." I nodded as the beast bellowed a challenge to all comers and then took to the air. We ducked as it arced above us, but we needn't have worried.

The dragon was merely taking the time to pick out its captor from the crowd. Spotting him huddled together with a group of friends outside a large tent, the great serpent folded its wings, swooped low, and rained down fire and brimstone upon them.

Their pavilion exploded into a fireball of bright, golden light. The dragon circled twice, just to make sure they were well and truly fucked, before uttering an eerily human laugh. Then it was gone, winging its way to the north, faster than I thought possible.

Nice exit! "He's intelligent too. When this is all over, I think I might try to recruit one onto the team. Can you imagine the fun we'd have disposing of prisoners?"

Nimrod grinned. "And on barbecue weekends."

Lights flashing and sirens wailing, a modern-day fire truck blared and crawled its way through the press of sightseers. In this kind of venue, the guys on board would be keen to reach the source of the blaze before it spread too far. A difficult task, for the ruckus had attracted a growing crowd. Good news for us, however, since the sudden influx of people to the blaze opened up a clear road through to our destination: the Sinotaph.

"C'mon, let's grab the opportunity while we can." I elbowed Nimrod in the ribs. "Hopefully, this commotion will have thinned the ranks of those waiting to make a deal."

We made our way through the remaining bystanders, up the steps, and into the main building. As we entered we shed our disguises, and I breathed a sigh of relief. I preferred black leather over cream latex any day.

Although I'd never been here before, I'd certainly heard of it, for it was the one place in all the endless levels of hell someone could come if they *officially* wanted to settle disputes, exercise grudges, or remove problems. Here you could buy the services of any type of assassin. Specters, demigods, reavers, or tormenters. Thugs, mercenaries, bravados. Or indeed, any idiot with something to prove, so long as they were prepared to kill . . . and the price was right.

And some fool had been willing to accept a contract on me. It made me wonder what the price on my head had been.

Despite my frustration, a large part of me could relate to the services provided here. Yes, I have a code. A set of values I strictly adhered to, which set me apart from the riffraff. But call me what you will, I am a stone-cold predator at heart. A reaper of souls for Satan. His executioner and destroyer of dreams. The people here were my kind of scum. Butchers, slayers, and slaughterer, who valued condemned life as the commodity it was; something to be sold to the highest bidder. I felt right at home.

The bartering floor was modeled on the Forum of the Roman senate, circular in shape, much like a miniature amphitheatre, with a central auction area, podium, and brazier. Public seating was arrayed around the floor in ascending tiers.

We waited in the wings as negotiations for a new tender were put forward.

I'll admit I was intrigued to see how things would progress, as it always struck me as odd that people would openly seek the services of an assassin in front of so many witnesses. My answer was soon revealed.

Murder was the number one pastime in hell, and Satan had simply capitalized on that fact. Only the most lucrative commissions would be found here, as these targets would be denizens who were either very important, or very hard to kill. Therefore, His Infernal Majesty had thought of a means by which he could ensure a healthy cut of the revenue generated.

Satan's plan was as brilliant as it was crafty, for no one ever actually died. They were merely reassigned upon their demise. So, if a particular feud ran deep the vendetta might continue in a series of tit-for-tat hits, each of which would merely serve to keep the royal coffers overflowing.

No wonder our Dark Lord could afford the very latest Hades Benz every year.

As proceedings continued I also noted that only the opening and closing of each bid was conducted from the floor. The client and chosen killer would discuss the actual specifics in secret, presumably in the private offices I had seen lining the corridor on the way here. Everything was done by the book. A presiding officer and auctioneer officiated. They were assisted by a state-appointed attorney and his recorder, who in turn were watched over by an independently assigned panel of six hellegal witnesses.

All very neat and tidy, as demonstrated by this fresh case, which concluded in double-quick time. We edged forward as the proposal drew to a close.

The presiding officer stood and brought client and assassin together.

"Have you both reached an agreement?"

"We have," they replied in unison, each with a slight bow.

"And have you prepared your documents in accordance with contractual guidelines, and with all the stipulations clearly expressed therein?"

"Yes."

"Then all that remains is for you to make public demonstration of your acceptance of those terms. Please step forward."

Approaching the podium, both parties unfolded similar cream-colored parchments, upon which I could see a great deal of writing. In the presence of the witnesses, they separately signed their names on each document. Next, they simultaneously placed their hands into the brazier. From my vantage, I could see the glassy-colored coals within, steaming with an otherworldly glow. The participants then individually placed their thumbs against both sets of signatures, to add a form of blood fingerprint. Finally each scroll was bound in black ribbon, and a charmed wax seal was added by the officiating lawyer. Job done, the newly obligated partners in crime walked from the auditorium to the polite applause of an audience consisting mainly of damned souls.

"Time to make an entrance," I whispered to Nimrod.

We strode confidently onto the floor. All eyes fell on us and the clapping stopped. An abrupt silence radiated throughout the room.

The presiding officer turned to see who had caused such a reaction, and the moment his gaze met mine he lost his balance and fell toward me.

I reached out to steady him and saw his nametag: *Cornelius*. He appeared confused. I didn't know if that was due to the shock of finding the Reaper in his presence, or because he was complicit in the plot against my life in some way. In any event, he then surprised me by simply saying, "Oh, it's you?"

"Yes, it is," I replied. "Why? Were you not expecting me, or did you not anticipate seeing me ever again?"

Without any hint of fear, Cornelius turned his back and addressed the onlookers. "Ladies, gentlemen, and other distinguished guests. If you would be so kind, the auction will take a short break and reconvene in, say, fifteen minutes? Thank you for your patience."

Before I could ask him what he was doing, Cornelius began strolling away. "Follow me, please, gentlemen," he called over his shoulder.

He led us a short way down the main corridor and in through a door marked *Private*.

Once inside, we found ourselves in Cornelius' personal kingdom. A huge antique desk dominated one corner of the room, its top buried beneath a pile of official-looking parchments and papers. Filing cabinets lined three walls, all overflowing with wallets and folders of varying thickness. From a rack beside the entrance hung a black bowler hat and umbrella, items completely at odds with Cornelius' formal Roman dress.

Nimrod remained by the doorway to ensure we weren't disturbed, and I got straight down to business. "I take it you know why we're here?"

"How can I help you?" Cornelius replied, as if listening to a different conversation.

"Did you not just hear my question? From the way you acted out on the floor, I suspect you may know the nature of my query."

"I'm sorry. I . . . I . . ." Cornelius stuttered, confused and agitated. "I couldn't help it, you see. It took me completely by surprise. I . . . oh, dear."

"What did? What are you talking about, man?"

"And so unexpected, to receive such an outlandish bid."

"Are you referring to the hits against me? Who proposed them?"

"Hits?" Suddenly lucid, Cornelius retorted, "I don't know what you mean, Reaper. Only one person ever came here. Just the one, mind. Very friendly fellow. Brought me a genuine bottle of Grand Dionysian ancient Greek wine to celebrate the deal."

Only one? But which *one?*

"And what was the name of this friendly fellow?" I pressed. "If he made a proposal, you obviously have his details, right? Where are they?"

Cornelius didn't appear to have heard. He was off in the land of unicorns again. "And all he did was tender a bid that had never been contemplated before. The Dread-Lock was quite charming, too. Do you know, it was kind enough to take away all my fear about agreeing to such a thing . . . ?"

Aha! At least I know which hit we're talking about. "And the customer?"

"A Blue Suit! Who could have anticipated something like that? I was helpless to resist. They invited me to listen in on their haggling. Most unusual. But we drank some wine, relaxed a little, and everything seemed fine . . ."

Or one of the Devil's Children? The mystery leak, perhaps?

". . . and their argument was so compelling. I felt I must help them."

As he talked, Cornelius reached toward his top drawer. "I'm just a businessman, you see. A servant, doing his own little bit to bring in the taxes. And these people looked very official and ever so important. We rarely get such distinguished guests."

"You're confusing me now," I said. "Was it just the one, or two clients you dealt with? Think, man." *Perhaps I'd better hex him.*

"I have to obey. They ordered me."

So calmly that I didn't immediately appreciate what he was doing, Cornelius removed an item from the desk and sat back. I sensed the presence of arcane energy. We made eye contact, and for the first time he appeared completely composed and rational.

"It's all my fault." He raised his hand to his mouth.

I just had time to register the Hell-Brass Magnum before a deafening report rang out. The wall behind him became a canvas splattered in gray and red goo.

He started to dissipate almost immediately.

"Shit!" Nimrod spluttered. "I didn't expect that."

I was too furious to think of a witty reply.

Without turning, I snarled, "Fetch me the bloody lawyer and the auctioneer. Now! I want that contract and any other paperwork relating to the transaction in my hands within the next few minutes or my scythe is going to start removing heads."

Nimrod recognized the threat in my voice and sobered instantly. He threw the door open and ran along the corridor, bellowing for the instantaneous presence of the presiding officer's lackeys.

While he was gone, I thought I'd check out a few things.

First off, something Cornelius had mentioned roused my suspicions. I looked to the opposite corner of the room and saw a small drinks decanter. Prominent among the bottles was an old-style earthenware jug.

I wonder?

Walking over, I snatched the flagon from the table, opened my senses, and popped the cork. The heady aroma of vintage wine warmed my nostrils, along with the subtle hint of something else.

Hidden toxins. Cream! You sneaky ratfucksonofabitch!

While I wasn't an expert on the pharmaceutical properties of certain herbs and chemicals, I knew someone who was.

I'll get these across to Bella and Donna. Hopefully, the compounds used will be exotic enough to narrow the field of source locations. One way or another, I'll use the information to narrow the gap and cut off his resources.

But I wasn't finished yet.

Speaking of which . . .

I replaced the carafe on the tray and returned to the desk area. The revolver lay where it had fallen after Cornelius' essence faded, and the smell of cordite still hung in the air. Thus I had to alter my perceptions entirely so I could focus on what had intrigued me just before he blew his brains out. A ripple of exotic energy.

Retrieving the gun, I flipped the catch and looked within the drum. Six bullets stared back, one of them spent. I tapped the shells out into the palm of my hand and sorted through them until I came to the empty casing. I held it to my nose.

The energy signature was hauntingly familiar.

That's when it hit me.

It smells like a triggered ripcord. Hey, these are new.

The door crashed open and Nimrod returned, escorting a very flustered individual.

"This is Benedict," he said, "the auctioneer. We'll ha–"

"Where's the lawyer?" I snapped. "I told you I wanted them both here."

"He had to leave, Reaper," Benedict replied before Nimrod could. "The Solicitor General demands we take all the ledgers across to the Halls of Injustice at least twice a day for verification." He had the decency to look apologetic. "I'm sorry. We didn't know how long you'd be with Cornelius, so we just seized the opportunity to . . . to . . . oh my!"

Benedict's voice trailed away as he registered that the space behind the desk had been redecorated, art deco style.

"Where's Cornelius?" he squeaked.

"That's all that's left of him," I replied, referring to the cranial matter still dribbling down the wall. "Evidently he felt compelled to end it all rather than speak with me. And I mean that literally."

"But . . . but . . . ." Benedict was too shocked to form a coherent sentence.

So I pressed on without him: "I could tell by the way everyone reacted when I arrived that you know who I am. Good, that'll save a lot of time. I need to see the official Deeds of Intent regarding the hit that was authorized on me."

Benedict's eyes widened in alarm.

"Yes, I know about it. And no, I won't reap your sorry ass *if* you assist in my enquiries. Do you know where the documents are, or not?"

"Er, yes." He sighed. "Hang on a tic, they should be over here."

As quickly as his bumbling feet would allow, Benedict shuffled across to one of the filing cabinets, opened the top drawer, and commenced rifling through the contents. He retrieved two honey-colored scrolls bound together by a ribbon of black silk.

As I took them from him I noticed a statutory blob of wax sealed the knot. It bore the Sinotaph's distinctive clasped hands monogram.

Just the pair? "So there's definitely only one commission? To which do these pertain, the deal with the Sibitti or the Dread-Locks?"

"Sibitti? Here?" Benedict gasped. "No, no, no. You must be mistaken, they'd never bind themselves to anything but their own aspirations. Believe me. I'm present at every auction when the bids are put forward. I'd have known if there had been further tenders on your life . . . other than the one made with the Dread-Master, of course."

Benedict's aura conveyed the truth of his answer. But it only raised more questions. Tamping them down—for now—I fought to conceal my excitement.

"So, this deed will contain the full details of all the parties concerned?"

"Yes, that's right."

At last. I handed the package back. "Open it, please."

Benedict took a moment to compose himself. Then he grasped the sigil in both hands, closed his eyes, and repeated a short phrase under his breath. A few seconds later, a surge of power thrummed in the air.

Crack!

The seals snapped apart, and the parchments unraveled. Catching the ends, Benedict smoothed them out on the top of the desk . . . and immediately frowned.

"Is everything okay?"

"No, this can't be right," he mewled.

He slid the top copy to one side and looked at the scroll underneath. His head bobbed between the two repeatedly as if he was a spectator at a tennis match.

"What is it? What's wrong?"

"This is most odd." He held out the copies for my inspection. "These aren't contracts at all. They're duplicate poems. Look . . ."

I did, only to be greeted by a familiar sight:

> *Unholy, undivine,*
> *Devout, with the deepest insincerity.*
> *We dress in shadows,*
> *And hear the sighs that whisper in the night.*
> *Like keys,*
> *They bare the contents of your soul.*
> *Black hearts for dark deeds,*
> *We flay your mind and risk the void,*

To unlock what was once so safe within.
Your memories know,
Listen,
For they tell their story.

"How could this possibly happen?" Benedict whined. "Our reputation will be left in tatters."

"There's much more at stake here than the Sinotaph's reputation." I snarled. "So if you *really* want to save your precious name, get that damned lawyer back here, along with anyone else who has the slightest bit of clout, and search these offices from top to bottom."

"Why? What do you want us to look for?"

"Crap like this!" I waved the false deeds in his face. "Or anything that might give us a clue as to who else is involved. Understood?"

My outburst appeared to help Benedict find his balls.

"By Anakim, I'll do it!" he swore. His expression became more determined. "I'll have them tear this place apart. We'll not be duped by the likes of that idiot."

I was startled by the sudden revelation. "Which idiot?"

"The client! He flaunted his cash in our faces, as if having such an exorbitant sum entitled him to special privileges. I can't remember his name because of the volume of customers we have, and . . . well, because handling such details was down to Judas and Cornelius. My job is solely floor-based—"

"But you remember what he looked like?"

"Yes, I bloody well do. Quite a robust, middle-aged fellow he was. Glasses, mustache, top hat and tails. Full of himself, too. He seemed to have the Dread-Lock eating out of his hand, and demanded everyone called him 'Doctor', instead of using his hel-legal name. He was quite insistent on having Cornelius join them in bashing out the actual details of the pact. Not good form at all."

Cream!

I glanced at Nimrod, who by his expression had made the same connection.

Nimrod coughed to draw Benedict's attention. "Who's Judas?"

"Huh? Oh, he's our lawyer. We're very glad to have him. The Legal Advocate's role is quite tedious. Form after form to fill in and all that. But Judas volunteered for the job. Just as well, really, as our previous advocate, Griffin, simply didn't turn up for work one day." He shrugged. "This is hell, after all. It happens all the time. We haven't seen him since."

"How long ago was that?" I demanded.

"Just over three months now. But don't worry, Judas is very efficient. If there's anything out of the ordinary in here, he'll spot it."

"Then we won't hold you up." I placed one of my cards on the desk. "The moment you have anything useful, call that number. My secretary will take a message. If it's important, I'll get back to you."

"I'll remember that."

"Good. Before we go, I'll send out one or two articles for sul-forensic examination. Make sure Judas is apprised of these items . . ." I quickly strolled around the office and selected the gun, wine and one of the parchments. "When I've finished with them, I'll make sure you get them back."

"Thank you, I'll make sure he knows."

I placed the evidence on a separate chair. Stepping back, I removed my scythe, opened my mind, and sent a long distance hail.

Bella? Donna? Can you hear me?

Whoa! Loud and clear, big boy, Donna came back. *It's just me at the moment, Bella's in the middle of an interrogation. By the way, are you okay? We heard you'd had a run-in with those Sibitti assholes.*

Nothing the Bālefire couldn't sort out, but we'll chat about that another time. Listen, I've made one or two breakthroughs regarding our most recent problem. I'm about to send you a few bits and bobs to look at. I'm hoping you'll find them useful. Watch out for the bullets in particular. I suspect they may be Tesla's latest toys, similar in function to a ripcord. A rather brutal method of ensuring information doesn't fall into the wrong hands, but effective nonetheless.

Really? How in the Seven Hells did he manage that?

That's what I'm hoping you'll *find out . . .*

I concentrated for a moment, depressed the second gem from bottom on my staff, and opened a portal. My scant pile of treasure disappeared.

The package is on its way. And Donna? Be as quick as you can, I'd hate to imagine the repercussions if ammunition like that became widely available.

Got it! We'll get onto this as a priority.

Excellent. Look, I've got to get going. I'm following up on a fresh lead. If you—

I know! If we get anything new, we'll call.

The ether went dead.

Good girl.

I nodded to Nimrod, and we made our way toward the exit. Benedict was already on the phone, shouting and screaming at someone to "move your ass, this is urgent!" He noticed us leaving, gave us a thumbs-up, and turned his back. The guy was on a roll and didn't want to spoil his momentum.

He'll do nicely.

As we walked briskly down the corridor, Nimrod edged closer, whispering, "From the way you're virtually skipping, I take it you know where we're going next?"

"I do. If the references to 'insincere and unholy behavior' weren't enough, who else do you know who dress 'in shadows, possess black hearts and do dark deeds'?"

"Besides the Dread-Locks?"

"Think about it. We're talking normal, quotidian citizens of the underworlds here. Those who have a special place where they can literally enact the line 'We flay your mind and risk the void.' Do you get it now?"

Nimrod mulled it over, and then slapped his hand against his forehead.

"Of course! The Gray . . . sorry, *Grey* Friars . . ." His face suddenly dropped. "Oh shit!"

"Yup! The Grey Friars. And to get there, we need to get past the Knights Tempter and their damned bridge. Ready for a spot of jousting?"

*

To describe Frédéric Chopin as vexed was an understatement. Lately it took far too long for him to recover following a seizure, and the gnawing ache that afflicted his joints all day and night made concentration increasingly difficult. His music had declined long ago—while he was still alive, in fact—and although he'd adjusted to the loss quite well, his condition now was deteriorating far beyond what he deemed acceptable.

My mind isn't what it was. I'm starting to lose it.

Frédéric suspected His Diabolical Majesty had arranged this malady so that no matter how he tried to cope, Satan would always have the last laugh. He picked up a drink from the salver beside him, extended the glass into the air, and whispered, "*Touché, mon Capitane.*"

Then he considered the extent of his plans, and a wry thought intruded. *Or so he would believe.* Frédéric raised a second toast. "Better still, *en garde.*"

He took a long pull of wine before he held his drink up to the light of the chandelier. The bubbles ascending from the bottom of the goblet refracted a thousand rainbows back at him. Unfortunately, their effervescence only soured his mood.

I need to distract myself . . . Aha! I know, I'll go and see how Cream is getting along in his laboratory. He's been down there for the past two hours, and only gets up to mischief when left to his own devices.

Although he wasn't a heavy drinker, Frédéric took his wine with him. This particular vintage was best served chilled, which meant the glass was always cold in his grasp, a welcome boon that helped ease his hands' discomfort.

As he descended the wide baroque stairway, Frédéric considered the compromises he had made to ensure his goals could be reached.

He loved his solitude, but had been willing to forgo seclusion to recruit the services of a most aggravating partner in crime, Dr. Thomas Neill Cream.

Cream is an unsophisticated, self-centered buffoon. What he lacks in finesse he more than makes up for by serving as the perfect distraction. The Reaper appears so consumed with catching him that he scarcely regards the real reasons behind the "good" doctor's miraculous successes. And so long as it stays that way . . . all well and good. Meanwhile, unmolested, I can collect the artifacts I need to prepare for the ultimate confrontation.

Then there was the involvement of Erra and his Sibitti assassins.

I thought them an unfortunate necessity, due to the attention they'd draw to this endeavor. But what a blessing in disguise that turned out to be, for it focused Satan's attentions onto a far grander playing field than actually exists. If I can keep him guessing and looking in the wrong direction, I just might be able to pull this off.

The face of Frédéric's beloved, his sole purpose for existing, briefly clouded his vision: *Not long now, my love. Not long now. Your patience will be rewarded.*

He pondered one more recollection of happier times, then banished such distractions from his mind. Fortunately, he had arrived at the basement. He opened the door . . . and staggered.

The stench was overpowering. Frédéric didn't at first know if the reek was due to the festering pall generated by the multitude of concoctions boiling and bubbling away in the tubes and jars strewn across every available work surface, or because the test subject had soiled himself again. But even from this distance, he could see the poor wretch was sitting in a huge pool of feces and urine.

He took another long draft to fortify himself against the assault on his olfactory nerves and asked, "How are things progressing?"

Ever full of self-importance, Cream refrained from answering immediately, merely raising one finger and continuing to work on his "patient."

Frédéric watched from the doorway as the doctor used a teat pipette to place three drops of a gelatinous amber liquid onto the puppet's tongue. Finally, Cream sat back.

The unfortunate subject convulsed for a moment, and such was the strength of his spasms that the restraints creaked in protest. Then, as suddenly as it started, the disturbing exhibition was over. A whoosh escaped the subject's lungs; his face relaxed; his tail went limp. As his ponderous head sagged forward, he let out a final sigh and fell asleep.

Only then did the Lambeth Poisoner turn from his work. "Fine. Everything is progressing as anticipated. This latest batch contains exactly the hypnotic element I was striving for. All I must do now is adjust the dosage, and we'll completely avoid the initial reaction you just saw as the neural inhibitors are circumvented."

"And the current side effects?"

"Thankfully, the bouts of confusion and altered lucidity already displayed by our candidates can easily be explained away by a combination of overwork, fatigue and stress. This new potion won't produce anything like that. Well, nothing *noticeable*, that is."

"But there will be an accumulative consequence?"

"Of course! Unless you've changed your mind and want our fall-guys to live?"

"No, that won't be necessary. The fewer loose ends we have, the better. How long do you think it will take to prepare this latest consignment for full delivery?"

Cream pursed his lips. "If I'm left alone to get on with it? By this time tomorrow."

"Excellent news." Frédéric cast his gaze about the room one final time. "Then I'll leave you to it."

He closed the door behind him and ascended the stairs. To no one in particular, he muttered, "No . . . it won't be long at all."

*

Cream watched as Chopin, his partner in crime, left the room. The door clicked quietly shut, and the sound of receding footsteps faded into the distance.

He followed the troubled genius with his mind's eye and hissed, "You are a fool if you think me blind to your machinations. I know what you crave, and how quickly you'd replace me given the chance. I'll not have you waste my future; yours alone is this fallacy of unrequited love. She deemed you a burden in life; she'll view you as an imbecile for even daring to think she would willingly join you here. And while I don't display your ability for uncovering arcane secrets, I do possess a rather potent concoction to help me retain the upper hand. A most fitting turn of events, I'd say, for all duplicitous acts have their consequences."

He turned back to his patient.

"Right, time to clean you up and get you back where you need to be." Leaning forward, Cream lowered his voice. "I'm going to count backward from ten. As I do so, all recollections of this place and the events that have occurred here will fade from your memory. When you wake, you will feel completely refreshed and relaxed. You will, of course, be horrified that you became so inebriated last night that you soiled yourself. But after a shower and change of clothing, even that embarrassment will simply slip your mind, leaving only an overwhelming compulsion to carry out your assignment. Nothing else matters. Nothing will distract you from your task. Once completed, you will end your life as instructed.

"Now, are you sitting comfortably? Ten . . . nine . . . eight . . ."

Chapter 14: A Moment of Clarity

In the Juxtapose level of hell, I found Olde London Town a conundrum at the best of times: a heady mix of the implausibly warped and secularly grotesque. Its denizens were the perfect accompaniment to their city, a stir-fried hotchpotch of condemned souls who took the geophysical and temporal irregularities of their hometown in their stride.

Everyday afterlife here was as much an enigma as a challenge. You'd think that, having lived here for centuries, I'd be used to it by now. Yet I was still caught by surprise from time to time, boundaries between eras being as fluid here as they were temperamental. In this place more than any other, I'd discovered that even if you knew a surprise was coming, forewarned was definitely *not* forearmed.

As was the case regarding my current predicament.

Nimrod and I were en route to the Grey Friars. In the land of the living, Greyfriars had been the site of a Franciscan friary that existed from 1225 – 1538, in a northwestern part of the City of

London called St Nicholas on the Shambles. That great establishment had included one of the largest conventional churches in the
capital. It had also been home to a Studium, an extensive library
of logical and theological texts so important it was rivaled only by
Oxford University, thus achieving a level of cultural prestige that
drew people from all over the then-known world, until Thomas
Cromwell—a man who became a good friend of mine—ordered
the transcripts seized during the English Reformation. Under
his enlightened guidance, the Greyfriars' estates were confiscat-
ed, the order itself disbanded, and most of its monks banished or
executed.

Of course, *we* couldn't let such a monument go to waste.
And with a gothic twist, the friary became the perfect establishment for the truly irreverent.

The Grey Friars were now Satan's very own thought po-
lice, an unholy order of hermits who regularly vetted the ranks of
the Devil's Children to weed out those with doubts or illusions of
grandeur. Every Sinday morning, the pews of the High Church
of Lucifer within the Friars' domain would be packed with Blue
Suits and spooks, all of whom would undergo their regular "con-
fessional" evaluation.

But the order also served another purpose: The site had retained its archives and was now one of the largest publicly known
repositories of occult knowledge and arcane mascots in the underworlds, matched only by the Hellexandria Library.

The Grey Friars defended that vault, and its treasures in their
care, within the Cloister of Scourging, a great castlelike tower situated in a separate annex. Constructed on a mound built from the
bones of those who died during the Great Fire of London some
one hundred years after the original monastery's passing, the
cloister's protections included a series of enchanted wards and a
powerful temporal barrier. The place was also guarded by the fri-

ars themselves, who were known to possess skills far more lethal than Shaolin monks tripping on amphetamines.

A heavy set of precautions, and yet all these measures were but a secondary line of defense. To reach them you first had to face the Knights Bridge. However, the "bridge" wasn't a literal construction of wood or stone linking one side to another, but an esoteric conduit from *here* to *there*, from *now* to *then*: A multidimensionhell link that spanned hydraspace to get you to where you needed to go.

Appearing much like a ground-level mushroom cloud from a nuclear explosion, the Knights Bridge encompassed the Cloister of Scourging in a haar of literally thought-stealing smog. This brume was so thick, so cloying, that unworthy individuals had been known to enter only to wander forever more, lost and alone.

And if the thought of facing such a barrier wasn't daunting enough, the entire pall was also protected by the Knights Tempter, an ancient heraldic order of warriors fanatically devoted to the glory of the Arch Deceiver and Father of Lies himself, Satan.

To get where I needed to go, this obstacle must be faced.

I stood outside the Old Bully—the main court of the Ministry of Injustice here in Juxtapose—and eyed the deceptively calm mists quietly tumbling and twisting over and over on the other side of the street.

"Okay," Nimrod breathed. "What do we do now?"

"*We* don't do anything." I cocked my head at the murky film on the other side of the street. "*I*, on the other hand, need to go into *that*."

"Are you sure it's wise?"

"There's no point in us both having our minds screwed with. You've heard the horror stories. Anyone attempting to traverse the bridge must pass a series of tests. What they are, exactly, differs from aspirant to aspirant. But whatever you *do* contend with, it measures your physical, mental, and spiritual fortitude in a way that flays your damned soul bare. Not a pleasant experience for a denizen of hell."

"Then why risk it, Daemon? People like us are especially wicked and depraved. The stronger we are, the more profound the experience will be. Why don't you simply try to phase through, or generate a short-range portal? For fuck's sake, if anyone's strong enough, it's you."

"Because that *would* be suicide, my friend. Don't forget, that stuff has built-in safeguards to prevent any kind of skullduggery. And if it were that easy, you'd get idiots like Tesla storming the place like hyenas on a fat juicy carcass."

Nimrod fell silent, then said, "And yet, Cream and his cronies managed to breach the Sphincter and the Grumbles gate-room without much difficulty. And one of their clues led you here."

"I know. I've been worrying about just that point, because if they've found a way around shields like this, we're all in trouble."

Nimrod clasped my shoulder. "I never thought I'd say this, but thank Azazel for the Knights Tempter."

"I'll let you know." I returned the gesture. "Remember, that fog is designed to neutralize whatever enhancements a candidate possesses."

"So you'll be completely ... ?"

"Normal? Yes. And I for one don't intend to have my head rearranged by a magically augmented club anytime soon." Pointing at myself, I tried to lighten the mood. "I mean, look at me. Would *you* want your features spoiled if you were a perfect specimen like me?"

"If I looked like you," Nimrod countered, "I'd be ashamed to be seen in public without a bag on my face. Two. Just in case the top one fell off!" His countenance suddenly became impassive. "But if you're afraid, I could always fit you with a set of baby reins to pull you back when you start crying."

I scanned his aura and could see he was attempting to mask his concern behind a humorous façade. I had to admit, I felt all emotional. "Fuck off, you pussy! Sitting here talking about it won't get the job done. I've had enough of your drivel. See you on the other side."

I pushed myself away from the wall, strode across the sidewalk, and headed toward the gently undulating wall of mystery. Passersby checked their step as they realized where I was heading. Cars screeched to a halt.

Seizing on the lull, Nimrod called, "Can I have first dibs on your apartment when you die? I've always wanted rooms with a view."

I gave him the finger, stepped in . . .

. . . and froze.

I'd expected a gradual transition from light to dark, a sense of being progressively enveloped and transported in some way to a new location. But I didn't get any of that. In an instant, I was someplace else entirely.

A thick gray soup surrounded me. I couldn't see the ground beneath my feet. When I extended my arms, my hands were swallowed whole, as if they didn't exist. Peering about me, I searched for a focal point on which to establish a bearing.

Not a goddam thing. Has the trial started already?

Suddenly wary, I realized it would be best to clear my head, so I took a deep breath, calmed my nerves, closed my eyes, and listened.

Thump—thump, thump—thump, thump—thump . . .

The sound of my heartbeat dominated, its steady rhythm providing an anchor around which to ground myself. I didn't need a cardiovascular system, of course, but I'd always found the sensation soothing, as it made me feel something I'd never been: normal.

For some reason the enfolding brume exacerbated that beat. It grew louder, and then more distant, as if my heart had suddenly been transposed beyond my flesh.

Thump—thump, thump—thump, thump—thump . . .

Now I was puzzled.

It sounds like it's getting louder. Drawing closer in some way. But how . . . ?

I opened my eyes and was startled to realize the vapors had folded back to reveal an open tourney field carpeted with thick, lush grass. White marquees formed a parade on either side of the meadow, each bedecked in red and gold pennants. In front of them, equipment racks had been arranged so that unseen champions might chose from a wide assortment of lethal-looking weapons. I completed a quick three-sixty and discovered behind me a fully decorated pavilion, resplendent in ersatz sunshine and festooned with ribbons and bows in the same heraldic colors.

The entire arena lay within a cocoon of milk-white fog, and despite my best efforts, I couldn't detect any other unliving soul.

Thud—thud, thud—thud, thud—thud . . .

As I spun toward the sound, a massive shadow detached itself from the mist at the open end of the field. My jaw dropped: there, not fifty yards away, sat an armored warrior atop a midnight-black charger.

Dressed from head to toe in steel, and with the distinctive inverted cross of scarlet and gold emblazoned across his surcoat and shield, I knew without a doubt that this was a Knight Tempter. The horse itself was huge, a courser, its broad chest and powerful body likewise protected by barding, spikes, and leather.

Armor and tack were coated in fine beads of moisture which glistened like diamonds in the illusory sunlight. Staring at them, I imagined for a moment what it must be like to face such a daunting team in battle.

My thoughts were definitely jinxed lately for no sooner had I contemplated that notion than the knight lowered his visor and raised his lance in salute. Then he then put his heels to his mount's flanks, and the horse jumped forward into a trot.

Mesmerized, I stood rooted to the spot and tried to fathom what it all meant.

Forty yards.

Their speed abruptly increased to a canter.

So, is this part of the process? Am I supposed to react . . . or not?

I chose to react and rolled to one side. As I came up, I unbuttoned my coat and threw back my hood.

Thirty yards.

Rider and steed altered trajectory, and the earth trembled beneath my feet. I gamboled again and drew my scythe. By the time I had dropped into a fighting crouch, I'd extended my weapon and primed it for combat.

Does he really want me to hamstring his horse? Or worse still, confront him directly?

They accelerated to a gallop. The beast snorted, its nostrils flared. Muscles bulged and the vibrations increased as divots flew. Like a portent of doom, the spear tip lowered.

Intuition kicked in.

No matter what's taking place, we're on the same side.

Twenty yards.

We're on the same side, we're on the same side, we're on the same side . . .

Despite the danger of the situation, my gut was telling me not to resist them. They were here to do a job. I had to work with them.

Ten yards.

Oh, bugger! I need a raise.

Against my natural instincts, I collapsed my weapon, stood tall, and threw my arms wide. At the very last moment, I squeezed my eyes shut and yelled, "I am no threat to you, or to the treasures under your protection."

It seemed like a good idea at the time, but my voice sounded as feeble as a wet fart flying in the face of thunder. As their shadow blotted out the sun, I decided I wasn't so sure anymore.

Shit! Shit! Shit! Sh-iiit!

"Oof-fuuuuck!"

The tip of the lance struck with the power of a runaway freight train. Piercing leather, fabric, skin and bone, it lifted me high off the turf and carried me through the air as if I were merely a rag doll. I couldn't breathe, I couldn't think. Nothing else existed except the pain of impalement.

The spear impacted against something hard behind me, and shattered. The shockwave ran along the length of the splinter still embedded in my body and multiplied the agony a thousandfold. As I slid to the floor, the knight disappeared, and an ethereal voice hissed, "Impressive . . ."

I landed in a heap, blood bubbling from my mouth and nose and streaming through the fingers clasped tightly over the hole in my chest. For some reason, my self-healing ability didn't appear to be kicking in, and there was nothing I could do to staunch the flow. I threw my sight inward to assess the damage and tried to stop my heart.

No use. I was locked within a mortal coil. A terrible, hollow ache crawled its way up from the pit of my stomach, only to give way to a wash of cold, then prickly heat. My vision began to waver and recede. The strangest of sensations wrapped itself around me: All discomfort faded and without knowing why, I suddenly felt heavy.

It took me a moment to realize—*this is death approaching.*

"There you go, old boy. Not to worry."

I twitched as an unexpected voice intruded.

"Don't you worry now, I'm a doctor. I'll soon sort you out."

A doctor? What's a doctor doing here?

Strong hands flipped me over and examined my injury. I tried to see who had come to my rescue, but my eyes refused to cooperate.

"Hmm. That's a nasty wound, but I have something here that will take away the pain. I take it you're not allergic to anything? Penicillin, ampicillin, cyanide? Ha! Only joking, I don't want you fading away on me just yet."

Great bedside manner.

Whoever this guy was, he wasn't gentle. He lifted my head by the hair, laughed in my face, and then abruptly let go. I saw stars as my skull slammed back down to the ground, but the impact helped clear my sight. My vision wavered and then came back into focus.

Someone was kneeling at my side. Dressed in a style reminiscent of a nineteenth-century physician, he had turned away from me to rummage around inside a black case adorned with a decorative motif—a silver skull and crossbones if I wasn't mistaken. I could hear clinking, as if glass bottles were being jiggled together. Sure enough, my mystery savior removed two small test tubes from his bag, humming a merry tune as he mixed their contents together in a separate vial.

Next, he extracted a syringe from his pocket, complete with needle, and filled the barrel with an evil-looking green liquid. Turning back to me, he said, "Normally, I'd let you ingest this little concoction, but where's the fun in that?"

Cream!

"How in the blazes . . . ?" I attempted to wriggle away from him, but discovered I couldn't move.

"Now, now," he cooed, "just be a good boy and lie back. This'll all be over soon."

He loomed over me and made a show of squeezing a drop of his foul brew from the tip of the needle. With a final leer, he stabbed down and impaled the side of my neck.

"That's it, that's it. Now I get to watch you die. Quite fitting, don't you think?"

A burning sensation exploded in my throat. Intensifying, it launched itself throughout my nervous system, quickly spreading into my heart, brain and spine. An involuntary spasm caused my teeth to clench, and my extremities started jerking with spasmodic convulsions.

Fury congealed across my brow, but all I could do was snarl at him.

Cream grinned in response and stooped to pick up my scythe. It responded to his touch, and began powering up.

Hey . . . ? That can't happen . . . !

A flush of realization washed through me.

None of this is real. It's part of the test.

A welcome sense of release trilled in the ether but didn't last long, as the taste of rising bile forced me to flip over onto my hands and knees. I heaved and vomited the contents of my stomach over the grass. Then, before I realized what was happening, my arms and legs commenced sinking into the ground.

Oh, for Azazel's sake, what now?

Wraithlike voices condensed out of the air, singing a hauntingly evocative refrain. As the melody clarified, the lyrics took on new meaning. Something deep within me responded to the call of the Knights Tempter.

They sang:

> "We have seen the places you have been
> And can never go again.
> Though dark and windswept
> And as bitter as a sea of souls,
> A bosom awaits to welcome you home.

Once lost but not forgotten,
You will be enfolded once more
Within light's eternal embrace,
Where you will rest,
Forever free of burdens . . ."

The words faded, snatched away by the breeze. Nonetheless, their import remained.

A paradox of some sort? But how does that relate to me?

As I tried to work out what it all meant, the foundations of the earth beneath me turned fluidic, and I found myself freefalling through thick white clouds. Wind howled as it hurtled past my face. As I broke free of the veil, majestic sunlight baptized me in coronal radiance. My insides heaved again; but instead of puking up my guts, my perspective shifted so that I somehow felt myself merge more fully into the unfolding drama.

A plummeting sensation seized me, body and soul, and sent me hurtling to my doom. Nonetheless, I drew comfort from an object grasped tightly in my right hand. I glanced to one side and saw a huge sword. It blazed like lightning, encompassing me within a violet and gold corona that bonded the blade to my flesh and inured me against the terrible drop.

Things happened faster. The rate of my descent increased. My internal alarm triggered. As I scanned the vicinity, something hurtled toward me across the vaulted sky, and my sense of danger peaked. Instinctively, I stabbed out. Glass chimed against glass, and a shower of prismatic light and sparks crisscrossed the heavens with glittering reflections.

My unknown adversary clamped his hand around my sword wrist. I returned the gesture and squeezed as hard as I could. Locked together, we tumbled out of control, over and over, each attempting to obliterate the other by sheer force of will. Vast ribbons of energy encompassed us in a living plasma field.

A suspended animation rush of impressions consumed me.

The terrible drop . . .

Pain.

Skin, glowing white-hot from devastating friction . . .

Intense agony.

Primary flight feather torn free by overwhelming drag . . .

Excruciating, prolonged torture.

A vast pit of malevolence rushing up from below . . .

Plunging.

Light receding above . . .

Forever plummeting.

A moment of clarity as the truth of my predicament finally registered.

I've fallen too far!

The endless spiral, down and down.

An overwhelming surge of heat as I pay the price . . .

Depravation.

The silence of eternal midnight . . .

Soul-crushing grief.

The inevitable pressure of all-consuming oblivion . . .

Anguish compounded a thousandfold.

Then an unexpected voice stabbed out of the darkness:

"You are more than you appear to be . . ."

Then why do I feel so emasculated?

"So much more. Do you not realize who you are?"

Who I am?

"What you are?"

I am alone. Stripped, barren, and darkened.

"Then why tolerate it? It is unnatural."

I deserve it.

"But you are a god!"

Don't be ridiculous, I am nothing. Debased, corrupted, and tarnished.

"A Titan to rival the likes of Lucifer himself."

That is preposterous. Outrageous. You shouldn't talk like that.

"Why? You are a colossus amongst insects. Why shouldn't you release the potential so artfully obscured and claim what could be yours?"

What are you saying?

"Overthrow the pretender, Satan. Why do you think Erra and his personified weapons were dispatched? He is insufficient for the task."

Blasphemy!

"Take the throne . . ."

Treason!

"Assume your rightful place as lord of the underworlds. Have you not personally consigned billions to such a fate? Who better to rule?"

No. Never!

Myriad images flickered toward me, each depicting the many realms of hell as they would be under the dominion of my governance. Desolate, inhospitable, and the epitome of pure misery . . .

Visions of magnificence. I felt emancipated, alive for the first time in millennia.

"This is who you were," the enticing voice cajoled, "and a portent of what you will become."

It was . . . it was . . .

A lie!

The very thought of it repelled me. Fueled by a sudden burst of unrighteous anger, I wavered on the brink of the Obsidian Rage, a deadly fury as harsh and abominable as all the levels of the netherworld combined.

"I know what you're doing," I roared into the night, "but you'll never break my resolve, Tempters. These are but fabrications sent to test my integrity. I refuse to play these mind games any longer. Now release me, or face Satan's wrath . . ."

My challenge pealed into the void.

"Very impressive . . ." hissed an unexpected voice above me. Its resonance echoed through the ether, then dissipated on the wind.

My skin tingled, and I found myself standing on a narrow gravel pathway leading up a small incline toward a fortified tower.

The Cloister of Scourging, I guessed.

A hulking great brute of a man dressed in simple gray robes stood before a lowered drawbridge. Behind him, a portcullis barred the way.

The welcoming committee? Or another test?

The guardian radiated great power and authority. Although he appeared to be in his mid forties, his aura betrayed the ruddy tinge of one who had served in hell for centuries. Arms like threaded tree trunks crossed a broad, finely-muscled chest. A combat scepter hung from a worn leather belt about this monk's waist. Something about the weapon set my teeth on edge.

Eyes like two chips of stone regarded me in silence. I was surprised to note a look of astonishment tinged with respect in their flintlike depths. "You made it then?" he stated.

"It would appear so." I patted myself down to ensure all the bits were in the right places and then turned to look about me. "*That* was one of the most unpleasant experiences I've ever had to endure and, believe me, I've suffered quite a few."

"It's supposed to be unpleasant." A brief look of anger clouded his face. "But sadly, not unpleasant enough, it seems."

"What do you mean?"

"I think it'd be better if I just showed you. As you've just tasted what it's like to face the Knights Tempter, you'll appreciate more than most just how daunting is the task. Hopefully, you'll put

a word in with His Nibs and be able to divert the heat of his anger."
He extended his hand. "I'm Friar Lemuel Tuck, the Warden."

"Friar Tuck? Seriously?"

Lemuel smiled. "No. Not that one. *I'm* the real deal, one of
the nastiest bastards you'll ever have the misfortune to meet in the
woods . . . but only if you cross me."

I grinned in return and took the proffered hand. Only then did
I notice it was a different color than the rest of his arm. In fact, the
stitching was exquisite, an outstanding piece of work.

I felt my fingers go numb through my gloves.

Unholy shit! How did he do that? "Did the Undertaker make
this modification?"

"He did, on His Satanic Majesty's instructions." He patted
the war hammer hanging from his belt. "If I didn't possess the
angel-hand, I wouldn't be able to wield the power of Godsbane,
my mace." He gestured along the path and began to lead the way.
"Please follow me, and I'll clarify a few things."

"I assume this all has to do with the reason why our Dark Father is going to be pissed at you?"

"I'm afraid so."

He took a deep breath and continued: "Tell me, would you
say the Knights Bridge was a formidable obstacle?"

"Are you kidding?" I couldn't prevent a claw from scratching its way down the chalkboard of my spine at the mere mention
of it.

"What did you find the most disconcerting aspect of your
experience?"

I thought for a moment. "To be honest, being confronted by
my nightmares made manifest, and being unable to do anything
about it except let the vision take me where it wanted. How did
they manage that?"

"*That*, dear Reaper, is due solely to the power of the mystery
we protect—the Key of Sighs."

"Key of Sighs?"

"Yes. Despite your high standing, it's a closely guarded se-cret and not something that you, even with your clearance lev-el, would have heard of. Don't feel insulted, it's a need-to-know matter."

"I'm not, believe me. My current assignment is emphasizing all the time just how little I really know. Seeing as you've men-tioned it though, what *is* this Key of Sighs?"

Lemuel shared a strange telepathic image with me. At first I thought I was viewing an oval piece of stone, but on closer inspec-tion the artifact had the texture of crystal, overlaid by the iridescent luster of a precious mineral.

"Is that a rock?" I murmured. "Silicate of some kind?"

"Believe it or not, what you're looking at is a chunk of the pearly gates themselves, taken during the original attempt to storm heaven. We call it the Key of Sighs because of what it can do. Any-one with sufficient strength of will can channel its divine nature to generate a sympathetic cosmic cipher—a key if you will—and . . . *Shazam!*"

"No way! Are you saying it can breach the Divide?"

My guide merely flared his eyebrows.

Fuck me!

Then a certain notion struck me. "But what does all this have to do with you? Or the Knights Tempter, for that matter?"

Lemuel responded by enlarging the psychic representation. The Key of Sighs circled idly, round and around; meanwhile I no-ticed what appeared to be two smooth areas along the upper quad-rant of its surface. From my perspective, it looked as if a gem cut-ter had excised two portions from the chunk itself.

He followed my gaze and explained: "As you can see, our Lord Satan had two slivers removed from the Key in order to augment its defenses. The surrounding miasma generated by the Knights is empowered by one of those flakes. Think of it as an environment laced by the very essence of God's Grace. A crux that acts as anathema to all who are hell-spawned."

I whistled.

The friar continued: "By its tincture, the Tempters are able to measure the physical, mental, and spiritual worthiness of all who seek to pass, for the Key searches out the darkest secrets of an aspirant's soul. From this, the Knights gain a foundation for each trial."

They certainly do! But I still had questions.

"And this is linked to your hand and the scepter?"

"Correct." Lemuel flexed his fingers and hefted Godsbane from his belt. "This weapon is forged from a subtle blend of medusanite and the second fragment of the Key. As I mentioned, were it not for the angel-hand, I would not be able to wield Godsbane's might in battle. Nor would I be able to do things like this . . ."

We arrived at the portcullis. Lemuel took a moment to compose himself and flipped the mace so its handle was uppermost. Then he pressed the heel into a small indentation next to an ornate ring-pull.

"*Lan khol yé zélah* (by all that is holy)," he intoned, "*pa-the eyl e-na shavat* (open to me now)."

"You speak the divine language?" I felt a familiar ripple of power as the metal grating rose ponderously into the air.

"A necessary evil, I'm afraid." He looked resigned. "The enchantments about this keep are comprised of both divine and occult essence; not that they seem to do much good, as I said."

I gasped. "Don't tell me someone's stolen the Key?"

"No! In a way, it's much worse."

Before I could ask him to clarify his remark, Lemuel gestured again and led me down a short flight of steps. We stopped before a solid oak gateway covered in metal studs and engraved with a host of cryptic sigils. The hairs along the back of my neck and arms stood up, and I realized we had arrived at the threshold of a powerful force field.

Lemuel removed a set of old-fashioned jailer's keys from a fold of his robe. He selected one, positioned it at the lock, and whispered a brief phrase in Hellanese. A spark of energy pulsed through the glyphs, and I heard a loud click. The entrance swung silently inward to reveal a similar corridor and identical-looking door about twenty yards away down a short slope. Braziers stationed within alcoves on either side of the passage burst to life as we stepped inside.

From the way he approached the next obstacle, I thought Lemuel would adopt the same procedure as before, but I was mistaken. This time, he used the shaft of Godsbane to operate the lock—as he had at the portcullis—and uttered a single word in the divine language.

At the next gate I spotted his pattern. The first doorway had been sealed by sorcery, the next by angelic wards. As such, Lemuel was patiently employing an overlapping strategy to overcome each successive barrier. We continued in this manner until, after more than fifteen minutes, we arrived at the final gateway.

This particular entrance was huge, fashioned from two great leaves of very dark timber. I examined its texture and determined it must be something similar to brazilwood, for the black grain was enriched here and there by knots of luscious red heartwood.

At chest height, the outline of two opposing hands had been fashioned into the surface of each panel; one on the left, the other on the right. The protective shield had power enough to make me feel as if a million insects were crawling across the surface of my skin.

My guide turned toward me. "Prepare yourself, Reaper. What you are about to see has only been witnessed by a handful of denizens in all the levels of the underverse. You might find it a little . . . overwhelming."

"Don't worry about me. My heart is black through and through and my soul belongs to Satan."

"Good to know. Nevertheless, I urge prudence." He winked. "You'll see why in just a moment."

Lemuel slung his scepter and removed a knife from the opposite side of his belt. He ran the tip of the blade across both his palms. As rich scarlet fluid flowed from the wounds, he placed each hand against the outline of its corresponding relief upon the panels. Conflicting energies blazed to life, red on the left, blue on the right, outlining his fingertips in coronas of lurid light.

He uttered a single word: "*Lem-esh* (Lemuel)," then stood back and made the sign of an inverted cross in the air.

His blood soaked into the wood's dark grain before my very eyes, and when I glanced at his palms I noticed the cuts had already closed over.

The background buzz cut off. The barrier dropped, as did the door, straight down into a hidden trench in the floor. My sensibilities were assailed by the pure, unadulterated glory of my personal opium made manifest.

The Bãlefire.

I staggered, and had to grasp the frame and lintel to prevent myself from falling.

A chamber lay revealed, similar to a one-hundred-yard vertical tube. The entrance I found myself occupying appeared to be the only one and had been positioned at the exact center of the chamber's height. At a point two or three feet below the ceiling, the Bãlefire erupted from thin air in a rush of pyrotechnic fury. It thundered down past our position to terminate in coruscating glory at the same distance from the floor.

I inhaled deeply and felt my potential swell.

"Careful, Reaper," Lemuel hissed, "so much tincture in such a confined space may present unforeseen hazards."

He's right, of course.

Only with the greatest effort was I able to prevent myself from leaping in, there and then, to feast.

Lemuel must have guessed my intentions. A firm grip on my shoulder refocused my attention away from the rose-tinted wonderland before me . . . and toward something else. "Look carefully," he advised, pointing with his other hand.

Having adjusted my sensitivity to compensate for the presence of so much limitless might, I was rewarded by the actuality of what I'd already seen by psychic representation.

"Behold the Key of Sighs," Lemuel breathed in a reverential tone, "a most puissant icon; and one of the great mysteries of the Divide, for by its sweet solace is the prohibition between our realms maintained."

Gleaming like a many-faceted precious stone, a basketball-sized chunk of the pearly gates hung suspended within the matter stream like the personification of tranquility made manifest. Its surface glittered as if dusted by a thousand mirrors, and in those reflections I saw an echo of the power of creation. It revolved slowly, over and over around its own axis while its hypnotic redolence called to me in ways I'd never imagined possible for one so dark-hearted.

The more I searched the mystery of its hidden depths, the more I found myself falling into it, meshing with it, and understanding the sublimity of its nature.

A dissonant tone grated on my nerves. Without thinking, I linked to the discord and manipulated the Key's position within the plasma strand. It twisted, revealing a portion of its surface that had previously been hidden; An ugly scar marred the beauty of its perfection.

"Bloody hell! Your thoughts presented a different picture. I thought you said an expert was employed to extract the samples for the defenses?"

"You are perceptive, Reaper. Rest assured, that wound was not inflicted by us. Our artisan was indeed skilled enough to take the cuttings without marring the Key's form or function. What you are looking at is much more recent. So here we come to the crux of our dilemma, for whoever committed this act of vandalism was making a statement."

"A statement, you say?"

"Of course. Think about it. They went to all the trouble of infiltrating one of the most heavily fortified locations in all of hell . . . and for what? Only to leave their prize where it was? Just so they could take a selfie and post it to Hatebook? No, they came here for a reason, and the realization of their plans involved a great deal of preparation. I dread to think what the bigger picture may involve."

Cream!

My visage darkened.

Lemuel noted my angry flush and moved closer. "You suspect someone of this outrage?"

"Am I that obvious?" I projected a sanitized précis of my dealings with Cream and his mysterious benefactors directly into Lemuel's mind, so he would better understand my recent frustrations.

He spent the next few minutes studying the data specifics, and then laughed aloud. "I see. *Now* it makes sense."

"What does?"

"Reaper, I suspect you've either been baited again, or been left another calling card."

"Calling card?"

"Yes." He pointed to the Key once more. "Please focus more acutely and tell me what you see."

I did as he asked and was surprised to discover that something had been wedged within the crudely-fashioned hole in the Key's perfect surface. Something small and shiny.

I frowned. "Do you know what this is?"

"Sadly, no. For all our arts, none of us possess the might to withstand the pure essence of the Bãlefire. Even I cannot enter, for the presence of the angel-hand might cause the wards about it to drop, giving away its location to those above who seek to recover it."

"So this setup effectively veils the Key from you-know-who?"

"Amongst others, yes. That's why I need your help. Because of your unique heritage, only you can hope to withstand such fury without triggering a catastrophic reaction within the shield's integrity."

Lemuel's statement puzzled me.

"Hang on a second, what about Satan and his fallen angels? Surely they could have helped you?"

"His Satanic Majesty fears to approach lest the mere presence of the Key prompt his ardor to attack heaven once more. Such a move requires careful strategy and execution, and he is determined upon certain success next time. When he comes for this blessed device, it will be at the hour of his devising, not before."

"And Samael and his brothers?"

"In all truth, he does not trust them to possess such might."

But he does me?

I didn't know whether to be shocked, honored, or downright insulted. Regardless, something Lemuel had just said hit a nerve:

"How do you think our intruder actually managed to enter? From what you've intimated, the barricades surrounding this site are formidable. If they're breached, there's a danger they'll fall. Our burglar didn't want that to happen, so he took precautions. But why? And how exactly would he do so? I could list the possible candidates on one hand, fallen angels and their mystic weapons included."

"Ah, I see what you mean," Lemuel replied. Then more quietly, "I fear the answer may lie in the realms of the forbidden. Things proscribed since the Time of Sundering. Understand,

Reaper, I only discuss such matters now because I wish to ensure the security of the treasure in my charge."

"By that inference, I take it you're aware of contrivances that could do this?"

"Of course. As the protector of the Key, it is my function to know of everything that might present a danger. Having studied the factors of this incident closely, I feel we may be forced to consider one or two utensils that should have been vitiated long ago. Such as the Sword of Damocles, or the Mermaid's Pin."

"What do these artifacts do?"

"The Sword, which in reality is a big dagger, negates all power, no matter who or what the source. The Pin is able to pierce the strongest barrier. They can only be used by the corporeal once, and even then at great cost. Both were ordered destroyed millennia ago."

Oh, fantastic. Another pile of shit I'll have to sort out along the way.

But I'd procrastinated long enough. "Right, you'd better stand back while I get this show on the road."

"Very well," Lemuel replied, "but if I may be so bold? Be careful to keep your aura under control. If the Key registers your presence, I fear your fortitude may trigger the divine wards, and that is something to be avoided."

"You don't have to worry on that account. The less I have to do with anything of heavenly origin, the better."

Yeah! I scolded myself, *you talk the talk, but how are you actually going to walk the walk, and pluck the item from the Key without touching it?*

I considered my dilemma from a purely practical point of view. *Physical exertion is out. If I make contact it'll activate the stone, and the Almighty's angels will descend on us like the proverbial avalanche, and damn the consequences. But if I use my hell-spawned abilities, that could also elicit an adverse reaction.*

I scanned the interior of the bore from top to bottom. My gaze came to rest on the spot where the Bālefire erupted from hydraspace. Opening my senses wide, I tasted the resonance of the matter stream as it cascaded through the chamber, and followed it down to the point where it disappeared.

Of course! It's so simple . . .

One of my primary attributes was the ability to phase through the ether. To do so, I incorporated a proficiency to blend with the very quintessence of hydraspace itself. However, I never actually breached the event horizon, as someone would do if they teleported. Instead, I merely skimmed the threshold between dimensions in a way that allowed me to jump between two proximate locations almost instantaneously. The point being, my molecules would temporarily mesh with those of the exotic medium through which I was traveling.

And if my essence is blended with the Bālefire, it shouldn't trigger . . .

In an instant, I was there.

At one with the roaring, writhing monstrosity that was the very heart-blood of infernity, I allowed its essence to sweep me along in a ferocious tide that took my esoteric breath away.

Part of my consciousness was aware of the expression painted all over Lemuel's face. My maneuver had obviously taken him by surprise. Fortunately, that didn't distract me from the task at hand: the Key of Sighs.

As the column of fire screamed down, it flowed across the dignity of the stone without generating the slightest ripple. Where the current impacted the mystery token, however, a violent eddy had been created. Swirling round and around, the miniature maelstrom concentrated the rushing energies so much that they threatened to vaporize the memento at any second.

Fortunately, that would no longer be a problem. Joining with the vortex for just an instant, I snatched the offending article from its perch. Then, indivisible from the plasma ribbon once more, I allowed the stream to carry me toward the terminus.

Moments later I was back, standing beside a startled Warden with a glowing—and exceedingly hot—souvenir in my grasp.

"Well, that was easier than I'd thought." *Makes a bloody change.*

Lemuel was dumbfounded. "How did . . . ?"

"Let's just say it's part of the unique heritage you mentioned, which makes me an effective Reaper. *Nowhere* is safe." I paused to carefully unfold my prize and take a closer look. "Now, what have we got here?"

The item in my possession was different from the messages I'd been left before. Although written by the same hand, and in blood, the author had somehow managed to stencil the words into a malleable, metallic sliver of paper.

This stuff feels like gold leaf . . . but far more flexible.

It was a very delicate piece of work, making me wonder how the text had been inscribed onto its surface without damage.

My latest clue said:

> *Kill jars,*
> *Pickled remains of past grievances,*
> *Both great and small,*
> *Marinating now upon their shelves,*
> *Preserves of the most succulent variety.*
> *Mine to savor when the fancy takes me,*
> *Sweet rich marrow,*
> *Toothpick finger-bones,*
> *Toasting your accomplishments,*
> *And flensing the taste of you from memory.*

"Well, well, well!" I fumed. "It looks as if I'll be settling some old scores much sooner than I expected."

"Is this from that Cream fellow you mentioned?" Lemuel asked. "And more importantly, do you understand what it means?"

"Oh, I understand it all right. And it's close enough to Cream to count as one and the same." I turned to the Warden and shook his hand. For some reason, the tingle running up my arm was much, much stronger this time. "Lemuel, thank you for your assistance. I wish there was some way I could repay you, but I've got to go. This clue tells me where I need to be. The sooner I get there, the better for all concerned."

Lemuel maintained his hold and grinned. "Then there *is* a way you can repay me. Simply fry the bastard who dared to make me look incompetent, then return the stolen piece into my care. None of us will be safe until the shard is reunited with the Key."

"I'll do my best."

"One thing more," he said. "Think of it as a parting gesture."

Before I could ask what he meant, Lemuel muttered something under his breath. I felt an icy-cold veil of darkness wash over my body. Everything went black for a moment and when I opened my eyes, I found myself standing on the sidewalk outside the Old Bully, right in front of a very surprised Hell Hound.

"How the fuck did you do that?" Nimrod spluttered. He jumped back, his usual composure totally blown.

"Do what?"

"You've only just this second walked into the mist on the other side of the street, and now . . ."

I grew quite concerned by the way he was staring at me. "What's wrong. Nimrod? You look like you've seen a long lost friend after far too long."

"That's just it, Boss, you haven't *been* anywhere. And all of a sudden you've appeared right beside me, glowing like a neon advertisement outside a brothel."

I stepped away and looked at my reflection in a window. Then I held up my hands. Power radiated from me in waves, and I

was shocked to discover I was indeed surrounded by a rich, strontium-red nimbus.

It must have been my exposure to the Bãlefire.

I sent my senses deep inside. *And come to think of it, I do feel
strangely invigorated.* "This is gonna come in handy."

"How so?"

I waved the latest clue in his face. "Thanks to the Knights
and the Grey Friars, we've gained a lot of time. *And* I know where
to go next. What say I use all this excess energy and take us there
in style, right now?"

"Sounds good, but where are we going?"

"We, my dear friend, are going to make a very public spectacle of a self-styled crime lord who thinks that attempting to murder
the Reaper won't have repercussions. You might want to get your
sword out. I have a feeling we'll be in the thick of it as soon as we
arrive."

Chapter 15: Consequences

A bitter wind pushed down from the distant mountains. Gaining momentum, the gale streaked across the pack ice. Its passage bullied the freshest layers of snow into outrageous twirling dances that only served to layer the frozen drifts in ever-thickening cloaks of white. The farther north they went, the stronger the squall, and the more Champ Ferguson's keen sight struggled to cope with the airborne needles being driven into his face at more than ninety-five miles per hour.

Perched as he was behind the pristine sail of a pressure ridge, Champ was afforded a degree of respite. Nevertheless, he was forced to squint and repeatedly blinked away the buildup of rime along his lashes that threatened to seal his eyes shut.

He glanced behind, where Yamato Takeru basked in the frigid gusts. Dressed from head to foot in seal fur, Yamato had thrown back his hood and allowed the length of his combat braid to stream behind him in the wind. A modern-day pair of Ray-Bans looked oddly out of place on this ensemble, as did the ivory-handled sword strapped to his back.

Lucky bastard! If I had his flair with the elements I'd do something about the blasted weather.

Champ peeked over the top of the ridge once more, only to be assaulted by a fresh flurry of flakes which proceeded to worm their way into his hood and down his back.

Dang my melt if I can see how I'm supposed to track this thing properly. Sunglasses screw up my ability to read spoor-sign, but without 'em I'm half blind.

He waited a moment for a lull in the storm, then tried again. So thick was the veil overhead that Paradise was barely able to punctuate the clouds; and where it did, the hurricane force winds ensured each delicate shaft of dappled light was soon obliterated by the grip of perpetual twilight.

We're in hell, for Azazel's sake. It's supposed to be all warm and toasty. Despite his own layered caribou skins, Champ shivered. *At least, that's what they told us in chapel . . .*

Yamato approached and squatted beside him. "Is it still heading toward Purgatory?"

"Straight as a die," Champ replied, "although Satan only knows what it's gonna do there."

"The Sibitti are a force of nature. They need no reason to wreak havoc on the weak and lowly, especially if it serves Erra's aspirations." He paused to scrutinize the glaring vista before them. "Has it shown any sign of slowing down?"

"Not really." Champ shrugged. "This one stopped dead in its tracks a few minutes ago, but it's still half a mile ahead of us."

"Really? Do you think it may be tired?"

"I doubt it. They don't seem to need a break, or a shit, or eat like the rest of us. It must be great to have the constitution of a personified weap– Jumpin' Jehoshaphat!"

"What? What's wrong?" Yamato's hand flew to his sword.

"It's gone!" Champ scrambled on his hands and knees to stare long and hard into the face of the storm.

"You mean you've lost sight of it?"

"Nooo. I mean the darn thing is *gone*, just like the others."

Yamato looked thoughtful. "It must have been communicating with someone, or receiving instructions."

"That's the third one we've followed that's upped and hightailed it away for no reason. Are you sure you can't track them in any way?"

"Tracking prey is your specialty, my friend. I merely employ the subtleties of my elemental gifts to keep us hidden from view while we're marking the sites of esoteric manipulation. Not a difficult task, seeing as the enforcers are incredibly powerful. However, once they manifest, or have teleported, it's down to you and your skills."

"C'mon then." Champ stood and dusted the latest layer of snow from his clothing. "Let's go and check. Perhaps we might be able to discover something useful at the site itself."

With no further need for caution, the Hounds quickly made their way to the approximate area where Champ had last spotted their quarry. Despite their proficiency, finding the exact spot was harder than they anticipated, and both spent a considerable time stumbling around in the worsening conditions.

"Are you sure this is the last place you saw our target?" Yamato called out. "I'm not . . . hang on . . .!" He froze, closed his eyes, and raised one hand in front of him.

Champ was at his side in seconds. He knelt and scanned the ground. "What have you got?"

"Ah, I see . . ." Yamato continued to probe the ether with his senses for a few moments. "It used a different method of travel. One we haven't seen before. That's why I couldn't detect it."

"Here you go. Shoot! Would you look at this?" Champ swept away a layer of frost to reveal a strange outline in the ice below.

Perfectly circular, the design looked similar to a kundalini yoga pattern used by ancient eastern mystics. "Can you see where the ground has melted and refrozen almost instantaneously? Whatever the Sibitti did, it must have generated a great deal of power to do this." He glanced at his companion. "Can you follow it?"

"I don't know . . . yet."

Champ hawked the contents of his nose and throat to the ground between them in disgust. "Shit! We're screwed then."

"Not necessarily." Yamato ignored the gesture. He was used to the quirks of his companion. "I'm sure Daemon will be interested in what we've discovered so far."

"Really? That his Hounds have developed a nasty habit of losing their prey?" Champ spat again. On this occasion, a trail of spittle froze instantly to his lip and chin, forcing him to wipe it away with the back of his hand.

Yamato moved closer. "You forget, these are Sibitti we're dealing with. Something is clearly fomenting for them to be moving about so openly. We've tracked them in New Hell, Hades, and now here, at the very borders of Purgatory. Why? What is their purpose? And who calls on them to abandon their quests?"

Champ was struck by a sudden thought. "If you manage to latch onto that new energy signature, perhaps you might be able to do one of your vision-quest thingamajigs? You know, scan the underverse and find out in which of the levels they're congregating?"

"And who with?" Yamato added.

"It'll be dangerous."

"And ripe with the potential for glory."

"If they catch us, those bastards will probably skin us alive."

"Since when has fear of the consequences ever prevented us from taking risks?" Yamato countered serenely. "This is the netherworld, after all. Even if we walk into a full-scale trap, it's not like we can actually die."

"But they can make us suffer." An evil grin cracked the ice coating Champ Ferguson's face. "I like it. Do your thing. The sooner we start, the sooner we can heat things up a little."

*

We crossed the threshold with weapons drawn. Nimrod ran forward a few steps to cover our advance, while I dropped into a crouch and spun back toward the portico.

I wouldn't put it past our Gallic friends to have installed something unfriendly to stab unexpected visitors in the back.

The geodesic plane continued to ripple for a moment, and the bridge flared a rich golden-yellow. Then it hissed out of existence. Up above, the phosphorous silver crescent horns that marked the terminus of the arch followed suit, dulling to plain white stone.

Clear, I yelled telepathically.

Same here, Nimrod replied, *although it won't stay that way for long.*

I skimmed our surroundings to get an idea of what we faced.

The foyer to the gate room atop the Awful Tower was much as I recalled. A metal gantry led down from the portal toward a circular reception area, which still bore the scars of my previous visit. Wide fractures lined the floor, walls, and ceiling in a spiderweb network of cracks that made the place look as if it might fall apart any second.

On either side of us, more than a thousand kill jars had been neatly stacked upon ledges, ranked in ascending tiers. Their contents bore stark testimony to the sadistic savagery of the vendettas still scourging the criminal underworld in Perish. A severed limb or excised organ here; a plucked eyeball or portion of flayed genitalia there; lone torso, coiled entrails, or the digits of one hand. All perfectly preserved with loving care and left to float in a personal sea of embalming fluid. Yet not one of the mementos could ever depict the full extent of suffering that went into their assemblage.

Nevertheless, these caught and held my attention for some reason.

Something's different . . .

Then it hit me. Although the main room hadn't been repaired, the shelves certainly had. From what I could see, they looked to have been rebuilt, placed on seismic stabilizers, and shifted back a few feet so they were now encased within the confines of reinforced glass.

That reminds me.

I checked to the front. The last time I was here I'd also damaged the special security screen separating the portal run-off from the rest of the top floor, and split the thing from top to bottom. It was missing.

The three fudge-monkeys I'd met previously—Speak only evil, see all evil, and hear nothing but evil—weren't.

I was swept by déjà vu as "Speaky" sat behind the reception counter, picked up the phone and began honking like a pregnant goose to someone on the other end of the line. Sadly, that was where the similarity to my past experience ended.

His buddies were ensconced behind upgraded defenses, two heavy-duty machine gun posts. Situated on either side and just behind the desk itself, both emplacements had been positioned on hydraulic rotational platforms and protected by a combination of armor plating and sandbags. To the left, I recognized a military issue He-XM313 anti-aircraft cannon; to the right, a Minigun and tripod setup peeped out from beneath a transparent bubble-cover.

Fuck me! They were waiting for us.

I thought back to my last encounter and realized Catraz had probably installed these precautions very shortly after his failed attempt on my life.

He's expecting repercussions at any rate . . . Best not disappoint him, then.

Just as I was about to move, demonic and human reinforce-
ments came pouring in through the door. They fanned out and
stood there, the men pale and anxious, the fiends twitching and
snarling as if waiting for some unseen signal to engage.

My gaze flicked across their ranks. As well as fangs and talons dripping with venom, I faced Hellishnikov 7.62s, M666s,
Hate-K submachine gun pistols, and even a few Tartarus EP13
heavy assault rifles.

So what are they waiting for, an invitation?

A split second later, I found out when a familiar voice blared
out of a hidden speaker: "Kill them! Kill them and stamp all over
their bloody remains. Don't be put off because he's the Reaper. A
bonus to the man who brings me his head!"

Crack-crack!

The chorus of multiple weapons simultaneously being
cocked served as a unified declaration of intent. In the silence that
followed, the distinctive whine of pneumatic barrels cranking up
only served to focus my resolve.

Nimrod? Left and center. I'll take this side. Enjoy yourself!

You too.

In such a situation I'd usually manifest, simply to ensure
the Phage boosted my perceptions sufficiently to meet the danger
head on. But having overdosed on Bãlefire, I was intrigued to see
how super-hyped my normal responses would be.

Blam!

The initial salvo was deafening. With so many rounds rain-
ing down all at once, there was no distinguishing one weapon
from another. I hit the deck and rolled for cover, leaving a scarlet
ribbon trailing behind me. I was still glowing from my encounter
with the Key of Sighs, and a swarm of metallic wasps following in
my wake buzzed angrily, blowing chunks out of walls and ceiling
as they tried to track my movements.

I laughed aloud. Not because of the adrenaline surge produced by the presence of so much danger, or from the heat of battle itself, but because I felt so alive. I'd never moved this fast without being augmented. The experience was exhilarating and fascinating, almost as if I were precognitive, and able to anticipate the flow and trajectory of each individual missile.

On a whim, I expanded my awareness even more, adjusting my reactions to compensate. The difference registered immediately.

In the background, a slower, rhythmic *thud—thud—thud* added a deeper counterpoint to the high-pitched serenade of the light-caliber bullets. The heavy machine gun had obviously opened up on the other side of the room, so I knew for sure Nimrod would now be just as busy as I, trying not to get his ass chewed to bits. But I couldn't spare much thought for him, it was taking every ounce of my hyper-energized concentration to avoid the lethal fusillade hammering toward me in a mesmerizing avalanche of glittering steel. Amazingly, I could see everything in a kaleidoscopic frenzy of slow-motion, altered reality.

Adopting a haphazard approach, I jinked, pirouetted, rolled, and feinted. Bounded, leaped, ducked and dived. Vengeful sparks flared and ricochets snapped back, impartially biting their originators instead of their intended targets. Men screamed and staggered. Muzzles fell, smoking and silent.

Regardless of the resistance, I snaked forward like a neon band of light.

Amid the tinkling cascade of spent rounds and ejected links, a rising sense of panic took hold. Some reckless fools broke ranks and tried to rush me. Their ill-thought maneuver only brought them within my reach and forced the Minigun operator to cease firing.

My scythe became a blur in my hands. Its ever-keen blade whirred like the wind, igneous and fluid. Heads rolled and limbs fell. Weapons clattered to the floor. Fingers still twitched, their dying nerves squeezing triggers in a hapless parody of impotent revenge.

And still I advanced.

Out of the corner of my eye, I noticed Nimrod was pinned down under a relentless onslaught from the .50 millimeter. Forced to stave off an unending deluge of shells big enough to demolish a house, he was unable to dispatch any of his opponents, who were slowly gaining ground on him. If this continued, I judged they would soon have him surrounded.

Time to even the score.

I slammed the heel of my staff into the deck and released a blinding surge of power. Opponents on both sides of the room covered their faces in fear and fell back a step.

I used the lull to my advantage. Twisting away from my antagonists, I leaped and pirouetted high through the air. Depressing the top stud on my sickle, I aimed the jewel toward a small group of hoods using the He-XM313 as cover. An unholy ribbon of lightning blazed from the gem and fried them all where they stood. I extended the discharge into a steady stream, and crowed with glee as energetic tendrils snapped and sizzled along the floors and walls, electrocuting those standing nearby as well.

But I wasn't satisfied. Not yet. Not with the sweet scent of death drenching the atmosphere, spurring me on and arousing my lust for darker deeds.

With a mighty roar, I compressed ever more potential into my efforts. The charred remains of my victims glowed white hot and then exploded, carbonizing bone and blackening metal in a paroxysm of rage that reduced cadavers to fine dust.

A high-pitched yelp rang out as tendrils of plasma continued to lick across the floor.

'Speak only evil' must have caught the tail end of the charge. How sad.

Only then did I drop to the floor. As I did so, I spun, side-stepped, and released two bolts of God's Grace straight at the He-XM313 emplacement. The entire post vaporized in a blue-white flash that left a steaming pile of molten slag behind.

Nimrod was amongst the survivors in an instant, his blade cutting a sanguinary passage through demon and human alike. Blood and gore sprayed the walls and ceiling in an ugly swathe of bubbling red and black potency.

I left him to it, for now only the Minigun remained between me and the door. That it was surrounded by a squadron of ghouls and the last detachment of hoods mattered not a whit, for they were obviously demoralized and confused.

I can help you with that.

To looks of mixed astonishment and trepidation, I sheathed my blade, stood tall, and slowly held up my naked hands. The radiant nimbus had reduced somewhat, but still grabbed their attention. I made eye contact with each and every one of them, cracking my knuckles repeatedly as I did so. Then I started forward.

Comprehension flared on the faces closest to me. Fear took hold and spread like the plague. As one, they let rip with everything they had.

But it was too late. Faster than anyone could follow, I was on them, weaving to and fro like the lethal instrument I'd been forged to be.

In less than ten seconds, more than thirty denizens lay dead at my feet.

Just one more to go . . . for now.

Even though I was too close for him to draw a proper bead on me, the Minigun operator was still firing blindly. I kicked the barrel of his weapon aside and then, with a cry of rage, clenched my fist and punched straight through the pod cover. The blow broke his neck. His eyes rolled into the back of his head, he slumped forward, and the ear-splitting crescendo abruptly ceased.

Within the confines of the gate room, the sudden stillness was deafening. A smell of cordite, scorched metal, and burnt flesh saturated the air. Dust and other particles swirled down from unseen nooks and crannies. I followed the flight of one particularly large piece of debris as it fluttered downward and then turned to survey the rest of the chamber.

The kill jars were my first concern. The rhyme had led me to this specific location, and I dreaded to think what might have happened to my next clue. But I needn't have worried. Amazingly, the armored glass had done its work. Despite a few ugly-looking scars and deeper pockmarks here and there, the glass had retained its integrity and protected the entire macabre collection.

I recalled how tough the roof of Infernos nightclub had been on my last visit.

Is that barrier made of the same material, I wonder?

Nimrod had hardly broken a sweat. I watched as he tore the shredded jacket off one of his victims and calmly used it to wipe the filth from his blade.

That's when I noticed something else. Something odd.

These bodies haven't dissipated.

I glanced back at the containers, and then at the structure itself.

Is there some kind of dampening field around this place that prevents dissolution? Or have they managed to extend the principle used for the jars themselves?

Spent links and empty casings tinkled and crunched beneath my feet as I ambled across to the nearest wall and tapped the metal plating with one bare finger. It felt as if an additional layer had been bolted on over the old panels; to my ear, it sounded quite dense.

Now that's a handy bit of intelligence to report back. Not only might this be a composite we've never seen before, but I'm itching to know how a thug like Catraz got his hands on it. Who knows, the Boss might even let me have some for the Den? The In-

quisitors would have a field day with this stuff lining the interrogation rooms.

I replaced my gloves and brushed myself off. As I did so, my thumb caught in a new addition to my attire; a fist-sized hole in the left-hand side of my trench coat. Puzzled, I checked further, and was shocked to realize my entire ensemble was peppered with a number of rents and bullet holes.

Only then did I take stock of my own situation.

While most of the damage was superficial, obviously having been caused while I'd pranced about like a demented ballet dancer, some of it was far more serious. My attention zeroed in on the site of several major injuries which still stung as they sealed over. I rolled up my sleeve. Sure enough, my skin wasn't glowing anymore. I clearly hadn't been quite as fast as I would have liked.

Of course it would wear off. And all the more so after what I've just been through.

I was a little pissed, to say the least. The wounds to my flesh would disappear in less than a minute. Those to my pride, however, would take longer to heal.

Suck it up, idiot! Pain is just weakness leaving the body. You should have thought of the consequences of using so much energy that quickly without manifesting. You have the Phage for a reason. Use it!

My fingers drummed against my leg in frustration.

No wonder Satan restricts my treatments. Such mastery could become quite addictive. Still, at least I know not to make the same mistake twice . . .

The muffled sound of shouting from outside disturbed my personal sulk session. I extended my senses and listened in.

". . . a move on quickly, boss, before those bastards get through. The CCTV's gone dead, so we don't know what's happening. *Merde alors!* Will you—"

Catraz!

I mentally relayed this new development to Nimrod, grinned, and inhaled sharply.

Nimrod guessed what was coming and ducked behind the remains of the machine gun emplacement. I exhaled, and released a massive pressure wave that blew the doors off their hinges. As luck would have it, they also took out the nearest guards ushering the so-called hardest crime boss in Perish toward his escape route.

That left only a half dozen heavily armed hoods, who quickly closed ranks about the Marlon Brando stunt-double hiding in the middle of their group. He appeared as panic-stricken as someone wired up to the national grid.

"Leaving so soon?" I bellowed.

Catraz screamed in terror. His goons reacted and leveled their guns. I phased and exploded into their midst before their first rounds had even been fired. The repeated thud of bodies and clatter of weapons hitting the deck was music to my ears.

I looked down through the transparent flooring and waved to the remainder of the security detail who had been caught flat-footed. Still inside the nightclub, they'd had no chance of getting here before it was too late.

Not that their presence would alter the outcome.

Adjusting my awareness, I sent a quick heads-up to Nimrod, and then stalked toward my prey. Catraz's face blanched white. He backed away and fumbled inside his jacket pocket.

Oh, no you don't.

As the Hell-Brass 6.66 Magnum left its holster, I snatched it from his grasp, back-handed him across the face, and tossed the weapon over the railing.

"Would you like to join it?" I asked. "I know you have a penchant for dropping things from a great height. I must admit, that displays a certain sense of karma I find most appealing."

"No, no, no. You can't. Don't you realize who I—?"

I slapped him again, harder this time.

Catraz flew across the deck and landed in a heap on the floor. He looked up in pained surprise, and his gaze jumped to my hands.

My grin was pure evil. I made the sign of the inverted cross, and then beckoned to him with my right index finger.

"C'mon, little man," I growled. "It's time to face the consequences of being a complete and utter dick."

"Leave me alone."

"I can't. You're in something up to your neck. I'll give you a clue. It begins with S and ends in HIT. Can you guess what it is?"

"I've got money, lots of money. Assets, too. Just name your price. Anything to make this go away."

For some reason, Catraz was finding it difficult to regain his feet and continued shuffling backward on his ass, heels and hands until he was pressed against the balustrade. Once there, he clung to the netting and began to sob.

I loomed over him.

The abrupt sound of combat behind me didn't break my concentration one bit. Nimrod would make short work of the latecomers, leaving me free to play.

"You should know by now that won't work," I warned. "I can't be bribed, and I don't have the slightest ounce of empathy for the likes of you. But seeing as you're so desperate to pay the price, let me tell you what your actions will cost."

He looked totally crushed, and yet seemed to cling desperately to the illusion that a ray of hope might appear out of nowhere to save him at the last second.

Time to spell it out.

I grabbed him by the throat, yanked him up so we were nose to nose, and snarled, "You really fucked up trying to kill me. And I mean *really* fucked up. So, I'm here to . . ."

My head dropped to his ear, and I lowered my voice to a bare whisper. Then I detailed *exactly* what was going to happen.

When I'd finished, I held him at arm's length. "Did you un-derstand all of that?"

The growing stain on his pants and the tears in his eyes showed he'd understood me perfectly.

Hell's bells, but I love my job.

Chapter 16: Testing the Water

I left Nimrod in charge of the mopping-up operations and instructed him to call the rest of the Hounds to assist. Searching the scores of kill jars for my next clue and removing the special wall panels would be long and complex processes, something the others could begin while I kept a promise.

Although I'm beginning to regret that promise.

My package was becoming rather tiresome. Although bound, gagged, and partially covered in a dusty old sack, my prisoner screamed and wriggled with every step I took. Mind you, I could appreciate that the thought of impending doom was probably spurring Catraz on to offer as much resistance as possible.

Not that it did him much good. The residents of Perish were as indifferent to the suffering of others as they were brutal and unfeeling. I thought of them as a "callous with a capital Tough shit sucker, so long as it's not me I don't care" kind of crowd. So the sight of the Reaper dragging a mysterious someone along by their ankles attracted little attention. And the closer we got to Pont

Snuff, the more deserted the streets became, and the less inclined people were to even glance our way.

On this occasion I was approaching from the direction of the Palais de Injustice, along the south bank. However, I had trouble spotting the difference between neighborhoods, for the congealing mists made it difficult to pick out any but the tallest major landmarks. By the time the first abutment came into view, the fog was so thick I could only see twenty to thirty yards ahead of me.

Catraz must have sensed the increasing chill and dwindling presence of traffic around us, for he fell mercifully silent.

Thank Purgatory for that!

At last, I stood before the spans of the oldest bridge in Perish, a place that epitomized the very spirit of hell. Eternal suffering, without a moment's peace. Moans throbbed out from the brume, exacerbating the mood a thousandfold. I took a moment to fortify my mind for the ordeal ahead, and noticed details I'd missed on my previous visit.

The bastions stationed along each side boasted the most ornate of embellishments. So lavish were they that each battlement could have been decorated by a master pâtissier. In defiance of the surrounding miasma leaching all color and substance from the air, so much thought had been put into the bridge's ornamentation that its arches reminded me of the side of a wedding cake.

I wonder why I never noticed this before?

A cackling chorus split the silence.

"Help me. For God's sake help me. I shouldn't be here—"

"No, help me. I'm the one who was wrongly condemned. I'm the one who—"

"Please, I beg you. Just look at me, anyone can see I'm innocent—"

"You bloody liars! You deserve what you got. I was merely tricked—"

"Ignore those fools. They just want you to step closer to the edge so they can grab you. I, on the other hand, have a genuine proposition—"

That's why!

Catraz must have heard the tirade as well, for he began to writhe and protest vigorously through his gag.

Someone's eager to get to his new home.

"C'mon, dipstick," I snapped, "let's get you settled in."

Prepared as I was, the siren calls were still hard to resist. Something in the tone of their voices and the emotions conveyed by their pleas reached deep down inside me to pluck at what little strings of humanity I had left.

I had to keep reminding myself: *This is hell. Everybody gets what they deserve . . . and then some.*

The enticements were as tenuous as the vapors through which they echoed.

"You've returned. We knew you'd come back. Just help me out so I can share the knowledge I've gained with you—"

"Bless you, Reaper. May Satan shower his fortunes upon you for the insight you've shown. Now, if you could just assist me—"

"This way, quickly, before the others interfere. I have the very thing to enable you to overcome the machinations of your adversaries—"

"About bloody time! Actions speak louder than words."

There!

"Don Pérignone? Is that you?"

"Read me, Reaper. You'll no doubt recognize what remains of my essence from when you were here before. It's not like I've had the chance to go anywhere."

Yup! That's him all right.

I zeroed in on his position and scanned the flickering residue of his aura. Barely readable, it nevertheless contained the acidic taint of one betrayed by circumstance and cursed by lingering impotence.

The surrounding entities shrieked in alarm, which only panicked Catraz all the more.

"No, don't listen to him—"

"He only seeks to betray you—"

"Don't be fooled. He's the worst of us all—"

"You can't be serious? He would sell his own mother for personal gain. You can't trust him. You mustn't."

It took every ounce of my concentration to weed out the distractions.

"Pérignone," I repeated, "are you still willing to trade?"

As emphasis, I lifted Catraz high into the air and dangled him over the edge like a wriggling worm. The resultant clamor from below pealed like thunder through my mind, and the murky waters exploded in a froth of seething agitation as spectral hands burst from the depths, groping imploringly toward a possible source of salvation.

"Silence!" I roared. "Or I'll see to it your miserable existence becomes even more wretched. How would you like it if I arranged for the Perishian Hellectricity Company to lay a few mainline cables into this stretch of the Inseine? Perhaps ask Satan himself to concoct a special power source, just for you? Fry your sorry assess all day, every day? You think it's bad now? Just wait until I've finished with you."

My threat did the trick. A thousand voices caught in a thousand throats, and the floating garden of puffy chalk-white fingers withdrew beneath the surface. In moments, even the ripples of their passing had disappeared. All except for the Don's, who managed to wave at me in a manner that somehow conveyed a sense of enduring patience.

"Of course I'm willing to trade," he spat, "and more. Just cut the crap and get me the hell out of this shithole . . . please!"

"Okay, but remember. The slightest sign of duplicity and you'll be back in there . . . eventually. My Inquisitors will get to play with you first."

"I wouldn't dream of double-crossing you, Reaper. As I already told you, you are unique in your value of honesty, so I've been totally straight with you. I demonstrated my willingness to trust you on the last occasion, by transporting you safely away. And I'll do so again, as soon as my feet are on dry land. Don't forget, even though I've been stuck in this muck-infested toilet for a few years now, I've kept my eyes and ears open. We get to hear things. Secret things. Whispers in the dark that filter their way down to the lowest dregs of society. And you wouldn't believe what's hidden under people's noses. Actions speak louder than words. Let me show you."

With infinite slowness I unwound the rope around my wrist and lowered Catraz, head first, toward the open embrace of his erstwhile mentor. Catraz felt the sudden motion and fought back with all his might against the inevitable outcome.

A pale face loomed from out of the depths. Eyes black as pitch and burning with desire fixed on their redemption. Skeletal arms twitched in anticipation.

They made contact. I felt a tingle of power and a transference of energy.

Two minds gasped as one.

Yes!

No!

A collective exhalation gurgled through the swirling current.

Once-gray flesh turned pink, flushing from the renewed vitality now coursing through its veins. Its opposite number stiffened and darkened. The rope perished, snapped, and dropped its load with a loud splash into the clutches of its new family. As it did so, Don Pérignone leaped away from the commotion, as hale and hearty as the day he'd been betrayed.

We both turned to watch as a waxwork profile sank to its doom. Clenched in the embrace of a score of pasty, bloated hands, Catraz trailed silver bubbles from his nose and mouth until obscured by shadow.

For some reason I found the experience strangely evocative and mused aloud, "Perhaps I ought to get onto the Hellectricity Company, just for the sheer fun of it? Can you imagine how the spooks will react? They won't have a clue when we'll actually turn the power on . . ."

"I couldn't really give a damn, Reaper." The Don emptied the contents of his nose and throat onto the ripples in typical Gallic style. "They're the biggest bunch of assholes I've ever had the misfortune to endure. I'm sure the latest addition will feel right at home amongst such company."

He paused to spit again, and cursed, "Bon débarras! Good riddance!"

Only then did I notice he was holding something in his hand, a box case of some sort that looked to be made of a marblelike substance. Covered in hieroglyphs, it was locked tight by an ornate seal of unknown material.

"A gift? You're spoiling me . . . and people will gossip."

"Thank you, Reaper. I knew you'd come back." He placed the box on the floor. "A mere token of what I hope will be a new and productive relationship."

I eyed the container dubiously. It was obviously warded, and I could sense the ancient magic that had gone into its fabrication.

"What is it?"

"As you know, those falling prey to the Inseine are shackled to their inception site by ethereal chains. They effectively moor you in place so you can't drift away from the area where this curse holds sway." He nodded along the watercourse. "It appears to run for a half mile in both directions. Those esoteric manacles are linked to physical things, big and heavy things; and the riverbed is littered with them: concrete blocks, burnt out cars, and so forth. Anyway, once I'd gotten over the initial shock of being double-crossed by that slimy, two-faced, no-good backstabber, I decided to make the best of my situation and examine my surroundings. Imagine my surprise when I discovered what I'd been anchored to . . ." He prodded the item on the floor with his boot: "This."

"And this is?"

"What I hinted at, the last time you were here. Did you think I was bullshitting?"

Don Pérignone opened his mind, and I was reminded of a vision I'd seen before.

A wide open valley stood revealed. On either side, two opposing armies waited. Selected champions marched forth to rousing cheers. One was a Titan made flesh. Towering over the other like a colossus over a gnat, his weapons gleamed in the midday sun and his shield bearers struggled to lift a spear more than nine feet in length. His opponent was diminutive; a mere herder of sheep whose only visible means of defense appeared to be a simple leather thong.

They approached one another. The man-mountain paused to peer down at the ground and deride the fool sent to confront him. The small figure ignored the taunts and concentrated instead on putting something into the sling he carried.

Closer now. A huge shadow blotted out the daylight as an insect whirred around the shepherd's head. A tiny dark object sped across the intervening gap, striking the giant square between the eyes.

The great warrior sagged. Massive knees gave way. The ground shook under the weight of a tremendous impact . . .

I staggered and shook my head clear. Time reverted to normal, and I stared at the box in astonishment.

"Are you telling me that's the Skull of Goliath? The actual skull itself?"

"Blind luck, eh?" The Don shrugged. "And true to my word, I make a gift of it to you . . . or whomever you wish to present it to."

"Why?"

"I'd have thought that was obvious. I'm in way over my head." He cocked a thumb toward the Inseine. "My time in there taught me that. Don't forget, we hear things in the river. I don't know how, but news from literally everywhere somehow filters down into the mud and silt, as if all the secrets in the underworlds can't stand being confined, so they find a way to squeeze through infernity's cracks. We've nothing else—sorry; I *had* nothing else to do except sift through the snippets. Listening here, learning there. Remember, I was better connected than most who wind up in there, so I understood only too well what was going down. Fanatics seem hell-bent on turning the natural order of things upside down, and I don't want that.

"And before you point it out, I *know* the underverse is supposed to be a place of eternal torment and suffering, where few ever manage to achieve a semblance of normality. But I was one of the lucky ones. My business connections had made life here better for me than it is for most. And while I had to contend with my own personal thorn in the flesh, as do we all, I still considered myself fortunate. Now knowing what I know makes me a liability. It puts a price on my head. So, I want my old afterlife back. And while it means I can't taste the finest wines and eat the most succulent morsels as I did when alive, I know that by working with you I'll at least get the opportunity to resume a more bearable existence."

As he spoke, I scanned the Don's aura closely. He was speaking the simple truth.

"And in return?"

"Just let me operate as I did before. I'm sure things will return to normal rather quickly now that Catraz is out of the way. I'll have to install a new set of lieutenants, of course, and clear out the lobotomized monkeys who helped him seize power in the first place. But once I've sanitized my staff, I will endeavor to pick up where I left off . . . with one important addition. My organization will now become a major source of intelligence for you—and for those from the Department of Injustice you wish me to work with."

Bella and Donna will be ecstatic, especially with the latest leaks.

"Oh, that reminds me," Pérignone added. "Just before I was released, I heard a little something about the identity of one of the leaks."

"A name? An address?"

"That's not the way it works." The Don's tone was apologetic. "No. We got information by way of images or phrases. Sometimes they were too cryptic to comprehend; sometimes you could understand them right away. While I know that some among the Blue Suits are involved, I don't know who they are."

"So, what have you got?"

"A phrase: 'Beware the betrayer's kiss.' I don't know if it'll do any good?"

*

Constructed from the shattered thrones of those he'd vanquished, Erra's divan had been erected atop a pile of rotting corpses and broken dreams in a huge chamber no denizen of hell could reach. Each year that mound got higher and higher, compounding his title as the undisputed lord of pestilence and mayhem.

Erra himself couldn't give two hoots. He was unconcerned with titles, and even less with what the damned thought of him. No, results were what mattered most to Erra, and results were what he continued to achieve.

The Seven had proven unstoppable thus far, causing a pall of fear to darken even the farthest-flung corners of hell as never before. He watched as the last of them arrived, personified weapons all, sons of heaven and earth, and champions without peer.

So attuned were they to each other that no sooner had the final enforcer materialized within the chamber than an unspoken signal passed between them, and they gathered at the base of the fleshy knoll in silence.

"You have done well," Erra began, "striking randomly and without mercy. The dread of you spreads throughout the entire underverse, and rightly so. However, brute force may have served its purpose, for terror can only do so much. We've all seen what happens to the weakest of insects when they are cornered. They can display a tenacity as frustrating as it is surprising. So, I've called you together because I want you to scheme amongst yourselves and come up with a fresh approach, one that undermines Lucifer's authority in a way that . . . that . . ."

The Sibitti waited patiently as their leader struggled to express the depth of his hatred, for this idea had obviously been fomenting for some time.

Erra sighed, changed tack and became more direct:

"Put it this way: you each represent the epitome of power, forces of nature and of chaos. Show me those qualities now, and foster a strategy by taking a leaf from the devil's own book. He thinks to dominate by taking from the weak and giving back what is precious in a way that perverts its true nature. His efforts have failed. Yours will not. The many levels of this netherworld are but a construct of his devising. Use them as you see fit. Employ your skills to turn the very fabric of his empire against him."

A thrum of approval radiated from the gathered champions, although only one, the second, dared to voice a question:

"And what of Grim? We were unable to fulfill our intentions in his regard, due to unfortunate timing. Does not the Reaper's office reflect on the integrity of his infernal master? A defeat for Grim is sure to be an embarrassment for Satan."

"True, Second, but be mindful of the fact that both you and your brethren caught Grim at an opportune time, when he was at his weakest. Three of you, where one should have been enough. And yet he displayed an unexpected resilience and resourcefulness that surprised you. Now he is fully recovered and empowered. Be wary of rushing in to finish what you started. Believe me when I tell you, there is more to that beast than meets the eye. He deserves further study before we face him again.

"I want you to plan on a far grander scale, for no matter how large an opponent, he will fall if you take his head. So aim higher. Satan is the primary target. Think! You are elemental creatures: How can we turn hell itself against him?"

Erra fell silent and watched in anticipation as the auras of his personified weapons flashed through all the colors of the rainbow with excitement. The Sibitti turned to face each other, and although not one of them expressed a word out loud, he could sense an animated telepathic discussion under way.

"Take your time," he told them. "Consider all the options at your disposal, and feel free to include the damned if you wish. Thus far, they have proven their worth repeatedly. Their insights and ingenuity may surprise you."

The buzz of mental conversation paused as the champions absorbed this latest snippet of information, and then continued apace.

Left alone with his thoughts, Erra turned his attention to another concern worrying him lately. The enigma that was Daemon Grim.

*

The overwhelming surge of dislocation receded. As the substance of infernity solidified about him once more, Frédéric Chopin felt the familiar embrace of his personal bane enfold him. Pain blossomed in his fingers. Radiating along his wrists and arms, it caused him to instinctively grip the lover's knot adorning his wrist. Only then was he able to relax.

"Are you back with us now?" Nikola Tesla enquired, concern evident on his face. "That looked to be a particularly virulent attack. Would you like one of my pulsar remedies?"

"Thank you, but no," Frédéric replied. "The discomfort reminds me of who I am and what's at stake. Without it, I fear I'd lose focus."

Piercing gray-blue eyes regarded the fallen composer closely, as if trying to read the many subtleties of the bitter battle Chopin endured.

"You? Lose focus? I doubt that. It's what drives you, and keeps you sane."

Stylish and meticulously elegant, Nikola rose from his seat and made his way to the modern-day mini-refrigerator. Seemingly at odds with the flamboyant furnishings of the Perishian apartment, the cold box nevertheless commanded pride of place next to the grand piano and drinks cabinet. Nikola poured a large helping of white wine over ice and hastened to his friend.

"Here, the chill should help ease the pain."

Frédéric received the beverage, closed his eyes and took a long deep draft.

Nikola studied his companion as he took his fill. "So, what did you see?"

"A change of direction, I'm afraid. It would appear my misgivings about our associate were entirely accurate. We are but a means to an end and, having served our usefulness, he deems us a dispensable commodity."

"What, he seeks to strike out on his own? Is he quite mad?"

"Amongst other things. In any event, the timing of his betrayal is both naïve and unfortunate, as certain roads have closed to us earlier I had originally envisaged. All I could see was overwhelming darkness, a veil of obscurity that clouded everything but the inevitability of eternal damnation—or obliteration."

"That is a handy gift you have, my friend. No pun or offence intended."

"None taken." Frédéric massaged his knuckles and grimaced. "But sometimes, I wonder if the cost is truly worth it? I've lost so much." His eyes clouded over as he contemplated former glories. "Still, *comme ci, comme ça,* beggars can't be choosers."

"What must we do?"

"Do? Why, we need to abandon ship, dear friend, with all speed."

"But what of the artifacts still in Cream's possession?"

"A necessary loss. For now at any rate. And later, who knows?"

Nikola reached into his pocket and removed another stringed bracelet, similar in design to that already worn by Frédéric. With an air of relief, he announced, "Just as well I have something prepared to counter him, isn't it?"

*

As Don Pérignone and I rode the elevator car back to the top of the Awful Tower, I continued to mull over the magnitude of recent developments.

We're standing at a crossroads. I can feel it in my bones. But with everything happening so fast, it's hard to determine which route to take. Is that a deliberate ploy, keeping me occupied, hot on the heels of one ghost after another so that I don't get the opportunity to stand back, jiggle the pieces, and see the bigger picture?

The image of a massive seaborne squall sprang to mind, and I snorted to myself.

Very appropriate. I need to step out of the storm and into the calm area. Once I find the storm's eye, I'll be in a better position to choose where to direct my efforts. And if I stay there, I can let things unfurl about me without being dragged every which way at once.

I transposed the impression into one more suitable to my purposes, and found myself looking at a cyclonic drama of all my most recent distractions: my topside assignment; Cream; the infiltration of the Devil's Children; plots and intrigue; ancient artifacts that should no longer exist; Erra and the Sibitti; relics that subverted the natural order of things; conspiracy by unknown adversaries; modern-day technology that replicated the most puissant arcane devices; Tesla; hell's most powerful wards subverted; Satan's rule undermined.

I found it difficult to know where to start, for each incident screamed past by me at a breathtaking rate. So fast, in fact, that I was hardly able to keep track.

So fast, in fact, that I was hardly able to keep track.

So don't! A voice inside my head whispered.

Eh?

A part of me, deep down in the furthest recesses of my mind, began to play devil's advocate. I decided to go with it to see where it led.

What do you mean, don't try?

I mean, don't try too hard. For a change, don't, especially when there's no need.

How did you work that one out?

You have rightly chosen the analogy of a storm. Expand that premise and a solution will present itself.

How?

Hurricanes form when disorganized areas of disturbed weather clash. That is what you face, a series of seemingly haphazard events, all thrown together in a manner that is churning up the restless sea of Hellkind. Breakers and whitecaps surround you at every turn. Trying to decide what to deal with first is distracting you. Don't. You're forgetting what lies at the center.

No I haven't, it's the eye. That's what I'm trying to step into.

Step into?

Yes.

Then you misunderstand. Don't step into the eye . . . be the eye. *Be the lodestone that attracts the convergence of all the waves. Currents have been set in motion that will run their course. Allow them to come, but instead of being sidetracked and attempting to label them in order of importance, just cling to the first swell that arrives and hold on, no matter how small and insignificant it might appear. Because . . . ?*

Because all the waves are generated from the same place, the actual source of the storm. And any of them will lead me back to where I need to go. Brilliant!

I decided I needed to argue with myself more often.

But only so long as I don't verbalize it. People think I'm strange enough as it is.

I smiled.

"Happy about something, Reaper?" the Don asked.

"Only that I seem to be making headway at last. So many questions have been flung at me lately that I haven't known where to start."

"I don't suppose I helped with that little snippet about the betrayer's kiss then?"

"It goes with the job," I sighed. "You've only confirmed what my own enquiries have highlighted . . ." *Someone wants out. This . . . pantomime is but a charade to cover the obvious. It's time to cut through the crap and start sanitizing. Thankfully, I know just the place to begin . . .* "And as I've come to realize, every little piece of the jigsaw helps."

Thinking of a jigsaw reminded me of something important.

I wonder if Bella and Donna have anything for me yet?

"Please excuse me," I added, "I need to make a private call. I'll see you at the top."

I phased from the carriage and materialized outside the gate room. Everyone else was still inside, so the place was deserted.

Perfect.

I took out my secure hellphone and dialed...

Bella picked up. "Daemon, hi. You must be psychic. Donna and I were waiting for one or two last-minute items to come back before we called, but you're gonna love some of the stuff sulforensic examination has turned up."

"Such as?"

"I'll start with the seizure from the Sinotaph . . ." The sound of a keyboard being tapped intruded. "Right, here we go. That ammunition you sent us, the Hell-Brass slug? They're definitely new. No one at the Special Weapons Division ever dreamed such a gadget could exist, yet alone fit into a bullet head. And none of our specialists here at the Fiendish Bureau of Investigation or at the Sintral Intelligence Agency has heard of them either. We even called the Satanic Intelligence Service, MI13, in Juxtapose. There's nothing like them out there. So, of course, we just had to try them out under laboratory conditions."

"And?"

"As you suspected, they do indeed work like a ripcord. The actual tip contains DNHA nanosoftware, very sophisticated and way beyond anything currently under development. They mechanically replicate an esoteric process by rewriting the subject's memory and residual cognitive function. It's abso–"

"Hang on. Are you saying these rounds have the capability to affect long-term awareness as well?"

"That's right. We've tested several bullets so far, and in each case the 'volunteers' have been completely wiped clean. They're a blank page, and have no recollection of their lives here in hell, or topside."

"Fuuuck! So what's Cornelius like now?"

"The Undertaker tells me he's acting exactly like our stooges. Extremely confused, unaware of the fact he's actually dead and condemned, and is so open to suggestion that if you asked him to bite off his own fingers, he'd happily do it. Needless to say, Bad Breath is pissed at the fact someone has managed to intrude into what is, essentially, his area of expertise, as it will make effective reassignment problematic."

And undermine Satan's credibility to make people suffer. Interesting...

"So we can't use his direct testimony as an eyewitness to identify any of the other players involved?"

"I'm sorry, Daemon, but no. Whoever's behind this has gone to great lengths to ensure they can't be directly implicated."

"As if we don't know it's Tesla!" I snapped. "With everything else that's happening, it can only be him."

"Our thoughts exactly. It seems the mild-mannered and benevolent philanthropist has turned a full one-eighty, and now wants the recognition and glory he spurned in life. Of course, with the company we think he's keeping, that's to be expected."

"I take it you've gained further info on Cream as well?"

"We certainly have. The lab results came back on the wine you sent us. Guess what? Our boffins have never seen a more elaborate concoction of naturally occurring hypnotics, hallucinogens, and suppressants. The volume of psychoactive ingredients contained in that one bottle alone was sufficient to run a small pharmacy. Together with the description already obtained, Cream's not shy in letting us know he's a main player. But we might be able to do something about that soon."

"Oh really?"

"Hang on a moment." The sound of slow tapping became more prevalent again. "Ah, here it is . . ."

"If this is good, you've both earned yourselves dinner at a restaurant of your choice."

"Well, get your tux to the drycleaners, big boy; you might be needing it."

"Please tell me you've got him?"

"We're getting there. Do you remember we had a tapeworm running on all recent hydraspace activity, especially trips of an 'unorthodox' nature?"

"You mean the search you were conducting on the tags that are secretly taken from everyone who travels through the Sheol-space continuum? Yes, go on."

"It's an ongoing process, but the field is rapidly narrowing. Cream is obviously working with Tesla, as their DNHA crops up all over the place at similar locations. Not necessarily at the same time, you understand, but close enough to point to an obvious connection."

I thought those prototypes masked their presence? "How are you going to proceed?"

"Because we've established a pattern, we're now concentrating our efforts on the identity of everyone else who turns up at those same places. And there's more than you'd think, as Cream and company are clearly offering all sorts of illegal shit for sale that will help the dissidents fight each other."

"Any names stand out?"

"Not as yet. There's the interest you'd expect from several of the more active rebel factions—Devo Pact, Che Guevara's lot, and the Democratic Resistance Freedom Fighters, to name a few. So we're focusing on individuals instead. Those who don't belong to any particular revolutionary cause, and who, therefore, might not have a legitimate/illegitimate reason to express an interest in such items . . ."

"Unless they were involved in their sale in some way, and therefore linked to Cream and Tesla?"

"You get my point. And I'm glad to say, we've narrowed it down to a mere few dozen candidates."

"Is that a fact?"

"Yes. The trouble is, because the obtaining of such information is highly classified and has to be conducted through the proper channels, we're still awaiting authorization for the next round of searches. But I know you're in a rush and want something in the meantime, so I conducted a wider, less restricted interrogation of the system. It picked out the most popular venue our mystery friends keep popping up in. I bet you don't know where that might be?"

"Don't tell me. Olde London Town? New Hell? Sulfurous Sands?"

"Close, but no cigar. I'll give you a clue. My HPS Satan-Nav indicates you're standing on one of its landmarks right now."

"Huh?"

The elevator carriage distracted me as it rumbled and rattled its way to a stop, so it took a moment for Bella's words to register. Don Pérignone waved at me from inside the cage and slid back the doors. Only then did the import of Bella's revelation hit me.

"Are you saying Perish is top of the list?"

"I am," she replied, "and of the twenty-six individuals we'll be taking a closer look at, nineteen have cropped up there. For some reason, Perish is a hive of activity."

The Don walked across the deck. The Skull was obviously heavier than it looked, as he was quite out of breath having to carry it any distance.

Time to test the waters, then, and see what the waves bring me.

"Bella, I've got to go. But thanks for that update. Let me know when you have something more . . . specific. And do me a favor? Split your list into those who are resident here, and those who live in one of the other levels. We might uncover something in the meantime to help us refine our efforts even more."

"Will do."

The line went dead and I turned to my latest partner in legitimate crime.

"There you are," he puffed, "is everything all right?"

"Better by the minute." I stooped to take the case from him. "Sorry about leaving you like that, but I had to make a sensitive call. It avoided the necessity of having to reap you."

Pérignone's eyes flared in alarm. "In that case, thank you. But if you're feeling the urge to kill someone, you can always help me clear out the dross in there." He cocked his head toward the gate room. "Remember, I've got to recruit some fresh meat, and you, dear Reaper, have an uncanny knack of knowing who to trust."

He's got a point. "Okay, I could do with a spot of fresh essence."

"Me too," he responded enthusiastically, "I haven't eaten properly in years."

Chapter 17: An Unexpected Journey

I was a bit disappointed to realize the guys hadn't uncovered the next clue while I'd been otherwise engaged, but when I saw the full extent of what they'd had to search through, I began to appreciate the scale of their task.

Over the years, Don Pérignone and Al Catraz had collected thousands of specimens, only a fraction of which were actually on display within the gate room. So while the various teams continued to busy themselves searching jars and dismantling walls, I dispatched the Skull of Goliath to His Infernal Majesty by way of UPDS, his very own Underworld Package Delivery System, and got down to the additional business of vetting hoods.

In five minutes I'd discovered exactly what the Don had meant by "not eating properly in years."

Nine out of ten of the first group were backstabbing schemers, loyal to no one in particular. I was ready to delegate them for immediate reassignment when Pérignone asked me to wait while he took a quick bite.

I thought it odd he'd want to delay proceedings while he skipped down to the kitchens to fix a quick sandwich. He didn't. Instead, Pérignone used Catraz's revolver to shoot the nearest unlucky dupe in the head, removed a handsaw from his pocket, and calmly detached the guy's arm at the elbow. Having completed his grisly task, he walked casually back to the desk and started munching away on the severed limb as if nothing out of the ordinary had taken place.

This took me completely by surprise.

Only then did our previous conversation at Pont Snuff really make sense.

"I had to contend with my own personal thorn in the flesh, as we all do . . . and while it means I still can't taste such fine wines and succulent morsels as I did when alive, I know that by working with you I'll get the opportunity to resume a more bearable existence."

When I questioned him about it, the former Parisian gourmet chef—and part-time black marketer—was entirely matter-of-fact about the way Satan had cursed him when he arrived in hell. Pérignone also went on to explain how that was where he'd got the original idea for the kill jars. Not because he was particularly bloodthirsty, far from it, but because the pickling process made the foodstuffs of his cannibal existence less disgusting. Of course, as he gradually immersed himself in the Perishian criminal underworld, the Don deliberately embellished the stories about his feeding process, which expounded his legend no end, and led to his rise to boss.

From the amount of heads he'd collected during a long and drawn out "evaluation" process—one that continued throughout the rest of the night and on into morning—it was clear my newfound informant had grown into the shoes he'd inherited.

Eventually, we reached the final batch.

This motley crew of six individuals were ushered in at gunpoint and paraded before us. Pale-faced and haggard, they dubiously eyed the growing pile of bodies and stacked pyramid of new trophies in their containers and began muttering amongst themselves.

To keep them on edge, I picked up my scythe and made a point of repeatedly slamming its heel into the decking as I walked toward them.

"Ladies and gentlemen, as you can clearly see there's been a change in leadership. Don Pérignone has resumed his rightful place at the helm, and I'm here to show my approval for the new regime. You should know I'm also here to ensure that only the most trustworthy employees remain on the workforce. So, let's cut to the chase . . ." I altered my perceptions so their auras stood out, dark and clear. "Do you promise to support the Don in this new endeavor and give him your loyalty?"

"Yes!" they replied as one.

Of course you do.

Their coronas flashed scarlet; and so did my blade an instant later, slicing through necks as easily as a hot knife through butter. The floor sprayed red and, almost immediately, their essences started to dissipate.

"Devildammit!" Pérignone cursed, "I was wondering when that would happen." He glared off to one side, where a cleanup squad from the GDSI—the *Directon Générale de la Satanique Intérieure*—Perish's special intelligence division of Satan's Children was carrying out the latest batch of the special wall plates that lined the gate room. "They've taken too many of my panels away. I installed them to create a dampening field around this entire structure. Without them, cadavers simply fade away and revert to reassignments."

The gang paused midstride, and the Don turned back to me. "I don't suppose you'd let me keep some, would you? Just enough for a samples chamber and perhaps a small interrogation room? It'd make keeping up appearances so much easier. "

I glanced at the team and shrugged. *Why not?* "Okay, if you go with those guys over there and show them where you want your panels, I'm sure they can help. They should have enough for a thorough sulforensic examination by now, anyway."

Before I had a chance to regret my decision, Pérignone bolted for the door and ushered them downstairs.

"Thank you, Reaper," he called back over his shoulder.

With nothing else to do, I ambled across to where Nimrod and the rest of the Hounds sat amid a cluster of urns. I could tell before I even reached them that frustrations were running high.

"Anything to report?"

Champ spat on the floor in disgust and proceeded to clean his nails with the tip of his bowie knife. Possessed of a more reserved nature, Yamato maintained his dignity and mentally updated me with the results of their Sibitti hunt.

I digested the contents of his report with interest.

"As you can see from my précis," he concluded, "we thought our pursuit a fruitless exercise until we drew a total blank here."

See what the waves bring me. "You're both positive none of the enforcers detected you before they flitted away?"

"Of that I have no doubt. Champ kept us at a reasonable distance to maintain our observations unhindered, and my abilities were more than sufficient to mask our presence. In each case, the Sibitti seemed intent upon their individual tasks, whatever that might be, until they simply froze in place for a few minutes. I was under the impression they might be receiving instructions, for each of them disappeared from sight soon after stopping.

"And have you been able to determine their location since?"

"Not as yet, although I *have* isolated the energy signature of their esoteric portals, which are extremely refined. I may need to be in close proximity, or within the actual realm in which they are congregating in numbers, in order for me to zero in on them. Obviously, our assistance here has delayed my experimentation in this regard."

"I didn't realize. Would you agree it's important we discover what they're up to?"

"Although it might not be connected to your current investigation? Most definitely. Their mere presence represents a threat to everyone's safety and to Satan's rule."

"Make it your priority then. And for Azazel's sake, maintain your distance. Your elemental affinity should keep you safe, but don't take chances. Use the portal here to take you wherever you need to go."

A quick glance at Nimrod revealed he was staring at me intently.

"Of course," Yamato replied. "We'll stop off at the Den first, resupply, and then get right on it."

"Yee-haw!" Champ leapt to his feet. "That's music to my ears. Something real to do, instead of just sittin' here looking through pickles and scratchin' my ass."

He was off, running toward the gate controls.

As the guys made ready to depart, I ushered Nimrod aside.

"Are you okay?"

"Are you?"

"What do you mean?"

"You're . . . different. Almost as if you left a part of yourself back at the Inseine. Did Goliath's Skull do something to you?"

"No, I've just had a change of focus, is all. With what's been happening lately, I've let myself get spread too thinly, and everything's unraveled. I've decided I'm not going to allow that to happen anymore. Each of these events is connected, so from now on I'll concentrate on one thing at a time and start pulling the threads tight. That way, the knot will come to me, and then we can do what we do best. Kill."

"Fair enough, I just wanted to—"

"Anyway," I said, "what's been the holdup here? I'd have thought the three of you would have unearthed something by now."

Nimrod gestured to the hundreds of jars surrounding us. "Where to bloody well start? It's been like looking for the proverbial needle in a haystack."

On a whim, I took out the last clue and read it again:

Kill jars,
Pickled remains of past grievances,
Both great and small,
Marinating now upon their shelves,
Preserves of the most succulent variety.
Mine to savor when the fancy takes me,
Sweet rich marrow,
Toothpick finger-bones,
Toasting your accomplishments,
And flensing the taste of you from memory.

We're obviously in the right place. But with so many jars to choose from . . . ?

As I considered the conundrum in front of me, Don Pérignone came blustering back into the room, spouting instructions.

". . . seen the dimensions of the chamber, I'll only need, what? Twenty of the medium-sized panels, twenty-four, tops? That way I can keep up the mystique, maintain my collection, and still leave you more than sixty to play with. So, if you let me. . ."

Of course! It's his collection. His accomplishment. He started it. If anyone would know the specifics of what's inside . . .

"Pérignone," I called, "a quick word."

The Don left off what he was doing and strode toward me. As he did so, I glanced at the last few lines of the rhyme again.

"Reaper?"

"How long have you been amassing body parts?"

"Phew, that's a good one." He pursed his bottom lip. "It must be going on fifty . . . yes, fifty years now."

"And how well do you remember your former victims?"

"Depending on how much they pissed me off, or how good they tasted, I can remember most of them. One of the quirks of hell, I suppose. Why?"

I showed him the section of the stanza that was bugging me.

"By any chance, would these words make you think of someone in particular? You know: because of what their death meant to you, or because of the opportunities their torture and execution opened up?"

Pérignone scrutinized the specified passage and narrowed his eyes. He read it again, and his aura flashed as the cogs turned over in his mind. Suddenly, a broad grin split his face and he mumbled, "The Snail!"

"The who?"

"The Snail: Sebastian Escargot. He was the first major boss I ousted to take charge of operations south of the river. Quite an achievement, as he'd built up his connections for over two hundred years before I came along. I'll always remember him screaming about how he would pluck out my eyes with his bare hands for daring to cross him."

He laughed at the memory.

"What did you do?"

"I ripped out his tongue and ate it in front of him. He still insisted on making a noise, so I cut off his fingers for good measure. Once I'd stripped them of flesh, I used them as toothpicks to clean my teeth. He was very stringy from what I remember . . ." The Don's eyes misted over as he recalled the experience. ". . . and then I smashed out each one of his molars with a hammer and chisel. I popped everything in a special jar and kept them on my desk for a while. Just like the Snail himself, actually. I kept him alive too, and gradually feasted on him, little by little, bit by bit, until there was hardly anything left."

My heart skipped a beat.

"And where is that jar now?"

"I'm not sure. Because it was so small, I ended up stashing it behind the main bar, along with one or two other little mementos. Al added some of his own, over the years. Whenever we got a bit melancholy, we used to get wasted together on Cursevoyeur cognac, and raise all sorts of crappy toasts to 'absent fiends'."

"Is it still there?"

"Your guess is as good as mine. I'll go and check."

Pérignone rushed off in the direction of the main salon. Time seemed to slow down, wade through treacle, and then stop. After what seemed like an eternity but was actually a mere three minutes later, my agony was over.

The Don blustered his way back into the chamber carrying an insignificant-looking pot in his hands.

"Here it is," he crowed, "the seal seems to have perished, but the contents appear intact."

A slight chinking noise became apparent the closer he got.

I took the jar from him and held it up to the light. Twelve white teeth and two sets of finger-bones clinked against each other inside the glass . . . and nothing else.

The sense of disappointment was overwhelming.

But I thought . . . ?

"Hang on a second." The Don sounded a little confused. "That doesn't look right."

"What doesn't?"

He tapped the side of the jar. "One of the molars looks as if it's got a filling. The Snail's teeth were perfect. So either that's not his, or . . ."

"Or someone went to the bother of removing it, drilling a hole, and putting it back."

I twisted the lid free, emptied everything into my hand, and poked through the contents.

"Here you go."

The tooth in question was now glaringly apparent, as the silver amalgam did indeed look oddly out of place against the otherwise pristine collection.

This is new, very recent in fact. There's absolutely no tarnishing.

Adjusting my senses, I looked within the crown.

There's something inside.

"Do you have any tweezers?" I mumbled. "Or anything else amongst your torture gear that will help me hold this without—"

Out of the corner of one eye, I saw Pérignone waggling a small leather wallet at me. It contained a set of dental instruments.

"I took the liberty of fetching these," he explained. "It seemed to make sense at the time. You want to examine a cavity, you need the proper equipment."

With a grin and a flourish, he held up a small torch in his opposite hand.

This one's on the ball . . . "Nicely done. Follow me."

We three trooped over to the reception desk and laid everything out. The Don switched on the flashlight, and held it above my head.

I selected a pair of pliers and held the tooth in place. Then I used the tip of a probe to dig beneath the cap of the filling. It lifted away much more easily than I expected, and I realized it must have been positioned like that deliberately.

This was just a plug. A temporary lid to protect whatever's inside.

Next, I chose the smallest excavator I could find to tease the edge of a tiny white-looking piece of fabric from within the cavity itself. Once the tip was exposed, I picked out some forceps and lifted the material free.

"Is that human skin?" Nimrod asked.

"It certainly is, treated to withstand prolonged immersion in chemicals."

Just what the doctor ordered, eh?

I shook the vellum gently, and because of its processing, it unraveled before our eyes to reveal a small rectangular message, measuring only half an inch by one inch. For the benefit of Nimrod and the Don, I linked with them telepathically and enlarged the parchment in their mind's eye so they could read the passage for themselves.

It said:

> *An apostolic number*
> *Lines the walls where vipers bite.*
> *But beware,*
> *My kiss can poison hearts*
> *And bring ruin to saviors.*
> *A bargain to slavery,*
> *For a mere thirty pieces of silver*
> *Revealed the hand of the betrayer.*
> *Remember,*
> *Everyone has a price.*
> *Who will you disown before the end?*

"This is written in a different hand," I mused. "Do you see how the letters maintain their form throughout the text? And the style is less . . . prosaic."

"Cream?" Nimrod suggested. "But what's he trying to tell us?"

"Er, isn't it obvious?" Pérignone said. "Don't forget what I heard while I was still in that bloody river. 'Beware the betrayer's kiss'? Does this relate to the identity of one of the Blue Suit traitors?"

"It must do," Nimrod enthused. "Jesus Christ was betrayed by Judas Iscariot, one of his apostles, for thirty pieces of silver. Judas literally screwed over mankind's savior for what was the price of a slave in those days. Look at the analogy."

"You're right," I grasped Nimrod by the arm. "And did we not investigate a certain matter recently where they employed a lawyer who just so happened to be called . . ."

"Judas!" we shouted together.

Pérignone spluttered. "Someone took out a contract on you?" He looked aghast. "Are they insane?"

"I'll tell you about it another time," I replied. "For now, I want the address of that bastard they use to legalize the contracts. Nimrod, we need to . . ."

The Don had gone abruptly silent and was staring intently at the clue on the desk. He seemed to be muttering something under his breath.

"What's wrong?" I asked.

He didn't answer immediately, and appeared to be working something out in his head. I cut him some slack, as he was proving to be as sharp as a button.

"I hope you don't mind my saying," he offered, "but you might be missing another aspect to the message."

"In what way?"

"Well, it's just that the poem tells us the apostolic number relates to a viper's bite. Now, I know my Bible as well as anyone else. Our Lord Satan was likened to a snake that bit God's savior in the heel. But that doesn't explain why the number twelve would 'line the wall' in the place 'where vipers bite.'"

"So what are you getting at?"

"This has a double meaning. It's giving us a location."

"A location?"

"Yes, an address here in Perish. I think the 'vipers bite' part is directing us to Place Venôme—a huge square in the First Horrondissement, originally built as a monument to the glory of Louis XIV's armies. Now it's an up-market set of apartments and hotels."

Bugger me!

"This may be the start of a wonderful relationship." I stared at the Don with newfound respect. "Just keep doing what you're doing, and I think you'll find your new lease of life quite rewarding."

Then I turned to Nimrod. "Put an info-request in on that address and grab your stuff. It looks like we're taking an unexpected trip."

*

The Hansom cab rattled past, forcing those pedestrians still out at this hour to jump for cover. Muddy water and goodness knows what other detritus sprayed in multiple directions at once, drenching those too slow or inebriated in a disgusting blend of festering liquids. Drunks and vagabonds lying in doorways or staggering along the sidewalk cursed and raised fists in outrage.

The hell-horse and carriage disappeared into the smog, the only evidence of its passing the resonant clip-clop of hooves and the clatter of steel-rimmed wood on cobbles, fading into the night.

Lambeth, in Victorian London, had been a dangerous place at any time of the day; Lambsdeath, its underworld counterpart here in the Juxtapose level of hell, all the more so. And yet a respectably dressed gentleman in top hat and tails sauntered through the vapor trails and dingy back alleys without a visible care in the world.

Every now and then he would tarry above a mysterious pile of rags or cardboard-layered den, and offer the occupants a pull from his silver hip flask. Very few refused; all were a source of amusement to their benefactor.

Doctor Thomas Neill Cream paused from his ministrations to chuckle and take his fill of the foul night air.

It's good to be back. I should have returned here long ago. He glanced about. This place holds so many memories, even if it is but a shadow of my former hunting grounds.

A drugged-up, spaced-out whore staggered past, one customer on either arm. Inured to the consequences of their actions, the trio ignored him as if he didn't exist and shambled off toward their inevitable appointment with flesh-eating insects and reassignment.

It lacks the sophistication of Perish, I'll admit that, but Juxtapose is the perfect place for those wishing to hide. So many eras, and little pockets of time. All out of sync, mixed together in a broth of menacing discontent and confusion.

Somewhere far off in the shadows, Cream's latest victims began retching and convulsing as the strychnine took effect.

Time to call it a night, I suppose, and see if my new subjects have managed to capture our prize. If this worked, it'll certainly put the cat among the pigeons.

As swiftly as he dared, Cream strolled out into the street and raised his cane.

"Good sir? Over here, please."

A large Clarence carriage rumbled toward him out of the gloom. Its lantern cut a fitful nimbus of light through the haze, and for a moment it appeared as if the cab with its asp-maned hell-horse would ride straight over him.

Instead it clattered to a stop and the teamster looked down, silent and suspicious, his whip raised and ready for mischief.

Cream waved an old godless florin between two fingers. "Lambsdeath Palace Road. And there'll be another where that came from if you can get there in less than ten minutes." He flipped it upward with his thumb.

The driver snatched the coin from midair and bit into its silver surface without the slightest sign of embarrassment. Satisfied, he pulled off his cap and placed his prize within a fouled handkerchief concealed beneath it. After a final check of the vicinity to ensure they wouldn't be accosted by thieves or worse, he sat back without a word and waited for his passenger to climb aboard.

They set off with a jerk, and soon Cream was surfing the mists toward his new home.

Yes, it's nice to be back. And although working on my own again will require some adjustments, at least I now possess certain utensils that should vouchsafe the success of my endeavors.

Chapter 18: Where Vipers Bite

The Don's description hadn't prepared me for *Place Venôme.* At seven hundred feet in length and four hundred in width, the opulent plaza paid tribute to the perfection Satan occasionally paraded before hell's denizens to tease the unwary and bait the ambitious.

Ornate Corinthian pilasters upheld a series of tiered pediments whose rustic yet ostentatious setting made one wonder if infernity's royalty had been invited to a "Palaces for Sale" extravaganza, an "in your face" taster of how sublime afterlife could be were it not for our Master's twisted perversions.

This is a bit flash for a lawyer. They either pay him far too much or he's definitely on the take . . . and I'm going with the latter.

The Venôme Column dominated the center of the square's broadest thoroughfare. More than one hundred feet in height, and originally built to commemorate Napoleon's greatest victory at Austerlitz in 1805, the column had been adorned by four hundred and twenty-five bas-relief bronze plates, each displaying a scene from Roman Emperor Trajan's conquests. But that was in the land of the living. Here in hell, His Satanic Majesty had commandeered the memorial and turned it into a testament to his enduring cruelty and ubiquitous authority.

I scrutinized the pillar from our vantage point at Rue de Talôn. The decorative frieze now portrayed the extent of Lucifer's domain and the depth of suffering inflicted throughout the many circles of the underverse. The statue on top had also been replaced by a colossal dragon rearing up on its hind legs, wings flared. Mounted upon a field of the dead and dying, its powerful jaws spat realistic flames toward the heavens, perfectly encapsulating the mood of eternal defiance.

Hateful rays of Paradise punctured the cloud base and flickered across the crown of the edifice, adding a final touch that made it appear as if the scales of the beast were engorged with power.

Way to go, Boss!

Inspired, I decided to study the lay of the land.

So, what have we actually got here? "Hmm. Apartments, houses, and a selection of consulates. A whole bunch of up-market hotels and several top-quality tailoring establishments . . ." I nudged Nimrod in the ribs. "Look at that! There's even an office of the local Department of Injustice. The sneaky fucker hid himself right out in the open amongst the Perishian elite."

Nimrod wasn't paying attention, being deeply engrossed in thought.

"I recognize this place from somewhere," he mumbled. Then his phone buzzed to alert him to an incoming text. "Hang on a minute. I think our request results are coming in."

While I waited, I altered my astral sensitivity so I could zoom in on the front doors and assess which was our target. My attention soon concentrated on the pristine exterior of a property in the southeastern quadrant. I refined my efforts and allowed my seeker-sense to bleed inside. Keeping things as light as I could, I gently expanded my consciousness to filter through the interior.

It appears to be empty. I'd better check the rear access points—

"By any chance, we're not going *there*, are we?" Nimrod said.

My expanded perspective snapped back into my skull like a released elastic band. Nimrod was pointing to the exact building I had been watching.

"Yes, why?"

"Bloody hell. I knew I'd seen this place. Chopin."

"Chopin?"

"That's right. Frédéric Chopin, the burnt-out musical genius from Warsaw in Poland. He was a true virtuoso until struck down by a series of mystery illnesses, which included temporal lobe epilepsy. His combined maladies robbed him of all ability to express his brilliance and, in the end, despite the care of his longtime lover Amantine Lucile Aurore Dupin, he simply wasted away. Because his life ended in Paris, Chopin is damned to serve out infernity here, in the Hellanese representation of his final home above."

My jaw hung open like a Venus flytrap. "How in Satan's name do you know that? Was it in the text?"

"The address check was, but the rest . . ." He shrugged. "That's down to National Gehennagraphic, every Frightday evening on PBS." In response to my look of incredulity, he concluded, "I'm a lot older than I look, don't forget, and I love most aspects of Hellonian history and culture. Chopin's exposé ran for a whole week only last month. You really ought to check out that show. It provides a lot of background information on all sorts of denizens, very handy in our line of work."

"Evidently," I muttered. Then with a sweep of my arms, I added, "C'mon, maestro, let's go find out how a true celebrity lives, and why he's mixing with the wrong crowd."

As we approached, I issued instructions based on my brief once-over:

"The property is a five-story house, and that includes the cellar. Apart from the main door, there are two rear exits; one at ground level and a smaller one from the basement itself. My scan showed nobody's home, but we need to confirm that. Neither did I sense the presence of esoteric wards or booby traps. But we're here because of Cream, so stay alert. When we enter, you start at the bottom and work up. I'll hit the roof space and head downward. Check for life signs only on the initial sweep. Once we're back together, we'll clear the premises slowly, floor by floor, until we can determine exactly why we've been led here. After that, I'll get Sulforensics in. Understood?"

"Perfectly."

"Okay, here we are."

We strode up the steps, and I removed one of my gloves. Placing my fingers to the lock, I said, "*Mi dreósgadh ânise!* (Open to me now!)"

The door opened with a sharp click.

"Go!"

As Nimrod sprinted forward, I phased and simply interpenetrated the structure of the ceilings and floorboards. My heightened senses pulsed outward like radar as I rose and skimmed across and through the constitution of the walls, furnishings, and fittings.

I was impressed by the quality of the décor. Whoever Chopin might turn out to be, he had good taste and high standards. Meticulous, if first impressions were anything to go by. Somehow, he'd managed blend eighteenth-century rococo glitz and modern-day efficiency without letting things become gaudy.

I completed my first round of inspection, and found myself in the loft.

No signs of human or demonic life whatsoever. Something caught my eye. *But what do we have here?*

Although tidy, the attic had nevertheless attracted the dust and detritus of sparse use and near abandonment. Mystery articles lay shrouded beneath large tarpaulins and old tapestries. Languishing in the far corner amid a pile of neatly stacked suitcases and chests I saw a rather large gap.

I hovered closer and examined fresh marks on the floor between the trunks. A sure sign that items had recently been moved.

He's gone, all right. Did he know we were coming?

After taking a moment to update Nimrod, I started my descent, concentrating on purely esoteric energy signatures. I took my time, slowly filtering down through the infrastructure, alert for traps and hidden danger.

An area on the first floor landing drew my interest. I scanned it again and, sure enough, my probe seemed to skip past a large storage cupboard. I materialized and stood outside the entrance. Moments later, I heard Nimrod thundering up the stairs behind me.

"Anything?" I called.

"It would appear Chopin and Cream did indeed know each other. There's a full laboratory setup in the basement that's now abandoned. Very extensive. Cells, too. So it looks like they were experimenting on people as part of whatever they were doing. Needless to say, any notebooks and files that might shed light on the matter are missing."

"Do you think that might explain the Blue Suit connection? Unwilling innocents as opposed to suicidal volunteers?"

"Hard to say. But I'm sure we'll find out soon."

"What about the ground floor?"

"Apart from a fully-stocked wine rack and larder, nothing useful. They obviously entertained guests down there. And from what I can surmise, they left in a hurry. Nothing personal is in evidence. No, it's this level where we really need to start . . ." Nimrod's voice trailed away and his brows furrowed as he noticed the closet for the first time. "What's *that*?"

"Yes, it caught my attention too. Somewhat out of place, isn't it?"

"I know my hunter's senses don't have anywhere near the finesse of your abilities, but when I look at it, all I see is a blank. It's like staring at a void."

"Precisely what I thought. And where better to hide something?"

I stepped forward to get a better impression of what I was dealing with, but every time I attempted to analyze the barrier, my probe was absorbed and compressed until it faded from existence.

Unholy shit, but that's strong! What are they keeping in here? Oh, it can't be?

Snippets from two recent conversations came back to haunt me. The first with François de UnBorn:

"It's just that . . . this person possessed a great deal of knowledge of things that shouldn't be spoken of. Things from . . . the Time of Sundering . . . in amongst his ramblings, he made specific reference to Vidium Swords, the Scroll of Divergent Union, some cup or other, and possibly—and I'm not quite sure about this—Goliath's Skull . . . he was not only aware of their existence, but was willing to part with a vast fortune to gain information as to the possible whereabouts of one or all of those artifacts."

François must have been talking about Chopin, our mysterious hand-wringing player.

Then I made another connection.

Damn. So that means Chopin's also linked to Tesla. I glanced about me at the corroborating evidence. *He has access to an absolute fortune if he's able to offer millions up-front for information, and can afford a place like this. But where did it come from?*

Then, part of my exchange with Lemuel Tuck struck a chord:

"How do you think our intruder actually managed to enter then? From what you've intimated, the barricades surrounding this actual site are formidable. If they're breached, there's a dan-

ger they'll fall. Our burglar didn't want that to happen, so he took precautions. But why? And how, exactly, would he do that? I could list the possible candidates on one hand, fallen angels and their mystic weapons included."

"Ah, I see what you mean. I fear the answer may lie in the realms of the forbidden. Things proscribed since the Time of Sundering . . . As the protector of the Key, it is my function to know everything that might present a danger. Having studied the factors of this incident closely, I feel we may be forced to consider one or two utensils that should have been vitiated long ago. The Sword of Damocles, or the Mermaid's Pin."

"What do these artifacts do?"

"The Sword negates all power, no matter the source. The Pin is able to pierce the strongest barrier. They can only be used by those in corporeal form once, and even then at great cost, and both were ordered destroyed millennia ago."

Hellfire! There could be anything on the other side, waiting to neutralize me once I've stuck my fat head in.

"Stand behind me," I ordered, "just in case."

As carefully as I could, I deployed my scythe and raised a powerful defense. Once I was prepared, I cast a spell similar to the one I'd used to enter the property itself.

"*Mi dreósgadh ânise!* (Open to me now!)"

A brief vibration juddered through the floorboards, and nothing else.

Okay, I'll use a hex instead.

This time, I placed the tip of my weapon against the handle, summoned my potential, and in a clear voice, said, "*An a' Satanas áinim, se thu àithen do ânise!* (In the name of Satan, I command you to open!)"

The air sizzled. Then the entire house rocked to its foundations, causing the chandeliers to chime loudly and plaster to fall from the cornices. Despite this, the way remained barred.

Nimrod and I glanced at each other in shock.

"That's an incredibly potent ward to be able to resist my hex," I acknowledged.

"What are you going to do?" Nimrod asked. "If you blast it open, it might destroy any evidence inside or, worse still, trigger a booby trap that could unleash Satan knows what upon us."

I had an idea. "Then I won't blast it. Remember, the Reaper has many attributes he can call upon. Brute strength and occult might are but two of the arrows in my quiver."

Before he could ask what I meant, I handed Nimrod my sickle, removed my gloves, and took a deep breath to calm my nerves. Then I leaned forward and pressed both hands against the door.

"*Tav yey qa-fé Ko- elaá, pa-the eyl e-na shavat.* (In the name of the Almighty, open to me now.)"

The resonance of the divine language operated on an entirely different pitch. Its purity breached the shield wall and negated the charms barring access to the threshold. The doorway vanished, revealing an open portal into a vaultlike cavern. Unfortunately, the only things I could see within were bare rocks and flagstones.

"That's impressive," Nimrod breathed, "to sustain an active wormhole leading to your very own Fort Knox, even if it has been emptied."

"It may be empty now," I murmured, "but only a short while ago, it wasn't."

The atmosphere inside was drenched in the vibrant residue of deviltry and angelic power, and I became lightheaded as soon as I inhaled its essence.

A fleeting glimpse of clashing energies flashed through my mind. I staggered, only to be steadied by a pair of strong, sure hands.

"Are you okay?" Nimrod's concern was evident.

"Yeah, I'm fine. Just an esoteric flashback. Even though the chamber is devoid of icons, the spoor is much more concentrated than I expected."

He steered me toward an open door just off the landing. "Then let's leave that for the investigators and check out what's in here instead."

He ushered me into a bright and spacious living area. Double windows at either end of the room indicated it ran the entire length of the house, and the open space was enhanced by a simple cream-and-white color scheme. A fireplace yawned opposite us against the far wall. Clustered around it were a large rectangular coffee table and three comfortable-looking sofas. The highly polished wooden floor was carpeted here and there with several strategically placed Persian rugs, focal points to catch the eye.

To my left, a Steinway grand piano filled one corner. Adorned with mother of pearl inlay, it made a dark and grainy island amid the sea of discarded sheet music scattered about its feet. A modern-day mini-fridge next to it looked out of place.

On the right, by the window, sat a simple writing bureau, easy chair and footstool. Various parchments and envelopes swamped the work surface, and crumpled paper spilled from the wastebasket.

Another beep alerted Nimrod to an incoming message.

"More info about our absent host?"

"Certainly is." He scanned the latest update. "After Chopin arrived in hell, the Undertaker compounded his earthborn afflictions a hundredfold, especially the unprovoked seizures caused by his epilepsy. It says here, Chopin would start to play a recital or compose a new work only to be kept from completing them due to the severity of his spasms. These convulsions were so powerful they actually broke his fingers." Nimrod chuckled. "And that's the way he's been ever since. Chopin is so deeply afflicted that he cannot finish what he starts, be it the playing of music, its composition, even the instruction of students. Satan has decreed that everything the maestro does remains unfinished."

A tingle skittered along surface of my skin.

"That's definitely our mystery player." I nodded toward the heavily laden desk. "Let's check over here first . . . Oh, and by the way, when you reply to that text, get another team sent over, pronto."

"I'm on it."

As Nimrod's thumbs flashed over his keypad, I strolled across to the secretaire, pulled out the chair, and took a seat. Every inch of the tabletop was littered with notes, part-written scores, and unfinished musings.

Where the heck do I start?

A notepaper with yesterday's date scrawled across the top caught my eye.

Hello? This is recent.

I picked it out:

'Dearest George,

Cling to hope. Soon, I shall acquire the means of true love's salvation, and free you from false grace. This past century has been fraught with bitterness and frustration, but fear not, our reunion will be christened upon a . . .'

Thereafter the handwriting deteriorated until it was unintelligible.

This is our man, all right.

I discarded the letter and started digging around for something else. Nimrod joined me and began sorting through a pile of communiqués neatly stacked within a wire basket.

I uncovered a leather-bound diary. The page was open at an entry from the previous week. Bold red letters declared: *'George—I will send for you upon your first awakening. False grace cannot hold you for much longer . . .'*

Even that short passage was marred by Chopin's bane.

"So who is this George fellow?" I mused. "Another bloody accomplice we've overlooked?"

I showed the pieces I'd already viewed to Nimrod, and his eyes widened in surprise.

"Oh! No, no, no. That would be George Sands, aka Amantine Dupin. I mentioned her earlier: Chopin's lover. He couldn't stand her when they first met, but, as is the way with human relationships, things changed the longer they were together. As his health deteriorated, however, their roles reversed. She cared for him to begin with, but Chopin developed an unhealthy interest in her daughter, Solange. Needless to say, that soured their affair, and she came to detest the sight of him. In fact, it was reported Sands began to view Chopin as another child, in the sense that he needed constant supervision. Because of his illness, Chopin never realized she despised him." Nimrod gestured. "Apparently, no one he met here in hell has thought to correct his misassumption."

"Ouch! Love's a bitch." I laughed aloud. Then I glanced through one or two passages again. "And he thinks he's going to rescue her from 'false grace'? Is he referring to the Almighty's Grace? As in heaven?"

Despite my bravado, something about Chopin's confidence made me uneasy.

How the bloody hell does he think he'll be able to . . .? Oh shit, the artifacts.

Nimrod abruptly jumped forward and snatched a large notepad from the desktop. He held it up to the light and looked across the surface of the uppermost leaf of paper.

"Excellent!" he purred. "You don't happen to have a pencil, do you?"

I rummaged through the secretary drawers until I found one.

"Here you go. What have you got?"

Nimrod laid the jotter flat and as lightly as he could drew the tip of the pencil back and forth across its surface.

"Because of his affliction," he explained, "I've noticed Chopin tends to use a heavy hand. He wrote something on the sheet above this one that I'd be very interested to read."

I watched as the white surface of the paper turned gray. As it did so, a uniform selection of words gradually stood forth.

Nimrod snorted. "It's a versed letter, to George herself."

"Here, let me."

Taking the pad from him, I expanded the stenciled message in my mind until we could both read what it said:

> *Most Precious George,*
> *I wish to bathe in the crimson pulse*
> *Of our hearts' fondest desire,*
> *Each beat, a wash of life*
> *Upon the shore of your prison's demise.*
> *The tide recedes,*
> *And my pursuit ends before it begins*
> *Across a sea of Bitter consequence,*
> *The fruition of our reunion grows near.*
> *So take heart, my love,*
> *For soon, your bosom will be free of grief.*

My eye was drawn to one reference in particular, and my blood ran cold:

A sea of Bitter consequence? But that's impossible. Not only is such a thing prohibited by law, under pain of unspeakable suffering, but those waters are murderous, even at the best of times.

I decided it might be best to keep this information to myself. At least until I could be sure.

Aloud, I said, "Can you see any reference here to a connection with the Devil's Children? You know, anything that might help us narrow down our search to fewer departments?"

"Daemon," Nimrod replied, "that'll take a lot of digging. You need to get someone in here you can trust."

Good point!

I refined a complex telepathic probe and sent it hurtling through the ether toward a pair of minds I knew were loyal to a tee.

Donna answered first: *Problems?*

You could say that. I paused to transfer a concise package of recent intelligence, including my concerns. *If you don't mind, I'd like you two to manage this stage of the operation personally. Choose your team carefully, and if you can, try to get bods from the Devil's Own. As you know, all those chosen for the special division of the Devil's Children are beyond reproach and I have a feeling we'll need their single minded devotion to cut through the chaff.*

Will do!

Bella chimed in: *Are you constrained for time? It's just that, the smaller the numbers, the better we can maintain control. Obviously, that'll mean it will take longer.*

I thought about it for a moment. *See what the waves bring me . . .*

Okay, good idea. While Nimrod and I continue to concentrate on Cream and Chopin, you look for anything specific to the Blue Suits and Devil's Children. I'm sure you appreciate my worry. We need to establish how many are involved and, dependent upon the actual division they work in, what kinds of personal data they can access.

You're fortunate then, Donna assured me. *The Den is very much in the public domain. Everyone knows who the Reaper is, and what his Hounds and Inquisitors do.*

Sorry, but you're missing my point, I countered. *If the leaks work in the wrong branch, our targets will not only have access to some very sensitive and private information, but you can bet your bottom dollar Cream and company will ensure they'll also have possession of items to negate our defenses and abilities. Until I can update the wards about the Den, my people are vulnerable.*

A sense of unified purpose and determination trilled through the ether.

We're on this, Bella and Donna replied in unison, *trust us.*

I do!

With that, they severed the connection.

Good girls.

I blinked my eyes back into focus to find Nimrod staring at me. "All sorted?"

"It is now. C'mon, we need to get back to Olde London Town; there's something I need to check out."

As I tried to stand, a powerful tremor rocked the building. My balance was slightly off from my long distance hail: I tripped and went to my knee

"What in Hades was that?" I snarled.

"I don't know. Does the metro run beneath us? Perhaps there's been an accident?"

I sent my astral sight powering down through the substrata.

"No, it felt deeper, much deeper."

"A hellquake then? No matter how stable a place might appear, everywhere gets them at times. His Satanic Majesty loves to remind us all of his overwhelming power and authority."

"Hmm." I wasn't convinced. "Our lord has a funny way of showing his stability, I might have . . ." A pungent, chemical tang assailed my nostrils. "That smell is familiar."

I looked down and discovered that I'd fallen close to the overflowing wastebasket. The aroma was coming from a scrunched-up sheet of paper near the top of the pile.

"Is that embalming fluid?" I sniffed the offending article to make sure I had selected the correct one, and started to unfold it. *Yes, it is!*

For some reason the smell reminded me of Don Pérignone's prized kill jar, where the preservatives had leaked from the dodgy lid.

But what if they hadn't? I experienced a revelation. "Hey, do you think Cream and Chopin have had a major falling out?"

"What do you mean?"

"The Don thought the seal on the jar of our last clue had perished and leaked. What if it hadn't? What if the leak had been caused deliberately, and whatever was originally inside had been replaced with a clue that led us here? Not to Judas or any other Blue Suit, but to Chopin's home address. Someone we didn't know existed, except by oblique reference to his mystery poems and shady descriptions at several of our target sites."

Nimrod appeared genuinely surprised. "You think they've had a falling-out? But this place is empty."

"No, it's abandoned, not empty. All the indicators point to Chopin leaving in a hurry."

The possibilities of this development were mind boggling.

"So what have you got there?" Nimrod asked as he helped me to my feet.

"Let's take a look, shall we? Hopefully it'll help."

I placed the crumpled piece of paper on the desktop and smoothed out yet another in a long list of rhymes. But this one was different.

"It looks to have been completed by two people," I murmured.

The first portion, clearly written in Chopin's declining style, read:

> *As passing as a paper cut upon fragile, gossamer skin,*
> *I leave my mark,*
> *Noxious, invisible, and uninvited.*
> *Escape is impossible, for once ingested,*
> *You are inclined to do my bidding.*
> *Fear not,*
> *Your scars will be an epitaph*
> *Of a life snuffed out before its time.*

Claret, rich, and thick,
Spilt from scarlet lips,
A birthmark, excised forever.

Cream had then added the following:

We mourn your passing, in red-bricked cathedrals,
Stately monuments to shadow and gloom,
Subterranean arteries
Of oily water and noxious fumes.
And screams, don't forget the screams
Echoing in vaulted chambers,
Where the dripping, gurgling resonance
Of carcass, garbage, and chamber pot
Fester in pools of stagnant abandonment.
Do you feel cast off?
Like a tuning fork that reverberates
To the flotsam and jetsam
Floating beneath our feet each day?

At the very bottom was an additional line:

Seeing as Chopin couldn't deliver, have this one
on me . . . for old time's sake.

Signed with a flourish, I could almost taste the twisted kick Cream had gotten from penning it.

"He's starting to get personal," Nimrod observed.

"*Started?* Do you know what I think this is?" I waved the note in the air. "I think Chopin wrote *this* as the original clue, and Cream replaced it with the one that led us here. Cream wanted us to discover the identity of his partner in crime, *and* where he lives. Then, realizing that Chopin would have fled, our worthy doctor came to this very house, added his little bit at the bottom, and left it here for us to find. I wouldn't be surprised if there's been a conflict of interests. Cream wants out. Has done all along. If what you say is correct, Chopin doesn't, *but* . . . he wants to bring someone in from heaven. These guys thought they were on the same team to begin with, but now they think they're nearing their goal, it's led to conflict . . . and Cream stuck the knife in first."

"Then why go to all that bother? What point is Cream trying to make here?"

We took another look at Chopin's segment.

"His whole poem is a definite threat," I muttered, "but who could be the target? Hang on! 'A birthmark, excised forever.' Hmm, birthmarks . . ."

Moles, bruises, café au lait. Then there's a stork bite, port wine stain . . . oh, and of course, a strawberry birthmark . . .

"No way! Strawberry?"

"But surely she can handle herself?"

"Tell me about it . . . unless she was caught by someone with arcane weapons in a place where she usually lets her guard down. Somewhere she goes to relax . . ."

I studied again what Cream had inferred from the second half of the clue.

Bastard! He is *making it personal.*

Opening my mind, I focused my thoughts along Strawberry's intimate mode.

Strawberry? Strawberry, this is urgent. Answer if you can hear me?

Nothing but telepathic static hissed back.

I went cold.

We have to go, now!"

Chapter 19: Divided Loyalties

The cenote had existed for millennia, an ancient cave-well with all-devouring limestone jaws. Always open to the elements and forever ravenous, its bowels displayed the evidence of perpetual hunger: they were lined with the detritus of root and vine and, of course, with the remains of those unfortunate enough to fall in from the realms above.

Overgrown in mold and decay, the atrium brooded in shadow. Stalactites hung from its roof, frozen like crystal tears at the moment of expression, paying homage to those pioneers now lying in their grave below. For only once they had fallen to their doom had those brave explorers rediscovered mysteries unseen for centuries.

The silence of the vault was punctuated by the constant *plink, plink, plink* of water dropping from far above into black-mirrored pools; and every now and again, eerie moans issued forth from the constricted throats of deeper tunnels.

A blinding pillar of transforming plasmic brilliance pierced the gloom. Lichens, roots, and ancient gut rock that hadn't seen the light of day for an age were bathed in phosphorous glory for but a moment, and then the cavern's interior found itself host to more than three dozen souls, once men and women.

Some barked orders, others illuminated lamps, the remainder opened equipment rolls. Two figures detached themselves from the throng and made their cautious way along a ledge toward an adjoining gallery. The first massaged the knuckles of his hands, while the second took great care to sheath a long silver cylindrical object within an oiled cloth.

"Congratulations," Chopin beamed, "your latest multi-phasic portal generator worked like the proverbial charm." He looked back at the combined squads of mercenaries behind them. "Everyone appears to have arrived safely, limbs and organs intact."

Tesla smiled. "I could say the same of you. Your vision was spot on!"

"Of course. While everything else I do is blighted by this accursed place, the unexpected consequence of the Undertaker's interference continues to prove faultless. Without it, I fear I may have gone insane."

They stared about themselves for a moment, taking in the splendor of broken columns and water-generated anthropomorphic carvings that looked as if, over eons, the dying had attempted to record their existence when faced with their inevitable demise.

"Whenever I visit these places to recover what I've seen," Chopin continued, "I always feel as if I'm intruding on sacrosanct landscapes where humans should never tread."

"Technically, we aren't human," Tesla jibed. "We gave that right up long ago, once we damned our souls to hell—or at this precise moment, Purgatory. So, by all means, intrude away, I'm sure no one will mind."

Both men chuckled.

"I wish we had more time to explore these hidden halls." Chopin's face adopted a wistful look. "Just think of what treasures we might uncover. But time is pressing and I need to recover the Moral Compass with all haste."

At the mention of their objective, Tesla focused.

"So what will this contraption do, exactly?"

"The Compass is an empyrean tool that acts as a combined lodestone and sextant and is designed to navigate regions of reality protected by wards of great esoteric power." Chopin sidled closer to his companion and lowered his voice. "I have foreseen a great upheaval, my friend, wherein the very fabric of the netherworlds will be threatened. Whatever the outcome of this cataclysm, I need to ensure that I can reach a certain destination unhindered. The Compass will allow me to do just that, for it remains true through any medium; heavenly, hellish, and mundane."

"Why not simply use one of my multi-phased generators? They'll get you to wherever you need to go in the underverse."

"Because I'm not going anywhere *in* the underverse, Nikola. I'm going someplace in between, where we can't be sure your orbs will work."

"I see . . ." Tesla appeared unnerved. "Then we had better hurry our friends along." He turned to the soldiers gathered behind them. "Colonel Banner? A moment of your time, please."

Colonel Severin Banner, a thirty-year fighting veteran and commanding officer of the "Cursed and Proud," one of the hardest, most vicious bunch of mercenaries ever to tarnish the realms of the damned, came skipping lightly across the rocks. "Gentlemen?"

"Remember, your men are searching for an old sea chest, about four feet square," Tesla began. "If you think of pirates, you won't go far wrong. That chest will have been down here for a long time, so the wood may have rotted and spilt its contents into the filth and muck you see about you. Tell your soldiers to look for black, tarnished pieces of metal. That'll be pieces-of-eight, your bounty. My colleague and I are interested in the arcane items amongst those coins, talismans of scientific value—"

"Yes, I remember," Banner said. "You only have to tell us once. I have my lads and lasses sorting out the metal detectors and thermal imaging equipment as we speak."

"Thank you for your tenacity," Tesla replied, "but I thought I'd better stress how time is of the essence. Our agreement of a fifty-fifty split still holds. That works out to ninety million in adjusted diablos. However, if your officers are able to locate what we require within the hour, your cut will increase to seventy-five percent. Is that clear?"

The colonel's eyes sparkled. Without a further word, he spun on his heels and began bellowing fresh commands. The mood permeating the cavern sharpened, and the makeshift camp shifted to a higher gear.

"This diversion has proven costly, but necessary," Chopin sighed. "But so long as it keeps us ahead of Cream and the Reaper, I will be content."

"Do you think our former associate will create more trouble?"

"Oh, I have no doubt of it. The items in his possession give him the advantage of both speed and surprise. Regardless, we have more than enough remaining to complete this venture." Chopin fingered the lover's knot tied about his wrist. "And don't forget, through the link we now have with him, I remain alerted to his machinations, sometimes before even *he* is aware of them."

*

Erra couldn't believe what he'd heard. The air above him boiled with malevolence and the ground beneath shuddered as he struggled to contain his surprise.

"Really? This is how you would seek to undermine him?"

"Yes, Lord," replied the First, spokesperson for the Seven, "for our experimentation thus far, although restrained, has shown the lithosphere, crust, and mantle responsive to our manipulation."

"But do you think it will work sufficiently to cause widespread doubt and fear?"

"Most certainly, for once we have achieved resonance with the quiddity binding each realm of hell to the other, we can sever the anchors holding them in place, disrupt hydraspace travel, and effectively isolate each circle. Sire, terror and anguish will rock Satan's empire to the core, and his domain will never be the same again. But please be aware, until we are ready to expose our machinations, we must confine our efforts to sparsely populated areas. Once we gain access to the geodesic arch, however, we'll hit the most fragile realm first: Juxtapose."

The charged atmosphere abated as Erra's agitation turned to satisfaction.

"As always, you have done well, my champions. By all means, proceed with your endeavors, and report back when you are ready to unleash hell on . . . well, hell itself."

*

In life, Vice-Admiral Horatio Nelson was one of the most inspirational leaders ever to exist. I admired his superb grasp of strategy and unconventional tactics and the "up and at them" attitude that had made him an absolute demon to face in battle. His reputation preceded him, so that after he arrived in the underworlds, we in Satan's service were very happy for him to continue his tradition of conquest and victory.

So focused was his dedication to duty that within a hundred years of being appointed, Nelson had effectively reduced the mayhem being wrought by feuding revolutionary parties across hell's endless seas to nearly nothing.

His Infernal Majesty rewarded Nelson by allowing his top-side monument to co-exist here, in the Juxtapose level of Olde London Town. Situated in Travulgar Square, the Darkmoor granite of Hellson's Column always drew the eye, providing a fine testimony to the ruthless character Satan expected from all his celebrity minions.

I liked it too, but for other reasons.

Below the statue, away from prying eyes, was a secret facility. A private set of rooms combined with a torture chamber belonging to Strawberry Fields, my most ruthless Inquisitor. We'd often enjoy coming here together on our rare days off, either to spend some quality time alone, or to refine our "interview" techniques on those subjects unlucky enough to have incurred our wrath.

Apart from a tight-knit circle of friends, no one knew about it.

Or so I thought.

Having left Perish via an emergency portal, Nimrod and I immediately made our way to the Den of Iniquity, just in case Strawberry was engaged in interrogating prisoners in a shielded part of the castle grounds. But she wasn't there.

Next, we tried the Black Tower and her private apartments, where we drew a similar blank.

Only then did I reveal my fears to Nimrod.

Cream's portion of the clue referenced the screams echoing from chambers within "red bricked cathedrals," and "stately monuments to shadow and gloom" where "subterranean arteries" literally festered with garbage and "the flotsam and jetsam" of Hellonian society ran beneath their feet each day.

Strawberry's little complex had been built directly below the stately monument of Hellson's Column, and could only be accessed from an entrance opening onto a major sewer junction—a hub, built from the finest blood-red bricks diablos could buy.

Nimrod and I finally made our way there with all speed.

"The door looks intact," Nimrod offered. He peered into recesses hidden in darkness. "And none of the defensive measures here have been triggered. But I suppose we have to expect that if Cream's using the . . . what was it again, Dagger of Damocles?"

"Close enough," I replied. "And remember, if he *has* got something like that, it'll probably negate our supernatural enhancements as well. So I'll not give him any advance warning by trying to use my astral sight, or phasing through the air. We'll go in the old-fashioned way: on foot, using eyes and ears only. If you spot him, employ your natural brute strength and agility and snap his spine. Try to leave him alive if you can. *I* want to be the one who sends him for reassignment."

"I'll do my best."

My recent experience with the strong room at Place Venôme gave me an idea.

For all their considerable strength, the barriers didn't nullify angelic power. Perhaps a bolt or two of God's Grace might be just the thing I need here?

Subconsciously, my left thumb shifted and came to rest against the second stud down from the top of my weapon. As swiftly as I could, with my other hand I entered the manual entry code into the command console, and then provided the necessary DNHA sample.

The vacuum seal disengaged, and the panels slid open with an audible hiss. Although quiet, the acoustics of the sewer tunnels made it sound like a leviathan having a gas attack.

Cursing silently, I led the way in.

The reception area, sparsely furnished, contained a desk, a few chairs, one filing cabinet, and two cells adjacent to the doorway. Those cells were empty, clean, and eerily silent. I sensed something amiss almost immediately. Strawberry was as meticulous in her work as in her private life, and yet here the security hatch leading to the private interior rooms was ajar. She wouldn't have left it that way.

Then I spotted her mobile phone on the desk. She never went anywhere without it. A quick check of its call log revealed the memory had been deleted.

I sent a telepathic warning to Nimrod: *We have company.*

Elusive as smoke, we drifted toward the next obstacle and waited at the threshold, listening.

It was as quiet as the grave.

Do you hear anything?

Nimrod gave a brief shake of his head.

Right, I'm going to edge the door open. You look inside and tell me what you see.

Nimrod nodded once, then pressed his back against the wall. He fiddled inside a pocket flap and produced a small extendable mirror. After adjusting for his desired length and angle, he positioned it at the sill and gave me a thumbs-up. I started to push.

Thankfully, the well-oiled hinges made no sound as they moved.

We linked minds so I could see through Nimrod's eyes. A crack of light spilling from the foyer into the passage beyond grew wider. Nimrod twirled the handle of the mirror back and forth between his fingers to extend our view.

We both knew the layout intimately. A short corridor led into a living area and kitchenette on the left, with a bedroom to the right. Along a further hallway stood a final door to the interrogation room. Strawberry had deliberately designed her outpost this way, since she always felt the act of torturing someone to be intensely arousing and liked her workplace to stay close at hand.

From what we could see, several lamps had been left illuminated inside. That would only be the case if Strawberry was actually here.

Without a word, we melted into the spider's lair, alert and ready for anything. Nimrod headed left; I peeled away to the right.

Strawberry had definitely been here: sheets were drawn back and her side of the bed rumpled. I smiled. Even when we weren't together, we tended to stick to our own sides.

Just like a couple. Eh . . . ?

I sobered instantly at that thought, as a number of other factors registered nearly simultaneously.

The first thing I noticed was her electric alarm clock, knocked out of position, facing the rear edge of the bedside cabinet. The top had been cracked open, as if someone had attempted to reach for the weapon she always kept inside: Strawberry's personalized Cobra's-Fang two-shot pistol. I pulled the drawer out the rest of the way and sure enough, the gun was missing.

But did Strawberry actually take it, or was she prevented?

Her scent still lingered in the air, along with a subtle hint of something else—something foreign. That scent didn't belong here and set my nerves on edge.

Poison?

I dropped to my hands and knees and looked under the bed. Ominously, one of Strawberry's ruby slippers sat upended in the middle of the floor, along with a piece of white gauze. I fished the cloth out, and the tang intensified.

She was *drugged . . .*

A sound from behind alerted me to Nimrod's approach.

The other side is clear, he thought, *she must have been in bed, asleep, when—*

There's only one way to know for sure. I turned to look at the only remaining barrier. *Let's get this over with.*

We moved forward, then stood listening outside the chamber. As before, silence ruled. With extreme caution, Nimrod tried the handle, only to find it locked.

I held up my hand, pantomimed counting down and then kicking the hatch.

He nodded.

We took up position, side by side.

Three, two, one, now!

Even without arcane augmentation, Nimrod and I were incredibly strong. Years of rigorous training and hard living had seen to that. With an almighty crack, the steel panel snapped free from its hinges and sprayed the interior with a lethal shower of concrete shards and metal splinters. The door itself flew through the air, clanged against the opposite wall, and landed upright. After teetering on its edge for a moment, it crashed to the floor amid a pile of debris.

Apart from the bloody remains of a lawyer draped across one of the torture racks, the room was empty. He'd been gutted, Jack the Ripper style, and a piece of paper had been left pinned to his forehead by a delicate jeweled knife.

Predictable as alw– What?

A very subtle but noticeable resonance permeated the area close to the body. I was intrigued as to its source, for I thought the odor might explain why the corpse hadn't faded yet and why our friend didn't stink like the rest of his fellow backstabbers. Fighting down my agitation, I looked closer and realized the victim's name badge was still pinned to what remained of his chest under all the muck and gore. I wiped the stain of his lungs away and identified him as Judas, one of the Devil's Children and our pet snake in the grass, now deceased.

"Well, there's no divided loyalties now," I mumbled, "coerced or not. Strawberry's missing, and I'm betting we're about to find out where she's been taken."

I yanked the blade from Judas' skull and slipped the note free. No sooner had I done so than his new reptilian carcass dissolved. A familiar, disgusting stench wafted through the air. I gagged, coughed, squeezed the tears from my eyes, and held our latest installment in front of me.

Written in Cream's own hand, it said:

> *I saw the life in your eyes,*
> *The energy of sunlight,*
> *And of Jovian vistas unseen.*
> *You were beautiful,*
> *But the Revelation Eight you away from inside.*
> *Now debased, you are darkened,*
> *Wormwood,*
> *Oh fallen star of heaven.*
> *Chained, with salvation in sight,*
> *Your redemption lies beyond your grasp.*
> *But fear not,*
> *A release is imminent.*

I knew it! "Oh, you are fucking idiots!"

"Who, me?" Nimrod asked, unaware I was venting my anger at absent fiends.

"This clue," I brandished the note in Nimrod's face, "reveals just how far Cream and Chopin are willing to go to outdo each other. It's bloody lunacy."

"What are you talking about?"

"You remember that love poem you found on the pad by using a pencil? You know, the one Chopin wrote for his beloved George?"

I broadcast the memory telepathically, so he could see it again:

> *Most Precious George,*
> *I wish to bathe in the crimson pulse*
> *Of our hearts' fondest desire,*
> *Each beat, a wash of life*

Upon the shore of your prison's demise.
The tide recedes,
And my pursuit ends before it begins
Across a sea of Bitter consequence,
The fruition of our reunion grows near.
So take heart my love,
For soon, your bosom will be free of grief.

"Yes, of course I do," he replied. "What's your point?"

"At first glance, it might appear that he was merely twittering away about reclaiming his lost love from heaven so they could be reunited here in hell, yes?"

"That's right. We discussed it at the time. Chopin doesn't realize how much George Sands came to detest him, so it's—"

"But did you ever stop to wonder *how* he might go about achieving his aims? I didn't say so at the time because I hoped against hope Chopin wouldn't be stupid enough to contemplate it, but his message contained some interesting references to things that obviously have a double meaning. Places he might go to ensure the success of his schemes. I'll give you a hint. Look again at the fifth through eighth stanzas of his note."

Nimrod adopted a thoughtful pose as he studied my mind once more.

I couldn't wait more than ten seconds: "Now look here." I held up Cream's latest breadcrumb and pointed to one line in particular. "This is another little pointer. "Revelation *Eight* you away"? Duh! Excuse me for blaspheming, but a certain book written by one who can't be named contains a passage in Revelation chapter eight, verse eleven, which says, and I quote:

"'And the name of the star is called Wormwood. And a third of the waters turned into wormwood, and many of the men died from the waters, because they had been made bitter.'

"How obvious do Cream and Chopin need to be? Put it all together. We've got prisons, chains, tides, fallen angels, across a sea of Bitter consequence?"

Nimrod's eyes popped in sudden comprehension and he gasped.

"No! The Bitter Sea?"

"Precisely."

"Hang on. Isn't that where ... ?"

"Yes, it is."

"But don't they keep ... ?"

"Yes, they do."

"Unholy shit! How in the seven shades of hell did they find out about that? And why kidnap Strawberry? It's not as if they can use her as leverage. If they survive the landing, the jailers will kill any unauthorized visitors on sight. Inquisitor or not, hostage or not, she's screwed if they drag her ashore without authorization."

"I know." Suddenly calm, I enjoyed a moment of clarity. "But I think that's why I've been baited all along. Think about it. Cream and Chopin have their own agendas now, that much is clear. But they've had a common geographical goal all along: the Isle of Cogs. They're heading toward their final destination, so they are keener than ever to ensure I know about it. Don't you see? They're hoping my presence will negate any resistance and some-how facilitate the success of their enterprise."

Nimrod almost choked.

"Are they really that naïve, to think you would compromise Satanic security just to save Strawberry?"

"That's what worries me," I admitted, "because they *aren't* that stupid. Up until now, they've displayed both tenacity and a resolve bordering on sheer genius. I doubt they'd suddenly stop."

So what do *they know that they think will give them an edge?*

"We have to notify His Majesty," Nimrod cautioned.

"I agree, but not just yet. With everything that's happened over the past year or so, Lucifer is bound to . . . overreact. Remember, he's still pissed at the challenge to his authority fomented by those damned poets last year. And there's Erra to contend with, don't forget. No, we will involve him, but only once we're sure of what's happening."

"And how are we going to do that?"

"I think a little trip to London's All Seeing Eye is needed. After all, there are only a few methods by which someone can approach the Isle unhindered. We need to know what they are."

"We'll need a gift, then."

"That's right." I held up the jeweled knife. "I'd like to give the Oracle this. It'd be right up his street. But I'm itching to find out how it prevented our erstwhile friend from dissipating. Cream and company have access to far too many goodies for my liking; the sooner we even the playing field, the better. So it looks like we'll have to go shopping." I clasped him by the shoulder. "Fancy a trip to the circus?"

Chapter 20: There's No Time Like the Present

Situated on the south bank of the River Tombs, the All Seeing Eye was easily the most distinguishable feature along the skyline of Olde London Town. When dormant, it looked like any other giant Ferris wheel, measuring over four hundred feet in diameter. However, once the Oracle had engaged his remarkable mind, the huge edifice transformed into an esoteric ocular enigma, unparalleled anywhere else among the many layers of hell.

The hub of the wheel would metamorphose into a super-enlarged pupil, the spokes into a scintillating iris with colors that shimmered through a thousand shades of blue. Finally, the outer edge of the structure—comprising the drive rim and capsules—would transmogrify into an ultra-thin sclera, encompassed within an electrostatic skein of arcane puissance.

Thus engaged, the Oracle could "see" any event, person, or circumstance anywhere and anywhen throughout infernity. A remarkable feat, given the fact that he was a mutant, one of those poor unfortunate souls permanently afflicted by the Undertaker on arrival. Rendered physically deaf, blind, and dumb, his extrasensory faculties were now second to none.

No one knew his name or, indeed, what he had done to deserve such punishment. Regardless, he was the go-to guy if you needed information and had the wherewithal to pay.

With no discernible skull to speak of except for the bottom half of his jaw—resplendent with a full set of pearly-white teeth but no tongue—the Oracle looked grotesque, an effect compounded by the fact that he dressed well and had surrounded himself with sumptuous luxury.

Dr. Thomas Neill Cream sat opposite his host, drinking tea from a bone-china cup and munching finger biscuits as if such circumstances were an everyday occurrence. An open fire snapped and crackled in one corner of the well-appointed room, and hundreds upon hundreds of scented candles burned warmly from silver holders scattered along every available surface.

The Oracle's naked brain glistened and pulsated with a strange sucking sound. The cerebrum itself oozed a steady stream of mucus which dripped down onto the shoulders of his midnight-purple jacket, where it soaked into the fabric in an ever-spreading stain. Dribble trickled from the corners of his half-mouth, fouling the front of his elaborate silk shirt a filthy green color that appeared leprous in the flickering firelight.

Cream didn't bat an eye, and waited patiently as the Oracle finished his own beverage through a modified straw.

A hiss from one corner drew Cream's attention. He turned in his seat to find a pair of baleful green eyes studying him from the shadows.

"Psst, psst, psst," he crooned, leaning forward and offering his hand for examination. "C'mon, there's a good kitty. I won't hurt you."

A dark shape detached itself from the gloom and clarified into a feminine feline form. Padding silently forward until barely out of reach, the cat stopped to test the air, nostrils quavering and whiskers twitching. Kitty obviously didn't like what she sensed, for dainty lips curled back to reveal pristine white fangs. With a final hiss, she dismissed Cream from her existence and wandered off toward the parlor.

You must excuse Esmeralda, the Oracle's mind intoned, *she's very particular when it comes to making friends.*

"Not to worry," Cream replied. *Mange-ridden moggy!* "I'm not here to make friends. I just need information so I can be on my way as quickly as possible."

The Oracle leaned forward in his chair, as if taking the measure of his guest.

A pity, for I could have saved you much . . . but so be it. Courtesy is such a rare commodity in this godforsaken place that people have forgotten how priceless it can be. An ethereal sigh whispered through the air. *You are aware, are you not, of the conditions of my services?*

"I am." Cream delved inside his briefcase and brought out a small crystal vial containing a clear liquid that glittered through all the colors of the rainbow. "I bring you the Tears of the Messiah, shed by Jesus himself at the death of his friend Lazarus. Not only does it contain the essence of hope revealed, but it acts as a restorative to all but the severest maladies."

A worthy gift, and one that must have cost you dearly. So tell me, what great boon do you seek for such a rarity?

"Passage to the Isle of Cogs."

By that I take it you mean the actual prison?

"Most certainly."

Then you are indeed fortunate, and right to act with haste.

"What do you mean?"

There are but a few methods by which the Isle can be approached in relative safety, and only one that avoids all hazards. Such an avenue is open but once a year. And tonight, my friend, as the bells of Little Ben strike twelve, the Infernal Equinox will manifest the portal, and those seeking safe passage may enter. . . if they know where to look.

Cream glanced at his watch, a thrill of surprise surging through him: *Midnight? Ha! There's nothing to stop me getting there first. I'm home free.*

With a smirk, he handed the bottle to the Oracle and purred, "That's good to know. So tell me, where must I go, and what do I do once there?"

Listen carefully, for my directions are precise and must be followed to the letter.

Cream took out a small notebook.

First, you must appreciate that time does not flow within the conduit as it does elsewhere. You will need . . .

*

Chopin knew there were certain areas in the underworlds where it would be unwise to venture unless brave, stupid, well protected, or skilled in the art of assassination. Lambsdeath, in Olde London Town, was one such district: an infamous hive of dingy cobbled streets and licentious back alleys where drunks, pickpockets, and whores of all shapes and sizes would commit bloody murder at the drop of a hat.

But, as dangerous as Lambsdeath could be, another territory boasted yet a darker reputation.

If you travel south for a mile or so along the River Tombs, you enter an area governed by the Pirate Lords, a merciless band of buccaneers, slavers, and bootleggers governed by a code so savage the term "cutthroat" would never do them credit.

Predatory to a superlative degree, the privateers sneered at those who chose to live in "safer" neighborhoods—which was saying something for hell—and didn't class souls as true residents until they bore a livid scar from ear to ear to prove their mettle. An odd state of affairs, for while they were ruthless with each other, these denizens had a radically different approach toward those with whom they conducted business.

Operating under a strict code as laid out by their leader—a mystery corsair known only as the Commodore—the Pirate Lords oversaw a huge enterprise from their headquarters, Davy Jones' Locker, in what the world of the living would have known as Battersea Station, a decommissioned, coal-fired power plant.

Here in hell, the Locker served as the main sea port for the whole of Juxtapose. Encompassing more than a hundred acres, the complex comprised a huge travel terminus, docklands, warehouses, tanneries and distribution center, all catering to the needs of those voyagers and traders who dared brave the worst stretch of interdimensionhell water in the underworld: the Bitter Sea.

But there was good reason why the Bitter Sea was so problematic. The Juxtapose level was saturated with random pockets of infernity, each snatched from one era or another and thrown together into a mishmash of conflicting realities. These kept the entire region in a constant state of flux, creating distortions throughout the Sheolspace continuum and generating eddies strong enough to disrupt the anchors linking Juxtapose to other underworldly circles.

The end results of all this organized chaos were some of the most vicious waterspouts and whirlpools ever witnessed by man or demon. Even elementals feared to venture into the heart of the maelstrom during stronger storms.

Yet that's exactly why Frédéric Chopin was here, waiting at the Celestial Mary Inn, Bitter Sea Port. Come what may, he had every intention of voyaging out into the Maw, as the churning mass was affectionately known; and to make matters worse, he wanted to be under way that very night.

Resplendent in a navy-blue frockcoat suit and contrasting Homburg hat, he stuck out like a sore thumb among the swarthy deckhands and salty seadogs filling the establishment with raucous cheers, bawdy songs, and a constant stream of explicit threats.

Accustomed to this rarefied atmosphere, serving wenches skillfully wove their way between tables. Hugging frothing tankards to their ample breasts, they dodged sudden lunges here and ducked repeated drunken advances there, all whilst engaging in good-natured—if somewhat graphic—banter.

Amazed by their wit and agility, Chopin wondered what it might be like to hire one's company for an hour. Then he immediately decided against it. Up until now, he'd managed to keep himself to himself; and although repeated glances were cast his way, he'd been left well alone.

No doubt I'm still alive because I look the part of a prospective client. He patted the stun grenade in his jacket pocket. *But just in case, I've taken adequate precautions.*

His mounting anxiety caused another spasm. As pain burned its way along his arms and into his spine, Chopin found his outlook shifting. His gaze melted down, through the woodworm-riddled table, on through the sawdust- and blood-covered floor, and deeper into the foundations of the tavern. Eventually, his consciousness arrived upon a wide expanse of shimmering bronze: somewhere else entirely.

Confused, Chopin blinked and shook his head.

Before he could clarify his position, the ground beneath his feet began to move every which way at once. He jumped back, thinking he might have stepped into quicksand, only to remember he wasn't physically there, but a mere spectator floating high in the air with a grandstand view of the most spectacular rock out-crop he'd ever seen.

Like a fist in the middle of a vast ocean, an island clenched its fist in defiance against the relentless assault of a vicious sea. Waves crashed against land from every angle, attempting to accomplish in seconds by brute force what wind and wave might hope to achieve over millennia by attrition. Resonating booms shook the shore. But to no avail, for each was followed by a hissing exhalation of surf through shingle, as the isle was given yet another breath of life.

Inland, away from the immediate battering, a buttress of weather-blackened granite stood out against the wet winds like the bow of a vast ship. Sharp as an arête, it faced north and sliced the approaching squall in two.

Chopin's attention was drawn to the top of the bluff, where an obsidian tower rose like an impossibly slender finger of contempt aimed at the heart of the storm. Dark and brooding, it pierced the gloom with an indestructible resolve.

He tried to scrutinize each feature of this new panorama, but no sooner did he attempt to focus than the vision wavered again, and he found himself swooping like a gull down toward the shoreline.

From this new perspective, Chopin saw that the undulations below him weren't due to the movement of a peculiar form of sand, but because of a vast network of giant interlinked sprockets and ratchets. Made from what looked like brass and blushed steel, each tine rotated in a different direction, churning up the beach until it was a lethal minefield of mechanical traps and snares.

The Isle of Cogs!

Then, everything went still.

What's happening . . . ?

A ticking sound, loud in his ethereal ears, lifted above the din of the tempest. Moments later, an abrupt *click* snapped through the air, whereupon everything started up once more.

Puzzled, Chopin watched the process unfold a second time, following the glittering shockwave as it clanked and clunked its way from the waterline up to the rocks leading toward the castle above.

In less than ten seconds the automated advance had wound to a close.

Tick, tick, tick, tick, tick, tick, tick, tick, tick—Click!

He continued to observe from on high as the clockwork process repeated itself over and over again.

Once accustomed to the ebb and flow of this harmony, Chopin could distinguish a pattern, a congruent course through the maze of flesh-grinding teeth that would avoid the danger of being rent limb from limb.

Well, well, well. How provident—

A surge of intense agony ripped through his hands. Chopin doubled over in pain, cursing as the fractured outlook of a migraine overcame his vision. He bit his bottom lip in an effort not to cry out, and soon the wave receded. He waited patiently for the refractive, kaleidoscopic rainbows to arch their way free of his sight. Once they had gone, he opened his eyes to find everyone within the Celestial Mary, staff and customers alike, staring at him.

The urge to explain himself was overwhelming. Fortunately, Chopin was saved from further embarrassment by the return of his companion, Nikola Tesla:

Tesla kicked the main door open, and it smashed into the nearest table with a bang. The sailors occupying that position jumped up cursing until they saw who was accompanying him, whereupon they resumed their places and ducked their heads.

A grizzled fellow with an authoritative air strutted into the salon. Obviously a pirate, he held his fists against his hips and glared around the room as if daring anyone to challenge him. They didn't. Instead, everyone fell silent.

At more than six feet tall, he certainly looked the part. Long dark hair, hook nose, eyes as sharp as slate. Barely visible above the cut of his slashed doublet and embroidered baldric, the telltale mark of a faded scar ran across width of his throat. His broad scarlet sash housed two pistols and a rather large cutlass. As the man drew nearer, Chopin could see a strange device sewn into the buccaneer's breast pocket: a red skeleton upon a sable background.

"This is Captain Edward Low," Tesla told Chopin, "and just the man we need for the job. Captain Low was born only a few miles from here—well, topside he was—in what we call Westmonster. He's sailed the Bitter Sea all his unlife, and knows her like the back of his hand. Like a friend, really, and . . . *oof!*"

"Avast, ye knock-kneed silver-tongued bedazzler!" Somehow, Low was able to doff his hat toward Chopin whilst managing to cuff Tesla on the back of the head in the same movement. "No one, and I mean *no one*, knows the Bitter Sea as well as I do. But let's get one thing straight. While I can tell ye every scar, every cut and blemish that adorns these mutinous hands o' mine, nobody can sail that murderous stretch o' water and say he knows her well enough to call her friend. Anyone who does is a liar!"

Chopin grinned. *Ooooh, I like this fellow.*

"But if there's a place ye need to be, *Flight of Fancy* and me will get ye there."

"Flight of Fancy?" Chopin asked.

"My ship, sir," Low replied, as if insulted his prospective client wouldn't know that, "and if truth be told, the only true love o' my life."

"And how stout is she?"

"Well, whatever that she-bitch of a Maw throws at us, we've taken. And more besides. We've weathered squall and tempest together, hurricane and doldrums. The Maw's tried to chew us up, swallow us down, and spit us out in bits, but we're still here. Her currents are as changeable as a woman's moods, and her weather fouler." He laughed. "Yes, the *Fancy* and I like it rough . . ."

Low waved to the barkeep for a round of drinks and took a seat opposite Chopin. Tesla slid in beside his friend and had the sense to keep quiet.

Chopin leaned across the table.

"Has my friend explained where we'd like you to take us?"

"He has. I thought *I* was the crazy one around here until he admitted that little doozy. Still, that's the name o' the game. If ye can pay, and we survive, I'll be able to milk this one among the captains for decades to come because no one has ever dared to land, unwarranted, upon the shores o' Cog Island."

"Oh, I can pay," Chopin whispered. "In fact, how would you like to *see* your bounty? Here and now?"

"Ye mean ye have the cash here?" Low was aghast. "Are ye truly insane? Ye don't know what I'm going to charge yet. And if the scum in here knew ye were minted so well, ye'd find yerself bleeding out in the gutter before winding yer way back to Slab A."

"I'm just focused," Chopin countered. He lowered his voice. "And well aware of your laws as laid down by the Commodore: once you accept the terms of the commission, along with pay-ment, we are bound by writ and I come under your protection."

Low paused while a serving girl laid the table with a semi-clean cloth, chipped glasses, and filthy bowls. Then she placed be-fore them one pot of bubbling "stew" that quivered as if still alive, along with three grubby spoons. The food smelt foul. The rum, however, was the genuine article. One hundred percent proof Cap-tain Gorgon's.

Low gave the wench a squeeze on the backside as she left, then resumed his interrogation. "Ye seem sure I'll accept? While I admit the destination doesn't put me off, ye might not agree to my price. It'll be steep."

"Steep or not, I'm confident we'll reach an accord, for what I have to offer is far more precious than mere blood or gold or money." Chopin glanced around and dropped his voice even further. "In fact, I have something that will guarantee your mastery of the Bitter Sea. Just imagine a future where vendors flock to you for custom and your fame spreads far and wide. Interested?"

"Show me," breathed Low the pirate.

As casually as possible, Chopin reached beneath his seat and produced an ordinary-looking oblong box about three feet long by fifteen inches wide, covered in stretched black leather. The lid was split down the middle and hinged on both sides, so that its contents could be viewed without removing the actual item.

Chopin beckoned and opened the leaves.

A golden glow sprang forth, bathing Low in its warm radiance. His eyes sparkled, and as he drank in the reality of every sailor's dream come true, he wore a beatific smile. "Is . . . is that the . . . ?"

"It certainly is," Chopin assured him, "and the only condition of my proposal is this: If you accept the Moral Compass as payment, you must use it to ensure I reach my goal unharmed. After that, we part ways, and this remarkable device is yours . . . forever."

In a flash, Low's dagger gleamed before Chopin.

"Yer right hand, sir," the captain breathed, "quickly, before others see what we barter over."

Chopin extended his arm.

With two deft slices, Low cut a gash first along his own palm, then Chopin's.

"Now shake."

They did, and the tablecloth stained red beneath their clasp.

Turning to the rest of the room, Low bellowed, "This man and I have reached an agreement, bound by blood. Both he and his companion are now protected by our code. Do ye all bear witness?"

"Aye!" The room shook to a thunderous declaration as pirates raised tankards and made toasts. The atmosphere became much friendlier.

Low slammed shut the lid of the box and scooped his prize to his chest.

"Our journey will take three days," he announced. "When would ye like to begin?"

"My bags are already in storage," Chopin replied, "and I'm a firm believer that when something needs doing, there's no time like the present."

*

To the north, a shattered plain rolled away as far as Champ's eye could see, broken and desolate. Flames burned constantly along parched ridges, and noxious gases burst forth from the myriad fissures, fracturing its surface with carbonized scars.

In the west, rivers of molten metal poured down from distant hills, adding their torrid potency to an already volatile mix. Fiery tornados rumbled across the horizon, blazing fulgurations that kicked up blinding clouds of cinders and dust. Hurled high into the air, each particle ignited, transforming into a storm of miniature meteorites that fell spitting and sparking from the sky in withering blasts that stung the eyes and burnt the lungs.

Champ Ferguson found the fumes and rippling heat overwhelming. He ducked down behind an outcrop of basalt, hawked up the contents of his gullet, and wiped the sweat from his brow with the back of his sleeve.

The spittle sizzled and bubbled on the scorched earth before disappearing in a puff of acrid vapor. His brow creased in frustration at the sight, and he clenched his fists in barely controlled anger.

"Are you all right, my friend?" Yamato Takeru enquired.

As serene as ever, Yamato stood a few yards behind his companion. Exposed to the searing winds that caused rocks to crack and living things to wither, he somehow managed to look as fresh as a daisy on a rainy day.

"Goddam fuckin' Hades," Champ spluttered. "First we were too cold, now we're too hot. My balls are swimming in gravy, for Satan's sake and . . . and"—he coughed, then gagged—"and *you*, with your bloody elemental magic keeping you all nice an' frosty, ask me if I'm all right? Unholy shit! I'm too frightened to fart in case I spontaneously combust and generate a mushroom cloud visible all the way over in Purgatory."

Yamato grinned.

"Now *that* I would pay to see." He shrugged. "Especially since you have no cause for complaint. I've already offered to encompass you within the cooling sphere of my influence, but you insisted it would interfere with your skills. I've let you have your own way, and *still* you bicker about it being too oppressive."

Champ was framing a retort when he felt a sudden concentration of heat around his nether regions, closely followed by the smell of burning. He glanced down and noticed his combat trousers were starting to scorch.

Shoot, I've been sitting still too long.

He jumped up, swatting at his thighs and buttocks, only to fall forward again as the ground beneath his feet flexed like a bubble.

What in tarnation . . . ? "Is that a hellquake? Quick, we'd better hightail it outta here before—"

"Hang on!"

Champ spun on the spot and noticed his fellow Hound had adopted the stance of a person walking a high wire. Yamato's eyes were closed, and he appeared to be concentrating.

Training kicked in. While his colleague was off in Wonderland, Champ drew his Abaddon 6000 pump-action shotgun from its back sling, racked a cartridge, dropped to one knee and scoured the immediate vicinity for danger.

Okay, perhaps it's not a hellquake?

His keen eyes caught sight of a distortion two hundred yards east of the cave where the Sibitti enforcers had installed themselves only half an hour before. Ignoring the pain in his leg, he watched the air flicker. After thirty seconds, the very fabric of reality seemed to bend in on itself.

I don't care what Yamato says, that *isn't natural.*

A great plume of sulfurous steam sprayed into the air. As it descended in a glittering mist, several huge fingers of rock punched upward out of the baked earth, bringing with them a brand new river of brimstone. The flow increased, flooding the valley floor below them.

Jumpin' Jehoshaphat!

When blobs of magma rained down from the sky, Champ had to jump from side to side and pat his clothes repeatedly to stop them catching fire.

"Erra's champions appear to have found a new way to amuse themselves," Yamato announced. Safely cocooned within a shimmering force field, not a hair on his head had been singed. "And whatever they're doing, it looks to be affecting the deepest levels of this realm."

"That can't be good for us, then?"

"It can't be good for anyone. We need to get closer to see exactly what they're up to."

Champ glanced at the cave. "You mean, in there? Are you fuckin' joking? There's four of them."

"On the contrary, I'm deathly serious."

It never rains—"Ow!" Champ paused to slap at the stinging sparks dancing through his hair. "And when were you thinking of enacting this death wish of yours?"

"Well, the sooner we get started, the sooner we can get out of here."

"And you're sure you'll be able to mask our presence sufficiently?"

Yamato casually expanded his protective field until Champ was safely inside. He smiled. "Of course."

"Against four of them?"

"You worry too much, my friend."

"No, I worry about getting torn limb from limb by personified weapons and forced to watch as they feed my liver to unfriendly ghouls. Call me possessive, but I'm rather attached to my insides: I'd like them to stay exactly where they are."

Yamato beckoned him forward.

"And you're getting soft."

"Soft? Me? There's only one of us here who's soft, and that's you. In the head. How dare you accuse . . ."

The bickering continued unabated until the Hounds were too close to the cave for comfort. Then the insults became much more personal, and purely telepathic . . .

Chapter 21: Cirque du Freak

Icepiccadilly Circus was an amazing experience, the one place in the entire underworld where a carnivoral atmosphere reigned twenty-four hours a day, seven days a week, all year round.

Not that Satan was growing soft. Far from it. Our Infernal Father was the very epitome of cruelty. And nowhere was this better expressed than at *the* major attraction he had fabricated especially for the Devil's Children. A unique locale where his Blue Suits and spooks could come to unwind after a hard day's incivility, to watch the grotesque and the fugly (those who had seriously fucked up and were mutated beyond recognition) and, of course, to witness the most invasive results of the Undertaker's warped sense of humor.

Erected at the junction of four main thoroughfares connecting the Worst End with Westmonster, this was also the site of a temporal nexus—an esoteric knot where five eras blended together in a frenzy of time-bending confusion: Modern; pre-Second World War; Victorian; Medieval; and Roman.

Everyday Joes were required to attend the circus at least once every year: a clever ploy, for although most denizens continually bickered about their lot or complained at the injustice of their banishment, a visit to this event reminded everybody of how bad things could get if they didn't shut up, buckle down, and make the best of what they'd been given.

And what a reminder it was.

Not for hell the tepid thrill of caged, toothless animals, or trapeze acts spinning gracefully through the air to land in the cosseted safety of thoughtfully placed nets. Oh, no. Here, in the Cirque du Freak that was Icepiccadilly Circus, you would witness rejects too hideous or repulsive to live a normal life, forced to perform for the public's displeasure.

The Upside-down Woman, for example, who had her limbs and entire gastrointestinal system swapped around upon her arrival in hell. Now made to walk everywhere on her hands, she could only eat laxatives or high fiber foods through her ass, and would defecate on demand through her mouth and nose until she passed out from asphyxiation while spectators vomited in disgust.

And she was only one example of these crossbred human chimeras, so deformed that the mere sight of them caused some amongst the gathered throng to experience heart attacks. Such travesties were usually goaded into gladiatorial combat unto death. Only a temporary reprieve, of course, for if they didn't acquit themselves well enough in battle or entertain the crowd sufficiently, they would receive further "adjustments" and be sent back to fight again. Wretches with no arms or legs, forced to cling by their broken teeth from piss-soaked high wires strung up just beyond the reach of snapping, rabid hell-wolves. None survived for long, and all screamed hideously as they were devoured. Clowns strapped into radio-activated suicide vests chased each other with buckets full of sulfuric acid, each dreading the moment a bored member of the audience would send them to their fiery doom.

Dwarves, bound and gagged, fired from cannons into cages where demented reavers had been starving for weeks. Wild West-style shooting stunts where the targets were sentient, gelatinous blobs of goo. Whatever the Undertaker had done to keep these travesties conscious was miraculous, for the only parts of them that looked even vaguely human were their ocular appendages. Deliberately left intact, their pop-eyed expressions conveyed the full depth of their terror before their eventual and inevitable demise.

My particular favorite was the Inside-out Man, who existed by strapping his externalized internal organs to his torso with masking tape. His was a funny act to watch, for he ran the gauntlet of a maze filled with razor-wire whilst pursued by a pack of slavering hellhounds with burning fur and poisonous fangs. Slipping and slithering about in blood, bile, and other bodily fluids, he never got far, and would go down pleading for mercy amid a circle of snapping incisors and slashing claws.

This soul must have really pissed off our Dark Father for he'd been filling the same slot for over two hundred years. Just thinking of the suffering he'd endured made me tingle with anticipation for Cream's forthcoming appointment with destiny: Me!

When I eventually catch the bugger . . .

But revenge must wait. First, I needed an appropriate form of payment to set before the Oracle, and I was in exactly the right place to find it.

Some kind of warped karma was in force here. While Satan had done his best to ensure that abject misery held sway, fate smiled upon the unfortunate to counter their maledictions in the strangest of ways . . .

These doomed and unrepentant souls could create the most wondrous gifts: fire-flake crystal pendants, carved from the flames of Gehenna made manifest; air-flute symphonies, orchestrated to the song of the northern storm as it grazed the ice forests of Higher Niflheim; the most intricate lifelike representations of Satan's favorite rose—worn only on special occasions—the dark red De-monkracie, fashioned from the yet-beating heart of a phoenix; liq-uefied nightmares, distilled from the horror experienced by those first awakening in hell and bottled for the connoisseur to savor, over and over again.

But more than the significant or cryptic flowed from the workshops of the aberrant; even their everyday offerings were also sublime in most spectacular ways:

The resonance of a hell-kitten shrieking, its tail pulled, was captured, amplified, and held to the ear of one deprived of hear-ing. Ablaze with color, cutterflies (miniature clockwork miracles woven from the purest strands of spider silk and razorblades) stut-tered and fluttered from thistle to thistle, deadheading other in-sects as they went, just like the real thing. Vicarious thrill-seekers shared the delicious sensation of a victim's body going limp as life was strangled from it, and the subsequent orgasmic relief, expe-rienced in the moments before the spiders and scorpions started their bloody work.

How they did it, Satan only knows, but I had a sneaking sus-picion that 'he who mustn't be named' was making a point. And to be honest I was glad he was, because without the Freaks' help I wouldn't stand a chance of gaining the Oracle's counsel any time soon.

The last time I'd traveled this part of Regret Street, I'd had to navigate the confines of a Roman Legionnaire stockade. Since then, however, hellspace had obviously twisted, for I now found myself somewhere in the mid 1930s looking at dated adverts for bootblack, fever cures, pickled herrings, and sanitized tapeworms.

Smoke blackened and soot covered, these reminded me of little windows of time through which passersby could catch a glimpse of lifestyles now abandoned or forgotten.

Except for here. Who would have realized the service Satan has provided for the annals of history, eh? Nice one, Boss.

We turned a corner and came to an outer circle of smaller tents and pavilions. Bordered by ramshackle carts, gypsy caravans, and a plethora of cooking pots in all shapes and sizes, the area was full of bizarre and extreme damned, relaxing and taking their ease. On one side, deformed acrobats practiced their act of dodging blazing arrows whilst balanced on sharpened stakes above a pit of vipers. On the other, a gryphon wrestled with a Minotaur.

Barbecued comestibles appeared to be their favorite, and from what I could surmise they weren't too fussy. I saw eyeballs, ears, livers, and an overwhelming assortment of limbs. Soiled underwear, old boots, and car seats were high on the popularity list too. One griddle even had the contents of a street bin strung out on a wire above the flames: used nappies, tin cans and all.

"Bingo! We've hit their living area head-on. Now I won't have to wade through all the booths and sideshows trying to find what I need."

"Shame..."

I glanced at Nimrod and caught him gazing toward the eaves of the brightly-lit pagoda with disappointment etched across his craggy face.

"I haven't blown up a clown in months," he complained. He had a wistful look in his eyes. "Do you know... if you wait until they're in a prime position and time things just right, you can set off a chain reaction that takes out a whole bunch of them? My record's seven, and that doesn't include the two who doused themselves in acid when they dropped their buckets. What an awesome night that wa–"

Nimrod's eyes suddenly focused. He spun on the spot and looked about as if searching for something.

"Are you seri–? What the fu–?"

I felt a vibration tickle my toes. Then the earth beneath my feet heaved and buckled. A high-pressure jet of steam burst forth from the ground only ten yards from my position, to be joined by another from across the street. A third one hit us, right in the middle of the big top itself. Hunks of rock and paving slab blew high into the air, along with a number of wagons and lean-tos. From the squeals I heard, many bystanders must have been swept away by the initial eruptions.

The trembling increased, and a loud crack heralded a crevasse appearing in the middle of the street. Tendrils of mystic potency writhed out, the rumbling deeper and more resonant. In moments, the chasm had widened. Although denizens ran hither and thither, many still fell into the growing abyss. They were closely followed by a shower of bricks and chunks of mortar when the nearest buildings started to topple. Sulfurous rain spattered down from the blood-dark vault, as if hurled here from another realm.

Somewhere, a siren started wailing.

This doesn't feel right.

My suspicions were confirmed by an overwhelming sense of foreboding. Black as midnight, it manifested a corporeal form and boiled up and out from the pit, latching onto anyone unfortunate enough to stray too close. Like a predatory cephalopod, its tentacles coiled around arms and legs or ankles and necks before dragging its victims, kicking and screaming, into the bowels of the earth.

But who's behind it?

I was in no mood to suffer further distractions and immediately took the offensive.

With a strenuous bound, I leaped high into the air, ripped my scythe free from its holster, and swung it back over my head in a double-handed grip. Then I called on the full extent of my mundane potential and channeled it into my weapon. The moment I touched down, I slammed the heel of my staff into the deck and depressed the scythe's top button.

A colossal surge of arcane power lanced into the rift. Instinct took over. I blended into the flow and, with a roar, bent it to my will.

"*Troh a'* lùthse ain mi sealbġh (By the power invested in me),

"*etom An a'Satanas aínim* (and in the name of Satan),

"*ràchaîs bi fádh etom Ilfrinn bi aiseghd*! (be gone, and hell be restored!)"

The vault above thundered in response to my command, and lightning split the air. My whole body became encompassed in bands of violet and golden augury. And as I hung transfixed in midair, the ground below me shook, and the teeming winds above the city were sucked inward from all points of the compass.

A tornado formed.

Undaunted, I redirected the sustaining essence of the underverse, pouring it down through my core and into the invading breach. The Phage beckoned, and I teetered on the edge of manifestation.

A glittering bubble ballooned away from me, huge and expanding exponentially. It grew in all directions until it encompassed the entire Icepiccadilly area in a shimmering corona of cabbalistic might.

No sooner had my countermeasure solidified than the upheaval ground to a halt. Deprived of whatever energy had sustained it, the menace retreated; the edges of the fissure grumbled and groaned their way back together. Soon, even the tremors died away.

A subliminal *pop* signaled the release of transcendent pressure.

Caught unprepared, I fell to my knees, momentarily overcome with nausea and weakness. I scanned my essence and took stock.

The outcome was exasperating. Although I had prevailed, the effort had cost me dearly.

Idiot! You failed to manifest again.

Nimrod came sprinting across the rubble. Before he could reach me, the atmosphere between us shimmered, turned gray, then bloomed outward like a convex viewing glass.

The face of Lucifer himself, in beatific form, appeared within the ocular. His eyes, however, betrayed his anger, and flashed like the fangs of a cobra.

"Well played, my Reaper!" Satan's voice boomed across the expanse of the square. The afflicted and ordinary damned citizens alike fell to their knees, cowering in fear. "I sensed the incursion the moment it began. I was gratified to witness the fortitude of one of my most vigorous subjects, and your unreserved commitment to defending my realm. If only more were like you, I could rest easier on my coals."

"Majesty," I acknowledged.

"You need not concern yourself further with this attack. Not for now, at any rate. Samael will investigate the circumstances behind it and devise an appropriate response. However, I am aware your Hounds are currently engaged in enquiries elsewhere. If there's the slightest indication that the two events are connected, let me know immediately, and we can revise our strategy. Understood?"

"Of course. It will be done."

The heat of His Infernal Majesty's gaze washed across the crowd once more.

"Let this be a lesson to you all," he growled. "Weakness and cowardice incurs my eternal wrath; bravery, my benevolent gratitude."

His visage wavered and disappeared. As it did so, a coruscating ribbon of Bālefire shot out from the vortex, striking me square in the chest.

Surrounded by a maelstrom of swirling, vital energy, I felt my entire being expand and then mesh with the animated tincture of infernity made manifest. Its resonance produced the highest high I could ever experience. Sadly, it was also far too brief.

As the helix contracted, the trailing edges of the plasma ribbon leached into every extremity of my body. Air exploded from my lungs, and the intensity of the rush left me twitching.

"He saved us," one of the survivors shouted.

"Yes, you saved us all," another joined in.

"Thank Purgatory for that," said a third.

"Stop!" I snapped. "I don't want or need your thanks. I didn't do it for you. It's my nature to protect Satan's name and reputation. You just got lucky."

The crowd around me grew larger; I looked to Nimrod for support.

"Nevertheless," the first voice continued, "what you did kept us all alive."

As if obeying some unspoken command, the gathering throng began to slither, stagger, and hobble forward to surround me. I stood up in an effort to look more frightening and put them off. It didn't work.

"Thank you, Reaper."

"Satan save you."

"Hex you, Reaper, hex you."

"Be careful what you say." I raised my voice. "All praise must go to our Awful Father. And I've already told you, I don't want—"

"How can we ever repay you?" wondered an elderly mutant standing right next to me.

Hello?

I peered closer at the wretched little fellow and saw the result of a failed chimera experiment: He had the face of a man but his skin had liquefied in some obscene way, so that it hung from his skull in rivulets that gave the appearance of melted wax. Weedy avian arms and legs poked out from an alpine bib and brace set. He cut a pathetic figure, hopping from one foot to the other, wringing a bright blue cap between his twiglike fingers.

"What did you say?" I asked.

"I want to know how we can repay you," he repeated. "Directly, indirectly, it matters not. *You* saved us. We may be the lowest of the low, but we have our pride and always pay our debts." He extended his claw. "My name is Obadiah. At your service."

I shook the proffered limb.

This guy has balls. "Now you come to mention it, Obadiah, we're not actually here for the show. My friend and I require the services of the Oracle and need—"

"Ah, the Hyde Price," he cut in, "of course, of course. Please follow me."

Obadiah led us toward a separate cluster of caravans and stalls congregated near the entrance to Gashouse Street. Because of their location at the extremity of the Circus environs, they had escaped the recent chaos with only minimal damage.

We drew closer, and I could pick out the various features of this part of the camp. To my left, a female hoopy was busy hanging gaily-colored washing from a makeshift line strung between a cart's wheel and the nearest shop, Bombs & Ignoble. Several younger ones sat nearby, on adjacent chamber pots. Trousers down, they were grinning at each other and eating highly laxative sticks of candy flush, obtained from one of the funfair's vendors. I wasn't sure, but from the way they were acting, they appeared to be engaged in a contest to see how long they could hold out before submitting to the bowel-loosening effects of their treats.

Typical; even in hell, boys will be boys.

I had to physically drag Nimrod along behind me, otherwise he would have stayed to watch until the bitter, pan-filling end.

At a stall just outside the caravan to my right, another elderly hobgoblin was braiding the nostril hairs of a fellow mutant, adorning each strand with a row of brightly-colored beads. Next to them, a distinguished-looking boglin was fashioning the most delicate little charms from lumps of freshly plucked earwax. Had I not seen them made before my eyes I'd never have guessed their origins, for each one was encrusted in moon dust and sparkled like the stars in a night sky.

We stopped outside a small pavilion, and Obadiah disappeared inside. He soon re-emerged carrying a small glass ball.

He explained: "Just over a year ago, I heard the Oracle was given a childlike mannequin by a grateful customer. As you know, youngsters are rare in the underworld, and such were the intricacies of the doll's design that the Oracle came to view it as his prized possession. In fact, he has grown to love it as if it were his own offspring and, over the past thirteen months or so, has sought to instill in it the many qualities of true life. In anticipation of future revenue, we at the Cirque du Freak have bent our arts toward creating the perfect accompaniments to his desires."

Obadiah paused to hold up the crystal orb. I studied it closely. It reminded me of a snow globe, except this one had swirling nebulas of rainbow lights inside instead of glitter.

"I recently completed this," he continued. "Called Tirion's Temptation, it contains the last living memories of a mother who died during childbirth. For some reason, her final recollections were of her eldest son, Tirion, as a babe who had just learned to laugh. The Oracle will be drawn to such a gift, which offers him a rare opportunity to animate his own progeny. And while he will be unable listen to it physically, Tirion's Temptation contains an esoteric vibrancy that will appeal to his peculiar . . . sensitivities. All he has to do is shake it, and *hey presto!*"

Perfect. "I'll take it, name your price."

"To you, Reaper, it's free." Obadiah placed the ball into my hand and bowed. "Please accept this with my gratitude."

"What? Are you sure? You know you can't buy my favor in any way, so trying that line of approach will be a complete waste of time."

"I was hoping you might view my request as a form of payment?"

"In what way?"

"It's . . . I'm due to fight in the arena again tomorrow. My centenary appearance, and I—" He had the decency to look ashamed. "I'm not trying to avoid it or anything like that, if that's what you're wondering. But would you mind passing my name on to the Undertaker? I want a better life down here, and being stuck in the Circus has prevented that. Don't get me wrong, I know I have to pay my dues like every other damned soul. But once you get consigned to the freak show, the Undertaker makes it nigh-on impossible to get out. I was hoping you might pay for this gift with a kind word in the right place? Stronger arms would be nice. Perhaps greater speed?"

The Bālefire coursing through my veins flared in response to his request.

"I'm sure they would," I replied, "but this is hell, and as our Infernal Lord reminded us only a short time ago, you have to earn his benevolent gratitude."

Obadiah's face dropped.

I removed my gloves.

"Still, you *have* done his Reaper a great service in providing the means by which he can more swiftly expedite the apprehension of a fugitive from injustice."

His eyes widened with hope.

"Here . . . At least this time you won't have to face the horror of battle."

I lightly touched Obadiah's forehead, and he collapsed to the floor at my feet, dead. In moments, he had melted from sight.

"You can be really cruel sometimes," Nimrod sighed. Then he smiled. "Just the way our Reaper should be."

"Why, thank you. Coming from one of the greatest hunters of men ever to exist, that's a great compliment." I paused to wave my prize in his face. "Now c'mon, the time for teasing minions is over. We have a gift to deliver."

*

The lights of Westmonster Bridge sparkled in the dusky glow of another dangerous evening in hell. At last, things seemed to be picking up, and the night air held a sense of anticipation I hadn't felt in a long time. From my vantage point outside the All Seeing Eye, I followed the curve of the opposite shoreline and the course of the capital's illuminations. Just opposite my position, they snaked along the Tombs itself, weaving inland along the length of Blackhall, then Hearse Guards Parade, and up to Hellson's Column in the distance. This was my hometown, and despite the recent ups and downs of existence here, the mere sight of it made me feel at peace and glad to be undead.

Things are heading toward a climax—and I, for one, can't wait.

Nimrod and I approached the wheel. Only one of the aboveground structures seemed to be connected to the Eye itself, the drive house at the base of the main support struts, and that crouched in total darkness. But I knew from experience that appearances could be deceiving.

I'd never had to use the services of the Oracle before and wondered how our meeting would go. I'd heard he was a mutant. Regardless, I knew as soon as we drew near the main entrance that he must have a wicked sense of humor, for it was held fast by a gargoyle door knocker. Instead of the usual features, however, the handle of this particular example happened to be a huge set of brass testicles hanging from an elongated scrotum.

Tongue in cheek, I hammered as hard as I could on the plate.

The chiseled features etched into the base panel grimaced. "Is there no peace for the wicked?" Its beady eyes snapped open. "What the fuck do you want at this time of night?"

Our door warden has a particularly foul mouth and bad temper. Mind you, I don't suppose it's much fun having a heavy set of balls smashed into your face on a regular basis.

I tried a civil approach. "Well, I'm not delivering pizza." I took out a full bloodstone and teased it toward his mouth. "But if you cut the crap and let us in so we can see your boss, you can have all of *this*. No change required."

That did the trick. Suddenly businesslike, the gargoyle's coppery tongue snaked out to accept the proffered gem. Having coiled around its prize, it snapped back faster than my eye could follow. A loud gulp was followed by a deep sigh of satisfaction. The door cracked open with a sharp clunk.

Please come in, a voice announced inside my head. *Esmeralda will show you the way.*

I jumped, but then reminded myself, *Of course, he's a deviant. That's how he communicates.*

We trooped inside and discovered the interior to be a rather mundane-looking entrance foyer and gift salon. From what I could see, only one exit led out to the passenger carriages. Not what I expected: apart from Nimrod and me, the place was deserted.

I glanced at Nimrod. He looked equally bemused, until something on the opposite side of the room caught his eye. When I gazed back across the shop, I discerned a sleek black cat sitting atop the main display case, washing itself. It hadn't been there a moment before.

"Aha! That must be Esmeralda?"

On hearing her name, Esmeralda stood up, twirled around three times, and disappeared.

The voice had said *"Esmeralda will show you the way."*

"Follow me," I whispered, "I think I know what we've got to do."

We hurried across and positioned ourselves in front of the same cabinet. I tasted the air. So far as I could tell, the ether was completely devoid of residual esoteric power.

"If I'm right, we've got to spin round and round like the cat did."

"I'm glad no one is watching then," Nimrod replied. "If I'm going to make a titting ballerina of myself, I'd rather do it without witnesses."

We did as instructed . . . although I couldn't get the shocking image of Nimrod in a tutu out of my mind.

No sooner had we completed the third rotation than a rippling curtain fell to the floor, and our perspective changed:

We found ourselves standing in a long hallway stretching into the distance before us and behind. Strangely, both directions seemed to curve away sharply. Esmeralda sat outside a room about three yards away, and a warm glow lit the corridor from inside. On seeing us, she let out a little chirrup, flicked her tail, and melted from sight. Her emerald green eyes were the last part of her to fade away.

"Goodbye to you, too," I mumbled.

I was impressed. We were obviously standing within a hell-space paradox of inestimable refinement, as I hadn't sensed its proximity at all.

This guy must have great power. We'd better tread carefully.

We entered the chamber, and I stopped short. A similar view to the one I had enjoyed only a few minutes ago lay before me. On this occasion, however, I was far above ground level and found myself looking down on the River Tombs via a panoramic window.

"How . . . ?"

We are at the top of the wheel, Reaper, the Oracle explained. *Once you have entered my home proper, the entire edifice blends into a composite whole, any part of which I can occupy at will.*

For the first time I noticed our host. Sitting in a comfy chair to one side of a roaring fire, he seemed completely at ease. From what I could see, he appeared human, apart from his head, which looked as if it was on inside out, for he possessed no skull to speak of apart from a lower jaw.

As I strolled toward him I had to navigate among a multitude of tables, each covered in candles. Despite his having no eyes, I got the distinct impression the Oracle was watching every step I took with infinite attention.

Hmm, he thought aloud, *it's not every day a denizen of hell gets to welcome the Reaper to his home. I must confess, I find myself intrigued by the notion. How may I be of service?*

"I am on official Satanic business, in pursuit of renegades who must be brought to injustice as swiftly as possible. Recent enquiries have led me here, for I believe the rebels may soon make an attempt on the maximum security prison at Cog Isle."

As I spoke, I removed Tirion's Temptation from within my jacket pocket, shook it gently, and held it up for his inspection.

The disgusting sound of an infant laughing heartily and merrily filled the room . . . and more! An arcane sub-tone lifted a submerged aspect of its cadence to the fore. The sound rose swiftly in pitch until it was beyond the range of the human ear.

The Oracle stiffened, and his head tilted to one side as if to savor every nuance of the experience. His brain quivered wetly, and he clapped his hands in obvious excitement.

But this is wonderful, he gushed, *and just what my own child needs to become more complete.*

"Then you should know this offering is made in exchange for information relating to safe passage across the Bitter Sea. You might think it odd that I need to approach you about such a matter, but I wish to conclude this affair speedily and without disturbing his Infernal Majesty, who has much to contend with at the moment."

I appreciate the sentiment, the Oracle replied. *The Isle of Cogs, you say?*

"Yes, that's correct."

Fate must be watching over you, for you are the second person to request information regarding the Forbidden Isle today.

Bong! As if adding emphasis to the Oracle's statement, the chimes of Little Ben commenced striking the hour. Its reverberating pealed echoed across the rooftops, adding a further layer to the combined resonance of Tirion's mirth.

Bong!

"Really? Today, you say?"

Yes, a Mister Lambeth was here less than two hours ago. If you are swift, you might catch him and enjoy his company on the journey.

Bong!

Fuck me, it's Cream! "Hang on . . . What do you mean, I have to be swift?"

Bong!

The portal manifests but once a year, on the Infernal Equinox. When activated, it only remains open for one minute, after which it dissipates.

Bong!

"Only a minute?"

I'm sorry, once it is shut, nothing can penetrate its boundaries. Not even you.

Bong!

"When?" I gasped. "When does it open?"

Tonight, at midnight, on the twelfth stroke.

Bong!

"Where, man? Quickly."

This year? Why, at Jekyll and Hyde Park.

Bong!

My blood ran cold. *Bugger!* I glanced at Nimrod. "We've got to go . . . now."

Wait! The Oracle's voice blared in my mind.

Bong!

"What?" I inhaled, and started to summon the power to phase.

Bong!

One facet about the portal you must understand is this: Thanks to the quirks of temporal dilation, time works differently within the conduit.

"How so?"

Bong!

While the traveler will only spend several hours travers-ing the length of the celestial pathway, three whole days will have passed here in the underworlds.

Bong!

"Three days! Are you joking?"

I do not jest about such matters. Safety is achieved at the cost of haste. This is hell; you cannot have both.

"Fair enough. I don't mean to be rude, but I need to leave. It just so happens Mister Lambeth is one of the fugitives I'm after. . . . Not your fault. Enjoy your gift."

I seized Nimrod by the wrist and blasted us west through the ether at breakneck speed.

Idon'tfuckingbelieveit!   *Idon'tfuckingbelieveit! Idon'tfuckingbelieveit!*

The River Tombs passed in a blur. We sped above Blackhall. Then Drowning Street. Hearse Guards Parade followed soon after. St Flames Park passed us by. We roared above Unconstitutional Hill like a meteor entering Earth's atmosphere. The Serpentine loomed in the distance, and Jekyll and Hyde Park drew ever closer in a giddy, kaleidoscopic rush of impressions.

Even at this distance I could sense telltale signs of a diminutive and expertly-concealed event horizon in the middle of the island on the lake.

Azazel! It must be incredibly potent.

Four persons were gathered before the vortex, one of whom looked to be draped across the shoulders of a much larger traveler.

Strawberry?

The edges of the geodesic threshold began flickering. The small party edged toward its entrance, as if happy to wait until the very last second to step inside.

No!

I began my descent and watched helplessly as Cream turned toward me and waved.

What? You are fucking dead!

Too late, I thundered to the ground scant yards from the terminus. Before the portal snapped shut, I glimpsed the briefest flash of honey-blonde hair inside.

"What in the blazes are we going to do now?" Nimrod seethed.

Cold with fury, I tried to think clearly. "If what the Oracle said is true, we have a three-day window. Three days to find a faster, more direct route."

"The pirates?" Nimrod suggested. "Or can we concentrate on finding Chopin or Tesla instead, and use their artifacts to help us?"

"Possibly. But either option will cost us dearly, in time if not resources." I teetered on the verge of violence. "C'mon! Whatever we do, we've gotta be quick."

Chapter 22: Storm in a Teacup

"This voyage is turning into a real pain in the ass," Captain Edward Low bellowed into the wind at no one in particular. "That's the fourth time the coordinates for magnetic north have changed in the last twenty-four hours. Neptune's beard, what in blazes is happening to the fabric o' our world?"

Crouching low over the compass, he slapped the gimbals with the flat of his hand, trying to make sense of the fluctuations that had bedeviled them since leaving Davey Jones' Locker in Juxtapose on the previous day.

He peered across the deck toward the mainmast, catching sight of Chopin and Tesla as they clung to the *Fancy's* guidelines for dear unlife. Green to the gills, both men looked ready to spill the contents of their stomachs.

Low grinned at the sight of their suffering. Spray and rain filled his mouth with a tangy brew of fresh water and brine. "Avast, ye landlubbers, I told ye the Bitter Sea was a cruel mistress at the best o' times. Ye can't say hello for the first time and expect her to withhold the passion of her vile temper."

His laughter cackled off into night until he spotted, near the aft castle, a deckhand who appeared to have nothing to do.

"Barnes! C'm'ere and take the wheel while I check our bearings again."

The sailor scuttled across and braced himself to take the wheel. He nodded, and Low released his grip. Ignoring the mad tilt of the deck, Low scooped the Moral Compass from its hidey-hole and positioned the base plate in the palm of his hand.

Good job this contraption doesn't need stars or the horizon to work, otherwise we'd all be buggered.

The arcane tool meshed to his aura, and its miniature gyroscopes commenced their synchronous dance. A gentle turquoise radiance bloomed from the crystal powering its core, which grew until the sextant part of the apparatus was encompassed within a phosphorescent cerulean nimbus. A glittering needle of light appeared within the corona. Flickering wildly, the indicator spun through all points of the compass and then stopped dead. A coherent beam of sapphire brilliance lanced out, puncturing the gloom and pointing the way to salvation.

Low sighed. *Of course. With an ocean full o' hate before me, I've got to take us even deeper into the jaws o' the Maw.*

"Three points to starboard," he roared, "and secure the hatches: we're heading into the tempest. Reef all spare canvas, stow all lines, and anyone on standby watch, get yer worthless bodies on deck now. Line the railings and 'ware the rigging."

Crew members rushed to comply. Low felt the timbers beneath his feet groaning in protest as the *Flight of Fancy* inched toward the desired heading.

"Is that wise?" Chopin complained. "We've endured nothing but stormy conditions since we set out. This ship has taken an awful battering. Surely she can't take much more? Isn't there an easier way?"

"If it's easy ye want, feel free to jump over the side and swim," Low retorted. "Ye wanted the Isle o' Cogs, so that's where we're going. I told ye the Bitter Sea was a temperamental, murderous bitch, and that was before all these . . . these unnatural interventions. It's as if Jonah himself is in league with the Leviathan o' the Abyss to bring us to ruin. The very nature o' the ocean is changing. But a little weather won't stop us, ye'll see. The Compass will keep us true. Learn to trust it."

The moment he'd spoken, Low wished he hadn't. For out of the darkness to the east rolled an avalanche of water that made the rest of the mountainous swells look like mere hillocks.

That bastard's moving against the current! If it hits us broadside, we'll lose the main mast . . . maybe more.

"Barnes, you slimy son of a whore, hard to starboard. Now!"

A trained hand, Barnes reacted without question. His muscles bunched as he wrestled the wheel into submission. Low flung the Moral Compass back into its locker and leaped to assist him.

With infinite slowness, the prow of the *Fancy* turned. A plateau of foaming peril bore down on them, revenant and hungry. The bow bucked, and planks flexed under the strain. Blocks and pulleys swung crazily, as if as poltergeist were loose among them. Hinges squeaked, and lanterns tilted as gravity went haywire.

The animated cliff of gray-green might tore into them, and the *Fancy* lifted. Higher they went, ever higher. The deck upended and the world twisted. Men screamed, flailing helplessly as they fell into the sea's raging clutches. Those that survived the initial surge grabbed at anything that might extend their meager grip on life. Unbelievably, they kept rising skyward until the ship was almost vertical. And still the wave's summit appeared to stretch on forever.

Low clung to the wheel with all his might and focused on the darker shade of black just beyond the frothy crest. Beside him, Barnes moaned under the relentless pressure of keeping the ship on course. Men were thrown from the rigging, and Chopin and Tesla hung like mere deadweight from the mast, the soles of their feet pointing directly toward Low.

Then they were over the apex and freefalling into the void. Down they plunged, gaining speed until they plowed into the sea like a hammer striking an anvil.

A tremendous shockwave tore through the keel. Water swamped the entire vessel.

Low instinctively clutched the wheel and scooped in the biggest lungful of air he could hold. The vibrations threatened to tear his arm from his shoulder. He gritted his teeth and squeezed with every ounce of strength he had. Eternity seemed to pass as the freezing waters tore at him, testing his resolve to hang on, enticing him to let go and take a last, welcoming breath.

I'll not go out this way. Not like this.

He started to thrash, his fingers grew numb, and lights danced before his eyes.

No!

Just as the world began to darken, they swept through an intervening curtain of cobalt turbulence and burst free into a welcoming gust of windblown air. Low experienced a moment's weightlessness before the ship slammed down into the ocean once more. Thrown off his feet, Low's chin smashed onto the deck, and stars flashed across his vision again. He spat out a tooth, and a coppery taste trickled down his throat as he pushed himself up on his elbows and looked behind.

A massive wall of roiling water surged away, eager to be someplace else as quickly as possible.

We were lucky.

Jumping to his feet, Low used his sleeve to wipe away blood and started issuing orders:

"What are ye lying there for? D'ye think this is a holiday excursion? Collins, get up to the crow's nest and see what's around us. Watson, Aspin? Go forward and sound for depth. Daubery, take a head count. Morris, damage assessment. Barnes . . ."

Barnes was gone.

Low caught sight of Chopin and Tesla lying in a bedraggled heap amid a pile of crushed blocks and pulleys against the port railing.

"Glad to see ye decided to remain with us, gentlemen. Welcome to the Bitter Sea. If ye think that little storm in a teacup was frightening, just wait until we face a real maelstrom. *That'll* be something to compose a tune to, I tell ye. Now, it looks as if I've lost a few hands. Nothing about this trip is turning out to be 'First star to the right, and straight on until mourning' so you'll have to make yerselves useful . . ."

*

Thomas Neill Cream hadn't enjoyed himself so much in a long time. Not only were the threads of his scheme pulling together rather nicely, but he also found himself experiencing an unexpected reprieve from pursuit.

Thick, fluffy white clouds graced the sky overhead. Through them, the shimmering radiance of an unseen sun grazed the landscape in the golden blush of a midsummer's grace. Above that expanse, an amethyst vault glittered to the frosted brilliance of a billion stars, each one humming with prismatic overtones of crystal clarity.

Before him, lush grasses and dense woodlands spread away to the horizon, encompassing the hills in viridescent blankets of luxury, and uncountable olive hues.

Arriving here only an hour ago, he had been sorely tempted to simply sit down, lie back and enjoy the scenery. Sadly, the temporal conduit didn't work like that.

He glanced behind where his spellbound thugs, Haggai and Micah, were bringing up the rear with his insensible insurance policy. These damned souls were not the focus of his scrutiny, however: just beyond them a huge stone archway slowly advanced, ponderously but inexorably marking the limits of his specially-fabricated personal world. Where the granite blocks grazed the ground, all evidence of this reality literally faded away, to be replaced by a featureless gray void.

Fortunately, there was no rush. Although relentless, the granite's progress was undemanding, its easy pace a delight to savor. Regardless, the point was clear: This was but a construct, a tool by which one traveled from A to B within the underworlds, and not a place to offer permanent respite from endless drudgery.

More's the pity.

Cream checked on how his lackeys were doing. Despite their large size, both were bureaucrats accustomed to sitting behind desks. The physical exertion was taking its toll.

"What appears to be the holdup?" he called.

"She's heavy," Haggai complained, "and my arms feel like they'll drop off at any moment. Can't Micah take a turn now? He hasn't even tried to carry her yet."

"Why should I?" Micah countered. "You obviously liked the look of the Inquisitor when we surprised her in her lair. Want her for yourself, do you?"

'No!"

"Yes, you do. I can see it in your eyes."

"Liar! I just wanted to protect her from you. *You're* the pervert, don't forget. That's why you ended up condemned. I don't really care what happens, so long as you don't get all sicko on her."

As if trying to prove a point, Haggai deposited his burden on the grass and jabbed a finger toward his associate.

Before Cream could say anything, Haggai stepped forward and drove the point of his toe into Strawberry's stomach.

"Careful, you idiot!" Cream thundered. "She must be unblemished to create the right effect. If you damage her, I'll have your head."

Micah rushed to intervene. "It's okay, it's all right. I've got her now." He stooped to lift the unconscious form into his arms. "Up you come, nice and—"

Strawberry's hands flew around the Blue Suit's head and pulled him close.

"Aaaaaaaargh!"

Micah's scream froze his companions. Dropping his charge, he staggered backward, hands clutching his throat. Blood welled between his fingers in an endless cascade that drenched the front of his shirt. Then he slumped to his knees, gargling, and fell forward. As he landed face down in the long grass, his body dissipated on the wind.

"Who'sh fucking nexht?" Strawberry slurred, attempting to wipe gore from her chin and gain her feet at the same time.

Cream was delighted by the unexpected resilience of his captive. "Miss Fields. Pretending to be drugged, were we? Naughty girl, we can't have you kicking and screaming until we've set the stage. Here, let me put that right."

He nodded to Haggai, who had moved up behind the stricken Inquisitor. The ruffian punched her to the back of her neck. Already stupefied from the powerful cocktail of drugs running through her veins, Strawberry's head snapped forward.

She must have been stronger than she looked, however, for she caught herself and attempted to rise once more. Then the abuse took its toll, and her eyes rolled into the back of her skull. She flopped to the floor for a second time and lay still.

Cream stooped to his bag and removed a large syringe containing a viscid, rose-gold fluid.

"This time I think I'll give you a double dose . . . just to make sure." He moved to her side, applied the needle to her carotid artery, and injected the syringe's entire contents into her. Only then did he sit back, satisfied.

"What now, sir?" Haggai asked.

Cream stood up and looked about.

"Now? My dear Haggai, pick her up. You don't get another break until we reach our destination."

The doctor spun on his heels and resumed his leisurely walk.

*

"Haven't we seen enough?" Champ Ferguson complained. "We've been here two days now. Two goddam blisterin' days. Shouldn't we be reporting this back to the boss, or even to Satan himself?"

"We will, my friend," Yamato Takeru replied. "But before we do, I must ensure to gain the whole picture. You know how vexed Daemon gets with an incomplete account, and our Master all the more so . . ." He paused to glance toward their targets. "So I need to understand exactly what they are doing. How else can I prepare an effective countermeasure?"

Champ continued to grumble until Yamato held up his hand for silence.

Once he had it, the former ninja warrior checked the integrity of his encompassing shield and extended his senses into the grotto, closing his eyes. So severe were the conditions inside that it was useless to attempt using his mundane sight, for the world he could see was swathed in a shimmering haze that reduced his vision to a greasy blur.

Despite being within a vast cave system, ash and cinders pattered down about them like snowflakes. These brought no relief, however, only serving to emphasize the intensity of the stifling furnace surrounding the Hounds. The ambient heat flensed the surface from the surrounding rocks and scorched them black. So extreme was this phenomenon, it even superheated the atoms of the cave walls. Their crystalline structure glowed as if powered by miniature suns, and the diamond-hard stalagmites and stalactites festooning the floors and ceiling gleamed like an army of laser scalpels.

Thick acrid fumes belched into the air, and spumes of acid sprayed every which way at once. Yamato eased his discomfort by ceasing to breathe.

The remains of a dozen Corinthian columns lay scattered across the floor before a wide marble stairway at the far end of the chamber, leading up to a boiling cauldron of flame. Yamato surmised this place must have once served as a site of worship for one of the many sects infesting hell. Now, it only served the needs of the four Sibitti crowded around it.

Yamato refined his sensitivity, allowing his astral probe to sample the character of their enemies' manipulations. He was deeply shocked by what he saw.

That can't be right? Surely they aren't that powerful?

A chill wormed its way down his spine, forcing him to consider a more prudent course of action. He opened his mind to share the scene with his colleague.

"Champ," he murmured, "this is important. If I don't make it out of here, ensure Daemon is apprised of what these monsters are doing."

"And what *are* they doing?"

Yamato enlarged the impression of the blazing inferno, labeling it clearly so Champ could understand.

"That is an access point to a cosmic chain," he said. "Think of it as an anchor that helps keep the circles of the underverse in their proper places. Every realm has a number of them scattered

throughout their esoteric foundations. They're important, because not only do they keep each reality secure in relation to its neighbor, but when we journey, say, between New Hell and Hades, or between Perdition and Niflheim, we use the gravitational vortexes those anchors generate to travel safely. Like *this* . . . see?"

Champ studied the diagram his friend presented to him.

"So, those are hydraspace lanes? The actual roads that run through the Sheolspace continuum?"

"That's right. Anyway, it would appear the Sibitti are trying to mess with the gravity wells that fasten each chain in place."

"They're *what?*"

Yamato tried to think of an analogy Champ would understand. He had a moment of inspiration: "Imagine sneaking up on your enemy when they've bedded down for the night. The Sibitti have just found out where we've tethered our horses, and they're trying to cut them loose."

"What? So all the different levels would float free like stampeding colts?"

"Exactly!"

Champ glanced around the outcrop and ran his fingers through his hair.

"Shoot! Can they even do that?"

"I don't know. But as I said, it's not preventing them from trying." Yamato nodded toward the enforcers. "Even though we're tucked out of the way, in a remote part of Hades, they've managed to access an anchor leading to Juxtapose. From what I can tell, that specific one is meshed to the Bitter Sea, just outside Olde London Town. Out of all the locations they could have chosen, that is the one most prone to fluctuation. Whatever they're doing will cause a huge seismic disturbance. We've got to warn them."

"About fuckin' time."

"And why would I let you do that?" a voice suddenly enquired.

The air shivered, and a demonic Sibitti folded out of nowhere.

Champ raised his Abaddon 6000 and discharged it full at the enforcer's chest.

Boom!

Glittering claws raked through the air, slapping the pellets aside.

"We're about to test the extent of our machinations," the entity hissed. "Wouldn't you care to stay and witness the results?"

Yamato whirled around to intervene. His enchanted blade, the Sword of Gathering Clouds of Heaven, came singing free of its sheath.

Something about his weapon caused the Sibitti to pause.

"A worthy foe," it hissed, "fearless, disciplined, focused. And elemental it would seem, as are we . . ."

A second Sibitti appeared.

Then a third.

Yamato's mind flared. *We must go!*

No shittin'?

Yamato spun an upsilon field and slammed it down over himself and Champ. Just as they were about to cross the threshold, the personified weapons reacted.

An almighty concussion turned the whole world white, and the Hounds fell into a yawning chasm of blackness.

*

How I managed to keep my temper, I'll never know. I needed a pirate, and fast. The first place I looked was Davey Jones' Locker, down in Bittersea—an area blessed wall-to-wall with brigands, buccaneers, and privateers. But these were also amongst the most superstitious folk in existence and ever since the attack on the Cirque du Freak, something had our seafaring denizens spooked. What it was they wouldn't say, but reports kept rolling in of strange occurrences out in the middle of the ocean. A bit of an understatement, in my view, as the Bitter Sea was renowned for unexpected squalls and storms.

Yet this strangeness was something different. It had them running scared and, due to the uncanny timing of events, I suspected it might also be connected to my current case.

Therefore, after more than forty hours during which pleading, sweet-talking and, in the end, outright threats had fallen on deaf ears, I found myself marooned on dry land and no closer to capturing Cream than I'd been two days previously.

Until fifty-five minutes ago, that is, when I'd had my first lucky break . . .

I was at the port, going from ship to ship, haggling with the Pirate Lords and trying to strike a deal, when one of them suggested I try a character called Jolly Roger.

A bit of digging revealed that Jolly Roger was none other than Roger Crossbones, an ex-sailor and one of the craziest men undead. About five years previously, whilst still a first mate to Captain "Rip" Tide, he'd been enjoying a day off, shark fishing with some of his crewmates. The group had gotten very drunk and had run out of chum—the mixture of fish-parts and blood fishermen use to attract prize specimens—so Roger had taken it upon himself to offer his own slashed toes as bait. This worked like a charm. The Great White had not only accepted the proffered foot but the rest of the leg as well: It had yanked in the whole of Roger, whereupon it chewed him six ways from Sinday. Due to his inebriated state Roger didn't feel a thing and died laughing, amid a frothing patch of blood, guts, and bubbling turbulence. Hence his nickname: "Jolly" Roger.

Upon reassignment, the Undertaker saw the funny side of this, and gave him a 'pugleg' instead of a pegleg. I was intrigued to find out what that meant, as I had been reliably informed that after the loss of his limb, Roger was taken under the wing of the

Commodore himself, and encouraged to expand into a new line of business: trading.

Except, of course, that "trading" meant smuggling, as well as exchanging goods, services and information to selected customers for the right price. Needless to say, Roger had taken to his new line of work like a fish to water, and was now one of the Commodore's most trustworthy white-market contacts.

An excellent bit of news, for if anyone knew of captains willing to risk certain death by venturing out into the Maw during this latest crisis, Roger most certainly would.

But how to ensure his cooperation?

That's when I requested the help of my newfound friends in Perish. Both Don Pérignone and François de UnBorn were delighted at the prospect of expanding their considerable network into Olde London Town.

On my behalf, additional calls were made, and not fifteen minutes ago I received my second lucky break. Roger agreed to see me, and I was given directions to his base of operations; a tavern called, unsurprisingly, Jolly Roger's. Only it wasn't in Bittersea, but over in Lambsdeath High Street, smack bang in the middle of Old Paradise Street and Black Prince Road, an area known for street gangs and unsavory dealings.

However, *that* had a plus side. Roger's establishment had built up a reputation, and now attracted the crazier element among the criminal underworld and pirate bands. In fact, certain captains known to frequent the inn would gladly stab themselves in the heart merely to increase their standing among the brotherhood.

These were exactly the type of men I needed to speak to, and as the carriage pulled up outside, I felt more positive than I had in a long time.

Jolly Roger's sat right on the boundary of several epochs. The property itself was encompassed within medieval times. The sidewalk outside and the road looked to be part of the Victorian era, with gas lamps and cobbled streets the norm. The opposite side of the river appeared most definitely modern-day.

Despite the cosmopolitan mix, this district had its own unique character. Other buildings along the block were shuttered and barred, a reflection of the natural order here. Mesmerizing vapors undulated across the ground from the River Tombs only yards away. For the most part the place was deserted, except for those determined damned souls still out to make a living or end a life.

Acrid smoke billowed from the Jolly Roger's chimney, which listed crazily to one side. Of its three levels, each floor leaned out farther than the one below. A sign swinging from the post outside depicted a fat man sitting at a table, a large tankard of frothing ale in his hand. He was laughing heartily and taking a long pull from a Gaelic pipe clenched firmly between his teeth.

At this crossroads, Jolly Roger's was the only place with its windows open; light spilled out from inside, along with the sounds of a popular sea-shanty. As tap houses went, it was one of the biggest I'd ever seen.

Nimrod opened the door and I followed him in.

More than fifty people cluttered the main saloon, a clear sign that most of the fleet was locked in port. Every single seat and table was taken. Even the table-free spots along the walls were packed with patrons leaning against thoughtfully-placed, waist-high shelves.

Background chatter fell away to nothing as we entered, and the smell of ale, roasting meats, and tobacco made me ravenously hungry.

As I glared around the room, a rotund, cheery, red-faced fellow behind the main bar waved and came hobbling toward me. A yelping sound rang out with every step he took, loud in the silence. He made his way between the tables, and I saw that his right leg disappeared at the knee into the butt-end of a fawn-colored, wrinkly-faced dog.

A Pug! The penny dropped. *A pirate with a literal pugleg. Oh, very good!*

Despite the fact he was a complete and utter tosser, I was forced to appreciate the subtle nuances of the Undertaker's humor a bit more.

Roger saw me smile as he drew near and grinned in return.

"You've heard, then?" he said, waggling the pug at me. Then he held up his right arm and showed me a gleaming razor-sharp hook. "And this is the hand I wipe my ass with. Our halitosis-ridden friend was inspired by the circumstances of my first reassignment after arriving here. He's kept me this way ever since."

Roger threw a beer-soaked cloth over one of his shoulders. The other shoulder was stained by white and black droppings of some sort. Whatever made the stains must have been acidic, for it had eaten away at the fabric of his shirt.

He noticed my scrutiny. "Yes, before you ask . . . I *do* have a parrot. Her name *is* Polly, and *nooo,* she isn't pretty. In fact, the Undertaker inflicted her with a severe bowel condition, so she gets screaming diarrhea. Regrettably, that only takes place when she's sitting on my shoulder." He sighed. "Anyway, your acquaintances across the water have told me why you're here. Follow me to the bar, and I'll see what I can do."

"So why is everyone so afraid?" I asked. "I thought the Pirate Lords ran a pretty tight ship to keep business flowing?"

"That's just it," Roger called back. "We're getting a buzz that the shorelines are shifting. Most trading is done along the coasts, but the captains who've just returned to port say the land is falling into the sea in one place after another. What's more, shallow reefs and new headlands are appearing where previously there was water. Tides are going haywire, as if following the lead of an entirely new gravitational anchor, and the Maw is experiencing all sorts of weird phenomena. One ship reported seeing a mid-ocean tsunami. It uncovered the seabed for miles in every direction, and then crushed three brigantines that had fallen prey to its currents . . ."

He fell quiet for a moment, conscious of the fact that the entire tavern was hanging on every word.

"Anyway, the *Talon* was the only vessel to survive that encounter. And her testimony ties in with the fact that we've lost seven crews since yesterday morning, and three more today. That's not good for business."

I grunted.

He turned to look at me. "You're Satan's Reaper. Do *you* know why any of this is happening? Is His Infernal Jester trying to punish us for something? Keep us on our toes?"

Patrons leaned toward us, waiting for my reply.

"I'm sorry, I don't," I answered. "The truth of the matter is that one of the attacks was aimed at me. And the only thing I *do* know is that I urgently need to cross the Bitter Sea. Tonight, in fact. Anyone with the balls enough to help me can name his price."

The entire inn fell silent.

"It'll be like pissing in the wind," someone called from one of the snugs, "all kinds of messy and disgusting."

"That it will," I countered, "but just imagine what it'll do for your reputation. The only captain with the guts to help the Reaper—and His Satanic Majesty—in their hour of need."

"Fortunately, I like messy," the same voice cried out. "Ah, fuck it! You only live repeatedly down here. I might as well do something that'll make life more interesting."

A tall, rangy pirate with short-cropped hair and goatee stood and made his way toward me. I was momentarily taken aback. Usually, his ilk favored the feathered tricorn hats, breeches and waistcoats of their era. But this guy was wearing a PFD vest over a Trident aquafleece spray top and leggings, rounded off with no-nonsense, modern-day sailing boots.

"Captain Charles Vane at your service," he declared, "although some here call me Allweather Vane, because I'm willing to take my ship into any kind of storm, any time of day or night."

"Just the man I'm looking for!" I declared. "Although you might have a problem from the word go."

"Why's that?"

"The people I'm after are heading for Cog Isle, a three-day journey from here. They have a two-day start."

Vane threw back his head and laughed. "Pah! That's nothing. What are they using, a galleon? Their best speed is a mere eight knots. Even the fastest clipper rigs we have are limited to a paltry twenty knots; and so far as I'm aware, they're too light to brave the squalls raging at the moment."

I decided to keep some details close to my chest. "My apologies. All I can say is it will take them a full three days to reach their destination. Can you help?"

Vane looked toward Roger. "Jolly? A bottle of Diabhalvulin 18 to toast my imminent contract." Then he extended his hand toward mine. "Reaper, you've got yourself a deal. The *Lone Ranger,* my cruiser, isn't like other vessels in the fleet. Perhaps you can tell by looking at me that I like things chic and modern. My baby is a Constantine Class Hell-Cat 6000 super-sport sea cruiser. She's one hundred and fifteen feet long, and powered by six HTV Kamikaze water-jet diesels, giving me a round range of eight hundred and ninety nautical miles, and an average cruising speed of forty-nine knots. I can get you where you need to go and back on one load of fuel in just over twenty-four hours. Is that good enough for you?"

"You have a speedboat?"

"More like a speed yacht. I've modified her, so she's watertight, submersible, and self-righting. Come hell or high water, I can plow straight through the choppiest water. In some circumstances we might reduce speed a bit, but we'll still get to the Forbidden Isle in less than a day, which I believe was the main stipulation of your request?" He held his hand and knife at the ready.

At last! Something's going right. "You've got yourself a commission. And if Diabhalvulin 18's your tipple, I'll have a case of it waiting for you for when we get back."

I held out my palm.

Two quick slashes later I was sealing the deal.

Vane held up my arm so the rest of the room could see the blood running down our wrists. He shouted, "The Reaper and I have reached an agreement, bound by blood. Both he and his companion are now protected by our code. Do you all bear witness to this fact?"

"Aye, we do!" The room resounded with off-color affirmations, and suddenly everyone was ordering a fresh round of drinks.

I glanced toward Nimrod for the first time. *Thank Azazel for that! I thought we were screwed.*

It would seem your record may yet remain intact, he replied, without a glimmer of emotion. *Just as well. You know how our Master loves untarnished service.*

Roger shouldered his way through the press, carrying the distinctive gold and green bottle I knew so well. I leaned closer to Vane.

"So, you like your whiskey?"

"I do. While most pirates stick to rum, I've developed a more refined palate. I was first introduced to Devil's Shore a few years back. A beautiful single malt if ever there was one. Then a fellow privateer suggested Corsairs' Rye and Armageddon while we were on a job across in New Hell a few years later. Now that was spectacular . . ."

He broke off as Roger laid out two glasses. Our host filled each one with sparkling amber nectar, and placed the bottle on the table.

". . . but all that paled when I discovered this little beauty."

Vane lifted his tumbler.

"Gentlemen, may I propose a toast to safe wa–"

The tavern rocked to its foundations. A deep, subsonic note infringed on my astral senses. Tables and chairs shook and men shouted as drinks spilled and display shelves toppled to the floor.

I heard detonations outside. Through a window I saw a solitary telegraph pole on the other side of the river swinging from side to side, as if in the grip of a giant's invisible hand. Then the transformers adorning its crossbars suddenly exploded.

Immediately after, another, much more powerful shockwave reverberated down into the roots of the fundament. Car alarms triggered as the distant rumble gathered strength and drew nearer. Roaring past, it shattered the Roger's windows in their frames and splintered the stone paving the floor.

A rolling motion seized us, shaking everyone back and forth like helpless fox cubs in the jaws of merciless hounds.

Dust billowed through the air. Falling from every ledge, crack and crevice, it filled my lungs and covered everything in a gray film of death. Following came chunks of mortar and larger lumps of plaster. Pressure built within my eardrums as if something were trying to crush my skull.

Are we under attack again? Nimrod called.

You can bet your ass we are. C'mon, let's go and see what hornets' nest has been stirred up this time.

I deployed my scythe, and struggled toward the door through dancing furniture and juddering bodies. The door's iron supports burst from their hinges and flew across the sidewalk, shredding passersby like wheat.

I staggered outside and stood on the embankment looking north. My head was ringing, and for a moment, everything went still. No hell-birds, no traffic, no noise.

Then reality returned with a vengeance:

Lambsdeath Bridge was gone, along with most of the in-frastructure lining this side of the Tombs. All that remained were the scoured frames of one or two of the larger properties, and two stumps of reinforced concrete: one on my side of the river, and an-other midstream.

Opposite me, Westmonster had been devastated. Although Little Ben was still intact, huge chunks of the Ministry of Infer-nal Affairs had been wrecked and now lay in ruins amid growing plumes of greasy smoke and spreading fires. The entire city looked as if it had just endured a blitzkrieg, only to come off second best.

I watched open-mouthed as a wall of magma sped away from me. Following the course of the river, it vaporized every-thing in its path and left the Tombs behind it empty but for an in-sipid trickle of mud.

Utter carnage raged. Sirens sounded in the background, and dark clouds gathered overhead as if Juxtapose had been laid upon a funeral pyre.

What the fuck?

"We've been marooned!" someone behind me gasped.

I spun to find Vane and Nimrod staring off into the distance, south toward Bittersea from where the magma had surged.

A part of me—a part deep down inside—liked what I saw.

This is what hell should look like. Make the bastards suffer . . . But not on my watch, not unless Satan actually sanctions it. "What do you mean, we've been marooned?"

Vane pointed toward the Satanic Intelligence Service, a mile away.

"The *Lone Ranger* was berthed not far from the MI13 build-ing, but look at it. The whole area is devastated. I'm betting this goes all the way back to the Bitter Sea."

"Really?"

"Yes. Perhaps even farther. Remember, that ocean borders on the junction of a number of realities. If whatever caused that upheaval came from another realm, it will have destabilized the entire region. That's why the River Tombs has run dry. Think of it as a mega form of hydraulic damming. There's such a huge difference in pressure, it's effectively holding the sea at bay. But this can't last forever. As gravity equalizes, there'll be a gigantic tidal bore hammering this way. Any ships that survive the initial fire surge will no doubt get smashed to pieces by the second wave. We need to evacuate."

"But that means—"

"I know. My deepest apologies, Reaper, but this is no storm in a teacup. We won't be going anywhere anytime soon."

So what the blazes can I do now?

Chapter 23: The Isle of Cogs

The chamber had no need for candlesticks or any other form of lighting, for tongues of God's Grace flickered everywhere. They sparkled within the constitution of the air as if comprised of the essence of suns, born amongst theomorphic clouds of infinite opulence. They glittered from the veined fabric of the marble columns holding the roof in place. They danced in a multitude of scintillating shades amid a waterfall that cascaded like molten silver into a pool of liquid serenity. And they clustered in corners, in every nook and cranny, so that the very idea of "shadow" could never taint the fidelity of unblemished illumination.

Yet those concentrations of glory congregated especially about the being that glided, like beauty personified, amongst the pillars of ancient enmity which endowed the cavern with strength.

The being's robes were simple and hung from slender shoulders like veils of purest silk. Pristine and unblemished, the gown was colorless, far too immaculate to be labeled with anything as banal as mere pigmentation.

The figure's feet were bare and perfectly formed, although bound about the ankles by delicate diamond fetters. Yet its movements still were graceful. It possessed no wings, for they had been taken a long, long time ago. Nonetheless, this creature was unmistakably an angel.

The angel's face was pale and ageless. While its countenance encompassed both majestic antiquity and the innocence of a child, its ravaged eyes looked beyond eternity into madness.

The troubled spirit tarried by the fountain and stooped to drink.

Bitterly cold, the water frosted when making contact with the angel's skin, and yet the temperature didn't concern it, for it was immune to the effects of mundane things.

Three sets of doors stood between pillars of living rock.

Two were within reach and seemed to be made of obsidian. Black as coal, they were heavily barred with iron and set inside ruby frames powered by the very lifeblood of infernity.

The third door was as white as snow and made of an unknown substance. Simple and unadorned, it stood positioned within an arched stone frame decorated by inlaid golden glyphs. This particular portico lay just beyond the reach of the angel's restraining chain and shimmered as if suffering a relentless assault from someplace else.

To one side of that entrance, a granite plinth housed a huge glittering sword. Buried halfway to its cross-guard, the weapon burned like ice, and the jewel that formed the pommel of its impossibly large hilt blazed silver, like a lunar flare in the night sky.

The entity drank its fill and then dipped its fingers into the mirrorlike liquid. As it trailed idle patterns across the surface, it sang, softly:

> "Hark the bonded angel sings,
> Curses on Earth's would-be king,
> Always vile and never mild,

Satan fallen and defiled,
Joyful Erra's plans arise,
See new fires in the skies,
Portents from the ends of . . ."

Distracted, the angel paused in its song and closed its eyes as if about to pray. Its head kinked to one side, and a sad smile crept across its face.

"Visitors?" it gasped, clearly bemused by the concept.

"Why, I haven't had visitors since, since . . . well, forever!"

*

Waves crashed against the small craft from every angle, as if attempting to beat it away from its goal by brute force, but it was too late. Despite the wild fluctuations that had harangued them since Bittersea Port, the boat's passengers had almost reached their destination.

With a heave, the longboat caught a final surge, lifting across the last of the shoals and onto the narrow strip of sand edging the waterline.

Frédéric Chopin ignored the driving wind and stinging rain, and breathed a huge sigh of relief. His exhalation mingled with the hiss of receding surf.

We're here at last. Not long now, my love.

Seizing the moment, he wrapped his oilskin tighter about his slight frame and crunched up through the shingle so he could better survey their destination. As he went, he absentmindedly massaged his hands and resolutely ignored everyone else.

But not for long.

"Is this it—our destination?" Nikola Tesla enquired, his eyes alight with energetic fascination as he took in the details of the land ahead.

"It would appear so."

Chopin thought back to his vision and brought the prerequisite details to the fore.

A jigsaw lay in front of them, unlike any puzzle you'd willingly want to solve, for this construct filled the beach with menace. Neither was it made of wood, but of iron and steel, of bronze and copper, perhaps of purest gold. And it was huge; a sprawling enigma of cogs and ratchets, sprockets and prongs in all shapes and sizes, stretching off toward the sand dunes fifty yards away.

Chopin was reminded of pictures from hellivision documentaries about breakers' yards and commercial sites where metal-based industrial waste was processed for recycling.

Those teeth appear capable of swallowing the Flight of Fancy *whole, galleon or not, while the smaller tines look sharp enough to snap an ankle or take a finger.*

Something nagged at the back of Chopin's mind.

So why aren't they moving, as they were in my dream?

He felt unnerved, for he'd seen enough of this maze at work to know it could mash a human body out of existence in seconds. Regardless, he was forced to dismiss the conundrum from his mind to assess the rest of their route.

Sure enough, a slender path led from the fringes of the shoreline up onto a cluster of stony hillocks. Following a series of switchbacks, the trail wound higher and higher, eventually climbing a massive rocky peninsula situated at the narrowest point of the island. Shaped like a vast wedge, this buttress faced out to sea like a colossal icebreaker, daring the atrocious weather to overwhelm its resolve. The black tower sat atop that fistula, as defiant and proud as in his vision.

"Yes," Chopin mumbled, "this is definitely the place, although its defenses seem to be lying dormant at the moment."

"Isn't that a good thing? Won't it make our task easier?"

"It would. But this is hell for, goodness sake, and I don't imagine for one min–"

"Well, it's good enough for me!" Edward Low interrupted.

Chopin turned to discover the captain had been busy whilst he himself had been otherwise engaged. Having unloaded the landing craft, his pirates now scuttled about on shore, preparing a few provisions.

"My job was to get ye here," Low said, "and that I've done. However, it feels wrong to just dump ye here, especially considering the prize ye've given me." He nodded toward the clockwork trap. "I know ye said it was dangerous, but the darn thing doesn't appear to be working. So, I'll have my men drop a few supplies off for ye among the rocks, and we'll be on our way."

"That's very kind of you," Chopin replied, "but completely un–"

He braced himself as an incredibly strong gust of wind caught everyone by surprise. Men staggered and struggled to remain upright. Screams alerted him to the fact something was wrong.

They all turned to watch as two of the sailors were swept into the air. They must have been unpacking something, for they were holding tight to a large piece of tarpaulin that now acted as a kite. Away they sailed, inland, only to be deposited in an untidy heap amongst the rocks.

Low burst out laughing. "Well, that was fortuitous. Raleigh and Brown completely overshot the beach. Perhaps we all ought to try that method of approach. Why don't ye—"

A bright flash interrupted his words.

Not seventy yards away, two gigantic apparitions appeared from thin air, close behind his stricken men. More than seven feet in height, both muscle-bound effigies wore executioner's smocks and hoods, and each looked able to tear a bull in half. Not that they'd need to, with the axes they were carrying, which seemed as large as the interlopers ahead.

And neither Raleigh nor Brown was aware of the danger.

"Jailers!" Chopin gasped. "Captain, you can't—"

"Hawkins, Blight," Low snapped, "get yerselves over there and help those men. Aspin, Daubery, go with 'em."

"Aye, Cap'n," they yelled.

All four pirates sprinted forward, drawing cutlasses as they ran. The dull, hollow reverberation of feet on metal rang out.

Clunk!

Oh, no!

A resonant ticking kept time above the steady drone of the gale.

Chopin reached out to grasp Tesla by the sleeve and backed away into the water. Low saw the movement and followed suit, dragging the two nearest sailors with him.

Just in time.

The sprocket just in front of where the captain had been standing spun to life. Its movement kicked two other cogs on its either side of into motion. Within the blink of an eye, four ratchets were moving; then eight. The escalating activation rippled forward, like a wave gaining momentum. In seconds, it caught up to the pirates at the rear.

A terrible grinding sound of meat and bone being levigated buzzed through the air. Aspin and Daubery went down as if pole-axed, amid a sickening spray of red mist.

Still a few paces ahead, Hawkins and Blight glanced over their shoulders, distracted by the commotion behind them. Panic set in. Both men leaped away from each other, dancing and jigging from side to side in a desperate attempt to evade the monstrous teeth chomping their way toward them.

Beyond the carnage, Raleigh and Brown jumped up and down, waving their arms like mad, yelling encouragement, still completely unaware of the presence of the jailers.

I can't watch, Chopin thought.

But he did, for the unfolding scene was as compelling as it was horrible.

Hawkins was the next to go, caught squarely in a crusher that would have squashed a sedan flat. One moment he was running hell-for-leather toward the refuge offered by a small seaweed-covered rock; the next, the ground simply opened up beneath him. Caught between two huge slabs of metal, he was instantly mangled below the waist. The slabs slammed together and flipped over for a second time, liquidizing what was left of the unfortunate Hawkins as they swept him from sight.

Up on the hillock, Raleigh and Brown froze in shock, just as the jailers' axes split them open from crown to crotch. Their sundered remains began to dissipate before they'd even had a chance to flop to the earth.

Now only Blight remained. A former circus acrobat, he'd managed to evade the wheels of death with remarkable alacrity. He was within yards of the mound when his heel came down on a needle-sharp point. He yelped in pain, stumbled, and threw himself forward, toward the temporary safety of the rocks.

He didn't quite make it.

The fabric of his trouser leg caught in a tine. Hooked, Blight was yanked to a standstill, whereupon he bunched into a ball and gathered his strength for another leap.

Ratchets and sprockets continued churning. A small prong latched onto his toes. Dragged backward, Blight screamed and started clawing divots from the earth as his legs were drawn, inch by morbid inch, into the workings of the trap, and pulverized.

A shot rang out, and Blight's head snapped back. His body fell limp and was consumed by ravenous teeth before it had a chance to dissolve.

Chopin turned to stare at Low, who calmly replaced his pistol in his cummerbund.

The Captain snorted. "I'll not have my men die like that."

Higher up on the rocks, another flash signaled the departure of the jailers.

"I did try to warn you," Chopin said. "This place might look benign, but it's one giant network of death. From what I can understand, arriving by sea requires aspirants to navigate the minefield. There is a safe path, and only by following it can we hope to deactivate all the other booby traps."

"Then I'll take my leave." Low tipped his cap. "I've lost enough men on this voyage. It'll take weeks for their reassignment to come through, an' even then I can't be sure I'll get them back; and if I do, what I'll get from that bloody idiot who calls himself an Undertaker might be next to useless." He started wading toward the longboat. "Morris, Christian, come along. It's time to be away."

Chopin and Tesla watched them go.

As the small pirate craft bobbed back toward the galleon, Tesla sidled closer to his companion.

"Are you sure you know the correct way?"

"We're about to find out." Chopin stooped to retrieve his knapsack and waggled his finger. "But just in case, we have our additional insurance right here . . . and a bonus I almost left back on the *Fancy.*"

"Insurance?" Tesla queried, "You think we'll need it?"

In reply to Tesla's questioning look, Chopin added, "We've waited a long time for this plan to come to fruition. I'll not have things spoiled now by the impatience of an idiot with a god complex. I've learned it's never wise to keep all your eggs in one basket, even with the end in sight. Sometimes, one makes sacrifices in order to ensure the day is won. At least that way, you survive to come back and play another day, yes?"

He paused to bring up the image of the elaborate pattern he'd seen in his mind. After replaying the events a few times, he felt confident enough to proceed.

"Are you ready, Nikola? Now, whatever you do, stick close to me and step exactly where I step. If anything triggers, for pity's sake, just use the orb and damn the consequences."

*

The gusts scouring the crown of Gibbets Hill on Cog Isle regularly exceeded two hundred and twenty knots. But that was understandable, for the prison had been encompassed within a permanent hurricane ever since its inception thirteen millennia previously.

Being so close to an established core of instability kept most things from thriving—except for a tree called the Scaffold. An ancient oak, fed on the blood of the condemned and fortified by the darkest necromancy, the Scaffold served as the prison's gallows for those rare few who managed to survive—in a more or less lucid condition—until the end of their sentences. For only if they satisfied the Dark Lord's perversions would they be permitted a death that freed them from torment. Of course, they then would face the corruptions of the Undertaker. But that was another story.

Except for one shattered spar, not a single leaf or bud sprouted from this weathered sentinel. And even so, the only thing to adorn its ruined limb was a frayed and tattered rope, fluttering wildly in the wind—a poignant reminder of how long it was since the tree had seen the last emancipation.

Below that bough, a wreath of stones marked the point of departure for the deceased; or, once in a blue moon, the site where new arrivals might take their first awestruck glimpse of one of the most desolate places in the underverse.

Today must be a special day, for as visitors made their slow way across the beach nearly a mile below, the ring of boulders here on the promontory began shining for the first time in an age.

A vortex condensed within the circle.

The outline of three people appeared there, infused with ethereal radiance. One traveler stood alone, distinct and separate, while the other two were superimposed as if one were carrying the other.

The light winked out, and they dropped down onto the bare dirt only to stagger under the wind's onslaught.

Dr. Thomas Cream's hat was snatched from his head in an instant. He ignored its loss, and scrambled forward as best he could to survey his surroundings.

Incredible. The entire island is shaped like a tooth, and we're at the root end.

Down below, within the scant protection afforded by a shallow bay, a galleon lay at anchor just offshore from the only beach the isle seemed to possess. Cream could just make out the shape of two people walking toward the low hills bordering the main outcrop while, out at sea, a small boat inched its slow and painful way in the direction of the ship.

Ah, my erstwhile associates. He smiled. *You're too late, my friends. I still think I'll get there just in the nick of time. And as they say, winner most definitely takes all.*

Cream glanced behind, where Haggai still struggled to retain his grip on their prisoner against the gale.

I suppose I'll have to do something about this now, or I'll lose the advantage I've worked so hard to achieve.

He removed the Sword of Damocles from his bag. As casually as possible, he strolled toward the swaying pair and made a deep incision in Strawberry's arm. As the blood flowed, he smeared some of it across the jewel adorning the weapon's hilt.

"You are in thrall to my will. Awaken now, and obey me in all things."

Although they remained glazed and unfocused, Strawberry's eyes snapped open. She stood upon her own two feet, somehow able to ignore the buffeting wind.

Excellent.

Freed of his burden, Haggai grinned and massaged his arms. "What do we do now?" he asked.

Cream sidled closer and pointed toward a black tower jutting up from the cliff less than half a mile away. "Well, Strawberry and I are going in there."

"And me?"

"And you . . . ?" Cream drove the tip of the blade into Haggai's temple. As Haggai's eyes rolled into the back of his head, Cream concluded, "You, dear boy, are going to enjoy a most wondrous day in the care of the Undertaker. Although you've not been a willing subject, and I can't guarantee he'll go easy on you." He chuckled. "But that's not really my concern, is it? Ta ta."

Haggai's essence dissipated, and Cream hummed a merry tune as he started down the slope. Passing Strawberry, he paused to trail a finger along her thigh. "Come along, my dear. Destiny awaits us."

*

I used the corner of my towel to wipe steam from the mirror and took a good long look at myself. This time, my gaze didn't crack the glass. Usually, a hot shower and change of clothing left me feeling refreshed and ready to face the challenges of a brand new day.

But not today.

Today, I was fighting the urge to rip off my trademark gloves, take my scythe, and go on a killing spree. I hadn't done that for ages—simply gone out and massacred a whole crowd of "someones" for the sheer, unadulterated joy of it.

I've been too focused on one thing lately. Consumed by it. That's going to change.

My bathroom door banged open.

"Glad to see you're dressed," Nimrod chided. "Everyone should be here within the next ten minutes. Have you worked out what you're going to say?"

"What is there to say," I retorted, "except the truth? We fucked up. Hidden away in our little tower and graced with all sorts of privileges, we've grown soft. Complacent. What started out as a straightforward assignment to recover a single renegade has somehow snowballed into stymieing an ever-growing plot to undermine Satan's authority. The devil only knows how many people are involved. I tell you now, we're only scratching the surface with Cream, Chopin and Tesla. Even though they have their own personal agendas, this conspiracy goes much deeper than we think."

"In what way?"

"Erra, for a start! How did he become involved? Hell, why did he become involved in the first place? And what about this apparently endless list of banned artifacts and weapons? Is there a link between Erra's insufferable enforcers and the encyclopedic knowledge that suddenly seems to be flooding the netherworlds regarding our strictest taboos? For Azazel's sake, I've been half expecting to see 'Read All About It, Everything You Ever Wanted To Know About The Time of Sundering' splashed all over the front page of the Sinday Times. I mean, c'mon! In what reality would someone like Cream be able find out about these things, and Satan's own Reaper not have a clue to their existence?"

As I settled into my very own 'throwing teddy out of the pram' session, I hurled my towel into the laundry basket and made my way toward the bedroom. Nimrod tagged along behind.

"Then there's the Devil's Children. How far has this cancer spread among them? Lackeys or not, each one of them is now a surefire security risk. I dread to think of other time bombs hiding away, just waiting for some subliminal signal to trigger further acts of mutinous mayhem. And which departments did Cream and

Chopin actually choose them from? What data can they access? If I had my way I'd cull the lot of them, and damn the inconvenience. The Undertaker could always draft additional assistants to help Gorgonous and his minions get through the backlog. It'd be safer in the long run because I'm now certain this . . . this pantomime has been in the planning for much longer than we originally thought."

I opened the door to my suite and ushered Nimrod inside.

"Strawberry's a prime example," I continued: "One of my own Inquisitors, abducted from a private, heavily-defended location that no one was supposed to know about. She's no slouch in a fight, and yet there was hardly any indication of a struggle. And to top it all, we can't seem to reach Champ and Yamato, and you know as well as I do what they were doing." Sparks danced along my scalp and down my arms, and I had to make a conscious effort not to let my passion take control. "There's a connection between every single event that has happened recently, I'm telling you. A common denominator that would help me reveal the mastermind behind it." I clamped my mouth shut and threw on my coat. "And Lucifer help them when I do."

Just mentioning His Infernal Majesty's name reminded me of another unsavory task I couldn't put off much longer.

Bugger! And I've still got to let my Dark Father know I messed everything up and need his help . . . "Fuck this, I need a drink. Care to join me?"

"Why not? But make it quick." Nimrod checked the time. "The team will be arriving soon, and we don't want to be partying when they get here."

The decanter was situated next to my writing bureau. I walked over to prepare a couple of single malts. As I did so, I glanced across to the fireplace, a welcome sight I hadn't laid eyes on in more than a week. Something on the mantelshelf caught my eye.

What's that?

A gray, baseball-sized object sat on the far side of my Napoleon-style display clock. Nestled between several figurines depicting Satan's daughter, Sin, in various stages of sublime rapture, it looked oddly out of place.

Hang on . . . I thought the Boss was going to take that?

Leaving the glasses where they were, I stalked over and picked up the item.

The orb's casing was warm to the touch.

Unholy shit! It's the prototype of the new multi-phasic portal generator François gave me. And it's still active!

Then I remembered a specific detail about the orb that made me go numb with shock.

Tesla specifically programmed these early models to operate twice before self-destructing. And I only used it once, to get away from the Sibitti. So that means . . . ?

I extended my other hand and exerted my will. My scythe flew from its resting place on the bed and into my grasp.

With a look of triumph, I turned to Nimrod.

"Cancel that meeting and grab your weapons," I crowed. "There's someplace we have to be. *Now.*"

Chapter 24: Eggs in a Basket

Tesla and Chopin braced themselves against the force of the hurricane and looked back over the obstacle course they had just completed. Already the bullying gusts were at work, covering large segments of the clockwork deathtrap with sand. Soon it would be utterly hidden, ready for its next victims.

"I can't believe it was that easy," Tesla muttered. "Torturously indirect, and sometimes heart-stopping, I'll admit, but . . . but . . ."

"A bit of a nerve-tingler?" Chopin said.

"Exactly. When you first neared the edge of the matrix so quickly, I was surprised . . . to say the least. Of course, that's before you led us back into its heart. Three times! I should have known better."

Chopin had to agree. Despite his foreknowledge, some of the maze's foot-snapping, bone-breaking undulations had approached frighteningly close. Snaking back and forth in a totally mesmerizing and completely random fashion, its automated operation had clearly been contrived to confuse and raise false hopes. He couldn't think of a single soul who could have guessed the safest route.

Tesla visibly shivered.

"And the ticking. Always the damned ticking . . ."

"Of course," Chopin agreed, "the entire construct was designed to place an aspirant under constant pressure. If you don't know the right way and are panicked into taking a wrong step . . . ouch!"

Tesla looked impressed.

"And yet, for all our meandering course, we didn't once need to run. Well played, sir. Well played."

"We can't relax yet," Chopin stressed. He beckoned to the trail ahead. "Come on, let's see what else awaits us before our eventual audience with destiny."

A storm was rolling in. They set off, pulling their cloaks ever tighter about them.

As Chopin's mind's-eye map had suggested, the path did indeed twist and turn through a series of switchbacks toward the looming bulk of the headland dominating this end of the island. The higher they went, the more barren the place became. Nonetheless, scattered clumps of dune grass and a hardy variety of beach-pea edged the path with green and violet glory. Chopin marveled how something so small and delicate could thrive in such harsh conditions.

But that's what life—or afterlife in our case—is all about. Clinging on and making the best of whatever comes your way.

The adventurers continued in this manner for a further fifteen minutes, during which time the biting wind increased, as did the chill factor. Then they wound their way around an outcrop of boulders and found themselves in a steep depression.

At more than twenty yards across, the bowl looked as if it had been scooped from the hillside by a giant hand. The effect was similar to walking into a hidden room, for although exposed to the vault like an amphitheatre, here the gales ceased abruptly and everything fell still.

Chopin came up short. To date, his visions had been incredibly detailed and accurate, and yet not once had the existence of this place been revealed. They were clearly meant to visit this shrine: although the path led in, there was no other way out.

A henge of stones stood at the center of open ground, rumbling to the resonance of hidden power. Surrounding the henge lay a shallow ditch from which eruptions of golden light sputtered into the air like exuberant soap-bubbles.

"What's the matter," Tesla asked, "was this not part of your dream?"

"No, it wasn't," Chopin admitted, "and yet something about this location seems familiar. Strange as this may sound, I don't feel threatened or worried."

"You don't feel threatened? But what are we going to do now? We're stuck."

"I don't think so. Don't forget, we're *supposed* to be here. We successfully traversed the shoreline trap, demonstrating we knew the official pattern, or code, if you like. The fact that I obtained the cryptograph by way of my prescient gift is neither here nor there. I did, I used it correctly, and we are safely through. Do *you* see any sign of jailers coming to rend us limb from limb? No. The island doesn't see us as a threat, and so long as we keep acting like we know what we're doing, I think we'll remain unharmed." He glanced toward the inner circle with its waiting moat of glowing essence. "The hard part is behind us. All we must do is . . . accept their invitation."

"Invitation? What the hell do you mean?"

"Watch this . . ."

They crept forward until they were standing at the very edge of the outer dyke. A spherule of aureate potency bloomed forth, and Chopin reached out to cup it with one hand. The bubble burst, spraying him with globules of shimmering radiance. A draft of unhellishly fresh, clean air wafted over him, together with the briefest snatch of a distant song.

Chopin gasped. *But that's . . .* that was wonderful!

The surge of vitality he'd detected had been absorbed by his skin, and now coursed through his veins. He flexed his fingers in delight.

"What was that?" Tesla asked, impatient to know what was happening.

"Hang on a second. I've sensed this energy before."

Ignoring all distractions, Chopin made a conscious effort to still his mind and look deep within himself. He soon remembered what was troubling him. His eyes snapped open, and he embraced his friend warmly.

"Are you all right, Frédéric?" Tesla blurted. The scientist seemed taken aback by Chopin's show of affection.

"More than all right." Chopin pointed toward the bottom of the moat. Simmering fissures marked several points where the fabric of Sheolspace had been torn open. "Those are natural rents, through which the very tincture of God's Grace can leak into the netherworlds." The ground rumbled beneath their feet, then subsided. "My visions have revealed such spots exist, here and there, throughout all the levels of hell; not because there's been a breach, but because such things are natural."

"Divine essence, a natural occurrence in infernity? Surely not."

"Oh yes. Despite the propaganda we've been force-fed, don't you recall some of the ancient texts we've discussed? You know, the ones my precognition revealed to us? Before the Time of Sundering, Satan and his angels could come and go from heaven at will. They even had their own appointed stations before the Almighty's throne. Our very own Ombudsman, Job, reveals such facts to us in the texts he wrote before his first death. Tell me, my friend. You're as sharp as a button, what core extract do you think our Dark Lord employed to kick off his little rebellion in the first place? What dominion did he share, to empower Samael and the rest of his cronies?"

Tesla pondered the conundrum only briefly. "I thought he used the Bālefire?"

"Eventually, yes he did, but not until he'd had time to work on it. Before that, the devil was forced to subvert the true nature of what was already on hand."

"Hang on, are you saying the Bālefire is corrupted Grace?"

"Ta-dah! How else do you think Lucifer was able to fabricate all this?" Chopin swept his arms through the air and spun on the spot. "He used the very power of creation itself, perverted to suit his aspirations. And he's the master of all corruption."

"Unholy shit!"

Chopin steered Tesla toward the ditch. "I've felt this potency before. Remember, the artifacts we recovered are ancient, leftovers from a time when the division between heaven and hell became established. The animating crux imbued into the angelic and demonic weapons was very faint. Mere echoes of what it once was. But it was so similar. I first credited this to opposing powers waning over time and blending together. I was wrong . . ."

"It was the same . . . or kindred, at the very least!" Tesla chipped in, showing he had caught Chopin's line of thought.

"Precisely. So, while we have to be careful of the potency boiling away within the fissures"—he paused to nod at another bubble as it floated past—*"these* are a very different kettle of fish. I think we're supposed to embrace their distilled essence before we make our way into the temple. This extract will provide the key to open the way forward, trust me."

They studied each other.

"Let's do it," Tesla declared. "You haven't been wrong yet, and I doubt you've brought us this far only to fall at the final hurdle."

They waited, side by side, until another effervescent discharge sparkled into being. As it rose into the air, they jumped forward across the gap, bursting the bubbles as they went.

The moment they landed, Chopin felt a prickling sensation crawl across his skin, along with a familiar reverberation. Then he heard a buzz coming from the middle of the circle. Walking forward, he discovered a series of blocks embedded into the floor at the exact center of the open area, forming an annulus.

Slightly submerged, the annulus had been invisible from outside the henge. But now, standing beside the feature itself, Chopin could see that each slab formed an exact representation of one outer, standing stone.

A small indentation in the middle of the disc drew his attention.

"I think this is a keyhole," he murmured. "Quickly, kneel with me and place your hand on this slab while a resonance of God's Grace still sings within us."

They placed their palms against the rock, then jumped in unison as thunder grumbled overhead and a series of hidden needles shot out to pierce their skin.

Too surprised to do anything else, Chopin listened as the thunder ebbed and the background hum intensified. Louder and louder it became, filling the air with a static charge that soon soared beyond the upper limit of human hearing.

A skein of energy blazed through the collar of the annulus. Round and around it went, faster and faster, circling them until one of the keystones burst into light. No sooner had it done so than a corresponding flare issued from one of the larger henge portals.

Air now shimmered across the plane of an invisible threshold, and a door appeared. As black as pitch and strengthened with heavy metal bands, this entrance glowed around the edges as if a sizzling hearth filled with Bãlefire were roaring behind it.

"It would appear we have been successful," Chopin declared. "Now prepare yourself, for I suspect our goal lies beyond . . . and the real battle is about to begin."

*

Cream staggered along the bluff, cursing his luck and trying to hide behind the scant shelter of Strawberry's slender body. To no avail. The reality of the Isle of Cogs was very different from what he had imagined, eavesdropping during those early days of Chopin's initial planning; and he had arrived ill prepared for the weather.

I should have paid more attention to his ramblings, he mused bitterly, or at least thought to pack more prudently.

He threw one arm across his face and peered, through tear-blurred eyes, out into the boiling cauldron of the ocean. So thick were the rolling thunderheads and so tempestuous the sea that it was impossible to distinguish where vault ended and water began. An all-consuming shroud rushed toward him out of the north, pregnant with rain.

And if I don't hurry up, I'll get soaked to the skin as well as chilled to the bone.

The first fat drops fell, blown ahead on a gale of bad tidings: an eager portent of what was to come. These were swiftly joined by the staccato beat of a myriad more, all equally desperate to make his acquaintance.

He sighed.

A flash of distant lightning illuminated the trail ahead. Cream noted that Strawberry, his unresisting captive, remained oblivious to the worsening conditions; secretly, he envied her. But then he spotted a dark gash just ahead, splitting the cliff face from top to bottom.

A gully? Perhaps it'll offer some respite. Not that I can tarry long. Chopin and Tesla must be well on their way by now.

He ducked as a tympanic peal of thunder blared, directly overhead.

At least I'm working my way down the hillside. I can't imagine how miserable they must be, climbing over wet rocks and sodden grass.

As swiftly as possible, Cream steered his bedraggled puppet into the defile and stopped dead. There, not five yards away, sat a huge block of stone. At more than seven feet wide and twice that tall, it almost filled the cleft, and loomed over them as if about to attack.

The vault above flared again, and by its light Cream was able to distinguish that the slab was, in fact, an obelisk. He also spied a series of steps cut into the rock on both sides of the culvert, giving access to small platforms near the top of the monument.

The breeze had abated considerably, and a tang of ozone spiced the air. Fumbling in his bag and fishing out a torch, Cream used its light to examine the edifice.

Whatever this was, its stone was extremely old and weatherworn. Faint symbols he couldn't distinguish had been carved long ago into its surface. Now, they were nothing more than vague indentations.

The doctor turned to his prisoner. Trying hard to ignore the way Strawberry's flimsy gown clung to her figure, he asked, "What is this structure?"

Milk-white eyes turned to regard the object.

"It is a sentinel and ancient ward-way. Although granted free passage by the conduit, you must still prove your mettle; for only those deemed worthy may enter the Black Keep."

"And how do aspirants prove their worth?"

"The blood knows."

Strawberry didn't explain further. Instead, she pointed to the top of the pillar and waited. Intrigued, Cream mounted the nearest stairway and made his way carefully toward the small ledge jutting out across the gully.

Once there, he shone the torch down a hole in the exact center of the monolith's crown. From it, a shallow trench led toward the outer edge, where another even tinier cavity awaited, along with a further set of narrow furrows.

He had an idea.

"My dear lady, tell me. Would an attractive Inquisitor of Satan's inner circle be deemed worthy to operate this device?"

"I do not know. Everyone is measured differently."

"Then let's find out, shall we? Slave, I order you to make the attempt."

Strawberry moved to the opposite steps and climbed them. Reaching the top, she knelt, extended her fangs and bit into her wrist, hard. Then she held her arm across the top of the block itself.

I didn't know she had fangs. So that's how she chewed out poor Micah's throat so easily. I really must learn to do my homework more thoroughly in future.

Thick, rich blood dripped into the center receptacle. Cream watched closely as it pooled before trickling toward the rim of the obelisk. The blood reached the plug and drained into a narrow channel running down the front of the pillar. The leading plane of this sentinel hissed as it heated. Soon it was white-hot, evaporating any rain falling near its surface. The characters adorning the shaft's face blazed to life, as fresh and precise as the day they were carved.

Cream scrabbled down to the ground and stood in front of his prize, beckoning urgently to his captive.

"Quickly, girl, tell me: what am I looking at here?"

Strawberry glided down, drenched to the skin but unhurried and unconcerned. Her blank eyes scrutinized impassively.

"These are ancient Hellanese glyphs," she explained, "not modern-day Hellonian as is customarily used amongst the so-called elite of the Devil's Children. By resorting to the language that birthed our culture, the jailers ensure that only those with the right heritage and breeding gain access to the keep. Even then, there are three elements that must be met: acoustic, telepathic, and physical. First, I must identify myself verbally, in Standard English. Second, I must enter the correct demonic mental sequence. As I do, I must also simultaneously complete the third requirement, which is to depress the hieroglyphs themselves. Only once I have completed these steps may I utter the plea, requesting passage into the inner sanctum."

"Do so, now." Cream, overcome and elated, danced a merry jig on the spot.

Strawberry stepped forward, wiping blood from her wrist onto the fingers of her opposite hand. In a clear voice, she said, "I am Strawberry Fields, known as Red Cap, aka Red Riding Hood, an Inquisitor of the First Order of Shâitan." As she intoned the words, the column started to vibrate.

Next, Strawberry pressed her fingers to the stone, a look of intense concentration on her face.

That must be the psychic phrase, Cream surmised.

Without missing a beat, Strawberry pressed a series of different glyphs. Her movements were swift and precise.

She clearly knows what she's doing . . . and her fingers aren't burning. *Interesting. I must discover wh–*

His thrall stood back, threw her arms wide, and intoned, *"Dàirit mi do leigh'd, ceadaîch* (Grant me permission to pass)."

The glyphs which Strawberry had depressed came alight as if illuminated from within by fire. A shiver rippled through the air, and then the monolith no longer stood before them. In its place was a huge door.

As black as midnight, and armored with iron studs set within reinforced mounts, the door gleamed coldly in the darkness despite the piercing scarlet light stabbing outward from around its gilded frame.

"Mercy me," Cream spluttered, "I didn't expect *that!*"

The portal exuded an air of sadness.

The faintest hint of a melancholy tune reached Cream's ears as he struggled to break its spell.

Then he looked toward his captive, all thoughts of lust forgotten. "Well, what are you waiting for? Let's get out of this insufferable rain."

*

The headlong downward rush receded, and Nimrod and I slammed into the ground inside what appeared to be a heavily fortified bailey, about thirty yards away from a tall dark spire. This, my first true experience with a multi-phasic portal generator, had been an eye-opener, a frigid helter-skelter ride of accelerated awareness and shifting glaciated perceptions. It was a pity I'd been so badly injured on the previous occasion, since the frosty euphoria that this method of travel produced was thrilling, even addictive.

No wonder Tesla's little toys have proved so popular among the mercenary and rebel leaders: just what they need to ensure their troops go into battle properly prepared or, in this case, hyped up on adrenaline and battle ardor.

My trip down psychedelic lane came to an abrupt end. Multiple bursts of light flashed around us. Our unscheduled arrival had triggered some form of defensive measure. Given the circumstances, this was something I'd have dearly wished to avoid, if I'd known. But, too late.

Back to back, Nimrod and I dropped into defensive positions, weapons drawn, prepared to face whatever came our way. Or so we thought.

We soon discovered what that might entail, for a death squad of hardened killers surrounded us.

Literally.

Not only were our overly-muscled hosts much taller than we, but they were dressed from head to toe in the distinctive leather jerkins, boots, and hoods of medieval executioners. What's more, each possessed vicious-looking ironware that captured the mood of their uniforms perfectly. A quick scan revealed they carried swords, cleavers, hatchets, and a wide variety of axes in all shapes and sizes. Every single weapon appeared well used and razor sharp.

Now I faced a conundrum. My need was urgent. Cream and Chopin had a head start; if they weren't here already, they soon would be. Their mere presence represented a huge threat to our security and safety. I simply didn't have time to waste explaining why I was here. Unfortunately, I saw no choice. The jailers had a job to do, and would resist me with all their considerable might if they considered me a risk.

Before any could advance, I stood tall and made a show of collapsing my scythe. As I put it away, I mentally instructed Nimrod to follow suit.

"Do you know who I am?" I lowered my barriers and let the unrestricted essence of my identity shine through. "In case you haven't been informed, I am Daemon Grim, our Lord Satan's bounty hunter and hellegally appointed Reaper. If you will be so kind as to exercise restraint for a moment, one of you can complete a psi-dentity and aura check and confirm it against my Infernal serial number: Six, six, six, alpha. Zero, zero, thirteen."

I glanced toward Nimrod. He adopted a similar approach.

"Nimrod of Ba'bel, in the land of Shi'nar. Our Lord Satan's bounty hunter, and first among those appointed as Hell Hounds. Infernal serial number: Six, nine, three, alpha. Zero, six, zero."

These guys were professional. Not one moved, although I was able to discern a butterfly sensation fluttering in the pit of my stomach.

At least they're scanning us instead of wading in to attack.

"Please be quick," I stressed. "This is an emergency. I suspect there may be an attempt on prisoner Alpha-One within the maximum-security solitary-confinement chamber."

A sizzling report, directly in front of the tower, announced the arrival of another jailer. From the gold braid across the shoulders of his waistcoat, I assumed he must be the guy in charge.

"Welcome, Reaper," he boomed. "Both you and your companion will be allowed to demonstrate your worth. If found true, an accommodation will be reached."

He lowered his hand. The ground in front of the keep shimmered and split apart. The fracture lengthened and widened, stretching across the entire width of the inner courtyard.

A rumbling sound issued from the crevice. Then a bright glittering veil of concentrated brilliance punched up, toward Paradise above.

That's God's Grace! How do they have access to such pure and unadulterated potency?

Sure enough, I heard the faint telltale harmony of an angelic choir, as if their song had been carried to us on a stiff breeze, full of the promise of spring. Try as I might, I couldn't make out the words. Nevertheless, their cadence remained, albeit just beyond the reach of my most finely-tuned perceptions.

"Pass through," intoned the chief warden, "and prove your mettle to the Black Keep."

"Very well," I replied. "But understand: If I pass the test, this is something Nimrod and I must address alone. I am under strict instructions to sanitize all knowledge of the issue I am investigating, and I'd hate for you or your brethren to become . . . *casualties*."

The warden nodded.

I made my way toward the barrier of rippling golden radiance and stopped a few feet shy of its threshold. There I extended my hand, and the chief stepped forward to make an incision along my palm.

Blood flowed. I clenched my fist and thrust it into the fire. The surface of my skin tingled. Then my form was enveloped by a curtain of emerald-green flames. Yet I wasn't consumed or hurt. Instead, I found myself invigorated, filled with an eager excitement I could barely contain.

The curtain reacted to my eagerness by falling in on itself. Its rate of collapse increased.

I stood transfixed by the roaring flame condensing until swallowed by the wound on my palm. The gash flared white, and my entire body flushed. When I glanced down, I wasn't surprised to discover that all trace of the scar had disappeared.

Now the keep itself beckoned.

When the process had started, the base of the tower had been nothing but a series of huge and uninterrupted obsidian slabs. Each one had been smooth, unadorned, betraying only the faintest seam where its artisans had fitted it in place.

Now, the flint-black exterior showed the glimmering impression of a massive double-leaved archway. Highlighted in silver, the outline contained thirteen translucent symbols: six to my left in classical Hellanese; an additional half dozen to my right in the divine language. The final character was fashioned into a keyhole at the point where both doors met.

I understood immediately what to do.

With the echo of divine resonance still coursing my veins, I approached the portal and studied its characters. These were ancient ideograms, each symbolizing the spirit of what I hoped to achieve. From what I remembered of such rituals, I had to select three appropriate glyphs from each side, press them in the correct order, and simultaneously pronounce their true meaning. If successful, I would then need to enter a final phrase.

Here goes nothing. Be forthright, be respectful, and above all, don't get cocky.

I started with my mother tongue, and chose what I hoped would be a fitting set of symbols from the left-hand sequence.

"Troh a' lùthse ain mi sealbgh (By the power invested in me),

"etom an a' Satanas aínim (and in the name of Satan),

"dàirit mi do leigh'd, ceadaîch (grant me permission to pass)."

Then I reverted to angelic speech:

"Lan khol yétev zélah (By all that was once holy),

"a na-khòr ené ne-phesh (recognize my spirit),

"pa-the eyl shal'tiél e-na shavat (and open to me with all haste)."

I studied the final hieroglyph. It represented a very rare and antiquated dual-tongued phrase—*sho-vâl*—which meant "qualify."

So, how do I sum this up?

A moment's inspiration almost had me choking on spit.

Of course!

As quickly as possible, I removed my scythe from its sheath and inserted the base of the shaft into the indentation forming the keyhole. Then I turned the whole thing in a clockwise direction. In Standard English, I added, "Allow me to complete my task."

Some arcane element within the weave of the Black Keep's defenses recognized me for who I was, and why I was there. The door disappeared.

Nimrod and I found ourselves within the tower itself, looking down into an open-sided stairwell winding its way around the
outer wall and dropping into the bowels of the earth. Even with
my keen senses, I couldn't find its bottom.

Snatches of song wafted up from the inky depths. A few
verses distinguished themselves. From what I could tell, it sounded like a dirge, and the words led into an obvious chorus:

> "My spirit has been sundered
> Betwixt light and dark,
> Eternal life unending
> Cursed by Satan's mark.
> What once was bright and holy
> Now tainted by regret,
> Paraded here for all to see,
> A championship rosette.
> But now he comes a-creeping,
> A-winnowing and reaping,
> Your next bounty he is seeking,
> Blood in rivers will be weeping . . ."

The voice was flawless and melodic, yet filled with a sadness
that pulled unexpectedly at the fringes of my own dark emotions.

Get a grip, Daemon. Next thing, you'll be taking it flowers.

Nimrod appeared affected by the tune as well, excited at the
prospect of meeting the prisoner face to face.

"Was that the . . . ?"

"Angel? Yes. It's down there somewhere and, from the
sounds of it, it's expecting us. Time was when I could sneak up on
a target without them knowing I was coming. If this continues, I'm
going to start developing a complex."

"I didn't actually believe until now." Nimrod breezed on as
if he hadn't registered my drab attempt at humor: "I'd heard the
rumors, of course, but I thought it was part of His Dark Majesty's

propaganda machine. You know, 'look how powerful I am, I've captured one of our celestial cousins.' I never really suspected it was true."

"Of course it is. Where else would Satan obtain seraphinite? At a million diablos a pop, it's his most lucrative form of currency. And exceedingly rare."

"But it's an angel! A real, live angel."

"Yeah, well, switch on, and fast. This is our first encounter with one. And although it's been captive for thousands of years, we don't fully understand what influence it might be able to exert. . . ."

A further snippet, this time from a different refrain, clarified from among the background echoes. Prisoner Alpha-One was obviously feeling perky and looking forward to company, for it was now serenading us with a quirky little ditty:

> "Death stalks these halls and smiles
> As it wiles away my bitter lament
> Of time ill spent in eternity's halls.
> How it calls to your soul, which is dank
> As it's rank, for your smile
> Does beguile, faded hopes . . ."

For all that the voice was pure and resonant, singing seemed a pointless exercise.

Now all he's doing is pissing me off.

We increased our stride to four steps at a time, round and round, ever downward. With every circuit, bits and pieces tempted us, fragments of nonsensical jingles or excerpts from deeper refrains. Not one stood out directly, and soon we reached the very bottom of the shaft to find ourselves in a stunning antechamber.

Simple and unadorned, the black slabs of this vestibule seemed to stretch off into the distance, extending for miles in every direction. Even so, the walls and floor sparkled from within, as if glittering dust motes had somehow been crushed and infused into the composition of the stones.

It looks like the Milky Way in miniature. Astounding . . .

And yet, for all its glory, the wonder about us paled into insignificance. For there, suspended in midair and blazing silently in the darkness, was a giant representation of the Greek letter *Pi*.

It revolved around itself on an unseen axis at the very center of the atrium, and a smattering of crystal snowflakes fell to the ground within its halo.

A sonorous ballad flowed out from the construct:

> "The blood you shed stains hallowed ground,
> The knife so wrought now rusts deep brown,
> The marrow you supped, now blushed pale yellow,
> But your memory, in lament, now fades in peril.
> The endless stain of treachery
> Leaches my soul and calls to me,
> It cries of death, and of bones bleached white,
> It whispers of shackles, from pits without light.
> I rot now, in halls of twilight hue;
> Longing for escape, I dream of you,
> A brother in my hour of need.
> Are you truly one of Satan's seed?
> O dark angel,
> I bid you welcome . . ."

In some strange way, I connected with the emotions embedded in the words. They were full of sorrow and crushed hope, crammed with an eternity of endless benediction at my inevitable presence. Then I noticed something else, something insidious and well hidden. Although transcendent, the angel's voice possessed a strange lilt that made me think of someone teetering on the edge of madness.

But that wouldn't be possible, would it?

Some unseen influence tugged me forward. Before I realized what was happening, Nimrod and I had crossed the threshold, and we were falling:

Time and circumstance changed.

I blinked my eyes clear.

Several things struck me at once but I ignored them all, for only one person mattered. There, not twenty yards away from me, the bane of my life in recent weeks, Dr. Thomas Neill Cream, was rolling around on the floor, fighting with someone—if you could call their bitch-slapping "fighting"—while a grinning Nikola Tesla looked on.

I listened as Tesla shouted encouragement to the other fellow involved, a man called Frederick.

Hang on . . . Frédéric Chopin?

Then I spotted Strawberry, off to one side.

Thank Satan for that!

She looked dazed and the worse for wear, but whole nonetheless. Even though my heart went out to her, Cream still acted like a lodestone to my attention.

"Cream!" My voice thundered across the confines of the room. I stomped forward, yanking off my gloves. "At last. While I'd have been happy to catch you on your own, I'm delighted you thought to put all my eggs into one basket."

"Strange," a familiar voice trilled from behind me, "I was just thinking that very same thing!"

Chapter 25: The Angel Grislington

I whirled around and came face to face with one of the most exquisite entities I have ever seen. Although it stood as tall as me, the angel was far more slender. And while it lacked my bulk, it exuded an unfathomable aura of strength that made me uneasy.

Its garment appeared almost fluidic in nature, draping its frame as if made to blend with its physique. Pristine and unblemished, the gown was devoid of all color and yet encompassed the entire visible spectrum in a scintillating display too refined to be limited to any particular color.

Somehow I knew this creature was male, but his finely wrought features were both sexless and ageless: a perfect blend of masculinity and femininity I would have classed as beautiful. Except for his eyes. His calm stare looked right through me as if he were gazing beyond eternity and into madness.

The Angel Grislington.

Grislington breezed past me without another word, looking completely at ease in the company of so many people. He tarried to watch Cream and Chopin's spat, and I grasped the opportunity to take in more of my surroundings.

The room had been modified from an existing cave. Stalagmites and stalactites meandered across ceiling and floor like vast pillars of living quartz. They'd obviously been here for an age, for even the smallest was thick enough to support an entire bank vault upon its gnarled shelves.

The natural pigmentation of the rocks was dark as midnight, as in the antechamber, yet they glittered with prismatic reflections. I couldn't detect a single shadow. In fact, I felt sure such a concept had never been given the chance to challenge the constancy of untainted effulgence. The canon of fire and ice seemed woven throughout the atmosphere. It flowed within the heart of a waterfall that cascaded into a pool of sublime clarity on the other side of the room, and threaded the essence of everything existing within the confines of this dungeon.

But especially did the radiance congregate about the angel.

When Grislington walked, a phosphorescent display danced in the air around him, as if every available facet of light paid him homage. Plasma flickered in his hair and through the fabric of his clothing. Sparks skittered along his skin and in the eddy created by his passing. Miniature tongues of flame rushed forth to clarify his way.

His feet were bare and perfectly clean, I noticed. And only then did I see the diamond manacle about one ankle. I opened my perceptions and staggered.

In Azazel's name!

Whatever theurgy was encompassed within that fetter was obscene. It stung my eyes and irritated my nose. The chain led past me to a central ring. The loop itself also reeked of occult power, and nowhere more so than in the anchor sunk into the bare rock floor at its core. From a mundane point of view, the chain didn't look capable of restraining a butterfly on a windy day, but my esoteric senses painted a different picture.

Despite the cavern clearly being his prison, Grislington's presence still suffused the place with a grandeur and permanence it otherwise would lack.

He saw me studying the gallery.

"Do you like my home?" he asked, gesturing to the bare walls. "I feel I must apologize, for it is somewhat lacking in the creature comforts you would expect." He smiled shyly. "But then, I am a creature the likes of which this place would never have hoped to entertain. For example . . ."

He waved his hand again, and two portals appeared fifty yards apart on opposite sides of the room. From what I could ascertain, they were barred, warded by dark sorcery, and yet within the angel's reach. Both were made of the same material as the Black Keep itself, obsidian. And Strawberry and Tesla each were standing just beyond the threshold of their own particular doorway. Because I'd been so intent on Cream when we'd entered, I now found myself closer to the left-hand gate.

I sobered instantly.

That must be where the different parties entered the vault. My eyes narrowed as I studied Grislington more closely. *And if he can hide the existence of such potent magic from me while restrained, he's even more powerful than I thought.*

Grislington blinked, and with that insignificant action dismissed me entirely from his concerns. Self-absorbed once more, he then bent to the outpouring I'd spotted earlier. He seemed fascinated by the texture of water as it trickled through his fingers, and I could understand why. Even from this distance I could taste its resonance. Majesty burst forth in a flood of vitality from a point just below the cave's ceiling, generating a gentle shower of ice flakes that pattered down around him. Where they burst, tinkling chimes in a variety of notes filled the air with music.

A mystic wormhole, identical to the one at the Cloister of Scourging.

Like a child at play, Grislington appeared content to let the stream of glory flow along his arms and down onto the floor, where it rapidly pooled to form a puddle.

I observed closely, noting something about the grotto I'd initially missed. Unlike the rest of the room, roughly circular in shape, the fountain had been positioned at the exact point where the cavern ballooned outward into an alcove. Why, I didn't know, as this made the aesthetics of the hall appear warped in some way. However, I spotted a clue in the behavior of the frosted crystals:

After they had shattered and their timbre had faded, each flake created a wisp of vapor. Those wisps became strands which flowed like silk across the edge of the pool and onto the flagstones, where they congealed into chilling haar. However, the mists failed to dissipate. Instead, they built up into a thickening brume that was coating Grislington from head to foot in a glazed rind that must be bitterly cold. Yet he continued to swirl the water as if neither temperature nor discomfort mattered.

He glanced at me again and raised one glistening finger from the fountain. The air distorted. A third arched entrance appeared, several yards behind him, within the recess.

He did it again. Hang on, is that where I came in?

I was shocked.

This portal was devoid of color. It reminded me of Grislington's robes in that its unknown texture shimmered like a glacier. One moment I couldn't make out a single tone I recognized, then its surface would flutter, and the slightest tinge of blue would appear. Then aquamarine. And then topaz. I even saw a hint of gold.

So mesmerizing was the play of light across the gate's surface, I was slow to register something else that had been positioned within the alcove. Something that had been driven more than half its length into an embedded granite plinth. Something that was the stuff of myth and legend, only discussed in whispers, but seen with alarming regularity in my dreams.

A Vidium Sword!

I froze.

What in the blazes is that *doing here?*

Its jeweled hilt shone like a full moon on a cloudless night, and the resonance of its song called me. My head dropped toward my chin, and continued to fall as if my body had become as insubstantial as smoke. Then the world expanded and my senses realigned to a new melody.

The weight of the cosmos arched away in all directions. A resolution had now been passed to respond to the greatest slander of all time. He Who Causes To Become framed a thought, and the heavens condensed into a single point.

A quorum gathered. Shrouded in nebulas and dark matter, they met to discuss a strategy. Debate raged until The Word issued a decree and passed judgment. From on high, He Who Causes To Become watched. Approval radiated throughout the gathered assembly, and a prodigious circular table made of purest jasper appeared. Upon it, a rainbow of prismatic brilliance glittered within an unquenchable fire. Each color represented an aspect of mastery, encompassed within the jeweled hilt of a sword of majestic power and purpose.

One by one, the host was called forward and the Chosen selected. They took their stand, drawn to the character of the weapon most suited to their nature. The celestial vault flared as each champion arose, flaming blade held on high.

A new hope was born, for this challenge could now be answered. They sallied forth, and dark clashed with light. Storms raged for an age of days throughout the firmament and quakes within the fundament. Outrage was answered by justice, terror by determination. A great dragon was hurled downward to the abyss, and a third of the stars were cast down with him. The heavens stood cleansed, and chaos was prevented.

But victory came at a price, for some were lost . . .

A measure of substance and sensibility returned to me. My eyes snapped open and recognition struck me like a thunderbolt. I scrutinized the layout of the chamber again. Then my gaze fell upon the totem in front of me, or, as it was known in heaven, the Sword of Celestial Arches: a weapon that could not only destroy fallen angels, but this particular blade could create a portal to anywhere and anywhen.

Now I understand!

As a demonstration of his supremacy, His Infernal Majesty had corrupted Grislington's constitution, so that the full nuance of his prisoner's former weapon was denied him. Then, in the ultimate act of cruelty, Satan paraded the means of his captive's salvation before him yet kept it out of reach, together with a doorway capable of transporting him home.

Oh, nice one, Boss!

From the way Grislington studied me, I could tell he knew what I had just surmised.

"A rather . . . felicitous manner of rubbing salt in the wound, don't you think? Not content with stripping me of my wings and binding me to hell, he sought to flaunt my very last hope for return." His eyes abruptly came into focus. "Still, I always have yo– Oh, look! Your friends appear to have tired of the novelty of our presence."

What the hell is he talking about? I glanced over my shoulder. *Oh, I see.*

Behind me, Cream and Chopin had obviously gotten over their shock at seeing an angel and the Reaper together for the first time, and resumed their quarreling.

". . . got it, you swine," Chopin cried, "at last!"

The diminutive composer stood above his opponent, brandishing a small bracelet in one hand. He backed away to the right, toward Tesla, victory contorting his face.

"What?" Cream gasped. He wiped away the blood from his nose and scrambled to his feet. "You've got the Reaper standing just across the room from you, and you're more concerned about wrestling my lover's knot from me? Are you insane, man?"

Grislington chuckled. "No, but I am."

Hey, Cream's got a point.

"You're too narrow-minded to see the larger picture, you fool," Chopin countered. "These bands we carry are more than —"

I blanked out the distraction of their wheedling voices and zoomed in on the angel's wristlet. From what I could discern, the cuff appeared to be made of thick braids of hair looped through various links of silver and agate-of-hell. It also employed an unknown gem on the clasp. That crystal was emitting a very subtle subharmonic field that called out to those worn by Chopin and Tesla.

The character of this crystal's presence reminded me of a very real danger, so I cast Nimrod a telepathic warning: *Heads up. There's unseen power at play here, despite the wards. Start making your way toward Cream, but stay on your toes. They all have artifacts that might neutralize us.*

Nimrod's hand came to rest on the hilt of his sword. Without relaxing his guard, he maintained his scrutiny of the room while backing slowly toward the nearest stalagmite. Once there. he used it as cover and began edging around the side of the chamber.

I noticed that Strawberry hadn't moved a muscle since we'd arrived and wondered what she was doing.

Strawberry? Are you okay? Don't worry, I'm here now; you're safe.

She didn't give any outward sign that she'd heard. But Grislington did, for he started to shuffle toward the center of the room. His eyes began to burn, as if fueled by an insatiable craving.

The argument suddenly got louder:

". . . why I was aware of your every move, fool?" Chopin was in mid retort. "Did you really think I cared about your self-aggrandizement? I needed to ensure this bracelet's return for the next stage of my plan, the retrieval of George's essence. With it, I will bind her soul to mine."

Chopin spun on his heel and nodded toward Tesla, who dropped to one knee and removed a large ornate goblet from the haversack by his feet. Made from some kind of burnished, rainbow-colored material, the goblet's substance glowed like a candle in the dark.

I knew it! The Cup of Tartarus, I presume?

Tesla took a tiny gem from his top pocket. It sparkled like captured sunlight, and its tincture immediately made me think of Grislington.

Seraphinite? Unholy shit! Is he going to try to control the angel? Or kill it?

"Idiot," Cream shouted, "you'll only make yourself a target. And your beloved George along with you."

He tore open his jacket to brandish a long, tapered dagger.

Oh great! I should have known. I was on the verge of panic. But then concern gave way to caution: *Hang on! Cream's got his own agenda. Will he try to use the Sword of Damocles to counter Chopin and —*

A sword of Damocles, Grislington's condescending mental voice interrupted. He seemed amused by my apparent faux pas, and I could sense his hunger increasing by the second. His eyes smoldered brighter, and his chest heaved beneath his shimmery gown.

The angel gestured toward Cream's weapon, then resorted to verbal speech to educate me:

"Only a hundred and forty-four thousand of those blades were ever made, one for each attendant who formed the echelons squiring the Chosen in battle. Such treasures reveal a heritage, both hinted and richly evoked. For they disclose a hidden purpose that He Who Causes To Become would have preferred remain secret."

Try as I might, I couldn't concentrate on everything at once. Grislington's words carried a profound weight of truth I found hard to ignore. I snapped a mental order toward Nimrod. *Watch what those clowns are doing!* Then I interposed myself between Grislington and his entertainment:"What the fuck are you dithering on about, angel?"

"My apologies," Grislington replied, his attention now fully upon me. "Although at times I might act without convention, you must remember, I have been disassociated from reality far too long. I am speaking of the true purpose of the Damocles daggers, and what Satan has striven to do with them ever since."

"True purpose?"

"Cousin, He Who Causes To Become couldn't have his holy angels and Vidium Swords falling into the wrong hands without *something* to counter them, could he? He was at war, after all, and a bloody war at that. He had to ensure an appropriate countermeasure was on hand to take away their edge, so to speak — you know, the danger they represented. Of course, bright Lucifer saw potential in that provision, and set out to vitiate his creator's intent from the word go."

As he spoke, Grislington crept ever closer. The intensity of his eyes bored into me, and he smiled like a serpent with a bear trap in its mouth. My sixth sense alerted me to a hidden danger. A static charge built in the air and sparks began dancing back and forth between us. Before I knew it, Grislington had used the diversion to close the gap considerably. He was almost within an arm's length of me.

Sneaky fucker! He's up to something, and it involves . . .

I circled to my right to put some distance between us and managed to position him with his back toward Strawberry. As a precaution, I also removed my scythe and held it ready. Just grasping it in my hands brought instant relief.

By now, Tesla had completed his manipulations on the portion of seraphinite within the cup. He held up the goblet, mumbled something under his breath, and then brought it to his lips.

Opposite him, Cream hastily cut one of his own fingers with the dagger and smeared his blood across the gem adorning its hilt. Pointing the blade toward Tesla, he started to chant.

I did my best to ignore the distraction their maneuvering created.

Strawberry! I called on her intimate mode. *Quickly, I need to remove obstacles.* I then projected an image of Cream and Chopin directly toward her. *Draw their attention, and I'll take them both down. You recover the artif– Strawberry?*

She didn't seem to have heard a word I thought.

What is it with her? Has she been hurt? I can't see any injury that might cause . . . I scanned her more closely. *In fact, I can't sense anything. Strawberry?*

Grislington didn't appear to have cottoned-on to my strategy, so I did the next best thing, striving to keep him occupied while Nimrod got into position: "So, angel, what do these Swords of Damocles represent, exactly?"

"Why, grand gestures and missed opportunities that the Tempter seized upon and expounded. They and all tools like them are the very contrivance by which Lucifer seeks to strengthen his position. He uses guile to mislead and —"

"Speak plainly," I cut in. "Are you saying Satan managed to corrupt them in some way?"

"No, you're not listening . . ." Grislington's voice trailed off as he regarded the weapon before him with reverence. "Don't forget, when those Damocles blades now in Lucifer's possession were taken from their rightful wielders, that diabolical task was undertaken by creatures recently ousted from their true dwelling place. They were all of heavenly origin. The Resister simply adapted the Zion-forged glaives to better suit the darkened nature of his fallen angels. Thus did Lucifer, ever fearful of rivalry, jealously insulate his own position." He stole even closer. "Don't you see? In their lust for greater power and influence, the devil's supporters lost themselves. Lucifer secretly added a most insidious spell, ubiquitous in scope; for in granting the wielder of a Damocles Sword what they most craved — the power to vanquish — he ensured they would surrender their own free will. Priceless, eh? But such is the way with all the Tempter's gifts." His gaze fell to my scythe. "They come with hidden costs. Do not be a pawn, Reaper. You are much more than you appear."

Me? "I am no pawn," I spluttered indignantly.

"And yet you reposition yourself on a game-board not of your choosing, the gallant dark knight, ready to sacrifice everything to protect his king."

"You border on heresy, accusing our lord in such a way."

"Lord? Pah! He is a weakling, a shortsighted fool who promises much and delivers little. Once cast down, he couldn't imagine a better kingdom to call his own, so he based his just proscription upon the foundations laid Above."

"Beware, angel. Prisoner or not, I bridle at your accusations. You condemn yourself by speaking out against him."

The Phage beckoned. Before I could call upon its power, Grislington pressed his advantage:

"Then look inside yourself, Reaper, and see if I am deserving of your judgment. After all, you have been granted the capacity to read hearts. How many have you adjudged to be deserving of condemnation over the centuries? Millions? Billions? As you well know, each soul is tried by being drawn out and enticed through its own dark desires. That desire, when fertilized, gives birth to sin. Sin, in turn, brings forth Satan's Reaper and an untimely death.

"Do not be misled, *brother.* Sin overreached your so-called dark lord eons ago. His procrastinations are prosaic, to say the least, but don't hide the fact that what we see around us, the discord, the malcontentedness, is naught but the inevitable result of a grand failure from a small idea."

Bugger!

The bait he dangled in front of me proved too thought-provoking to ignore. Something within me, buried deep down, responded, for in his words resounded a ring of truth I couldn't disregard.

His argument is sound. But why . . . ? how . . . ?

I glanced away to give myself a break and tried to make sense of what this creature alleged. Only then did I notice that Tesla and Cream were yet cancelling each other out. No matter what trick or tactic they employed, the purity of the arcane devices in their hands countered each soul's strategy.

Enchantments clashed and the atmosphere bristled.

The angel lingered, as if waiting for something.

Nimrod rounded the base of the final stalagmite, and I could see he would soon be in range of his prey.

Thank the stars someone's making progress.

Before Nimrod could reach Cream, Chopin joined the fray. The composer ran to Tesla's side and smeared blood from his fist onto the chalice's lip. Then he held up a long blonde hair between his thumb and forefinger. This too he lowered into the device.

"Swiftly, man!" he shouted. "The Cup of Tartarus won't be foiled easily. It remains at your service till your will has been done or you choose to withdraw. Change target."

Isn't that Cream's blood and Strawberry's hair? Clever idea.

Cream also heard the exchange and guessed Chopin's intent. He looked horrified for a moment. Then a crafty smile bent his face into a sneer. He pushed the Sword of Damocles at Strawberry, pointed at his erstwhile associates and snarled, "Kill them!"

No, Strawberry. I tried to compel her with all my might. *Kill him. Kill Cream instead. Strawberry, for fuck's sake, just kill him.*

Once again, my thoughts were absorbed without impact. It felt as if Strawberry's consciousness were absent, leaving nothing behind upon which my coercion could gain purchase. Nevertheless, a few moments after Cream uttered his command, an overwhelming surge of hostility leaked from Strawberry's mind.

Where did that come from?

Grislington noticed my concern and pressed his line of reasoning.

"Choose, Reaper. Are you a mere puppet or *more* than you appear to be?"

Those words struck a chord.

I've heard that before. Somewhere recently . . . The Knights Tempter!

Recollections of an ethereal voice within the miasma of the Knights Bridge came flooding back:

"You are more than you appear to be . . ."

Then why do I feel so emasculated?

"So much more. Do you not realize who you are?"

Who I am?

"What you are?"

I am alone. Stripped, barren, and darkened.

"Then why tolerate it? It is unnatural."

I deserve it.

"But you are a god!"

Don't be ridiculous, I am nothing. Debased, corrupted, and tarnished.

"A Titan to rival the likes of Lucifer himself."

That is preposterous. Outrageous. You shouldn't talk like that.

"Why? You are a colossus amongst insects. Why shouldn't you release the potential so artfully obscured and claim what could be yours?"

What are you saying?

"Overthrow the pretender, Satan. Why do you think Erra and his personified weapons were dispatched? The Deceiver is insufficient for the task."

Blasphemy!

"Take the throne . . ."

Treason!

"Assume your rightful place as lord of the underworld. Have you not personally consigned billions to such a fate? Who better to rule...?"

I shook myself alert.

But that was just a trial to test my integrity. They only said such things to analyze how I'd react. To see what was in my heart . . . didn't they?

Grislington licked his lips, reprising his hell-bound impression of a Cheshire cat.

Concentrate, Daemon. Pull it together for fuc– Nimrod!

Forgotten by all but me, Nimrod had at last maneuvered to within a few paces of where Cream now stood, blissfully unaware of his imminent death.

Nimrod made eye contact, and I was on him like a rash.

I can't leave Grislington alone for one second. He's up to something, and I don't yet know what. I glanced toward Cream. *But when you get an opening, kill that little shit where he stands. I think Strawberry's in thrall, and we need Cream dead.*

On the other side of the room, Tesla threw back his head, gulped down the contents of the goblet, and contemplated his new quarry: "Strawberry, my dear, be a good girl and place the sword on the floor, then kick it toward me. Do it now."

Because my attention was divided, with Grislington getting in the way, I only glimpsed part of Strawberry's reaction. She staggered, and the kris dipped, ever so slightly, toward the flagstones. Just as quickly, however, she righted herself, an ugly look of determination on her face.

A network of conflicting sorcery thrashed the air between her and Tesla.

"Fool," Cream bellowed, "you chose the wrong target. Her mind is now obedient to me. She is *my* puppet to command, not yours."

Puppet? I don't think so, sunshine. Not with my girlfriend, you don't!

Enraged, I called upon the full extent of my mundane capabilities. A reservoir of untapped potential flowed toward me. Seizing it, I tried to form something tangible — only to feel it skip away at the last second.

What?

I tried again.

Once more, the rippling energies that bound the hellspace medium together bent to my will, but just as they reached optimum mass, they pulsed and frittered off into the ether.

I cursed myself. *Fucking retard! The security protocols must apply to me as well. I was confused. But the head warden promised me an accommodation would be reached. Unless something else is at play here?*

On a hunch, I stabbed forward with my scythe and depressed the top button. The trigger clicked but the weapon didn't activate.

Okay, if hell's essence won't operate, perhaps God's Grace will.

I repeated the exercise, but this time flicked the second stud.

When the same thing happened again, my blood boiled.

Frustration added impetus to my rage. I tried to restrain my temper, but it was too late. A rising thirst for blood hampered my resolve. With scant regard for anyone's safety, I switched to an alternate form of theurgy — deviltry of the darkest kind — and added a steadily increasing concentration of demonic power to my summoning.

This time, an agonizing bolt of pain nearly burst the top of my skull. Defeated, I was forced to release the accumulating reservoir of thaumaturgic malevolence or die.

How the . . . ? I'm not strong enough like this. I need to manifest.

Grislington's eyes were as round as saucers. Fascinated by my efforts, he reminded me of an owl contemplating a fresh kill. Part of me wondered if he was reading my mind, but I couldn't dwell on the angelic prisoner right now. Dismissing all thoughts of him, I plunged inside my heart, where majesty resided.

I called, and a heady free-for-all of Bãlefire rushed to do my bidding. As I assumed the mantle of the Phage, my awareness expanded exponentially.

A concussion jarred the local region of the Sheolspace continuum, indicating the Black Keep's wards had been triggered. Nonetheless, I was confident they wouldn't be able to resist the exuberance of the most puissant force in infernity. Neither would the artifacts within the chamber.

Tesla, an expert on theoretical physics, must have deduced what I intended, for he redirected his attack my way. Or to be precise, *our* way: Grislington was nearly on top of me again.

The all-encompassing halo of light surrounding the angel flared as it negated a barrage of abuse. Grislington neither broke a sweat nor looked away, but continued staring at me through the flickering curtain of his defenses.

So he's protected, despite the wards riddling this place? Now that's good to know.

Strawberry countered Tesla's attack, and by the way those two acted I could tell their mystic stalemate had recommenced.

The glittering display diminished.

A movement behind her indicated Nimrod had reached a prime position from which to attack Cream.

Nimrod, this has gone on long enough. That little fucker isn't leaving here alive. Take his head off, now.

With pleasure.

So silently even I couldn't hear it, Nimrod slid his sword from its sheath and positioned himself for a killing blow. I decided to help by causing a distraction. Now empowered, I threw back my head and howled. A rippling wall of magenta flame sizzled along the extremity of my corona, and everyone looked my way.

Grislington chose that moment to make his play.

"Of course, those for whom the blades were originally fashioned also know a thing or two about their manipulation." His voice was as chill as a bitter breeze skating across a forest of bones. "We *were* bonded to them, after all."

The façade of beatitude dropped from his face, and I saw a deranged monster standing in his place. So bitter, so twisted was the hatred radiating in waves from every fiber of his being that had Satan himself been here, he might have been afraid.

I knew he was hiding something. Time to pay the piper.

My scythe swept up, charged and ready to strike.

Then two things happened at once:

Nimrod stepped forward, raised his sword and, with a mighty heave, slashed down.

Strawberry leaped into motion so fast her body blurred. But not at Chopin or Tesla, as I'd expected. Her target was . . .

Too late, I tried to shout a warning.

Strawberry landed on Nimrod's back. Her legs and one arm wrapped about him in a lopsided bear hug as her fangs bit deep into his neck.

Caught completely off guard, Nimrod staggered and tried to counter. Although he managed to fend off the dagger, Strawberry's teeth wrought terrible damage.

Blood sprayed across the walls and floor, drenching Cream in a crimson wash that sent him scrambling for cover behind the nearest column.

Chopin and Tesla hesitated, horrified, and their esoteric blitz faltered, frittering away to nothing.

A trained warrior, Nimrod adjusted his balance and threw himself backward, into the nearest stalagmite. A sickening crack resounded. Strawberry managed to hang on, but the Sword of Damocles fell from her grasp and skittered off toward the far wall. Nimrod tucked and gamboled, throwing both himself and his attacker to the floor, Strawberry underneath him. The sound of more bones crunching indicated that she, too, must be seriously injured.

Strawberry went limp, and Nimrod rolled away, onto his knees. With one hand, he tried to stanch the scarlet flow pulsing between his fingers, while with the other he groped for his weapon.

Our gazes locked. I could see his aura wavering as his life force waned.

Shit, he needs help fast, otherwise —

Nimrod's eyes widened in alarm. The tip of a blade appeared, sprouting from his chest like the mutated stigma of an oversized lily. Cream loomed right behind him.

You cowardly little fuck!

Nimrod coughed, blood welled from his mouth and nose. Then he went limp. A sudden inrush of air warned me of what was coming next. Barely in time, I dropped to the floor . . .

Nimrod's remaining essence crushed his body inward, like a collapsing singularity. Then it exploded outward, swatting everyone back against the walls. Weapons and artifacts were torn from stunned fingers, and prismatic reverberations chimed through the crystalline rocks around us.

My Phage was in full bloom now, and at last I had someone on whom to vent its fury.

"Cream!" I roared.

Jumping up, I scanned the room. The sound of feet running on flagstones drew my attention. Instinctively I let rip with everything I had. Still sprinting around the outer edge of the chamber, Cream ducked behind a stalagmite. A coherent beam of vitriolic menace scorched a molten path along the charmed walls and floor, pursuing him.

Somehow, Cream managed to evade my gaze long enough to be able to check his step and double back on himself.

Frustration multiplied, I sucked in more dark energy. My vision went black. My heart stopped. I became death incarnate.

Cream ventured out at last, and scooped a dazed Strawberry into his arms.

Strawberry! No . . .

A cutthroat's razor snapped open. With his self-preservation gene working overtime, Cream held the blade to Strawberry's neck and dragged her backward, toward one of the obsidian doorways.

I balked at the thought of hurting her, and my power wavered.

Two silver ribbons of lightning stabbed out, transfixing Strawberry by their light. The bolts intensified, growing to encompass her in an argent halo. Then the unthinkable happened:

One moment Strawberry was there in front of me; the next, the love of my life was gone, obliterated in a blinding flash.

I blinked my eyes clear in time to watch a smattering of ashen flakes patter slowly to the ground, like petals from a broken flower.

Oh, Strawberry. Not you!

Cream stared beyond me, open-mouthed in shock.

I turned, bristling with resentment.

Grislington stood beside the Sword of Celestial Arches. While the weapon remained safely ensconced within its restraining block of stone, the angel's fingers rested lightly on its pommel. The jewel flashed as if a conflagration raged within it, straining to escape. The display drew a corresponding echo from the Sword of Damocles, which the angel held in his other hand. Grislington's chains lay on the floor, cold and inert.

His eyes, completely devoid of empathy, still shone from focusing the onslaught that ended Strawberry's life.

"As I said," chided the angel, "those of us for whom the blades were originally fashioned know a thing or two about manipulation and mastery. Remember that, for next time."

"You're dead!" I screamed.

"Oh, I don't think so," he replied.

He caressed the Sword of Celestial Arches, and it blazed once more. The white portal seemed to absorb the purity of the light emitted by the gem. At one with the nature of everything around him, Grislington meshed to the newly generated esoteric resonance and stepped backward into the newly-opened doorway. He disappeared.

I dropped my staff in surprise.

"You . . . ? You bastard. Come back and face me. Do you hear me? Grislington! I'll hunt you down, I'll —"

"Au revoir — au revoir — au revoir — au revoir . . ." His fading voice reverberated, taunting me. As did his final embellishment: "Brother — brother — brother . . ."

Furious barely described my feelings at that moment. I almost released the pent-up energy within me in a cataclysmic retort that would bring the Black Keep tumbling down about my ears. Almost . . .

As I fought to control myself, the ruckus of another argument drew me into the here and now. From the sounds of it, Cream was whining, for a change . . .

"... love of heaven. I beg you, take me with you. I prom–"

"I don't know what disgusts me more," Chopin said. "The fact that you'd make such a request in the first place, or your gall at imagining I'd ever agree. After what you've done, hell will freeze over before I'll even want to think on your name. Let alone see your face."

"No one is going anywhere," I said, "except the Mortuary, where I'm sure the Undertaker will be only too ready to get 'creative'. Let's just say, by the time he's finished, none of you will be ever in a position to contemplate rebellion again."

I stomped toward them. While Chopin and Tesla held their ground, Cream was a different kettle of fish: The *un*worthy doctor scuttled away until his back pressed against the wall. He stared wide-eyed at my hands as I advanced, so I made a point of replacing my gloves, pulling them tight across the stretch of my fists.

"Don't worry," I assured them, "it's not going to be quick or painless. For any of you."

I contemplated my options. With the guts Chopin and Tesla had shown in the face of death, the choice was easy.

I phased and lifted Cream off the floor by his ears. He yelled and began kicking helplessly.

"You can't do this. You can't. Not now, it isn't fair! After all the —"

"Oh. But. I. Can. And. I. Will."

As I bit off each word, I slammed his head against the rock behind him until his skull ran red.

"Please," Cream whimpered, "I beg you, show mercy."

"Mercy? Like you showed to Nimrod? One of the finest warriors to ever grace the Seven Hells, stabbed in the back by a complete and utter waste of skin?"

My thumbs edged round to his eye sockets. With a jerk, I thrust as hard as I could.

Cream's shriek of anguish almost drowned out the satisfying pop of his eyeballs. I meshed with his perception of the pain and multiplied the agony, reveling in the severity of his torment until he was on the verge of passing out.

Not yet, little bird. Not yet.

Keeping a grip on my victim with one hand, I gestured with the other, and my scythe flew from where it had fallen and into my outstretched grasp. Then I embedded it in the wall, right through Cream's sternum.

I pressed my lips to his ear.

"Now, the shock of the impalement will kill you in about thirty, maybe forty seconds? So I'll have to step things up a bit." I released my hold. "But where to start?"

I rubbed my palms together as I inspected his pathetic body.

"I know. It's always amazed me how intense the discomfort can be when you catch your fingers on something, or stub your toe. Such little bones. Such a lot of *potential.*"

"No, please. Don't, don't . . . stop."

I grinned and commenced to work my way through the knuckle of each and every digit Cream possessed. He screamed. Oh, how he screamed. But by the time I'd finished, his wails had subsided to mere sobs, and I could sense his failing heart fluttering within the fragile cage of his chest.

I said not yet, little bird.

Cream's skin had taken on a deathly pallor. Sweating profusely, he felt cold to the touch. The growing ruby stain on the floor indicated he'd lost more than half his volume of blood already.

Okay. Now *it's time.*

"By the way," I whispered, "I'm going to ask the Undertaker to take special care of your reassignment. Because on top of whatever else he does, I'll make sure he programs your mind to relive the memories of these last moments. I want you to drown in them, over and over again, for all eternity, every time you start to fall asleep. Think of it as a sweet-dreams reminder from me."

He could barely reply, so I gripped his head between my hands and pressed them together, tighter and tighter.

His final groan ascended into an ululating cry, and then a high-pitched squeak.

I bunched my muscles and squeezed harder.

A resonant *crunch* snapped through the air as I shattered his skull. His body went limp as gray matter splattered my face and the front of my jacket. Blood and mucus ran down my arms and across my boots.

Cream's remains dissipated, leaving not a smear behind.

I stepped back, feeling more alive than I had for a long, long time.

And there's more to come.

I spun to face my next delight, only to find the other idiots waiting for me, Tesla in the forefront with the Cup of Tartarus in hand.

"Just let us go, Reaper," Tesla pleaded, "and we'll stay out of your way." Behind Tesla, Chopin hunched his shoulders as if anticipating a blow.

"And why would I want to do that, after the merry chase you've led me?"

"Be aware, the power of your Phage has shattered the safeguards surrounding this keep. Those restraints acted like a dampening field, soaking up lethal energy that otherwise would have destroyed us all. Now nothing prevents us from using *this* on you . . ." Tesla brandished the chalice at me. "Even as strong as you are, I doubt you'd be able to negate the full force of its Almighty compunction, manifested or not."

Chopin winced and made himself even smaller.

Tesla's hands were trembling.

But they're not so sure.

"Let's test your theory, shall we? You should know by now how dark my soul is. Even at the best of times, I can't be tempted, bribed, or reasoned with. And despite my sense of humor, I don't have a shred of empathy for anyone I'm sent to reap. And while on occasion I might respect the courage someone shows in the face death, it doesn't alter the fact that I would still kill them as soon as look at them. Unfortunately for you two, today hasn't been the 'best of times.' One of my closest friends got speared like a stuffed pig, and someone" — *Oh, Strawberry* — "very dear to my glacial heart was taken from me. Reassignments aside, I'm pissed and in the mood for a fight."

I stepped toward them.

Tesla seemed reluctant to act, but Chopin shook him by the shoulder until the scientist put the goblet to his lips, evoking the full authority of the holy talisman.

I felt the first flush of intent begin to coalesce in the air about me.

Tesla lowered the cup, and simply said, "Die!"

Heavenly power bloomed, and rushed to swamp me. With nothing to impede its sovereignty, that force gained the impetus of an avalanche and smashed against the might of my mystic defenses. A storm-wind of celestial savagery lashed the room with tentacles of incongruous, livid destruction.

I moved toward them through the maelstrom.

The vitality of two opposing forces amplified each other, generating a supercharged tornado. Confined to our immediate vicinity, it ripped chunks of quartz from the ceiling and stones from the floor. Loose blocks were torn from their sockets and smashed to pieces. A shower of weaker stalactites followed. Then everything pounded together, whirling in a fusillade of lethal debris.

I took another step.

Celestial vitality continued to respond to the dominion of Tesla's command. It crushed in on me from all sides, until I felt as if I had the weight of a mountain on top of me.

My knees buckled under the strain; my eyes bulged.

I refused to consider defeat. Fighting against these tornadic stresses, I extended my sickle to its full battle configuration and took a hard-won pace forward.

Heavenly light thundered against hellish dark. What was holy beat against all things profane. A rising tide threatened to engulf me. Terrible, endless pressure mounted.

I had an idea.

Can my weapon handle this amount of energy? Absorb it and channel it?

Obsidian walls were glowing white hot, and the columns had begun to melt. My clothes started smoking, then burned along with them.

Although Chopin and Tesla were cocooned within a protective sphere, I could see them becoming increasingly worried. The closer I got, the more they glanced at each other and backed away.

Tesla leaned closer to Chopin, shouting something over the banshee scream of the cyclone. Because of the din, I couldn't hear everything they said.

"... is now without the protection of ... so the wards will be deactivated. That means we can ... the orbs. It'll ... completely safe."

"... sure? If you're wrong ... end up goodness knows where ..."

Tesla shrugged. "If you don't think ... can always use ... to ... ship? What have ... to lose?"

Only a few more steps ...

My thumb inched toward the bottommost stud on my scythe.

Chopin dropped to his knees and rifled around inside a military-style kitbag lying at Tesla's feet. He soon found what he wanted: a small spherical matte-gray object that fitted in the palm of his hand.

Oh no you don't!

The trouble was, I could barely stand, let alone move. The tempest was whirling about me so viciously, I felt as if I'd be ripped away any second and pummeled into a bloody mess against the rocks. And even if I survived, so much razor sharp chaff whizzed about the room that I'd be cut to shreds if I allowed my concentration to slip.

So, despite my keenest desire, I couldn't do anything to stop them.

I gritted my teeth against the strain, leaned into the storm, and did my best to hold my hands steady.

Slowly but surely, I raised my scythe and leveled it at them. They were now huddled so close together I couldn't miss.

Just a few more sec–

The Cup of Tartarus clanged to the floor as they winked away. For some reason, the cup seemed immune to the effects of the destruction being wrought within the cavern. It merely lay there on its side, spewing forth an endless cataract of godly energy.

What the fuck do I do now? How do I turn that thing off?

"Fool!" an ethereal voice whispered, clear above the tumult. "Did I not say you are more than you appear to be?"

A majestic resonance bounded around the chamber. Something within me fluttered in response. Whatever it was, I refused to recognize it. But it was there, buried so far down I'd never accessed it before. Older than the Bālefire, it strained for release.

Before I could examine this unknown incongruity, my perspective shifted and fresh worries took over:

The chalice was still active and, like a black hole linked to a bottomless universal well, continuing to funnel into my world a raft of cosmic forces that could eventually consume me. My natural inclination was to destroy it . . . if I could.

However, something alien within its tincture called out to me.

Feed!

I had nothing to lose, so I opened to it.

Part of my mind tried to prevent what was happening, and threw up a shimmering veil of incandescent fury.

That veil was vaporized in an instant.

How in Satan's name—?

Never had I tasted such potency. Undiluted dominion screamed toward me: so much, so quickly that it generated a gravity-well which threatened to bring the entire edifice down around my ears.

Unadulterated might filled me. I felt myself swell, expanding beyond the constraints of mere flesh. Exhilarated, I burst into astral flame. Glory roared out from the goblet to quench me. And there, in the eye of the storm, I discovered a paradox.

I was the Bâlefire. Brimstone incarnate, made flesh.

I was also part of the Heavenly Light, celestial beauty eclipsed.

Perpetual discordance personified. At war with myself — within myself — because of myself, I was the very anathema of my own existence.

But how can this be?

A realization of my predicament struck home. *I won't survive this.*

The Cup of Tartarus, now united with the very genesis of the creative matrix, would continue pouring out its energies until either the Light or the Bâlefire was extinguished. Or until I was consumed.

And I was under no illusions as to which would expire first.

Unless . . . ?

A similar notion to one I'd had earlier came to mind.

My weapon need only survive long enough to absorb the combined capacity and redirect that energy to where I need it most.

Before I could talk myself out of it, I leaped high into the air and exposed both myself and my scythe to the empyrean vigor drenching the atmosphere. My potential instantly swelled. As I descended, I inverted the handle and triggered all five buttons. Dropping to one knee as I hit the floor, I slammed the hilt onto the chalice.

The scythe's gem blazed, and the Cup of Tartarus shattered. A livid flame of blue-white anger stabbed out. Piercing my chest like a fang, the scintillating ribbon of boiling puissance blasted into my body. Impaled on a spike of agony, I hung suspended in midair.

The Bãlefire rushed to respond and the topaz plasma strand was joined by another coil; this one silver and scarlet: my torment magnified a thousandfold.

I caught sight of my hands and feet. My clothes were gone, extirpated an eternity ago. Yet neither was I naked, for my skin shone translucent, a fickle reminder of who I once was. Too shocked to regret, I stared in amazement at a photonegative image of my skeleton, and pondered why I was still alive. Pain returned in blistering waves, and I doubled-up into a fetal ball.

Still fighting for ascendancy, the two bands of power intertwined, enveloping me within a coruscating helix. In the mad rush to cancel one other out, the polar opposites were, in fact, still augmenting each other's capacity. Tendrils of chaotic energy multiplied. Snapping out like whips, they screamed for oblivion.

A multitude of fissures opened around me, snaking their way through the cavern and beyond. The obsidian portals ruptured, and effervescent bands of neon-red light burst forth. As the process accelerated, the fracturing stretched onward and outward like fingers of forked lightning. Now, only the white door stood in their way.

There was nothing I could do. I was but an embryo, hovering in arcane amniotic essence amid the very stuff of creation and destruction.

The block securing the Sword of Celestial Arches shattered. As the glaive fell free, its gem flared like a star, drawing a response from the capstone above the final gateway.

A tone of purest clarity rang out. The fabric of the door shimmered and was gone. In its place, a window into eternity beckoned, containing visions of such wonderment that for the first time in my long and lonely life I knew what it meant to be truly insignificant.

Oh my . . .

The scales dropped from my eyes.

Limitless potential waited within the nucleus of the smallest atom.

Memories, hidden within a vortex of confusion, tugged at the edge of comprehension.

Something significant clawed for air within the very core of my soul.

Then, as if the multiverse had taken a breath, everything went silent.

When this happened, the overwhelming surge of incandescence blasting out of the portal shattered what remained of my broken husk and swept my shadow high into the air, out of the light and into the chaos beyond.

Now it became as if I'd never existed.

Nonetheless a part of me remained aware, conscious of the fact that I clung tenuously to life, yet able to bask in a freedom and exultation long denied me.

If only Strawberry were here to see this with me.

But, eventually, an end came.

I knew it would.

An unfathomable source of gravity claimed me once more, and my terrible descent into darkness began.

As I fell, a poignant thought intruded.

Haven't I done this before?

Epilogue

"Ship dead ahead,"

The warning barely registered on Captain Edward Low. So strong blew the squall that his lookout's words were snatched away and scattered to the four winds.

He peered up through the blinding rain and spray and could just make out the shape of his crewman, outlined by the glow of the lantern, peering down at him from the crow's nest.

The sailor waved his arms and pointed.

Low hurried forward with the sure step of a man who's spent most of his life at sea, Chopin and Tesla tucked in behind. Like drunken revelers, Lowe's two passengers rolled and swayed with every stride, providing amusement to those crew members they passed.

"Is this it?" Chopin yelled.

"We'll see soon enough," Low answered across his shoulder. "The Moral Compass indicated we're at the coordinates ye

449

provided. Moving shorelines or not, we're in the right vicinity. Keep yer eyes peeled."

The three men reached the bow and leaned over the rail.

The silhouette of a brigantine materialized out of the gloom. Without lights, the ship rode low in the water and listed heavily to one side. Even from a distance, Low could see her sails had been shredded. One of her two main masts was missing, and spoiled rigging played out into the ocean, working with the currents to drag the craft to her doom.

Low's first look told him she was beyond saving.

Blast! I could have done with the salvage price.

The gusts eased, and the *Flight of Fancy* sailed into a patch of calmer weather.

"Ahoy there!" Low called.

No reply.

"Ahoy, unknown craft," he called again, cupping both hands to his lips, "d'ye need assistance? Is anybody there?"

The only response was the resonant groan of stressed timbers and creaking pulleys.

The rise and fall of the sea masked just how rapidly the *Fancy* was bearing down on the brig. Soon, they were alongside. Everyone fell silent, and several ratings held their lamps high in the air. Tesla produced a modern-day flashlight and played its beam up and down the other ship's hull.

A particularly large gash had been ripped along the starboard bow, and her gunnels and oar-ports were tattered.

"It shows all the signs o' being abandoned," Low murmured. *Or worse. I'm sure some o' those gouges are teeth marks.*

"It is as I suspected," Chopin explained. "The crew of that vessel failed to take into account the respect due to Scydia, and paid the price. She is a female hydra, as I explained the other day, and although the whole of the Bitter Sea is her home, she is drawn like a moth to the vibrancy of the objects we seek here, at the center of this island. To pass her safely, we must appease her with a suitable distraction. That's why I insisted we stop at Clam Bay on the way."

"And yer sure that'll do the trick?"

"His visions have never been wrong," Tesla interjected, "as you witnessed on the Isle of Cogs."

Low's face clouded at the reminder.

Aye, I did that. "Expensive business though. The loss o' one old salt is cause for grief. But I've lost fourteen. Fourteen! It'll cost me dearly to replace them with experienced hands I can trust."

"You'll be able to afford it, and more," Chopin rushed to reassure him, "for the chamber that awaits our discovery contains more gold than you can safely fit in your hold."

Low turned to study the composer.

So ye say. "And ye don't want *any* of it?"

Chopin shook his head. "Not a doubloon, diablo, bar, or ingot. My interests remain focused on other totems we will find. Like you, I seek to replace what I've lost. The Angel Grislington was quite a talkative fellow before he chose to flee. What he said leads me to believe I'll discover something here that will allow me to do just that. Hopefully, it'll be one of many I get to recover, and with it I intend to—What's that?"

Chopin's eyes grew round as saucers. Low turned to look at what had so alarmed the composer.

Another shape, vast and imposing, loomed out of the mist. The sound of breakers could be heard nearby, surging across unseen shallows.

Cliffs . . . I'll be damned. He grinned.

"We're here," Chopin enthused. "How soon can we get ashore? From what my dream indicated, we'll have an eight hour march to the mausoleum."

"Just ye hold on a second," Low advised. "I'll not have the *Fancy* wrecked because we were too hasty. Afore we do anything else, we'd better get the lady's gift ready. Davy Jones' Locker's goin' to wait a while longer before claimin' any more o' my crew." Low turned away and signaled to his new first mate. "Morris? Quickly, man, get below and bring the Olympian Pearl topside."

*

The stench of rotting corpses filled the air. Erra found its bouquet a soothing distraction from the irritation before him.

His enforcers had captured his guests four days previously while completing their final preparations for the next stage of his campaign of terror. Not only had the prisoners proven remarkably difficult to subjugate at the time, but since then both had shown exceptional fortitude against injury and pain.

It must be why they were chosen as . . . what was the term they used? Hell Hounds?

The oriental warrior in particular proved most resistant to the interrogation techniques employed by the Sibitti, and in addition to an elemental capacity that demanded respect, possessed a sword that caused Erra's champions to become troubled in its presence.

This Grim fellow surrounds himself with a most capable retinue. If I can ascertain what is so different about them, I'm sure I could accelerate our timetable.

One of the Seven left the captives in a heap on the floor and came forward to the base of the throne mound.

"Sire."

"Please tell me you've been able to achieve a positive result?"

"Alas, no. They continue to show a remarkable resilience to our questioning. But we did follow your suggestion, and gelded them both. Following that, we took out their eyes and burned their limbs slowly away."

"And?"

"The most uncouth specimen, one Champ Ferguson, roared his defiance throughout. So much so that we cut out his tongue as a lesson. One he failed to . . . appreciate. Thereafter, he took to spitting at us on every occasion until we cauterized his mouth shut. Since then, he has continued to insult us telepathically with an endless and inventive tirade of vulgarity."

"And the warrior?"

"As ever, the warrior Yamato Takeru maintains a serenity that detaches him from our ministrations." A tinge of respect clouded the enforcer's emotions. "Impressive."

Impressive indeed. "So, after four days we are no closer to discovering what makes our guests different. Nor, indeed, can we glean any intelligence regarding the full potential of their illustrious leader."

"I'm afraid not, Sire."

Unfortunate.

Erra considered his options.

"Continue your interrogations around the clock, no breaks. But whatever you do, exercise extreme caution. If we inadvertently kill them, I doubt we'd be able to prevent their essences from dissipating and returning to source. And if that happens, we'll have more than a mystical sword to worry about. From what I have learned, Satan's Reaper would be vexed to discover our treatment of his aides and seek to redress the perceived slight to his honor. Such a confrontation should be avoided at all costs; at least until I have had an opportunity to ascertain more about him. So, move them to a more secure location and keep them alive, if barely, while continuing to inflict the most exquisite misery upon them."

"I have just the place in mind."

The enforcer retreated and signaled for the prisoners to be dragged back to their cells.

Erra watched them go in silence.

The one called Champ Ferguson littered the air with mental threats and promised horrors of certain vengeance. Meanwhile, Yamato Takeru remained aloof, secure within a psychic cocoon that defied all attempts to breach it.

Four days? Erra mused. *How much longer will they hold out?*

*

Grislington peered across the heads of the passing crowd. A sign within the shop window on the opposite side of the street caught his attention:

Dirge & Skinners—Suits to die for
So'vile Row
Bespite Tailors & Shirt makers
Dirge.Skinners.co.jux.doom

Perfect, exactly what I need as part of my new identity.

Choosing his moment, Grislington crossed the busy road and made his way to the entrance. The brass doorbell tinkled as he entered. Inside, Grislington was relieved at how insulated was the premises' interior from the traffic noise outside.

He closed his eyes and leaned back against the glass to clear his mind. After an age held in solitary confinement, experiencing so many new sensations was proving both overwhelming and novel.

"May I help you, sir?" a voice called out.

Grislington shook himself. Ignoring the query, he surveyed his surroundings:

The shop floor was dominated by a huge central desk. Around it, fussy clothes racks, over-filled shelving, and more than a dozen suits in various stages of assembly made the place appear cluttered. Pictures of satisfied customers filled all available wall space, and Grislington was intrigued by the pedigrees of the tailors' clientele.

"Good day to you, sir." An owlish and distinguished elderly gentleman, complete with measuring tape draped from his neck, approached. He nodded formally. "My name is Crispin Dirge. How may I be of assistance?"

Grislington returned the nod and shook the proprietor's hand.

"Without wishing to overstate, I'm here to purchase an entirely new wardrobe. I've been transferred from the Perish branch, and one of my new underlings at the Ministry recommends your fine establishment as *the* tailors to visit before I start work next week."

Dirge simpered, "Then you've certainly come to the right place. We have been serving His Infernal Majesty and his Blue Suits for well over a hundred years now. May I ask what it is *exactly* that you require?"

"Both formal and informal attire." Grislington feigned indifference, fingering several cloth reels as he spoke. "I'll be here for some time, so as well as a dozen pinstripes solely for the office, I hope to acquire at least twice that number of suits for both business and casual wear. I was thinking, perhaps a combination of pure wool worsted and mohair might be a good place to start. Oh, and sports jackets. I'll need sports jackets, too . . . say, half a dozen?"

Dirge's eyes flared as the size of the order grew.

Damned souls. How easily they are swayed by the thought of material gain.

Grislington grinned, and Dirge responded to the expression with approval:

"That would be a most excellent start," the tailor gushed. "Needless to say, with an order that size, I'll ensure to put our current commissions on hold until we've completed say, half your request? Forgive me, but it takes at least four fittings and seventy to seventy-five hours to prepare a suit meeting our exacting standards; and even with my staff working around the clock, the first part of your batch won't be ready for three days."

"That sounds ideal. I wouldn't want you to rush. With the monumental task I have ahead of me, I must look my very best." Grislington reached into his pocket and removed a small gem-like object that sparkled like a thousand stars in a moonlit sky. He placed it on the counter. "Would this be enough for a down payment?"

Dirge's jaw dropped.

"Is tha– Is that seraphinite?"

"Yes, of course. My only condition in securing your services will be your absolute discretion." Grislington flashed a winning smile. "Due to the nature of my work. I'm sure you understand."

"But . . . but that's over a million diablos. Your complete wardrobe, with shirts, pants, socks and ties won't come to more than sixty, perhaps seventy thousand . . ."

"Then it looks like you'll have my custom for some time to come, doesn't it, Crispin?"

"Er, yes, sir. That you will."

Grislington studied his latest catch closely.

I do believe I have a winner.

The realization of what this new order would mean for his business suddenly registered on the elderly man's face.

"If you don't mind, sir, I'll need a name and address to open your account."

"Of course. The name's Giseldone, Angelus Giseldone, and I've moved in just around the corner. I'm staying at Number One Brute Street."

"But that's perfect, your being so close will help expedite your request. I take it you have no objection to providing your initial measurements now? With something this important, one wants to get straight down to business."

A man after my own heart. "Then by all means, Crispin, please lead the way, and let's get to it."

*

The Undertaker rushed along a final passageway and emerged onto the central corridor. Once there, he slowed his pace to straighten his necktie and be sure the buttons of his lab coat were properly fastened. He caught sight of his reflection in the glass of one notice board, and hastily smoothed his hair back into place.

That'll have to do.

Arriving outside his office, he took a final deep breath to calm his nerves, grasped the handle, and opened the door. His Infernal Majesty already sat inside, occupying the Undertaker's favorite high-backed chair, next to the bureau.

The Undertaker couldn't have hoped for better. Satan was wearing his businessman's guise of pinstripe suit and cashmere overcoat. That usually meant he'd come to discuss things, rather than punish outright. But the devil didn't like to be kept waiting. Long fingers rapped like a squad of drummers on the desktop, and from where the Undertaker stood, he could see chips of wood and green leather on the floor about his master's feet.

"Your Majesty," the Undertaker intoned, "to what do I owe the pleasure?" *As if I can't guess.*

"It's been four days, and for some reason I can't fathom, you haven't yet updated me as to the condition of the renegade . . . or my people. Why is that?"

"Your Majesty, you must understand—"

"I *must* do nothing," Satan cut in, "except make certain that the Devil's Own within my intelligence teams have all the particulars they need to protect my realm. Mayhap you've not noticed, hidden away in the bowels of this mortuary, but hell is under attack. Not only have we suffered a string of unexplained seismic incidents, but the Juxtapose level has been wrecked. Huge areas along the banks of the River Tombs have been completely destroyed or reduced to rubble. While Samael and his brethren are doing their best, such investigations are not their area of expertise. I need my primary teams back on the job. I want to know *what's* happening, *where* Yamato and Champ are, and *why* everything has gone tits up. Obviously, I can't do that while Cream, Nimrod, and Strawberry languish here in blissful inactivity. So tell me, please, I'd love to know. What's the delay?"

"Sire, let me assure you, I am aware of your concerns. I have made haste to secure the particulars you require. Cream's memories proved an absolute goldmine of information. I have wiped them clean whilst preserving his every thought, every nuance for your scrutiny. You will find what I have discovered most informative. Due to the stresses of late, I was merely waiting to revive both Strawberry and Nimrod before updating you, so I could present a bundle of good news all at once. I apologize if I erred in that regard."

The Undertaker sighed. Would Satan take the bait?

Visibly relaxing, the devil asked, "By that inference, I take it both Nimrod and Strawberry are ready?"

"Of course."

"So why did you take so long to revive them?"

"My Lord, you know the constitutions of the Hounds and Inquisitors are vastly different to those of the riffraff. I had to ensure the nucleus of each identity fully integrated before resuscitating them. Not only that, but their recollections were chock-full of fresh intelligence regarding what influence the artifacts, once triggered, had on each soul. We might have missed something had I not been so careful. And, of course, there was the other matter of the modification you wished added to Strawberry's genetic profile."

"Ah yes." Satan's eyes narrowed. "I take it that has proved successful?"

"Completely. She will no longer be able to embrace Grim without . . . consequences."

"Excellent. There's much to do, and their attachment was interfering with their efficiency. Both of them need to be focused in the days ahead, especially Daemon."

The Undertaker seized his opening: "Talking of the Reaper, have you decided on the option you'd prefer?"

Satan pondered for a moment.

"Is he conscious?"

"Part of him is, and always has been, although you might look on it more as a state of suspended animation while his body strives to repair itself. As you know, there is no love lost between us but, I must admit, I am fascinated by his constitution. The enhancements you bestowed on him when he arrived in the underworld are truly remarkable. He lost his epidermis, dermis, and subcutaneous fat layers. His muscles and connective tissue were vaporized, as were most of his organs. In fact, the only parts of him to survive intact are his brain, heart, skeletal structure, and the core essence of his psyche. And yet, despite such appalling injuries, he has refused to die." *Here goes nothing.* "May I ask . . . *what* is he?"

"You may not." Satan's eyes hardened in warning. "Fulfill your obligations and leave his spirit untouched. I will see to that aspect personally, after his reanimation."

"As you wish. Nevertheless, I still require your direction as to your preference."

"I need him sooner rather than later. Which is the speedier alternative?"

"Without a doubt, the second choice I listed in my report is quickest. As I mentioned, his wounds were so severe even his self-rejuvenating matrix was damaged. This takes time to recover. Because you do not wish him tainted by spare parts, we must wait months while the plexus repairs itself. Even then, the process may be delayed by any trauma he suffers in the meantime. Therefore, prudence suggests arresting his regenerative process until his core recovers. I can do that quite simply. In effect, his body will remain frozen in its current condition. Autonomous and esoteric function will be unaffected, as will his ability to operate. The consequence of such a choice is that he will appear to be nothing more than a skeleton."

"How he looks has little significance. He is my Reaper, not an Adonis seeking the adulation of fawning masses. I know Daemon intimately. He is as unconcerned by vanity as am I."

That's exactly what worries me.

"I appreciate what you say, Lord, but what of his face?"

"His face must remain as it has become, veiled within a skein of darkest necromancy."

Oh shit!

"Your Satanic Majesty, I take it you will explain these . . . 'modifications' you are requesting? As I mentioned, there is no love lost between us, and he might think I have deliberately sought to interfere with him. Forgive me, but I have no wish to end up on the receiving end of his ire."

"*I* will explain nothing! *You* will do as you are told, as will Daemon. If he is ready to be revived, do it quickly. Have him report to my private suite over in Juxtapose by this time tomorrow. Believe me, once I have empowered him, he will be occupied by more pressing matters than your petty jealousy. Rebels must be brought to injustice, ancient relics must be recovered, hot and bloody revenge must be wrought. Do you understand?"

"Completely, Sire."

The Undertaker bowed. As he did so, a sharp "phhft" announced the moment the Dark Lord vanished in a puff of smoke.

Charming!

With the pungent aroma of rotten eggs filling his office, the Undertaker saw with irritation that once again his master's departure had scorched his favorite carpet.

He pinched the bridge of his nose between thumb and forefinger.

No wonder I'm getting so many headaches lately. So much to do, so little time.

Then he considered the task ahead of him and sighed deeply. *Oh well, I'd better get this over with.*

*

Through my bedroom window atop the Black Tower I surveyed the sprawling grounds of the Den of Iniquity. As usual, the high-pitched screams of those being questioned by my Inquisitors far below serenaded the regular gathering of hell-ravens lining the battlements.

They jostled each other for position and croaked at each other, their harsh counterpoint serving as a reminder to the interrogators that they were hungry, and still waiting on the daily allowance of bloody morsels and shredded tidbits they took as their due.

Beyond the walls, Olde London Town smoldered where fires still raged from the recent attacks. Her soot-stained rooftops and smog-laden streets appeared somehow darker, more somber, and their brooding sense of menace more pervasive than I'd thought possible.

Well, this is hell, after all. Uncountable damned souls survive, and they'll learn to adapt. I turned to regard the image of a stranger in the full-length mirror. *As must we all.*

I strode across the room to give myself a closer once-over.

My mind was still wonky after the revival process, my memories patchy at best, so whenever I caught sight of my new reflection out of the corner of one eye, I'd think an impostor was shadowing me.

"I'll get used to it, I suppose," I mumbled, "not that I have much choice in the matter."

The joy of finally apprehending Cream had been soured by the flight of Chopin and Tesla, as well as the artfully-crafted escape of Grislington. For some reason, His Infernal Majesty hadn't been all that pissed.

It's not like him to be so understanding. An awful lot of extra shit was dredged up that I never realized even existed, let alone imagined I'd need to deal with along the way.

I studied my new look.

And, of course, his impatience has probably got something to do with this.

Most of my physical body had been extirpated in a cataclysmic release of celestial energies. My life force also should have been extinguished by such a blast, but wasn't, emphasizing I was much harder to kill than even I had realized.

How in Azazel's name was I not obliterated? Or at the very least consigned for reassignment?

Still, as tough as I was, there'd been a price to pay.

And then some . . .

Fortunately, Lucifer had stepped in to assist me by donating an extraordinary legacy: a suit of armor he himself had worn during the original rebellion.

Made of palladinium, its variegated gray-and-black coloring made it look as if the metal had tarnished, like antique silver. In truth, the armor might be far more durable than even my medusanite scythe.

Polymorphic in nature, this gift was one of a kind, fitting around my skeleton like a synthesized second skin. I could feel sensations through its structure, as if the nature of the palladinium now compensated for the loss of my mundane nervous system.

Lightning played within its depths, a sure indicator of reserves of arcane might simmering just below the surface. And if there was any doubt that this armor was the result of the darkest theurgy, its surface had been gilded in occult embellishment and Hadean glyphs of diabolical power.

As I stood there, I could sense its vitality coursing through my ethereal complexus and marveled at the way it responded to my every thought.

I allowed my gaze to wander over its facets.

Because the palladinium was liquescent in nature, the cuirass had been forged out of a single measure, without seam or crease. The gorget was a more intricate affair. Molded in the form of an aegis, it had been gilded with flying serpents.

The pauldrons adorning my shoulders were emblazoned with Lucifer's own standard, while the vambraces had been configured with retractable battle spurs, each of which carried my own crossed-scythes emblem. Shaped like dragon claws, the spikes were razor sharp, designed for offense as well as defense. They were a particular favorite of mine, and appeared capable of tearing a hole in the side of a tank.

The cuisse, greaves, and sabatons were equally fluidic and resilient, allowing for a remarkable range of movement. In fact, despite being armored from head to foot, the entire ensemble was so light I truly felt as if I were naked.

I raised my hands and clenched my fists. Poison-tipped and studded spikes sprang from each knuckle. Not that I'd need them. From what Satan had intimated, the influence of my death touch had been increased tenfold. Now I need only will it so, and my authority could kill on contact *through* my gauntlets.

Finally, I leaned forward and peered at the space where my face had been.

Although I knew my head was protected by a Spartan-style helm, I couldn't see it. I reached up and illuminated the strip-light above the mirror. No difference. My profile didn't exist. My face was only a veil of dense smoke, as if the very pits of Hades were smoldering in a condensed brume above my shoulders. As luck would have it, my Dark Lord had seen fit to spare me the accompanying stench of sulfur, and supplied me with a brand new cowl to replace my trench coat.

While it fitted snugly across the crown of my skull and gave me a vaguely human silhouette, the shawl remained loose enough to complement the flow of the rest of my cloak, and ensured the interior of the hood remained in shadow.

To be honest, I liked it. It added a certain *je ne sais quoi* that would cause everyday denizens to shit themselves from looking at me.

"Perfect." My voice sounded completely natural. "Thus equipped, I'll be able—"

Daemon?

A telepathic hail thundered into my head. I instantly recognized the mind of His Infernal Majesty.

If you'd care to leave off admiring your new look for a moment? I'm in my drawing room in the adjacent tower, and we have revenge and bloody murder to plot.

Yes!

My new eyes flared in delight, and twin stars ignited within the miasma that my face had become. Strontium red in color, they shone from swirling depths with a promise of the violence to come.

I extended my arm. My scythe flew across the room and slammed into my hand with a satisfying *clang*.

"I'm on my way."

www.ingramcontent.com/pod-product-compliance
Lightning Source LLC
Chambersburg PA
CBHW031141050726
47495CB00018B/261